James Craig has worked as a journalist and consultant for more than thirty years. He lives in Central London with his family. His previous Inspector Carlyle novels, *London Calling*; *Never Apologise, Never Explain*; *Buckingham Palace Blues*; *The Circus*; *Then We Die* and *A Man of Sorrows*; *Time to Kill* are also available from C

For more information  , or follow him on Twitter: @byjan

Praise for *London Calling*

'A cracking read.' BBC Radio 4

'Fast paced and very easy to get quickly lost in.' Lovereading. com

Praise for *Never Apologise, Never Explain*

'Pacy and entertaining.' *The Times*

'Engaging, fast paced . . . a satisfying modern British crime novel.' *Shots*

'*Never Apologise, Never Explain* is as close as you can get to the heartbeat of London. It may even cause palpitations when reading.' *It's A Crime! Reviews*

Also by James Craig

Novels

London Calling
Never Apologise, Never Explain
Buckingham Palace Blues
The Circus
Then We Die
A Man of Sorrows
Shoot To Kill
Sins of the Fathers

Short Stories

The Enemy Within
What Dies Inside
The Hand of God

NOBODY'S HERO

James Craig

Constable
is an imprint of
Little, Brown Book Group
Carmelite House
50 Victoria Embankment
London EC4Y 0DZ

An Hachette UK Company

Constable • London

www.littlebrown.co.uk

CONSTABLE

First published in Great Britain in 2015 by Constable

Copyright © James Craig, 2015

1 3 5 7 9 10 8 6 4 2

The moral right of the author has been asserted.

*All characters and events in this publication, other than
those clearly in the public domain, are fictitious
and any resemblance to real persons,
living or dead, is purely coincidental.*

A CIP catalogue record for this book
is available from the British Library.

ISBN 978-1-47211-510-2 (paperback)
ISBN 978-1-47211-511-9 (ebook)

Typeset in Times New Roman by TW Typesetting, Plymouth, Devon
Printed and bound in Great Britain by CPI Group (UK) Ltd, Croydon CR0 4YY
Papers used by Constable are from well-managed forests
and other responsible sources

MIX
Paper from
responsible sources
FSC
www.fsc.org FSC® C104740

For Catherine and Cate

Thanks to Gary Carverhill for his help in all things related to Stiff Little Fingers. For more SLF info, please go to www.slf.com

ONE

Struggling to shift away from the damp patch sticking to the small of her back, Sandra Middlemass wrinkled her nose. With the benefit of hindsight, opening the window would have been a good idea. Even the waves of pollution rising up from the thousands of vehicles making their way along the road outside would have been an improvement on the fetid atmosphere inside the room.

From the other side of the thin glass, the relentless hum of early evening traffic rumbling past at six miles an hour was suddenly interrupted by a series of screaming police sirens trying to force their way through the capital's near-gridlock.

'Ugh.' With his tongue hanging out of the side of his mouth, the fat man half-pushed himself up as he gave a nervous glance towards the window.

The idiot thinks they're coming for him, Sandra thought, feeling him beginning to soften inside her. *As if.* Scratching her nose, she watched the guy struggle to put his tongue back in his mouth. *Who was he?* She tried to remember the name. *Steve something or other.*

Whatever. He was one of Aqib's white mates. Not the kind of bloke to waste any money on deodorant. And not very good when it came to putting on a condom.

Had she screwed him before? Sandra had no idea.

'Fucking coppers,' the guy grunted, still looking through the window at the milky sky.

1

Don't you worry, Sandra thought wearily, *it's not like they're coming to save me. They never come for me.*

As if on cue, the sirens immediately reached a crescendo and began dying away.

See?

Sandra had learned over the last six months that there was no danger of any of her abusers being caught in the act. Once, she'd even been to the police station to beg for help; ended up sitting in an airless waiting room for four hours without even an offer of something to drink.

No one came then, either. In the end, she just walked out. An hour or so later, she had been back on the job.

Most likely, the coppers dutifully rushing across West London tonight were responding to reports of another gang of shoplifters targeting the nearby shopping centre. It was a routine occurrence – one that always got a prompt response from the boys in blue at the nearby police station. That was the thing about the police in this city – they only dealt with the right sort of crime. Protecting iPhones and Rolexes was one thing. People, on the other hand, were nowhere near as important. Leave them to their own devices and they would eventually go away. Crumble to dust. Disappear.

If that was the name of the game, well fine. She would play the game. She would disappear. Problem solved.

Mumbling to himself, Steve – if that was his name – rubbed at the tattoo on his left forearm. It was a crude drawing of some bloke's face. The bloke had spiky hair and shifty eyes. Underneath the face, in small letters, was tattooed *Captain, Leader, Legend.*

Legend? Bell-end, more like, Sandra thought, stifling a giggle. Inside her, Steve was continuing to wilt. She hoped that the Durex would stay on. Even more, she hoped that he managed to restore his erection. Otherwise, there would doubtless be a beating in it for her.

As the sirens faded further into the distance, she felt the guy's attention finally return to her naked body. After toying with

Sandra's left nipple for a couple of seconds, he flopped down on top of her and began grinding away. The weight on her chest was crushing and she could barely breathe as he picked up speed.

Get on with it, you stupid bastard.

Looking past the punter's left shoulder, Sandra noticed that there was a large cobweb in the far corner of the room, near to where the ceiling met the wall. Next to it was a massive spider. It looked like the spider was watching them. For some reason, the idea struck her as amusing. This time she allowed herself a laugh.

'What's so funny, huh?' The fat man pushed himself off her chest, balling his right hand into a fist as he did so.

He just can't manage it. Taking a deep breath, the girl braced herself for the inevitable blow. When it came, his wedding ring split her lip. Sandra hadn't noticed the ring before. What kind of idiot would marry a loser like this?

Running her tongue across her gums, she tasted the salty blood. 'Is it still in?' she grinned, sticking out her chin, defying him to hit her again.

'You little bitch,' the man hissed, sliding off her. Standing by the bed, he tore off the empty condom and tossed it on to the floor.

Wiping the sweat from her left breast, a sense of giddiness enveloped her. Sandra finally realized that she knew how this should end. *What was it called? Short-term pain for long-term gain.* A few more minutes and it would be all over. She could say goodbye to all the fat men and their tattoos, forever.

It was time to disappear.

'I'm sorry,' she propped herself up on her elbows, 'it's just that for such a big man, you have such a *small* cock. Tiny, in fact.'

The guy stepped forward and Sandra was sure that she could see his dick shrink even further, getting smaller and smaller until it had almost disappeared into an unkempt nest of black pubes. Her grin grew wider as the second blow rammed her nose back into her face. Her head bounced back onto the pillow but immediately she lifted herself up again, inviting more punishment.

'I've never had anyone who couldn't get it up before,' she managed to say. 'But I'm sure there's an explanation. Maybe you're gay?'

The look on the guy's face as he reached for her throat was a mixture of confusion, hatred and pure rage.

Got you. 'Not that there's anything wrong with that,' she smiled sweetly as his hands tightened around her windpipe. Then gurgled: 'Nothing at all.'

TWO

Overwhelmed by a sense of ennui, Joseph Belsky pushed his chair back from his desk, stretched out his arms and yawned theatrically. Closing his mouth, he looked past his reflection, gazing out of the window at the orange glow of the lurid metropolitan sky. From somewhere in the heavens came the whining of jet engines as an aircraft made its descent towards Heathrow. Were the flights becoming more frequent, or was it just his imagination? *One day*, Belsky thought unhappily, *one of the planes would inevitably fall from the sky, for some reason or another.* Still staring blankly at the rain, his thoughts turned to long-gone skyscrapers far away as he listened to the aircraft's Rolls-Royce engines slip off into the distance.

The city below lay silent and uncomplaining. Not for the first time, Belsky wondered just how he had managed to end up living so far from the ground. Never having a head for heights, he had been the most reluctant buyer of a seventeen-hundred square foot, three-bedroom home on the twenty-second floor of the Whitehouse Apartment building on the South Bank. It was his late wife, Winnifred, who had chosen it. At the time, Belsky had been too meek to resist; after Winnifred keeled over – felled by a fatal heart attack during a visit to a garden centre in Elephant and Castle – he simply didn't have the energy to pack up and move on.

From the moment she first walked into the place, Winnifred had been hooked on the views that the flat offered across the historic centre of the city. When he had tried to complain that the price was way beyond their budget, the look on her face had sent him scurrying back to the bank to beg for a massively increased loan, underpinned by a ludicrously optimistic assessment of his future income. When the teenage mortgage adviser had signed it off with barely a second glance, Belsky knew he was sunk. Those were the days before the credit crunch, the sub-prime crisis, the banking crisis and the seemingly endless recession that had seen home loans for ordinary people dry up. Thank God London property prices hadn't crashed too, otherwise he would have been taking his monster debt with him to the grave.

Following Winnifred's funeral, her ashes – those that Belsky hadn't tried to smoke, *à la Keith Richards* – had been kept in a small Chinese lacquer box on the windowsill. He had been keen that – even in death – she should still be able to enjoy the vista. Tonight, however, there wasn't much to see; the weather had closed in, cutting visibility to a minimum. Two hundred and fifty feet below him, even the mighty River Thames was barely visible. *Jeez*, Belsky thought, *it's almost June but it feels like November*. More than forty years had passed since he'd left the sunny optimism of California and headed to Europe, finally settling down and making his home in London. It was a decision that he rarely regretted but sometimes, boy, this city could be hard to love. Maybe he would bring his summer holidays forward this year and head for the South of France, or maybe Barcelona – anywhere with some light and some warmth.

Scratching his two-day-old stubble, Belsky glanced over at the iMac sitting in the corner of the room. Maybe he should nip online and book something for next week. 'No, no,' he mumbled to himself, 'back to work.' Before he could properly rouse himself, however, the strains of the theme tune from the Mickey Mouse Club began percolating through from the living room. *Good old Mickey; a constant in an ever-changing, endlessly disappointing world.*

Resisting the urge to sing along, he felt the merest ripple of guilt. Belsky had faithfully promised Stephanie, his daughter, that he would not use the TV as a babysitter for Joanne this evening. Then again, he *was* on a deadline. And floundering, at that – a not so uncommon occurrence these days.

Anyway, his daughter had gone out dancing and left Grandpa in charge. Joanne, nine, seemed more than happy with a can of Coke and a cartoon – just as her mother had been, thirty years before. Hopefully, his granddaughter wouldn't shop him in the morning, but even if she did, what would Stephanie be able to do about it?

After carefully refilling his glass from the bottle of Bordeaux perched next to Winnifred on the windowsill, Belsky took a mouthful of wine and considered the rough sketch taped to his drawing board. The drawing – of a jolly fat woman dressed as a circus performer being fired out of a cannon – was shit, but it was too late in the day to rip it up and start again. Lifting the glass back to his lips, Belsky sighed. How much longer could he keep churning this stuff out? His editor had wanted him to poke fun at the latest politician caught fiddling their expenses – some junior minister Belsky had never even heard of. 'The problem is,' he mumbled to himself, 'it's just not very funny, is it?' More to the point, after a long succession of such scandals, it was hardly *news* any more. A sense of despair washed over him. Maybe it was time to start thinking about retirement.

Belsky's stomach growled; the wine was giving him the munchies. His thoughts were turning to pepperoni pizza when he became aware of a loud banging noise.

'Grandpa,' Joanne shouted over the sound of Donald Duck's sniggering, 'someone's at the door.'

Putting down his wine glass, Belsky forced himself out of his chair and shuffled into the living room.

'Someone's at the door,' Joanne repeated, giggling as Goofy fell over Donald's outstretched leg and webbed foot.

'Why don't they ring the goddamn doorbell then?' Belsky grumbled as he headed for the hallway. 'That's what it's there for.'

7

Sucking down some Coke, his granddaughter did not lift her gaze from the TV. 'It's probably Mum.'

Belsky grunted, knowing full well that the child was most probably correct. The likelihood was that Stephanie would have had another row with her boyfriend and the dancing would be off. They were a disastrous couple, it seemed to him; unable to do anything without arguing about it, loudly and at length. Why Stephanie hadn't stayed with Joanne's father . . . well, Belsky didn't want to go there.

As he switched on the hall light, there was a crash, as if someone was trying to kick the door down. Belsky shook his head; it looked like Stephanie had forgotten her key again, as well.

'Hold on. I'm coming. What's the hurry?' Just as he was about to reach for the lock, there was the sound of splintering wood and the door burst open. 'What the . . .' The cartoonist jumped backwards as a young man appeared on the threshold. About Belsky's height, the man was wearing a pair of dirty jeans and a heavy parka zipped up to his chin; the invader was sweating from the exertion of breaking down the door. As Belsky caught sight of the axe in the man's hand, his mouth fell open in disbelief. Belatedly, he realized that this was the moment he had been waiting for. For a split second, he felt paralysed. Then, as the adrenaline kicked in, he turned on his heels and fled back through the flat.

THREE

A steady stream of tourists passed aimlessly through the lobby of the King's Cross Novotel. Almost all of them stopped to admire the banner, thirty feet wide and ten feet tall, covering the wall next to Reception. Quite a few pointed. Some laughed. On the banner was an image of a spaceship travelling serenely through the cosmos, heading towards a bright shining sun in the far distance, above the rather cryptic message: *A fantastic journey.*

Standing in the middle of the lobby, Elma Reyes sucked her teeth in annoyance as she watched a couple of Dutch tourists in replica Arsenal shirts pose in front of it, giving the thumbs-up, while a third took a photo. As the person who would ultimately have to pay for the banner, Elma was not happy.

She was not happy at all.

The damn thing had cost more than six hundred pounds and the end result was something that looked like an advert for a Sci-Fi conference. Space – the final frontier, and all that nonsense.

The photographer turned to her, holding the camera in his outstretched hand. Unlike his mates, he was wearing the shirt of a team that she did not recognize. She was fairly sure that it wasn't a London team, at any rate. 'Will you shoot the three of us?' he asked, switching on a friendly smile.

Gladly, Elma thought, and marched away. Taking the brusque rejection in his stride, the Dutchman went off in search of someone who might be more accommodating of his modest request.

A spaceship? 'God, give us grace,' Elma mumbled, 'to accept with serenity the things that cannot be changed.' Not that she had much option; it was far too late to do anything about it now.

Beneath the banner was a board bearing the greeting which was the only real clue as to the event's true purpose: *The Christian Salvation Centre™ welcomes you to the First Annual Miracle & Healing Conference™ (Motto: 'Believe and it will happen.'™).*

I should've just told them to put my picture up there, the CSC's CEO and Life President thought sourly. *If you don't keep it simple, these boys are simply guaranteed to get it wrong.*

A diffident-looking young man allowed himself to be intercepted by the photographer and set about taking a series of pictures of the Dutch trio. After handing back the camera, he walked over to Elma.

'Which spaceship is that?' she scowled, pointing at the wall.

Melville Farasin, Elma's special assistant, was caught taking his iPhone from the pocket of his trousers. 'Huh?'

'The banner,' Elma said irritably, 'the spaceship on the banner. Where did you get it from?'

Melville reluctantly returned the phone to his pocket. 'No idea.'

'What do you mean, you've no idea?' The woman felt her hackles rising. 'If you've no idea, why did you let them put it on there?' The boy had always tried her patience and, if anything, the problem was getting worse. Indeed, if it wasn't for the fact that he was the son of her best friend, Wendy, there was no doubt that young Melville would have been sacked long ago. As it was, keeping him in gainful employ was stretching her definition of Christian patience to breaking point. Wendy had never confessed the identity of the boy's father – Elma was sure that was because the man in question must have been an out-and-out imbecile.

Melville took a deep breath. His boss was a small woman with a big mean streak; how she had been chosen to spread the word of God was something of a mystery to him. If it wasn't for fear of upsetting his mum, Melville would have packed this job in long ago. Burger King would have provided more spirituality, not to mention money. 'You told me to get something that indicated a long journey,' he reminded her, trying to keep any kind of whining tone from his voice. 'Terence will have sourced it from the internet or something.'

Grimacing, Elma picked a piece of lint from her designer kaftan. Terence McGuiver was another troublesome youth, steadfastly refusing to allow Jesus into his heart. But he was cheap and somehow managed to keep the Salvation Centre's digital operations on the road, so he would probably last longer than Melville. 'This is the Church of God,' she said wearily, 'not *Star Trek*. Probably a breach of copyright too.'

'Don't worry,' Melville replied, 'it's not the Starship *Enterprise*.' He pointed at the poster. 'The USS *Enterprise* – the ship from *Star Trek* – has kind of wings at the back.'

'Whatever.' Elma waved away his explanation with an angry hand. '*Star Trek*, *Star Wars* . . .'

'*Star Wars*? That's not really Terry's kind of thing either. It's more likely from *Prometheus*, somethin' like that.'

Pushing back her shoulders, Elma tried to give the boy a hard stare. Even in her heels, however, she barely came up to his chin. 'Regardless of its name,' she hissed, 'it has got *ab-so-lute-ly* nothing to do with the sweet Lord Jesus, has it?'

'Well,' Melville stroked his chin in mock contemplation, 'I think I read somewhere that there are those who think that Jesus was some kind of spaceman.'

Resisting the temptation to give the boy a sharp clip round the ear, Elma moved on. 'How many have we got?' she asked, looking around the largely empty foyer.

Melville tapped a couple of keys on his phone and gazed enquiringly at the screen. 'One hundred and twenty-six, so far.'

'Is that all?' Elma shook her head in disbelief. If she didn't get at least double that into the Novotel's theatre and conference centre, the CSC would struggle to cover its costs. *Miracle & Healing*™ was supposed to be a flagship event. Elma had shipped speakers over from India and the United States; if the conference was a flop, her chances of breaking out of the London market and going international would take a serious hit. 'Don't people in this God-forsaken city *want* to be healed?'

'We have three hundred registered attendees,' the boy said quickly, 'and after leafleting the local neighbourhood last night, we are anticipating walk-in of up to a hundred.'

'Let's hope they bring their credit cards,' Elma snapped, 'and are ready to spend big.' Checking her Rolex Oyster Perpetual – a gift from a grateful member of her flock – she felt exhausted, completely devoid of the energy she would need for her sermon, which was due to start in less than two hours' time. Closing her eyes, Elma pushed her mantra to the front of her brain:

God will not give me anything I can't handle. I just wish that He didn't trust me so much.

God will not give me anything I can't handle. I just wish that He didn't trust me so much.

God will not give me anything I can't handle.

With a sigh, she pointed towards the Business Centre, past the reception desk towards the back of the hotel. 'Go and check that my speech is ready. We'll do a final rehearsal later.'

'Hm.'

'We will,' Elma insisted. 'Right now, I need to go and get some rest. If I'm not at my best, you know I won't be able to perform.'

'I suppose so.'

'You *know* so, boy.' She brusquely waved him away. 'Now go and get busy.'

Melville looked at her blankly. 'Doing what?'

'Whatever it is you do,' Elma said tiredly. 'Whatever it is you do.'

FOUR

'You're already in the paper.' Inspector John Carlyle casually tossed his copy of the *Evening Standard* across the desk before pulling up a chair and plonking himself down.

Putting down his mug of tea, Seymour Erikssen picked up the newspaper, unfolded it and brought it up till it was about three inches from his nose. Squinting at his photograph, he smiled. 'That's from quite a few years ago now,' he mused. 'I was looking good back then. Had more hair, for a start. Not so many lines around the eyes.'

'We're all getting older.' The inspector took a bulging file of notes from under his arm and placed them carefully in front of him.

'Yes, we are.' Seymour dropped the paper back on the desk. 'I remember you when you first arrived here at Charing Cross nick. That must have been about . . . what, fifteen, sixteen years ago?'

'Something like that.' The old guy was a few years out but the inspector wasn't minded to correct him.

Seymour looked him up and down. 'You've put on a bit of weight since then. Lost some hair yourself.' He gave a sympathetic cluck. 'And when did you start wearing specs?'

'A while ago now.' Carlyle reflexively touched his Lindberg frames. He was long due another eye-test, but with glasses at £450 a pair it could wait.

Seymour patted his jacket pocket. 'I'm not sure where I put mine. I think I might have lost them earlier this evening.'

'When you were running down Monmouth Street with three iPads under your arm, trying to evade WPC Mason?'

'Could be,' Seymour acknowledged breezily. 'She's quite nippy, that girl.'

'They all are,' Carlyle sighed, 'once you get to your age.'

'Don't I know it,' Seymour replied wistfully, 'But back in the day . . .'

'Back in the day,' Carlyle reminded him gently, 'you were still getting caught.'

'Hmm. I must have been one of your first arrests when you got here.'

'Yeah.'

'Remind me, where did you come from?'

'Bethnal Green.'

'Bethnal Green, that's right. A bit grim out there.'

'Quite.'

'Poor pickings compared to the West End.'

'Doesn't make any odds, does it, if you keep on getting caught?'

Seymour gave him an amused look that made the inspector wonder just how often the old burglar *hadn't* been caught, and asked, 'How many times is it now?'

'That I've nicked you?' Carlyle looked heavenward. 'I dunno, seven maybe? Eight? Too bloody many, anyway.'

'Come on, Inspector,' Seymour chuckled, 'lighten up, it's just a game.'

'A game you keep losing.'

'It's not the winning, as my old ma used to say, it's the taking part.'

'Seymour . . .'

Lifting the newspaper from the desk, Erikssen scanned the story of his latest arrest for a second time. 'Still, at least I made page four.'

'It's nothing to be proud about.' Leaning across the table, the inspector tapped the headline under Seymour's nose: BACK BEHIND BARS: LONDON'S MOST HOPELESS CRIMINAL.

Seymour finished reading the article and noted, 'The press got on to it quick.'

Sitting back in his chair, Carlyle shrugged. 'You know how it is.'

'Who's the journalist?'

'No idea.' The inspector didn't need to check the byline. Bernard Gilmore was one of Carlyle's long-term journalist contacts. The fact that he had tipped Bernie off the night before was not something he was going to share with Seymour. 'Anyway, it's not exactly something to tell the grandkids about.'

'They know already.'

God give me strength, Carlyle thought.

Taking a sip of his tea, the burglar sniggered. 'At least I'm famous.'

Under the hard strip-lighting of the interview room, Carlyle noticed that Erikssen's hands were shaking quite badly. His silver hair was thin on top, almost to the point of extinction, and his cheeks were hollow. Not exactly a great advert for a career in breaking and entering. *The guy must be pushing seventy by now*, he thought. *Maybe he's ill.* 'Are you okay?'

All he got in reply was a non-committal grunt.

Opening the file, Carlyle looked down at his papers. Seymour's criminal record ran to twelve pages of A4.

Seymour pointed at the file. 'I would have thought you'd have all that on computer by now.'

The inspector flicked through the pages. 'Not when your first conviction is from Dorking Juvenile Court in 1957.'

'Convicted of larceny.' Seymour smiled at the memory. 'A year's probation and ten shillings in costs.'

Carlyle looked up from the papers. 'Nothing wrong with your memory, then.'

'Not at all.' Seymour tapped his temple with an index finger. 'Sharp as a tack.'

'Still, I don't think that two hundred and fifty-two convictions over a period of fifty-three years is the kind of claim to fame that most people would want.'

'It's a living.'

'Seymour, you are the worst bloody burglar I've ever met. Maybe it's time to retire.'

'What would I do?'

'I dunno.' Feeling quite old himself, Carlyle made a face. 'Something.'

'Inspector?'

Swivelling in his chair, Carlyle turned to see the aforementioned WPC Mason with her head stuck round the interview-room door and a serious look on her face. She glanced at Erikssen before telling her superior officer: 'We've got a situation.'

FIVE

The corridor was so full of people he could hardly get through. Nodding at the uniform stationed at the front door of the flat, the inspector brushed past a couple of forensics guys and headed inside. In the living room, he clocked the girl watching cartoons on the sofa, studiously ignoring all the excitement going on around her, and headed towards the grinding sound of metal on metal coming from further back inside.

Stepping into what looked like a study, he nodded a greeting at Umar Sligo. Hands on hips, the sergeant was watching a man on his knees, trying to drill a hole in a door in the far corner of the room. Carlyle shot Umar an enquiring look. All he got back was a weary shrug.

The workman was clearly getting nowhere. Waiting for him to stop, the inspector looked around the room. On the far wall was a large framed poster from the recent *Art as Life* Bauhaus exhibition at the Barbican. Carlyle recalled his wife dragging him along to it a few months earlier. It had been vaguely interesting but tiring; for some reason, museums always seemed to exhaust him, almost from the moment he walked through their doors.

Scrutinizing the image of a woman in a gimp mask, it took the inspector a moment to notice that the drilling had stopped. He waited for the ringing in his ears to die down before turning back to his colleague.

'What's been going on here then?'

'Man locked himself in the bathroom,' Umar chuckled, 'and can't get out.'

'And we can't get in?'

The workman struggled to his feet. 'It's a panic room; reinforced steel. Looks like the lock has jammed, or something.' He dropped the drill into an outsized bag of tools. 'You're going to have to get the company that installed it to come round and get him out.'

'They're on their way,' Umar explained, 'but it could take a while.'

The inspector felt a spasm of irritation. He hadn't eaten all day and knew that if he didn't get some sustenance soon, someone would suffer. 'How long?'

'Hard to say,' Umar replied. 'It's gonna take an hour or so for the engineer to get here. When he does, it might take five minutes to fix, it might take five hours. We just don't know.'

Carlyle stared at the door. To his highly trained eyes, it looked like a normal bathroom door. 'The guy in there, is he okay?'

'He's a bit embarrassed, but fine.'

'You've talked to him?'

'He's got a landline installed in there. I spoke to him on the phone about ten minutes ago. He's got enough food and water in there to last for twenty-four hours, apparently.'

At least he's getting fed, Carlyle thought grumpily.

'And Triple RXD says the panic room has its own dedicated clean air supply.'

'Triple RXD?'

'The specialist security company that installed the panic room.'

'And who's the kid sitting in the living room watching TV?'

'That's the guy's granddaughter.'

So the guy ran into his panic room and left the kid? Carlyle was less than impressed.

'We're trying to track down the mother at the moment,' Umar continued. 'Meantime, I've got a female PCSO to sit with the girl. She seems fine.'

The inspector hadn't seen any support officer on his way in but he let that slide. 'So, what exactly happened here?'

'Well . . .'

Before his sergeant could explain, Carlyle raised a hand. 'First things first,' he said sharply. 'Let's go and get something to eat.'

Laura Stevenson flipped the Closed sign and locked the door. Carlyle and Umar were the only patrons left in the 93 Coffee Bar but Laura had known the inspector a long time and she was not going to hurry them out.

'Take your time,' she said, heading behind the counter. 'I'll be a little while yet.'

'Thanks, Laura. That was great.' Pushing away his empty plate, the revived inspector leaned back in his chair and smiled in satisfaction.

'More coffee?'

The inspector held up a hand. 'Not for me, thanks. I'm fine.'

'Are you sure?'

'Yeah. I drink far too much already as it is. I get loads of grief about it at home.'

'Addicted,' Laura tutted, coming back over to take away his plate.

Carlyle waited until she had gone before turning to his sergeant. 'How long had you been at the flat before I got there?'

Umar made a face. 'Half an hour or so, maybe forty-five minutes. It was pretty clear from the off that it was going to take a while to get him out.'

Carlyle raised an eyebrow. 'You got there quick.'

'I was on my way home when I got the call. Christina wasn't best pleased.'

Carlyle gave a sympathetic shrug. 'She'll get used to it.'

'I don't know about that.'

'She'll have to.'

Umar said nothing.

'Still not getting any sleep?'

19

Umar shook his head. The dark rings under his eyes told their own story. Parenthood had begun chipping away at his youthful good looks. All in all, it made the inspector feel decidedly chipper.

'Don't worry; you just have to muddle through as best you can. It's the same for everyone. And it gets easier as they get older.'

'Let's hope so,' Umar said wearily. 'Ella's still waking every couple of hours. Christina's walking round like a zombie and I just feel knackered all the time. It's almost been a year . . .'

Birthday alert, Carlyle thought and made a mental note to mention it to his wife. Helen would know what kind of present to get for a one year old. Some kind of fluffy toy, probably. He gave his colleague a gentle pat on the shoulder. 'Don't worry. One down, only another twenty or so years to go.'

'Thanks a lot,' Umar laughed. 'You're always such a great help.'

'My pleasure. Tell me about the guy in the bathroom.'

'Ok-ay.' Umar pulled a small notebook from his jacket pocket and flipped through the pages until he found his notes. 'His name is Joseph Belsky and he is a cartoonist.'

Carlyle seeing a sketch taped to a drawing board in the flat. 'So?'

'He works for various newspapers,' Umar continued. 'Apparently, a few years ago he drew a cartoon of the prophet Muhammad . . .'

'Uh oh.' Carlyle was not liking where this was going.

'. . . which was considered blasphemous by various Muslim groups around the world. One of them put a million-dollar bounty on his head.'

'So that explains the panic room,' Carlyle said. 'Looks like he's a kind of poor man's Salman Rushdie.'

Umar gave him a quizzical look. 'Who?'

'Never mind.'

The sergeant looked back down at his notes. 'Just before seven, a man smashed his way into the flat with an axe.'

Carlyle frowned. 'If he had a panic room, why didn't they reinforce the front door?'

'Good question, to which we do not yet have any answer. There was supposed to be twenty-four-seven security on the ground floor but the guy there had gone to take a dump.'

'Urgh. Too much information.'

'Probably just as well. The guard was an old bloke of about seventy.'

'Everybody has to work longer these days.'

'If he'd tried to stop the guy with the axe he'd have come a cropper and we might have a death on our hands.'

'God. Imagine getting your skull split in two because of a bloody cartoon.'

'Stranger things have happened.'

'Yes, I suppose they have.' An image of Jack Nicholson in *The Shining* floated into the inspector's head. 'How big was the axe?'

'Not that big.' Umar held his hands in front of his face like a fisherman illustrating the size of his catch. 'About this big. A four-inch blade.' He pulled out his BlackBerry, hit a few buttons and passed it to the inspector. 'That's it.'

Carlyle looked at the image on the screen. '*Estwing Sportsman Axe*. Nice bit of kit.'

'Not the kind of thing you would normally have much need for in Central London.'

'No, I suppose not.'

'So, the axeman smashes in the front door and chases Belsky through the flat, screaming, "*Your time has come!*" '

'But he didn't touch the kid?'

'No, he didn't pay any attention to her at all. When the first uniforms arrived on the scene, approximately twelve minutes after Belsky called 999, he was still trying to smash the bathroom door down.'

'So this guy's not the sharpest tool in the box then?'

'Boom, boom.' Umar gave him a sickly smile. 'But they never are, are they?' With an Irish father and a Pakistani mother, the sergeant had considerable experience when it came to dealing with nutters of all persuasions.

'No,' his boss agreed, 'they never are. Who is he?'

'When they arrested him, he gave his name as Taimur Rage.'

'That doesn't sound very Islamic militant to me,' Carlyle noted. 'Not that my knowledge of this kind of thing is that great. Once you get past Osama bin Laden there isn't much brand recognition.'

'He's from Shepherd's Bush.'

'Osama?'

'Taimur Rage.'

'Mm. Nothing good ever came out of Shepherd's Bush,' said Carlyle with feeling. In the early 1980s, as a young constable straight out of training college, he had pounded the less than salubrious West London streets. His experiences of the Shepherd's Bush station were not particularly good ones.

Umar stroked his chin. 'What about QPR? Or the BBC? Or that giant shopping centre?'

The inspector shook his head, as if trying to dislodge the unhappy memories. 'I rest my case.'

'Anyway,' said Umar, getting back to the matter in hand, 'we need to check out the address that the axe man gave us, but it looks like he's local.'

'Excellent,' Carlyle groaned. 'A home-grown terrorist. That's just what we need. Why couldn't he just go on the dole and lounge around playing computer games all day? Loot the odd pair of trainers when there's a riot going on. That's what normal British kids do, isn't it?'

'I thought that you were supposed to be the parenting expert.'

'Is our man on any of the databases?' Carlyle asked, ignoring the jibe.

'Not as far as I know, but we're still checking.'

'Good. Where is he now?'

'They took him back to Charing Cross.'

Carlyle suddenly remembered Seymour Erikssen. 'Shit.' He

22

glanced at his watch. Time was running out. If he didn't formally charge the burglar in the next hour or so, the old bugger would walk.

'What?'

'Need to get going.' Jumping to his feet, Carlyle fished a twenty-pound note out of his pocket and signalled to Laura that he wanted to settle the bill. 'Let's go and see if they've managed to rescue our cartoonist yet – then I've got to get back to the station sharpish.'

SIX

'*Oooh*, that's good . . . that's so *good*.' Elma Reyes reached for the large glass of very expensive wine that was perched on the edge of the massage table near her head. Conscious of a delicious tingling sensation at the base of her spine, she smiled and purred, 'Don't stop,' arching her back as she pushed her thighs half an inch wider apart. 'Deeper. You know what I like, Harry.'

Warming some Raw Gaia oil in his hands, Harry Gomes, Elma's regular masseur for the best part of a decade, laughed quietly to himself. 'Yes, I do. Deep-tissue massage to relieve the tension. And you've got *lots* of tension.' Lazily letting the oil drip onto her buttocks, he began drizzling it into the crack of her ass, chasing after it with the tips of his fingers.

'*Deeep* tissue . . .' Elma took a slurp of the wine – you couldn't beat a decent Bordeaux in her book – and breathed in the scent of the lavender candle burning in the corner of her hotel bedroom. As Harry's probing intensified, she wondered if she should have had a shower before climbing on to the table. *Too late now, girl*, she thought to herself. *Anyway, Harry's not the sort to complain, he can take most things in his stride*.

Placing the glass carefully back down on the table, she lowered her head onto the towel. 'Those thumbs of yours get into places . . .' She sighed as his hands gently prised her buttocks apart. The foreplay was over and now it was time to finish her off.

'You ready?'

'Uhuh.' She gasped slightly as he entered her.

24

'Just relax.'

'I'm relaxed, Harry.'

'Good. Leave everything to me.'

'Sure thing.'

Harry was a squat, fifty-something guy who originally hailed from Jamaica, arriving in London with his parents in the late seventies. After winning three medals (two silver and a bronze) in power lifting at the Auckland Commonwealth Games, he had taken a three-year course in Healing Therapies and Eastern Philosophy at the University of South Berkshire and set up as an out-call masseur, servicing primarily athletes and minor celebrities. He first met Elma at a *Let Jesus In* conference in Crystal Palace. It was one of her earliest gigs, supporting Silas Spelman (the Guru of South London), and as the time approached for her to leap on stage, Elma was so stressed that she could hardly speak. However, after twenty minutes with Harry and his healing hands, she had knocked them dead. As far as Elma was concerned, it was just about the best fifty quid she had ever spent. As soon as she bounded off the stage, the whoops of the congregation ringing in her ears, she had made a regular booking. Since then, Harry had been 'working on her issues' for an hour once a week, plus an extra hour immediately before any performance. Their relationship had grown over the years, surviving the collapse of Harry's business after he was convicted at the Old Bailey of sexually assaulting thirteen clients. Following Harry's re-emergence from Wormwood Scrubs, Elma was one of the few people who stood by him. Despite, or rather because of, his controversial technique, she valued his ministrations more than ever. Put simply, Harry was the only guy who had been able to make her orgasm – or even brought her close – since she'd left her husband.

He was, she acknowledged, her gift from God.

Elma Reyes was well on the way to heaven when there was a knock at the door. She tried to ignore it but, fatally, Harry

25

hesitated. As his fingers stopped their insistent probing, she immediately growled, 'Don't stop.'

'You want me to get that?' Harry mumbled.

'No, no,' she gasped. 'Keep going.'

'Elma?' The knock was sharper this time, more insistent. 'Are you in there?'

'Shit.' Elma felt Harry's hands slip over her backside as he stepped away from the table. With a sigh, she rolled over, giving him a full view of her goodies, and reached for a fresh towel.

Embarrassed, Harry looked down at the stains on his shirt. 'The door.'

'I know. I heard it.' *You've never tried to fuck me*, Elma thought sourly as she slipped off the damp massage table. She tried to stare him down, demand that he contemplate her nakedness, but he wouldn't catch her eye. *I've not even seen the remotest sign of a boner. Not even a lick of those thin old lips of yours. What in the world is wrong with you, man? Are you gay or somethin'? How can that possibly be? Didn't you want to screw those white women who took you to court for tryin' to touch them up?*

The third knock was louder still.

'Who is it?' she shouted, giving in to the inevitable, finally wrapping the towel around her diminutive frame.

'It's Jerome.'

'Uhuh.' Elma glanced at Harry, who was now busy cleaning his hands with a handiwipe, and rolled her eyes towards the heavens. The Reverend Jerome Mears was Elma's star turn for the Miracles Conference. It had cost her fifteen grand, plus expenses, to get him over to London for this one single appearance – a ridiculous amount of money, but a sum she deemed it worth paying if it ended up helping catapult the Christian Salvation Centre into the big league of international worship.

Billed as America's leading healing evangelist, Jerome Cameron Mears III came with an impeccable pedigree. Voted Texan Church of the Year in three of the last seven years (a record), the Mears Ministry had taken twenty-first-century churchgoing to a whole new level. In its digital database were lodged thousands of documented cases of believers who had been cured of a broad range of ailments and injuries, thanks exclusively to Jerome's hotline to God and the power of his preaching. According to his promotional literature contained in the Ministry's online Media Pack, there were also 'at least eleven documented cases of people who have been raised from the dead' as a direct result of the Reverend's blessing.

To date, Elma Reyes could not claim to have cured anyone of anything, never mind brought a parishioner back from the dead. On first reading about Jerome's claims, the street-wise South London girl in her had been doubtful as to their veracity. Even allowing for the fact that she was dealing with a bunch of Americans, the language of it all struck her as odd. *At least* eleven cases? How could you not be sure of the number? Surely if there was anyone else out there who had been reanimated as a result of your silver tongue, you would know about it?

Before handing over the down payment on the Reverend's fee, Elma had toyed with the idea of asking to see his 'documentation'. In the end, however, she decided that such a request would have been demeaning to their professional relationship. As her dear, late father – a thirty-year veteran of the 171 Tabernacle and the Forest Hill bus depot – used to say: doubt, scepticism and an empirical-based approach to life were the way of the dullard and of the apostate. And, God knows, there were enough of both of those in the world already.

Stifling a yawn, Elma made no effort to move towards the door. 'What is it that you need, Jerome?'

'Can I have a word? We should talk.'

'I'm kinda busy right now.' Elma reached for her glass and took another mouthful of wine. 'Can I come and grab you in ten?'

'It's kind of urgent.'

Elma sighed. 'Okay, okay. Hold on.' Feeling deeply unsatisfied, she padded across the room and flicked open the lock. Pulling the door open she waved Jerome inside.

'Come in.'

Following her through the tiny hallway, the Reverend sniffed the air suspiciously. 'You havin' a party?' Resplendent in a bespoke yellow MacLeod dress tartan suit, he looked like a refugee from children's television. The suit had been created by Lewis & Hayward on Savile Row; Elma knew that it had cost more than two grand, but it made the man feel good and that was what counted. Plus, it would go down a storm back home.

London, however, was a different matter. Elma frowned. 'Are you wearing that on stage?'

'Sure.' Jerome's grin grew so wide, it looked like it might eat his entire face. 'Ain't it great?'

I'm gonna need some sunglasses, Elma thought.

Looking her up and down, the American did not seem that impressed. 'Are you good to go?'

'Just getting myself in the zone,' she said defensively.

'Hm.' Jerome nodded at Harry, who avoided his gaze.

I'm never gonna come now, Elma thought miserably. 'Harry . . .'

Finally realizing that the session was over, the masseur blew out the candle, made his excuses and quickly left.

As the door clicked shut, Elma tried to smile at Jerome while he took in the details of the chaotic scene. 'I need to relax before a performance.'

'Indeed.' The Reverend smiled lasciviously. As a man who had been arrested in a hotel room not unlike this one with two fifteen-year-old girls, a quart of Jack Daniel's and three grams of cocaine (scented candles were not his thing) just before his keynote address to the 2013 Jesus Gets You More conference in Atlanta, Jerome knew exactly what the woman meant. Performance anxiety was a terrible thing – you couldn't let it bring you down or someone else would take your place in the spotlight in the blink of an eye. God suffered from Attention

Deficit Disorder just the same as everyone else. 'Gotta be at your best when you hit that stage.'

'That's right.' Elma belatedly became aware that she was feeling more than a little drunk.

'Gotta be all loose.' Jerome waved his arms around like a dancing jellyfish. He liked to think of himself as God's answer to Charlie Sheen; he did the sinning so that his grateful flock didn't have to engage in any of that unfortunate behaviour themselves. If others took a similar approach he was cool with that. As long as he got the balance of his fee, he was not going to judge a small-time player like Elma Reyes one way or the other.

Elma waved the wine glass in front of her face. 'Fancy a drink? A little loosener before the show starts?'

'I'm good, thanks.' Hands on hips, Jerome stood in the middle of the room, looking not unlike a middle-aged Eminem gone badly to seed.

'Sure?'

'Sure.' The preacher stepped over to the window in order to let out a small but surprisingly pungent fart. 'I don't want to sound a note of alarm,' he drawled, laying the Texan accent on thick for the Brit woman, 'but we are due to start quite soon and the crowd out there,' he pointed over his shoulder with his thumb, 'is still rather thin.'

And you're worried about the rest of your money. Holding her towel closed with one hand, Elma grasped her wine glass firmly in the other. 'Don't worry, there's plenty of time.' She tried to force a smile on her face. 'People here arrive late.'

'You tend to do things differently here in England,' Jerome mused, not exactly happy about it.

'Exactly. The general assumption is that we will start at least half an hour late.'

Jerome grimaced. He had plans for this evening; they included hanging out with a magnum of bubbly and some party girls. He didn't want things to be derailed by poor timekeeping.

'It's not a big deal,' Elma continued. 'We are committed to

making this a truly unforgettable experience for all of those who attend.'

'I understand that,' Jerome persisted, 'I truly do. But if I'm going to put a live feed of this . . . event on my website, the place is gonna have to look full; fuller than it is right now, at least. How will it look to my congregation if they see that I came all the way over here to perform in front of a mere handful of people?' He gave Elma an embarrassed shrug. 'You promised me a sell-out crowd.'

'Don't worry.' Elma tried to sound reassuring. 'My people will make sure that the venue fills out in good time.' If the worst came to the worst, she would have to get Melville to pay some of his mates again. For thirty quid a head, those boys could go crazy like the best of them. 'Depending on developments, we can, ah, mobilize significant numbers at very short notice.'

'Well, mobilize them, then,' Jerome said, a testiness creeping into his voice that she hadn't heard before. 'We haven't got time to waste here. Don't people here in London town need to have miracles performed for them?'

I certainly do, thought Elma. There was an awkward pause before the sound of Lincoln Brewster's 'Let Your Glory Shine' started up from inside her Victoria Beckham satchel. *Saved by the bell*, Elma thought, *halleluiah. Ask and He shall deliver.* 'Sorry,' she smiled, 'that's my phone. I'm afraid I need to get it.'

Looking less than pleased, Jerome gave her a curt nod. Reaching into the bag, she let the towel fall to the carpet as she pulled out her iPhone 6. 'Hold on one second, please,' she said into it, and placing her hand over the mouthpiece, she turned to face the Reverend, who had gone slightly pale. 'Let me deal with this and I'll see you downstairs in a couple of minutes.'

'Sure thing.' Trying to keep his gaze somewhere above her head, Jerome was already skipping towards the door with a certain alacrity. 'I'll see you there.'

'Alrighty.' As the American disappeared, Elma returned her

attention to the phone. 'Sorry for keeping you waiting,' she trilled. 'This is Elma Rayes, Founder and CEO of the Christian Salvation Centre. We promise you more miracles for your money, guaranteed. How can I be of assistance?'

There was a snort from the other end of the phone. 'Cut the shit, girl. Are you high?'

'No, I am not high.' Hurling the wine glass across the room, Elma watched it bounce off the bed without breaking. 'As you well know, I am working. And I am working *sober*.'

'Good for you,' Michelangelo Federici laughed, 'good for you. And how are things in King's Cross? How is the conference going?'

'It's going fine.'

'Uhuh. Making money?'

'Of course.' Elma scratched absentmindedly at her chest. Her mouth felt dry and she had a strong desire for some more wine. Gazing at the bottle, she estimated that there was at least another glass and a half in there before it was empty.

'Good. Your cash flow could do with some extra *oomph*.'

Elma tip-toed around the end of the bed, looking to retrieve her wine glass. 'You're my lawyer, Mikey,' she said, grunting as she bent over to pick it up, 'not my damn accountant. What do you want?'

'Sorry to be the bearer of bad news,' the lawyer replied, 'when you're busy saving people and stuff . . .'

'But?'

'But you've got a problem.'

'Oh Christ,' Elma mumbled, wedging the phone under her ear as she reached for the booze.

From the other end of the phone came the gentle chuckle of the true non-believer. 'You can try calling the Boss,' Federici said, almost gently, 'but I don't think He's going to be much help to you on this one.'

SEVEN

They returned to the South Bank to find that Joseph Belsky was still securely locked inside his reinforced toilet. With much headshaking and sucking of teeth, a perplexed-looking panic room consultant refused to be drawn either on the precise nature of the problem, or the amount of time it might take for it to be resolved. Leaving Umar in charge of proceedings, the inspector quickly headed back towards the relative safety of the north side of the river.

Normally, there was nothing that Carlyle liked better than a stroll across Waterloo Bridge. With the Palace of Westminster on one side and St Paul's Cathedral on the other, and the murky, mighty Thames under your feet, it offered, in his humble opinion, the best views in the capital, especially at night. Tonight, however, there was no time to stop and dawdle; Carlyle was rapidly running out of time if he was to charge Seymour Erikssen and keep London safe from the capital's most prolific, if incompetent, thief.

'Idiot,' he chanted under his breath as he steamed northwards. 'Idiot, idiot, idiot.' It was beginning to look rather as if he'd been a bit too cute in leaking the story to the press; if 'London's worst criminal' walked free thanks to a bureaucratic cock-up, Carlyle would get it in the neck for sure. He knew from bitter experience that Bernie Gilmore, with his sources deep inside the police force, would be on the phone even before Seymour had managed to nip to the bar of the Jolly Friar on Charing Cross Road and order his first pint of London Pride. And where Bernie went, others followed, all of them full of the manufactured bemusement and outrage that was handed out to all journalists at birth.

'Idiot.' The last thing Carlyle needed was a lashing in the press – especially when he deserved it. Patting the mobile phone in the breast pocket of his jacket, he wondered if he should call his boss and give her a heads-up. Happily, Commander Carole Simpson had quite a high pain threshold when it came to the inspector's occasional errors of judgement. Over the years she had demonstrated a creditable willingness to watch his back. Carlyle liked to think that this was the result of her appreciation – almost unique among commanding officers during the course of his career – of his positive qualities. In reality, he knew it was as much to do with her desire for a quiet life as her own career began to wind down.

'Idiot.' Should he call Simpson or not? If he marked her card now, the fallout later might be less severe. On other hand, he didn't want to flag a problem that might not, in the end, materialize. The basic rule for all top brass – the less they know the better – still applied to Simpson, despite her positive qualities. Skipping past a shabby woman pushing a baby buggy, he lengthened his stride, keeping his gaze focused on the patch of pavement immediately in front of his feet.

The police station in Agar Street was at least five minutes' walk away, even at a brisk pace. Heading north, on the west side of the bridge, the inspector continued to curse himself for not paying more attention to the time as he slalomed between the promenading tourists, theatregoers coming out of the South Bank's latest hit show, *Frankenstein the Musical*, and straggling commuters coming the other way as they headed for Waterloo station.

As he reached the middle of the bridge, a familiar voice appeared out of the background hum.

'What are you doing here?'

'Huh?' Letting his head fall even closer to his chest, the inspector had no intention of stopping.

'John.'

Reluctantly slowing his pace, he half-turned to face the cheery smile of Susan Phillips.

The Met pathologist gently placed a hand on his arm. 'You're not trying to avoid me, are you?'

'Um. No. Not at all. Just a bit pushed for time.' Sticking a brittle smile on his face, the inspector finally came to a reluctant halt, stepping into the narrow cycle lane in order to get out of the steady two-way flow of pedestrians on the pavement. As he did so, a taxi advertising the latest Tom Cruise movie slid slowly past, moving out into the middle lane as the driver sought to slip round an obstacle that lay up ahead. Carlyle checked and saw that a yellow-green ambulance less than ten yards in front of him was blocking off the nearside lane for motorists. The back doors were open and a couple of paramedics were lifting a body on a gurney inside. Their unhurried manner indicated that their patient hadn't made it.

'So this one's not yours?' Phillips asked, gesturing towards the ambulance as she reached over to give him a kiss on the cheek.

Carlyle felt himself redden slightly. He had worked with Phillips for decades; she was one of the colleagues that he liked the most. But he couldn't remember her ever pecking him on the cheek before. When had they become so . . . *European*? The thought floated through his head that maybe she had acquired a continental boyfriend. Phillips, more than attractive even as she reached her fifties, went through men faster than other people went through shoes.

'The stiff?' he answered. 'No, no.' Momentarily forgetting that he was in a rush, the inspector watched one of the paramedics slam the doors shut and move round to the driver's door. 'Not at all. What happened?'

'Some guy dropped down dead on the pavement. Looks like a heart attack. I don't really know why they bothered calling me out. Nothing suspicious, as far as I can see.'

Carlyle sighed. 'Shit happens. Who was he?'

'Dunno.' Arms folded, she watched as the ambulance began slowly pulling away from the kerb. The small knot of rubber-neckers who had been hovering on the pavement to catch the free show began dispersing, and the backed-up traffic started moving more freely. Within seconds, it was as if the dead man had never existed.

Apart from the battered black leather briefcase left standing in the gutter, next to a drain cover.

Still standing in the bike lane, forcing the oncoming cyclists to give him a wide berth, the inspector frowned. 'Does that belong to the dead guy?'

'What?'

Carlyle pointed at the case. 'That.'

'Shit.' A look of irritation swept across the normally relaxed pathologist's face.

Carlyle glanced up and down the bridge. 'Where are the uniforms?'

'There was a PC and a plastic,' Phillips explained. 'Plastic policemen' was the less than flattering name that regular offic-ers had chosen for their volunteer colleagues, the Community Support Officers who were drafted in to beef up the numbers. 'They must have buggered off back to the station.'

'Brilliant.' Carlyle shook his head in disgust. 'Absolutely brilliant.'

'It happens,' Phillips said philosophically.

'Where were they from? Charing Cross?'

'I don't think so. I think it was Waterloo.' She mentioned a couple of names.

Carlyle made a face. 'Don't know them.' But he would cer-tainly make a point of tracking them down.

'I can check.'

'Don't worry.' Glancing up at the digital clock on the façade of the National Theatre, he remembered why he had been hurrying back north. 'I really need to get going.' Grabbing the briefcase, he jumped back onto the pavement. 'Don't worry though, I'll sort this out.'

'Thanks, John,' Phillips shouted after him as he scuttled away.

'No problem,' he called back over his shoulder, but he was already too far away for her to hear.

EIGHT

Carlyle's eye was drawn to the picture of the young woman wearing nothing but a cyclist's crash helmet and a smile. With her back to the camera, she had a bright red handprint emblazoned on each buttock. *Is that PhotoShop?* he wondered. *Or did someone actually plant their hand on her backside?*

Dropping the briefcase he'd recovered from Waterloo Bridge onto the floor, he felt a stab of regret. Why had he never met the kind of girl who would let you paint her bum and photograph it for posterity?

Story of his life.

Underneath the image was the legend: *Don't forget WNBR Day.*

Painted Bum Day.

Looking up from his copy of the *Daily Mail*, the desk sergeant caught him staring. 'Not bad, eh?'

Trying not to look sheepish, Carlyle mumbled something noncommittal.

'It'll stop the traffic,' the sergeant went on.

'What will?'

'World Naked Bike Ride Day,' the man explained.

What? 'Ah, yes, of course.'

'The London ride comes across Waterloo Bridge, down the Strand and round Trafalgar Square.'

Carlyle took another look at the girl in the poster. 'So what's it got to do with painting your bum?'

The sergeant shrugged. 'Who knows? It's some kind of protest about something or other.'

I suppose there are worse things than people riding round in the altogether, Carlyle thought, unable to decide whether he found the event amusing or annoying.

'But really,' the sergeant scoffed, 'who cares?'

An image popped into the inspector's head of a sea of colourful arseholes riding past Nelson's Column. 'What about public decency?' he asked. 'Won't there be a lot of complaints?'

'Yeah. We'll get some. Usually from the people busy taking the most photos.'

'But isn't it illegal?'

'Of course it's bloody illegal,' the sergeant snorted. 'Not to mention cold and uncomfortable. But it's been going on for three or four years now. They are expecting as many as six thousand riders to turn up this time around.'

'Bloody hell.'

'It's described as "clothes optional", so not all of them will be naked, but most of them will – at least, they will if the weather's good.'

Carlyle shook his head. Why anyone would want to cycle through Central London in their birthday suit was totally beyond him. Biking in London was dangerous enough, even if you kept all of your clothes on. What if you got knocked off in the buff? It didn't bear thinking about.

'And at the end of the day, there's not a lot of point in arresting them just for getting their kit off, is there?'

'I suppose not,' the inspector agreed.

'Apart from anything else, think of the practicalities.'

'Yes.'

The sergeant raised an inquisitive eyebrow. 'Have you ever tried to arrest anyone who didn't have any clothes on?'

Carlyle thought about it for a moment. The only person that came to mind was Christina O'Brien, Umar's partner. He recalled with some admiration the night he had witnessed

Christina's brisk and expert assault on a uniform on the stage of Everton's Gentleman's Club. That, however, was not something he was going to share with the desk sergeant.

'Not that I recall,' he lied.

'It's difficult to know where to put your hands.'

'I can imagine.'

'And the press go bananas – any excuse to publish a photo of someone getting their tits out.'

'Mm.'

'You've got to be realistic. There is only so much we can do.'

'Yeah,' Carlyle nodded, having no idea what the sergeant was talking about. 'When it comes down to it, our priority will be to keep an eye out for any lurking perverts using it as an excuse to get their todgers out in public.' He thought about that for a moment. 'Of course, distinguishing the pervs from the legitimate protestors will be a doddle.'

'Ultimately, it's not my problem,' the sergeant observed. 'As you can imagine, we are not short of volunteers to cover the event.'

'I bet.'

'After all, it beats bike marking outside Tesco.'

'Sure.' Carlyle wasn't sure what bike marking was, but it didn't sound like much fun.

'Want me to put you down on the rota? It's guaranteed overtime – should be at least three or four hours.'

The promise of additional cash caused the inspector to hesitate. Once an inalienable right, a key component of an officer's income, overtime was now an occasional perk and getting rarer all the time. When it came your way, you normally didn't think twice. As always, he could do with the money. Alice's school fees would be due soon and the family finances were feeling the squeeze.

At the same time, however, Carlyle knew that he needed extra shifts like a hole in the head. He had little enough time off as it was. And, perhaps more importantly, explaining to his wife that

39

he was off to observe naked girls with painted rears would be difficult.

Very difficult indeed.

Actually, it would be impossible.

The sergeant looked at him expectantly.

'It's okay,' said Carlyle, somewhat reluctantly, 'I'll pass.'

'Suit yourself,' the sergeant replied. 'Anyway, back to more pressing matters . . .'

Knowing exactly what he meant, Carlyle's heart sank. 'Seymour Erikssen?'

'Gone.'

'You let him walk?'

'Not that I had any choice in the matter. You ran out of time. He left about ten minutes ago.'

'Shit.'

'On the way out, he gave me a cheery wave and asked me to give you his best regards – said that he'd see you next time.'

'The cheeky old bastard,' Carlyle grumbled.

'There's no messing about with Seymour. He knows the drill.'

'Well, he bloody would, wouldn't he?' Carlyle said, hoisting the briefcase he'd recovered from Waterloo Bridge onto the desk. 'It could be his specialist subject on *Mastermind*.'

Studiously ignoring the briefcase on his desk, the sergeant went back to reading a story in his newspaper. The headline, as far as Carlyle could make out, reading it upside down, was about a woman who had been impregnated by a squid. Not for the first time, he contemplated the benefits of the internet destroying the newspaper industry completely.

'Bloody hell,' the sergeant mumbled to himself.

Bloody hell indeed, thought the inspector. The phone started vibrating in his pocket. With a sigh, he pulled it out, checked the name on the screen and said, 'Hello, Bernie.'

'What's all this I hear about Britain's most notorious criminal being allowed to walk right out of your nick?' was the journalist's cheery opening gambit.

'He was London's most hopeless criminal, last time I looked,' said Carlyle wearily.

'Whatever his bloody moniker was is irrelevant. I wrote about him yesterday. What's going on?'

'Nothing much.' Even to his own ears, the inspector's attempt at insouciance fell completely flat.

'Don't muck me about, I'm on deadline,' Bernie huffed, bashing noisily away at a keyboard to make his point.

'You're always on deadline,' Carlyle pointed out.

'Exactly. So, why did you let him go?'

'No comment.'

Bernie started typing even harder. It sounded like he wanted to break his computer, such was the fury of his news-gathering frenzy. 'Don't try and play that bloody game with me. After all, you're the one who wanted a puff piece only yesterday.' There was a menacing pause as he hit some more keys. 'You don't want to see your name in print, do you?'

'No,' Carlyle said testily, not happy at being threatened. 'Of course not.'

'Stop messing about then, and give me something.'

'Okay, okay.' Stepping away from the desk, Carlyle lowered his voice. 'On background, not for quotation, we haven't let him walk: investigations are continuing.' He tried to explain the essence of what had happened without having to actually spell out the reality of the situation.

'So,' Bernie asked suspiciously, 'Seymour's still under lock and key in the station?'

Pushing through the front doors, Carlyle jogged down the steps and across the street. 'I'm not at the station at the moment.' A motorbike roared by, providing a convenient alibi.

'You know less than me,' Bernie scoffed.

It wouldn't be the first time, Carlyle mused. 'Why don't you just quote a source familiar with the investigation saying that Seymour Erikssen is a priority case and will be dealt with accordingly.'

41

'Meaningless crap,' the hack snorted, typing the quote straight into his piece.

Should fit right in then, Carlyle thought.

'Let me know when you find out more.'

'Will do.'

'And the next time you want me to run a story, make sure it has a happy ending.'

'You don't like happy endings,' Carlyle grumped.

'I don't like stories where a cop tries to claim a much-overdue win,' Bernie thundered, 'and then, after I've put my name to the story, somehow contrives to snatch defeat from the jaws of bloody victory.'

'But Bernie—' Before the inspector had the chance to say any more, the call was terminated. He thought about calling the journalist back – but what was the point? Carlyle knew that he had nothing more to say about Seymour Erikssen. For a moment, he contemplated trading something on the axeman, but decided against it. His media-handling skills simply weren't up to it. Putting the phone back into his pocket, he took a couple of deep breaths and headed back inside.

NINE

During the couple of minutes that the inspector had spent on the pavement outside, a large mug bearing the image of a crown and the legend KEEP CALM AND GO AWAY had materialized by the desk sergeant's elbow. As he approached the desk, Carlyle saw that his slow-reading colleague had moved on two pages. Now he was engrossed in a story about tourists dying – allegedly – of blowfish poisoning in Bangkok.

'Are all the stories in that paper about fish?' Carlyle quipped.

All he got by way of reply was a blank look.

'Never mind.'

The sergeant pointed to the briefcase which he had moved to the end of the desk, as far away from his person as possible. 'What d'ya want me to do with that?'

'A guy had a fatal heart attack on Waterloo Bridge,' Carlyle explained. 'The uniforms left his case sitting on the pavement.'

The sergeant's gaze started drifting back to his paper.

'Book it, stick it in the evidence locker and we'll sort it out later.'

The sergeant made a noise that could have been a grunt or perhaps indigestion.

The inspector took that as a, '*Yes, of course, sir, three bloody bags full, sir,*' and decided to move on. 'Right now, I need to speak to Taimur Rage.'

'The mad axeman,' said the sergeant languidly, not looking up. Finally tiring of international fish news, he turned the paper over and began scanning the sports pages.

'That's the one,' said Carlyle, beginning to get ever so slightly annoyed.

'He's in Interview Room Three – or maybe Five. Mason is keeping an eye on him.'

'Good.' WPC Sonia Mason was that rarest of creatures – a uniform that Carlyle could actually pick out of a line-up. Mason, barely a year out of officer training at Hendon, was one of the most sensible young officers that the inspector had come across in a long while. She had a good manner, to boot, and he was sure that she would go far in her police career, unlike the essentially inert lump in front of him. 'Has the axeman had his call?' Normally, Carlyle wasn't keen on allowing suspects to get on the phone too quickly, to make their statutory phone call to their lawyer. In this case, however, with the guy completely bang to rights, he was rather more relaxed.

'I believe so.' The sergeant looked up, to let Carlyle know that he was getting pretty fed up himself with the constant interruptions to his reading. 'Maybe. We haven't had a lawyer turn up yet.'

'Okay.' As he was about to leave, Carlyle was conscious of someone arriving at his shoulder. Turning, he faced a guy much taller than himself, maybe six foot, give or take. Tanned, with a light five o'clock shadow, he was wearing a grey pinstripe suit with a blue shirt, open at the neck. Ignoring the inspector, the civilian addressed the sergeant in a businesslike tone. 'Michelangelo Federici. I'm Mr Rage's legal adviser.'

The sergeant shot Carlyle an *over to you* look.

Turning to the inspector, the lawyer held out a hand. 'Michelangelo Federici,' he repeated.

With no particular enthusiasm, the inspector took his hand. 'Inspector John Carlyle. I'm in charge of this case.'

'Good. In that case, I wonder if you could show me to my client, please.'

'Come this way,' said Carlyle, gesturing towards the doors leading to the station proper. 'We can go and see him together.'

* * *

Downstairs, Carlyle paused at the door to the interview room. Turning to the axeman's lawyer, he adopted what he hoped sounded like a worldly-wise, *we're all in this together* tone. 'The basic situation here appears to be very straightforward,' he said quietly. 'Your client smashed his way into the victim's flat and then tried to kill him. Taimur is lucky that Mr Belsky was able to lock himself in the bog or we would no doubt be looking at a murder charge.'

Federici nodded in polite agreement. 'I understand all of that, Inspector. Taimur explained to me very clearly what happened. And I know that you will want to pursue a quick and uncomplicated investigation.'

'Always.'

'For my part, I have no intention of dragging this out any longer than is necessary. No one benefits from turning this into a circus.'

Carlyle could feel a *but* coming on. Taking a deep breath, he braced himself for the weasel words that would inevitably follow.

'But, as you know, things are rarely as simple as they seem.'

Exhaling, the inspector replied, 'On the contrary,' trying to sound as philosophical as possible. 'In my experience, things are often *exactly* as simple as they seem.'

Federici dropped his case onto the threadbare carpet. 'As I said, you will get no interference or obfuscation from me.'

That'll be a first for a lawyer, the inspector thought sourly. 'I appreciate it,' he said aloud.

'And I don't think you'll have too many problems with Taimur himself. He's a nice, quiet boy.'

'Who tried to put an axe in a guy's head,' Carlyle interjected.

'For what it's worth,' said the lawyer apologetically, 'I don't think he would have gone through with it.'

'Mm.'

'Have you spoken to him yet?'

'No.'

'He's not some kind of religious fanatic, rocking backwards and forwards, mumbling passages from the Koran.'

'I'm sure, like you say, he's just a normal kid who took a wrong turn. But you know better than I do that all that stuff should be saved for the judge. All I want to do is get the facts down on paper and then it's a matter for the CPS.'

'I understand perfectly.' The lawyer held up his hands. 'But surely you are interested in the boy's backstory? Presumably you want an explanation of what happened?'

'Explanations . . . excuses. It's all the same thing. Keep it for court.'

'Fine, fine,' the lawyer snapped. 'What are you going to tell the media?'

Carlyle thought about his run-in with Bernie Gilmore. 'As little as possible.'

'Good.'

'It'll be quite the little shit storm as it is.'

'Yes.' The lawyer did not seem that distressed by the prospect.

'I would suggest the less all of us say, the better,' Carlyle went on.

'Agreed.' There was a moment's reflection before Federici added, 'However . . .'

Here we go, Carlyle thought. 'Yes?'

'I fear that we will have some problems with the boy's parents.'

'What do you mean?'

'They can be difficult.'

'If they're that bothered,' Carlyle snorted, 'where are they?'

'Sorry?'

'If they are that worried about their son,' he repeated, speaking slowly, 'why have they not come to the station to see what's going on with him?'

'They're working,' Federici said lamely. 'At least, the mother is. Technically, she is my client.'

'She pays the bills.'

At the mention of money, a pained expression crossed the lawyer's face. 'Yes.'

'And the father?'

'I have only met him a couple of times,' Federici explained, 'but he doesn't seem to have any problem with me representing his son.'

'So this is not the first time Taimur has been in trouble?' Carlyle asked, looking through the window in the cell door and nodding at the youngster who still sat, staring vacantly into space.

'There's been nothing like this before,' the lawyer said hastily. 'Have you not read the file?'

'Not yet,' Carlyle admitted. The reality was he hadn't even seen the damn thing yet. 'Anyway, the parents have not been able to keep him on the straight and narrow.'

'They are long divorced, which is part of the problem.'

Carlyle scratched his head. He was about as interested in dysfunctional families as he was in religion. What was it that Tolstoy had said? *'All happy families are the same, each unhappy family is unhappy in its own way.'* The quote was one of the few things rattling around his head from his largely long-forgotten school days. 'However . . . *strained* the domestic arrangements, I would impress upon both parents,' he said, slipping into his best approximation of social worker mode, 'the need to support their son at this time.'

'Of course.'

'You should stress that they will not do that, however, by shouting their mouths off to the press.' The thought popped into the inspector's head that Bernie Gilmore was probably tracking them down already and Carlyle realized that he was almost certainly wasting his breath.

'I will see what I can do, but there are no guarantees.' The lawyer reached down for his bag. 'I'll talk you through the family situation in more detail later. Let me speak to my client first and then we can deal with your questions.'

'Okay,' Carlyle agreed, suddenly distracted by the smells that had started coming down the hallway from the nearby canteen. Despite his recent visit to the 93 Coffee Bar, he was still feeling hungry. In the back of his mind the idea was growing that an egg roll, smothered in ketchup, and a mug of green tea would be just the thing to hit the spot. 'Talk to your client,' he said. 'I'll be back in fifteen minutes or so.'

Pushing open the door, Federici gave him a broad smile. 'Perfect.'

TEN

Having sauntered out of the police station at Charing Cross without a care in the world, Seymour Erikssen decided to celebrate his unexpected release from the cells with a pint of ridiculously expensive Estonian lager in the Enclosure Bar, just off Seven Dials. All black paint and chrome fittings, the Enclosure wasn't really Seymour's type of place, but the clientele – a mixture of loud Eurotrash, gormless tourists and working girls – potentially provided some interesting pickings. Thanks to the best efforts of the Metropolitan Police, his timing was good. It was getting late; people were becoming drunk and drunks made good victims.

Sipping his £8 beer, Seymour settled down for some people-watching. It crossed his mind that someone might recognize him from the story in the *Standard* but, then again, the Enclosure crowd weren't the kind of people who read newspapers, even free ones. 'Bloody journalists,' Seymour clucked to himself. 'They write rubbish that nobody bothers to read any more.' The papers might think of him as hopeless, but that was because they only knew about the times when things *hadn't* worked out. In his line of employment, being arrested was an occupational hazard – and it didn't happen nearly as often as those poking fun at him liked to think.

By the far wall, a platinum blonde with a pageboy haircut was pawing a smug-looking pretty boy. On a large TV above their heads, a music video was playing. The sound was muted and Seymour slowly realized that a completely different song was

49

playing over the bar's sound system. On the screen, some girl singer and a group of dancers in combat uniforms were stomping around a derelict factory in front of a burned-out car. The whole thing looked exactly like a million other videos before it, and even the performers themselves appeared bored by what they were doing.

Seymour drained the last of his drink and was unsuccessfully trying to signal to the barman that he wanted another when he caught a flash of yellow out of the corner of his eye. Turning his head, he clocked a man in the most outrageous suit he'd ever seen – some kind of yellow tartan number – flanked by a couple of girls whose short skirts, perfect teeth and ridiculously inflated chests immediately screamed hookers.

Pulling out his wallet, the guy waved a black credit card and a barman came scurrying. In a comedy American accent that was clearly fake, the punter ordered a magnum of Bollinger champagne. Placing his empty glass on the bar, Seymour smiled. His guests had arrived. It was time to get back to work.

ELEVEN

Did she have a condom in her bag? Did she care? Feeling more than a little drunk, Carole Simpson slipped off her T-bar sandals and scrunched her toes into the carpet. 'Aahhh, that feels *nice.*'

After a long, boring day at the Home Office's Modern Policing Conference (Theme: 'Accountability and Value Delivery') she felt recklessly exhausted. Ten hours stuck in the windowless basement of a Central London hotel, listening to presentations on delivering policing and justice reforms i.e. keeping your crime stats looking reasonable while sacking as many people as possible in order to meet the Government's budget cuts – was enough to sap anyone's will to live. The day's events had been followed by a drinks reception and an interminable Awards dinner. And all that tomorrow offered was the prospect of more of the same. No wonder she had downed two G&Ts, a bottle and a half of wine and a very large cognac at dinner.

Taking a swig from her glass of Sancerre, she staggered against the wall.

'Carole.' Laughing, her companion picked up the shoes and began weaving his way down the corridor.

You're as drunk as I am, Simpson thought, hiccupng. Somewhere in the far recesses of her mushy brain, the Commander knew that the sensible course of action would be to go home. She started to look at her watch but thought better of it. Really, she should have gone home hours ago. Instead, she watched the

Deputy Chief Constable of Cleveland – or was it Cumbria? – stop in front of the door to his hotel room and begin fumbling with his key card.

Swaying gently in the air conditioning, she watched as it took Lover Boy three attempts to unlock the door. *Correction*, said the distant voice inside her head, *you're even drunker than I am.*

Holding the door open, he threw her shoes into the room and beckoned for her to follow. For a moment, her legs seemed unable to move. When was the last time she had had sex? The sad truth was, it was too long ago to remember. Another hiccup. She started to giggle like a teenager. *I wonder – will he be able to get it up?*

'C'mon,' slurred her host as he fell through the door.

'Hold on,' she giggled, embarrassed if anyone should hear, 'I'm coming.'

Trying to look thoroughly pissed off, Carlyle tapped an index finger on the sheets of paper lying on the desk in front of him. 'I'm sorry, but this isn't anywhere near good enough.'

Looking at the paint peeling on the ceiling, arms folded, the would-be axe murderer, Taimur Rage, licked his lips, saying nothing. The inspector had to admit that the youth sitting in front of him wasn't quite what he had expected. Cleanshaven, with curly chestnut hair and intense brown eyes, the boy appeared considerably younger than his stated age of nineteen. Wearing jeans and a *Rage Against the Machine* T-shirt under a stylish navy cardigan, with an expensive pair of grey trainers on his feet, he didn't much look like a poster boy for al-Qaeda either.

Still, Carlyle thought, *stranger things have happened.*

Michelangelo Federici gave his client a gentle pat on the shoulder before turning his attention to the inspector. 'All in all, it looks like a full confession to me.'

'A confession, but hardly a full one.' Carlyle looked at Taimur.

'I need the names of his associates and the details of his . . .' he struggled to find the right word '. . . cell.'

'His cell?' Federici frowned. 'What is the narrative that you are trying to create here? We have explained what happened and my client has already expressed contrition for his momentary lapse of sanity. There isn't any—'

Carlyle held up a hand. *Whatever happened to no obfuscation?* he thought wearily. 'The attempted murder of Joseph Belsky is clearly a terrorist hate crime,' he snapped, cringing at the way the words sounded coming out of his mouth. 'It was conducted against a man with a price on his head. And you are telling me that this – this kid – did it all on his own?'

The lawyer shrugged.

Eyeing both men carefully, Carlyle sat back in his chair. 'When I walk out of here,' he said slowly, 'if all I have in my hand is this pile of . . .' he waved his hand dismissively at the statement '. . . *shite*, this investigation will take a most unfortunate turn.'

'You have to do your job,' said Federici equably. 'We are co-operating fully.'

'If I am not able to do my job, the security services will be down here in the blink of an eye for a quick waterboarding session.' Carlyle jabbed a finger towards Taimur's face. 'Do you want to end up in Guantanamo Bay?' He knew that he was talking bollocks – waterboarding was so last decade – but in the absence of anything else, he reckoned it was worth a try.

Finally meeting his gaze, the boy gave him a blank look.

'Well?'

Taimur started to say something but was quickly stopped by his lawyer. 'My client has nothing to add to his statement which is both truthful and very comprehensive. He is adamant that he acted alone, having been radicalised on the basis of information gleaned from the internet.' Pulling a pen from his jacket pocket, Federici handed it to Taimur and pointed to the bottom of the page. 'Sign it there.' The boy did as instructed and Federici handed the statement to the inspector. 'There you are – a full confession.'

We'll see about that, thought Carlyle, reluctantly taking the sheet of paper from the lawyer.

Pushing back his chair, Federici got to his feet. 'I told you that we would not waste any of your time this evening.'

'My investigation is continuing,' Carlyle said lamely.

'No doubt.' Scooping up the remaining papers, the lawyer tidied them into his briefcase. 'In the meantime, I'm sure that we could all do with some sleep.'

He had barely made it to his desk on the third floor of the station when a call came in from Umar.

'Tell me you've got the guy out,' Carlyle said.

'Not yet. They've now decided to try and smash through the wall.'

Carlyle frowned. 'Why didn't they think of that earlier?'

'It's not as easy as a few blows with a sledgehammer,' Umar explained, the weariness in his voice clear. 'The walls have steel reinforcements as well.'

'Hasn't it got a window?'

'Nope. Basically, the guy has locked himself in a big metal box. The door has a computer-generated lock and there's been some kind of IT meltdown.'

Sounds all too plausible, Carlyle thought.

'It looks like it's gonna take a while longer to get him out.'

'Yeah, but how much longer?'

'No idea.'

'Great.'

'Look at it this way,' Umar chuckled suddenly, 'it's a good advert for the people who make the panic rooms. No one can get into the bloody thing.'

'No,' Carlyle mused, 'but the issue here is how you get *out* of it. Are you sure that Belsky won't suffocate in there?'

'He's fine. He's got food and water in there. Even some books. His mobile can't get a signal but he has a landline. I spoke to him an hour or so ago and he sounded very chipper.'

'Okay.'

'Meanwhile, how are you getting on with the axe man?'

'Axe *boy*, more like.' Carlyle talked the sergeant through the highlights of his interview with Taimur Rage.

'That's great,' Umar observed, 'that he's confessed.'

'We'll see,' Carlyle said.

'It's a total result!' Umar exclaimed, ignoring his boss's grumpiness. 'A nice, quick win. Good news.'

'Perhaps.'

'I can feel a press conference coming on.'

'I'll leave that to you.' Carlyle thought of Seymour Erikssen and Bernie Gilmore. 'But let's try and keep this little drama out of the media for the moment.'

'Too late for that,' Umar said. 'The press have turned up already.'

'What?' Carlyle groaned. 'How did they find out?'

'Belsky rang up the BBC and gave them an interview.'

'What a genius. I hope you told him to shut up.'

'I've asked him not to speak to any more press until we get him out. So far, we've got a couple of TV crews and half a dozen reporters on the street outside.' Umar yawned. 'At least the uniforms managed to stop them getting into the building.'

'Mm.'

'Are you coming back over here?'

You've got to be kidding, Carlyle thought. *I'm going to bed.* 'I've got stuff to do here,' he lied. 'Anyway, sounds like you've got things well under control.'

Umar registered his displeasure with a grunt.

'What about the girl?' Carlyle asked, ignoring his sergeant's obvious dismay at the way in which his night had unfolded.

'Her mother finally made an appearance and picked her up. They've gone home. She seemed to be fine.'

55

'Children can be remarkably resilient,' Carlyle mused. 'What's her name?'

'Joanne . . . Joanne Belsky. Nine years old. She fell asleep after you left. Seems a nice kid.'

Joanne *Belsky*. Carlyle thought about that for a moment. 'Mother not married?'

'Maybe not. Does it make a difference?'

'No, I suppose not.'

'Anyway, you can ask her yourself. I told her to bring the girl to the station so that she could make a statement.'

'Fine.' Carlyle glanced at the clock on the wall. It was already a lot closer to 10 a.m. than he would have liked. As he got older, the inspector found that a lack of sleep could seriously impede his performance on the job. Eight, or even nine hours, was the minimum required if he was going to trot into work fresh and ready to go. Tonight he was only going to get a fraction of that. On the other hand, he was going to get a lot more than Umar. The realization made him feel a little better. 'Let me know when you finally get Grandpa Belsky out of Fort Knox.'

Umar laughed. 'Will do.'

'Seeing as we've supposedly "solved" the case already, there's no rush.'

He was woken by his daughter flopping onto the bed. 'Da-ad. Get up. Mum says you're taking us out for breakfast.'

'Urgh,' Carlyle groaned, burrowing deeper under the duvet.

'Get up,' Alice demanded, stripping off the covers.

'Bloody hell.' Yawning, he scratched himself. 'Shouldn't you be off to school?'

'It's Saturday,' Alice trilled. Grabbing her father by his ankle, she made a half-hearted attempt to pull him off the bed.

'Bugger off,' he hissed, his eyes clamped shut against the light streaming through the window.

'It's almost ten o'clock,' Alice laughed, letting go of his foot. 'Mum says you've got one minute to get out of bed.'

'Yes, it's time for you to get up.' Helen appeared in the doorway waving his mobile in her hand. 'Your phone's going mental and I need some coffee. So hurry up.'

'Okay, okay, you win.' Slowly, slowly, Carlyle edged himself off the bed. Opening one eye, he stumbled towards the bathroom. 'Give me five minutes.'

TWELVE

Entering the Caffè Nero at the top of Long Acre, the inspector wished he was back in bed. It was hot, noisy and, as usual, the place was full of tourists who couldn't find the piazza. Luckily, his arrival had coincided with an elderly couple getting up to leave. Plonking himself down in an armchair, Carlyle commandeered a third chair and settled in to guard the table while Helen and Alice went to buy the drinks. In his hand was a bag of goodies smuggled in from the Patisserie Valerie next door. The neighbouring café did the best pastries, Nero did the best coffee and the inspector liked to mix and match. Sticking his hand in the bag, he pulled out a chunk of almond croissant and slipped it into his mouth under the bored gaze of the wan-looking girl who was briskly clearing the used cups, plates and empty packaging from the table. Alice and Helen were chatting away in the queue, stuck behind a family who seemed incapable of agreeing on their order. Muttering unhappily, Carlyle pulled out his mobile. The screen told him he had eight missed calls, annoying him even further. Grumbling, he hit 901 and pulled up the first message.

It's Bernie Gilmore, call me.

Grimacing, Carlyle hit 3 to delete the call and waited for the next message to play.

It's Umar, nothing much to report—
3.

Inspector, it's the front desk at Charing Cross. There's a guy here wanting to speak to you called Chris Brennan—

3.

After an almost interminable delay, Helen appeared with a coffee in each hand. Behind her, Alice was drinking an outsized orange and mango smoothie through a straw. Under her arm was a copy of the *Daily Mirror*. Carlyle noted the front page headline – MY SEX GANG SHAME – and sighed. *When's she going to start reading a proper paper?* he wondered. Long of the view that they would all be better off if they didn't read any newspapers at all, the inspector really didn't like the thought of his daughter reading that kind of stuff. But she was growing up and he realized that there simply wasn't anything that he could do about it. Like so many things, if he made it an issue, he made it a problem.

'Here you go.' Helen placed his cup carefully on the table as Alice jumped into the next chair. Kicking off her sandals, she swung her legs over the side of the chair and began reading her paper.

'Thanks.' Taking a cup, Carlyle took a mouthful of coffee – nice and hot, just how he liked it – and checked out the rest of his missed calls. Umar had called him another three times, most recently just before nine. *Looks like he's had to pull an all-nighter,* Carlyle thought. Grabbing the remains of his croissant, he handed the Patisserie Valerie bag to his wife.

Taking a seat opposite him, Helen pulled a chocolate muffin out of the bag and began cutting it into quarters with a plastic knife.

Mm, Carlyle thought, *that looks good.*

'Tough night?' Helen asked, popping a sliver of muffin into her mouth.

Chewing on the last of his croissant, Carlyle told her, 'More for Umar than for me.' Keeping his voice low, he explained the situation with Belsky and the axe man.

'Yeah. I heard about it on the radio this morning. He jumped in a panic room and can't get out.'

'Some problem with the lock, apparently. At least the panic room did the job it was supposed to do.'

'Seems like it – a bit too well, maybe. Is he still stuck in there?'

'As far as I know.' Relaxing into his armchair, Carlyle was in no hurry to check in with Umar to find out.

'Will he be okay?'

'Belsky? Yeah, he should be fine. He could probably survive in there for weeks, if not months, if he had to.'

'In a prison of his own making.'

'Kind of. If the worst comes to the worst, I suppose they can smash through the outside wall or something.'

Picking up her cup, Helen took a sip and settled back in her chair. 'Serves him right.'

Carlyle frowned. 'What do you mean?'

'Well, it was a deliberately provocative thing to do.'

'What? Drawing a cartoon of the prophet Muhammad?'

'Under the circumstances, it was a rather juvenile, *male* thing to do.' A look descended on Helen's face that Carlyle knew only too well. Stupidly, he had risen to the bait and she was going to educate him on a few basic facts of life. 'Publishing a cartoon that they knew would cause offence and wind up a whole cross-section of nutters was just self-indulgent and totally irresponsible.'

'Ha.' Carlyle laughed. Working for an international medical aid charity, his wife was the social conscience of the family. However, that did not mean that she was a stereotypical, lentil-sucking liberal. Helen judged everything – and everyone – on their merits, as she saw them. And her husband liked the fact that she could regularly surprise him with her trenchant views on random subjects. 'What about freedom of speech?'

'It has its limits,' Helen declared, 'like everything else. A greedy publisher publishes a controversial cartoon, in order to sell newspapers. It's a commercial business decision, nothing to do with free speech.'

'Mm.'

'And you have a willing dupe like Joseph Belsky, who is more than ready to play along, in order to get his fifteen minutes of fame.'

'Rather more than fifteen minutes,' Carlyle said. 'This palaver has been going on for years.'

'You know what I mean. It's just a way of saying *look at me.* Like,' she waved a hand in the air, 'like the American author who shot himself in the head to get publicity for his book.'

That sounds like a good idea, thought Carlyle. *Maybe it'll catch on.*

Tuning into their conversation, Alice looked up. 'Did he kill himself?'

'No, I think he survived.' Helen took a sip of her coffee. 'It was in the paper last week; some guy you've never heard of.'

'Not really serious then, was he?' Not waiting for a reply, Alice ducked back behind the pages of her paper.

Looking at her husband, Helen raised an amused eyebrow. 'That's exactly the point. It's just dilettantism.'

'Either way, the police still have to clean up the mess.'

Reaching across the table, Helen gave him a consoling pat on the arm. 'Poor you.'

Yes, Carlyle thought, *poor bloody me.* He was momentarily distracted by two pretty girls in short skirts wandering into the café.

'I've met him a couple of times.'

'Eh?' Worried that his gawping had been noticed, he quickly turned to meet his wife's gaze.

'Belsky.' If Helen had noticed his wandering eye, she was too polite to mention it. 'He's a regular donor and has attended a couple of Avalon's fundraising events. He was at the Congo event a while back. Even gave us some drawings for the charity auction. They raised a few hundred quid.'

'If he's a supporter of the charity, shouldn't you be supporting him, rather than biting the hand that feeds you?'

Finishing her coffee, she gave him a stern look. 'We don't support people willy-nilly, just because they give us some cash. You can be a berk and still manage to support a good cause.'

'I suppose so.'

'Belsky struck me as being more than a bit smug. He knew what he was doing when he drew the cartoon. In the blink of an

61

eye, he went from being an anonymous cartoonist to some kind of poster boy for western democracy, which, as we all know, is a long way from being perfect.'

'True.' With the conversation veering off at a tangent, the inspector glanced at his watch, wondering if he really shouldn't be getting on his way.

'At the charity do, I was on his table and he was holding court all night,' Helen explained. 'It was all about him, if you know what I mean. He's a man with a monster ego.'

'Umar will get him out. By the way, before I forget, it will be baby Ella's birthday soon. What shall we get her?' i.e. *Can you organize a present from us?* He flashed what he hoped was a winning smile.

'God. Is it a year already?' Reaching into her bag, Helen pulled out a diary and a biro. Scribbling down a note, she put both pen and diary back into the bag. 'Time flies.'

'Yeah.' Instinctively, they both looked over at Alice, still engrossed in her paper, and exchanged a knowing smile. There was nothing that accelerated the passage of time like being a parent.

'Alice and I can see about getting something in the market this morning.'

'Thanks.'

'I've got plans,' said Alice flatly.

Her mother took a deep breath. 'Well, it won't take long. I can give Christina a call and see what she thinks might be good to get.'

Carlyle brushed the remains of his pastry from his shirt. 'That would be great. Umar says she's having a bit of a hard time right now.'

'It's a hard time for anyone, after having a baby.'

'Sure.'

'Maybe she's missing work.'

'She's hardly going to go back to Everton's, is she?' Everton's was a strip club round the corner from the Carlyle family's flat, close to Holborn tube. Christina, an American student, had first met Umar there when the Met had raided the place, looking for illegal immigrants.

'No,' said Helen, her voice tart, 'but she might want to do something.'

'Who works at Everton's?' Alice asked.

'No one,' said her father.

'Maybe we should do some babysitting,' said Helen. 'Give them some time off to go and see a movie or something.'

I don't know about that, Carlyle thought. As far as the inspector was concerned, his babysitting days were long gone. 'Er, yes,' he replied, trying to hide his lack of enthusiasm. 'Why not?'

'It would be nice to at least offer,' his wife replied, picking up on his downbeat tone.

'Yes.' *Just as long as they don't take us up on it.*

'It's been a long time since you changed a nappy,' Helen pointed out.

'Not that long.'

'Dad,' Alice protested, not looking up from her reading.

'Well . . .' Suddenly his brain disengaged from his mouth as he recalled the voicemail from the desk sergeant at the station. *Chris Brennan. Chris bloody Brennan. What did* he *want?* Jumping to his feet, he was in two minds. Should he head for the station, or head back across the river to Belsky's apartment? Making a decision, he reached over and kissed his wife on the top of her head. 'I'd better get going.'

'Okay.' Reaching down, Helen picked up the *Celebs* section from Alice's newspaper, which had fallen on the floor as she waved him on his way. 'See you later.'

'See you, Dad.' Standing over his lounging daughter, he could see that Alice had reached the newspaper's problem page and was checking out the agony aunt's response to the question *Is my boyfriend gay?*

That's one question I don't have to worry about, he cheerily told himself as he headed for the door.

THIRTEEN

Sitting in the gloom of the VIP Room at Everton's, he watched Christina, naked from the waist down, slowly remove the bra from a slender blonde girl that he didn't recognize. His breathing accelerated as the two smiling women moved towards him . . .

'Sergeant.'

'Huh?' He felt a hand on his shoulder.

'Sergeant, wake up.'

Slowly opening his eyes, Umar focused on the WPC standing over him. She was neither blonde, nor smiling. Fortunately, she didn't seem to notice the monster erection in his jeans as she stepped away from him.

'Sorry,' he mumbled. 'I just dozed off.'

'Don't worry, you haven't missed much. But it looks like problem solved. They're just about to get Belsky out of the panic room. The engineering guy says it should be open in a couple of minutes.'

'Good. Thanks. I'll be there in a moment.' Waiting for the uniform to turn away and head back towards the cartoonist's study, Umar pushed himself up from the sofa and got unsteadily to his feet. Half-lifting an arm, he tentatively sniffed his armpit. *Urgh, not good.* His body ached with tiredness and all he wanted was a piss and a drink, in that order. Both, however, would have to wait.

Pulling out his phone, he checked the time, calculating that he'd managed about forty minutes' sleep. Tapping a few buttons, he checked his missed calls. There were two from Christina but none from Carlyle. Umar shook his head.

Big surprise. The boss was happy enough to hide when it suited him.

Pulling up Carlyle's number, Umar hit call.

He was still waiting for the inspector's voicemail to kick in when the WPC reappeared in the doorway with an excited look on her face. 'We're on.'

'Okay. I'm coming.' Quickly ending the call, Umar followed her inside.

At least his erection had quickly subsided. Too tired to feel frustrated, Umar let the Senior Security Director of Triple RXD Security Systems explain at some length the reasons for the unfortunate technical fault that had resulted in Joseph Belsky being locked in his panic room overnight. None of it made any sense to the policeman but the guy – a small bloke with a nervous twitch that was exacerbated by a lack of sleep and too much caffeine – clearly had to get it off his chest.

'So,' the policeman asked when the man finally stopped spouting technical gibberish laced with excuses, 'is it open?'

'It is now.' With a flourish, the engineer tapped a couple of keys on a temporary pad that had been wired up to the door. After a moment's silence, there was a satisfying metallic click, signalling that the lock had finally disengaged.

The director let out a long breath. 'Thank Christ for that.'

'Better late than never,' Umar quipped.

'At least we didn't have to try and go in through the wall,' said the director, wiping his brow with a paper napkin from a nearby café. 'That could have taken days.'

'Always good to look on the bright side,' said Umar, trying to keep the sarcasm from his voice. Stepping past the engineer, he carefully pulled open the door a couple of inches.

'Mr Belsky,' he said gently, 'it's the police. Apologies for the delay in getting you out of here. Apparently it was caused by some kind of computer glitch that kept the lock . . . er, locked.'

'A computer error that was not something we could have anticipated,' the director piped up from behind him. 'It was just a very unfortunate set of circumstances.'

That'll be a matter for your lawyers to sort out, thought Umar, irritated by the guy's intervention. Shuffling forward, he put his head closer to the crack in the door. From inside the bathroom he could hear the sound of a tap running. 'Mr Belsky?' Turning away, he signalled for the WPC to clear the room. Once he was alone, he took a deep breath to prepare himself. Then, pulling the door properly open, he stepped up to the threshold and looked inside.

'Oh shit . . .'

FOURTEEN

She wanted to move.

She couldn't.

The ceiling, however, was moving – gently lurching from side to side, as if she was on a ship, rocking up and down on a gentle swell. With a shudder, Carole Simpson realized that she was going to throw up. Tossing back the duvet, she jumped out of bed and sprinted into the bathroom. Making it just in time, she deposited the remains of last night's partially digested *risotto capesante* into the empty bath in a series of satisfying retches. Turning to the basin, she rinsed her mouth with water from the tap before slumping on to the cool tiled floor.

Resting her forehead against the rim of the tub, she listened to the blood throbbing in her temples. It had been the kind of heavy night that took her back to her university days – well, almost. Had it been fun? Or just an embarrassment? She was too wasted to tell. Trying to tune out the headache that was relentlessly building from the base of her skull, she took a couple of slow, deep breaths and waited.

After throwing up for a second time, the Commander was reasonably confident that there was nothing more to come from her stomach. Reaching for the shower attachment, she carefully washed away her vomit, before stepping into the bath and taking a quick, lukewarm shower. Feeling marginally better, she padded back into the bedroom encased in a hotel bathrobe.

Her new friend was still face down in the bed, snoring loudly. Catching sight of his hairy back, she feared that she might throw up again. When the moment passed, she allowed herself a wry smile. 'In the end, you couldn't get it up,' she mumbled to herself, 'could you?'

By way of reply, the Deputy Chief Constable issued a loud fart and pulled a pillow over his head. With an amused sigh, Simpson began recovering her clothing from the floor. She had just put on her bra and was looking for her knickers when the strains of 'I Vow To Thee My Country' began issuing from her DKNY leather clutch.

'Damn.' Glancing at the bed, she grabbed her bag and quickly retreated back into the bathroom. Pushing the door closed, she perched on the lid of the toilet seat and answered her BlackBerry, cutting off Katherine Jenkins in full flow.

I must change my ringtone, she thought. 'Hello?'

'Carole,' came the brusque voice down the line, 'it's Dudley Whitehead.'

Whitehead was her line manager, one of the Met's Deputy Assistant Commissioners. What the hell did *he* want? The Commander suddenly felt a desperate urge to pee. Sliding off the seat, she opened the lid and tried to go as quietly as possible.

'Carole?'

'Yes?'

'Where are you?'

'I'm . . .' for a moment, her mind went completely blank. 'I'm at the Home Office conference. The one at . . .' she struggled to remember the name of the hotel '. . . the one on Park Lane.'

Whitehead thought about that for a second. 'Good. Be in my office in thirty minutes.'

So much for the bloody case being closed. Umar had been sent home to get a couple of hours' sleep and the inspector was back in charge of the scene. Ignoring the ambulance crew hovering behind him, Carlyle stood in the middle of Joseph Belsky's study, staring into space as he waited for Susan Phillips to emerge from the bathroom. In his mind he was going through a checklist of all the people he needed to speak to in the light of this most unfortunate development. Each addition to the list added a notch to his level of frustration.

How had something so simple managed to become so complicated?

After a few minutes, the pathologist appeared in the doorway and gave him a rueful smile. Dressed in faded jeans and a crisp white shirt, with her hair pulled back into a girlish ponytail, she was looking good.

'We've got to stop meeting like this,' he quipped.

'Hm.' Phillips' smile quickly ebbed away. 'Nico isn't best pleased. He had plans for today.'

Nico? That must be the current boyfriend. Carlyle didn't ask – there would be another one along in a minute. Phillips was high maintenance. Unlike Helen. He thought of his wife and gave silent thanks for her many qualities.

'We were supposed to be going to the races.'

'Shame.' The inspector glanced towards the door. From here, all you could see of the body were the bright red Converse All Stars on Belsky's feet. 'What happened?'

'Hard to say.' Phillips pulled off her latex gloves. 'Maybe he had some kind of stroke.'

Carlyle wondered about Taimur Rage. Should the boy now be charged with murder? He would have to talk to Simpson about that. 'Presumably it was stress-related?'

'Possibly. It might have been triggered by the attack or it might have been brought on by being stuck inside the panic room.'

Triple RXD are not going to like that, Carlyle thought.

'Or it might just be a coincidence. The guy was in his late sixties and not in great shape. Maybe it would have happened anyway.'

'That would be handy,' Carlyle said hopefully. 'Less paperwork.'

69

'It will be what it will be,' Phillips said flatly, not appreciating the quip. 'I'm not going to commit myself now.'

'No, no, of course not.'

She signalled to the paramedics that they could take Belsky away. 'I'll let you know when I've had a look.'

'Thanks.' Following Phillips into the living room, he stepped over to the window and peered out at the city.

'Nice view,' said Phillips, gesturing at the river as she appeared at his shoulder.

'Yeah.'

'Expensive.'

'No doubt.' Placing his forehead against the window pane, he tried to make out the press pack waiting on the street below. Unsurprisingly, it had grown after Belsky's death had become known and there were at least three satellite trucks broadcasting live from the scene.

'Are you going to say anything?' Phillips asked.

'Not if I can avoid it,' Carlyle mumbled. 'Seeing as I've got nothing to say. That kind of thing is best left to the Commander.' It suddenly struck him as odd that Carole Simpson hadn't yet given him a call. With the news all over the TV and the internet, she would normally be hassling him for updates at every opportunity.

'And what about the other one?'

'What other one?' Carlyle frowned.

'The man who keeled over on Waterloo Bridge.'

'Oh, him.' The inspector made a face. 'Haven't seen any paperwork yet. And I haven't had time to check the contents of his briefcase.'

Phillips shot him a disapproving stare.

'Have you taken a look yet?' Carlyle countered. 'Was it a heart attack?'

'That's still tbc. With no suspicious circumstances, he's not a top priority. We've got a bit of a backlog at the moment.'

Just for a change, the inspector thought.

'And Belsky, of course, will jump in front of him in the queue.'

'I don't suppose he'll complain.'

'But his family will.'

That reminds me, Carlyle thought, *I'd better see if someone's checked the Missing Persons list.* 'If he has one.'

'It's a really shit part of the job. Having to explain to people why they can't have the body of their loved one back. They think we're just lazy and slow, but it's the bloody cuts. They're killing us.'

'Yes.'

Realizing that he wasn't interested in listening to yet another complaint about government incompetence and their draconian cuts in police spending, she quickly returned to the matter in hand. 'Anyway, my best guess is that our Waterloo Bridge Guy won't be done up for a couple more days yet at the absolute earliest.' She gave him a winning smile. 'Don't worry though, I'll get him cut open before the end of next week.'

Lovely, Carlyle thought, fighting to keep a mental image of Phillips with a scalpel out of his head. Squeamish at the best of times, he didn't like to dwell too much on what happened to her clients once they reached the slab.

Aware of his weak stomach, the smile on Phillips' face grew wider. 'You can come and watch me do the autopsy, if you like.'

'That's very kind,' holding up a hand, Carlyle was already heading out of the flat, 'but not really necessary . . .'

FIFTEEN

'Oh, my.' Slowly, the Reverend Jerome Mears lifted up his left foot and carefully removed the used Trojan that had stuck to it. Lifting the condom a couple of inches in front of his nose, he carefully inspected the contents. Who said London girls didn't know how to party? The fact that one had been Danish and the other had been what – Irish? – was neither here nor there.

Looking slowly around the hotel room, Jerome couldn't spy a trash can. After a moment's contemplation he dropped the offending article into a dirty tea cup sitting on the desk by the far wall. Scratching his balls vigorously, he breathed in the familiar smells of sweat, spilled juices and sex. The girls had long gone, leaving the hotel room looking as if it had just hosted a Guns 'N' Roses after-party. 'We are all slaves to sin,' Jerome said aloud. 'Some more than others.'

However, rather than feeling wasted after his night of debauchery, he felt energized. Despite the three of them putting away seven bottles of champagne, he didn't have any trace of a hangover. And the alcohol certainly hadn't negatively impacted his performance. Thinking about the events of last night was giving him a boner – but a few quick tugs were enough for him to realize that the tank was empty. He needed food. Letting his dick fall from his hand, he reached for the room service menu and ordered a Full English breakfast.

After he had showered and dressed, the Reverend began packing for the flight home. He had a sermon to preach in Houston in less than twenty-four hours. It would be a blessed relief to be back in the fold among true believers. The King's Cross crowd had been so lame he had been seriously worried that Elma Reyes was indeed going to try and stiff him on the balance of his fee. Recalling the moment when she dropped her towel and stood in front of him buck naked, he shuddered.

In the end, after a lot of grumbling and a half-hearted effort at renegotiating, Elma had come up with his cash. But, from a professional point of view, the whole experience had been deeply unsatisfactory. By his calculation, there had been less than a hundred people in the audience and Jerome strongly suspected that many of those were ringers, stand-ins who had been rounded up by some of Elma's little helpers. Before the first *Halleluiah* had issued from his mouth, the Reverend had already decided that he would not be coming back. The First Annual Miracle & Healing Conference™ would also be the *last* Annual Miracle & Healing Conference™ as far as he was concerned. This had been a one-time gig. London? What a total dump. Even the good-time girls couldn't save it.

Stuffing the last of his toiletries into his Louis Vuitton weekend bag, Jerome pulled open the closet door – and froze. 'Oh, my good Lord.' He stood there, willing the evidence of his eyes to be false. At the back of the closet, the mini-safe was wide open and his cash – the fee from Elma – was gone. 'I've been robbed,' he breathed, not willing to believe it. 'God give me strength. I've been robbed.'

It must have been quite a party. Unable to open any of the windows, Sonia Mason wrinkled her nose at the stale smell. Looking towards the door, the WPC wondered how long it would be before she could escape. Her partner, an amiable galoot called Joe Lucas, had disappeared, leaving Sonia alone with the weirdo in the funny suit.

Standing by the closet containing the empty safe, the guy was making no effort to hide his thoughts. He was looking Mason up and down like . . . well, suffice to say, his tongue was hanging out and he was dribbling on the carpet. It was almost as if the guy had forgotten why he'd called 999 in the first place. Sonia realized that it was less about her and more about the uniform. She didn't feel threatened but the whole thing was depressingly gross. Why did the sight of a WPC's outfit give 90 per cent of guys a hard-on? Okay, maybe not 90 per cent, but certainly a majority. Off duty, she only received a fraction of the attention that came her way when she was on the job. Maybe it was a power thing.

Taking a half-step away from the guy, she glanced down at the scribble in her notebook. 'So, *sir*, you estimate that there was approximately nine thousand pounds in cash in the safe?'

'Nine thousand, six hundred,' Jerome corrected her. The remains of the twelve grand he'd got from Elma minus the money for the girls. The latter were the most likely suspects. All he knew about them, beyond a certain lack of inhibition, was that they had answered to the names Hannah and Jocelyn. Unless the hotel management managed to identify them from the CCTV, there was next to zero chance of tracking them down.

Looking up, Mason frowned. 'Wasn't that rather a lot of cash to be keeping in your hotel room?'

'I don't know,' Jerome said cheerily. 'Is it?' His initial dismay at losing the cash had been replaced by a certain philosophical detachment. *After all*, he told himself, *the Lord works in mysterious ways*. More importantly, he was fairly sure that his insurance would pick up the tab. 'Money isn't really my thing.'

What a load of old bollocks, Mason thought. *Money is everybody's thing.*

'In my line of work . . .'

'Which is what exactly?'

'I'm a consultant.'

'Okay.' Who cared what the guy did for a living? They were all going through the motions here. This wasn't an investigation, just a bureaucratic procedure. Mason tore a blank page from her

74

notebook and scribbled an address on it. 'You'll need to come down to the station,' she said, handing him the piece of paper, 'and speak to the desk sergeant. He'll give you a crime number. You'll need that if you are intending to make a claim on your insurance policy.'

A pained expression slipped across Jerome's face. 'But I have a plane to catch,' he whined.

Mason gave him an unconcerned smile. 'It's not far from here, it shouldn't take you long.' The door opened and she turned to see PC Lucas finally reappear, a paper cup in each hand. Stepping forward, she reached out to relieve him of one of them. 'Thanks, Joe.'

'No problem,' Lucas mumbled, avoiding eye-contact.

He fancies me, Mason thought, taking a sip of her latte. *Shame he's not my type.* It was always good, however, to have a few tame admirers around. 'Joe?'

'Yes?'

'Maybe you could take Mr . . .' she suddenly realized she had forgotten the guy's name.

'Mears,' Jerome reminded her.

'Maybe you could take Mr Mears down to the station and sort him out with a reference number for his insurance claim while I go and talk to the management.' Without waiting for a reply, she sidled past her colleague and out into the corridor. Heading for the lifts, she took a succession of deep breaths, clearing the stale air from her nostrils as quickly as possible.

SIXTEEN

It was an outrage. Looking up at the TV screen hanging from his ceiling, the inspector shook his head. The Clash's 'London Calling' was playing over an airline advert. What would Joe Strummer have made of it? One of Carlyle's pet hates was advertisers using songs that he liked. It just seemed so . . . invidious, something that it was impossible to escape. He regularly started singing snippets of 'London Calling' to himself as he walked down the road, but he didn't want to be reminded of a bloody travel company while he did so. He remembered reading not so long ago how one of the Beastie Boys had written into his will that advertisers could not use his music. Good for him.

As the advert finished, he watched his sergeant slowly make his way across the third floor towards his desk and said, 'Where the bloody hell have you been?'

'I went home to get a few hours' kip.' Unshaven and rather dishevelled, Umar looked like he'd slept on the streets. 'In the end, it was more like a couple of hours' babysitting.'

Carlyle grunted unsympathetically. 'Christina not very supportive then, was she?'

Umar's look said it all.

'I remember that. Helen was just the same.'

'It's like she thinks I just sit around the station all day, having a rest,' he yawned, 'so that when I get home—'

'Tell me about it.' Contemplating their fate, the inspector felt a familiar pang of self-pity. As far as he was aware, his father,

Alexander, had never changed a single nappy when he was a nipper. In terms of looking after the baby and running the house, his mother had done it all. Nowadays, 'new men' – or whatever the hell they were called – couldn't get away with simply putting bread on the table. Social expectations had changed. Carlyle and Umar were definitely on the wrong end of history when it came to doling out the chores. Now that Alice was older, he could be more philosophical about it, but there were times when it still rankled.

'I'm completely shagged . . .'

'Don't worry,' said Carlyle, jumping to his feet. 'I've got plenty to take your mind off things.'

At the conference. Where r u? Oh God. Lover Boy was sending her messages. How did he get the number? Carole Simpson deleted the text message from her BlackBerry and sat up straight.

'Carole?'

Looking up, the Commander tried to smile. 'Yes?'

Dudley Whitehead leaned forward, his oversized belly spilling across the desk. 'Are you all right?'

'I'm fine,' Simpson snapped, letting her irritation show. A couple of paracetamol, washed down with a triple espresso had effectively suppressed her hangover. Even so, she avoided staring at the Deputy Assistant Commissioner's fuchsia-pink polo shirt. It looked as if Dudley had been diverted to New Scotland Yard on his way to the golf course and wasn't too happy about it.

'How's the conference going?' he asked.

'Very interesting.' Simpson felt the BlackBerry vibrate in her hand. This time she ignored the message. 'It is nice to be able to get the chance to . . . engage with colleagues.'

'I'm glad to hear it. These things cost a bloody fortune. And I sometimes worry that you just don't spend enough time bonding with your peers.'

Simpson looked at him curiously but said nothing.

'Right, anyway . . .' Whitehead picked up a sheet of paper

from his desk and waved it in front of his face. 'I need an update on this Belsky situation.'

Simpson nodded sagely. *What Belsky situation?*

'The Commissioner is worried that it could go all over the place.'

'I can imagine.'

'He needs to know that it will be dealt with as quickly and as quietly as possible, with the needs of all stakeholders given full consideration.'

Stakeholders? What the hell was he talking about? Simpson vaguely recalled the Met had sent Whitehead on an MBA course the previous year. He must have picked up this jargon at business school. 'Of course.'

'So, what do you think?'

'I think we can manage it.'

The Deputy Assistant Commissioner looked at her, unconvinced. On the other hand, his tee time was in little more than an hour. His driver would be pushed to get him out of London in time. 'Have you got the right people on it?'

'I am happy for now,' Simpson replied, 'but we will be keeping it under close review.'

'The Commissioner mentioned your man . . .' he looked down at his sheet of paper '. . . Carlyle.'

Simpson's heart sank. The one bloody inspector in the whole of London known – by name – to the Commissioner and she was responsible for him. 'What about him?'

Whitehead wiped his porcine brow. 'He's . . . controversial.'

'He's effective,' Simpson shot back. This was not the first time she'd had this type of conversation and the Commander knew her lines off by heart.

'Are you keeping him on a tight leash?'

As if. 'Of course.'

'I suppose that's the best we can hope for at this stage,' Whitehead sighed. 'Just make sure that he keeps you fully informed at all times.'

The little bastard never keeps me in the loop. Simpson stifled a laugh. 'That won't be a problem, sir. The inspector is extremely competent when it comes to lines of reporting.'

'Good.' Whitehead glanced at the clock on the wall behind Simpson's head. He really was pushed for time now. That Calloway RAZR X driver he had his eye on would have to stay in the Pro's Shop at least until after his round. 'And be quick. We don't want MI5 coming in and taking over our investigation, do we?'

'Absolutely not.' Taking her cue from the Deputy Assistant Commissioner, Simpson jumped to her feet and headed for the door. MI5? What the hell had Carlyle dragged her into now?

SEVENTEEN

Dabbing at the corner of her eye with a paper napkin, Elma Reyes shot an accusing stare at her lawyer.

'The amount of money I pay you, I'd have thought you could get him out.'

Michelangelo Federici shook his head sadly. Clients were unrealistic at the best of times – and this was not the best of times. 'Elma,' he said gently, 'the boy attacked a guy with an axe. The guy died.'

'Keep your voice down,' Elma hissed. Looking around the café, she took a moment to satisfy herself that no one was eavesdropping on their conversation. 'Taimur didn't kill the guy, did he?'

Federici stared into the dregs of his elderflower tea. 'That depends on your view of cause and effect.'

'Huh?'

'Never mind. Look, at least you got to see him before they remanded him.'

At the mention of prison, Elma's eyes started welling up again. 'You should have got him out,' she sobbed. 'Now he's locked up with a bunch of hardcore criminals. God knows what will happen.'

I'm sure you've said a prayer for him, Federici thought tartly. All this maternal grief would be more convincing if it wasn't for the fact that their visit to Charing Cross was the first time that Elma had seen her son in almost a year. Since he had been a teenager, the boy had chosen to live with his father. All Elma's energy had gone into building up the Christian Salvation Centre. This was one family for whom charity most definitely did not begin at home.

'Have you spoken to Calvin?' he asked.

For a moment, it looked like Elma might choke on her tea. She cleared her throat. 'Why in God's name would I want to do that?'

Gazing out of the window, Federici watched a young woman stroll past with a poodle on a leash. The poodle's fur had been dyed pink. *People can be such dicks*, he thought. 'He is the boy's father.'

Elma grunted her displeasure at being reminded of such an unsavoury fact.

'Look,' Federici took his wallet from the inside pocket of his jacket and pulled out a twenty-pound note to pay their bill, 'I know that you and Calvin are not in regular contact.'

'I haven't spoken to that . . . we haven't talked in almost ten years.'

'But the point is that you have to now, for Taimur's sake.'

Staring at the ceiling, Elma Reyes said nothing.

Carlyle breezed past the front desk, doing a double-take as he took in the man in the crazy yellow suit. *Some kind of dress tartan*, he mused to himself, digging down deep into his Scottish DNA. Waving his arms around, the guy was clearly irritated as a young PC fluttered aimlessly at his shoulder.

'How long does it take to get a damn piece of paper around here?' The accent was American, the body language universal.

Just another tourist who has come a cropper in the world's greatest city, the inspector thought disinterestedly. Slipping through the doors leading to the station proper, he skipped up the stairs and into Interview Room 1C on the first floor. As he entered the room, a young girl who had to be Joanne Belsky looked up from behind her *Beano*.

The *Beano*. He didn't even know it was still going.

For a second, his thoughts drifted back to memories of Calamity James and Alexander Lemming. Maybe, if he asked nicely, the girl might let him have a quick peek. 'You must be Joanne.'

Saying nothing, the child slid back behind her comic.

'Where's your mother, then?'

'I'm here.'

He turned to find an harassed-looking woman standing in the doorway. 'I'm Stephanie Belsky.' Slim, almost as tall as the inspector himself, she was wearing a brown leather jacket over a pearl-grey silk blouse, not too much make-up and her hair cut short, but not too short. All in all, a fairly standard *yummy mummy* look.

Belsky offered him her hand. Pushing back his shoulders slightly, he shook it limply and said, 'Inspector John Carlyle.'

Removing a stray strand of hair from her face, Stephanie Belsky looked him up and down, giving no indication that she was in any way impressed. 'And you've met Joanne.'

'Yes.'

'Are you in charge of the investigation?'

'That's correct.' He invited her to take a seat next to her daughter. 'I was one of the officers on the scene after the initial attack. Our condolences . . . to you both.'

Pulling out a chair, Stephanie Belsky acknowledged the stilted expression of sympathy with a curt nod. 'Were you the one who found him?'

'Your father?' Carlyle glanced at the child but she did not look up. 'No, that was one of my colleagues.'

The admission seemed to sour her mood still further. 'So, what is it that you need from us now?'

'Well,' Carlyle took a deep breath, 'as Joanne was there . . .'

To further illustrate her exasperation with the forces of so-called law and order, Stephanie Belsky began drumming her bright red nails on the table.

'. . . we would like to get a statement.'

'Is that really necessary?' She eyed him suspiciously. 'I thought that you had a confession?'

How did she know that? 'Yes, but . . .'

'So why do you need to put Joanne through all that again by making her give you a statement?'

'Mum.' With a theatrical flourish, Joanne placed her comic on the table. 'For God's sake. It's not like I saw the guy put an axe in Grandpa's head. I'm hardly traumatized. We're all going to die in the end.'

An awkward silence descended on the interview room. Her mother looked like she wanted to give the girl a clip round the ear, but reluctantly thought better of it. Biting his lip, the inspector tried not to smile. He was liking Joanne Belsky just fine.

Stephanie Belsky shot the inspector an apologetic look. 'I'm sorry. She's always been very . . . forceful.'

'Not at all.'

'She got into trouble at school,' the woman added ruefully, 'for telling the other kids that Santa Claus didn't exist – she was only four at the time.'

'Well, he doesn't,' Joanne said flatly, 'does he?'

'You sound like my daughter,' Carlyle laughed. 'She is very forceful too.'

Joanne gave a sympathetic nod. 'How old is she? As old as me?'

'A bit older. She runs rings round her old dad.'

Both females gave him a look which said *that shouldn't be too difficult.*

Joanne let her gaze fall to the desk. 'My dad ran away when I was little. Mum says that he was a right—'

'That's more than enough,' said Stephanie Belsky, placing a hand on her daughter's shoulder. 'If you are going to give the inspector a statement, let's get on with it, shall we?'

EIGHTEEN

'The kid left her comic in the interview room.' The desk sergeant waved the well-thumbed copy of the *Beano* at Carlyle. 'I used to read this as a kid,' he smiled.

'Me too.'

'I didn't know they still published it.'

'Yeah. A bit of a miracle in this day and age.'

'Yeah,' the sergeant agreed. 'Shame about the *Dandy*, though.'

Carlyle suddenly felt a twinge of nostalgia for *Desperate Dan*, *Korky the Cat* and *Bananaman*. 'What happened to the *Dandy*?'

'They closed it down,' the sergeant replied. 'It might still be online. But the comic was only selling eight thousand copies a week. When we were kids it sold millions, literally.'

'Long time ago.'

'Tell me about it,' said the sergeant, with feeling. 'Kids don't read any more. God knows what they teach 'em in the bloody schools these days. They just play bloody computer games all day. Can't be right, can it?'

'Things are different now.'

'S'pose.' The sergeant didn't seem too happy about it.

'Anyway, Joanne Belsky still reads. She seems a very smart girl.' Carlyle stepped over to the front desk and took the comic from the sergeant. 'I'll get it back to her.' He half-turned away and then remembered something from his mental To Do list. 'By the way,' he said, turning back to face the desk, 'Chris Brennan.'

The sergeant's face soured. Ambulance-chasing lawyers

were never popular at Charing Cross, and Brennan, an ex-public schoolboy with the face of an angel and the morals of a sewer rat, was one of the worst.

'I got a message that he was looking for me yesterday. Any idea what he wanted?'

'I wasn't on yesterday.' The sergeant began flicking through the outsized day book on his desk. 'And I don't think there's a note.' He ran a finger down the relevant pages. 'Nope . . . can't see anything.'

'Never mind,' Carlyle mumbled. 'I'm sure that if he's after something he'll track me down soon enough.'

'You can bet on that.'

Yes, thought Carlyle unhappily, *I suppose I can.*

Where the hell was Calamity James? An increasingly disgruntled inspector flicked through the pages of the *Beano* for a second time, just to be sure that he hadn't missed it. With a sigh, he had to admit the truth: at some point over the last forty-plus years, it looked like his favourite cartoon character had been axed. 'Ridiculous,' he hissed. 'Bloody ridiculous.'

'So this is how you spend your time, is it? Reading comics?'

Urgh. Looking up, Carlyle saw Carole Simpson hovering at his shoulder. He had been too busy agonizing over Calamity to notice his boss sneaking up on him.

'Good morning to you too.'

Simpson pointed to the clock on the far wall. 'I'll think you'll find it's now the afternoon, Inspector.' The meeting with the Deputy Assistant Commissioner had left the Commander in a foul mood. Her headache had returned with a vengeance and she needed some sleep. Worst of all, Lover Boy was texting her every two minutes from the bloody conference.

'Good afternoon, Commander.' Tossing the comic on his desk, Carlyle made no effort to get up. 'How are you today?'

'Fine,' Simpson lied. Perching on the corner of his desk, she folded her arms. He was trying not to stare, but the inspector could see that she looked knackered. Washed out. Or, perhaps she was just hungover? He gave a discreet sniff. Was that booze he could smell? Maybe.

Facing conflicting emotions, Carlyle played for time. Seeing his boss looking like shit always brought out his cheery side. On the other hand, the Commander – based up the road at the Paddington Green station – rarely appeared at Charing Cross. Her arrival invariably meant that someone was going to get a bollocking; and usually, that 'someone' was the inspector himself.

'So,' he asked, 'to what do we owe this pleasure?'

Simpson leaned thirty degrees forward in a vaguely threatening manner. 'Why didn't you tell me about Joseph Belsky?'

Belsky, of course. He had deliberately avoided the media reporting of the cartoonist's death. Ultimately, it was just another freakshow for so-called 'normal' people to gawp at. All the inevitable bullshit handwringing was intensely annoying. Scratching his head, the inspector tried to sound as casual as possible. 'I didn't want to disturb you unnecessarily. It's all sorted. I was just about to write my report.'

'It's all sorted,' Simpson parroted.

'Yes,' Carlyle said evenly, beginning to wonder if she knew something that he didn't. 'Done and dusted. We have a full confession from Taimur Rage, the unfortunately-named axe man, and I got a statement this morning from the young granddaughter, who was in the flat at the time. Forensics are doing their thing. Once the autopsy on Belsky is in, the CPS or whoever can take a view on the precise charges and then the lawyers can sort it out.' He tried to go for an innocent smile. 'Simple.'

Swaying slightly, Simpson looked at him with a deep suspicion based on years of experience.

You're not going to throw up over me, are you? Carlyle wondered. As a precautionary measure, he began edging his chair away from his desk. 'What?'

'This mad axe man. What about accomplices?'

The inspector made a face. 'He says he did it on his own.'

'Come on, John. Terrorists don't work alone.'

'Nutters who go around waving axes do.'

'Belsky had a bounty on his head.'

Carlyle edged away a little more, until he could go no further without it being obvious. 'Look, Taimur looks very much like your average brainless teenager. He's probably spent the last couple of years sat in a dark room watching videos of IEDs going off in Afghanistan whereas, if he was a normal lad, he'd be sitting with a jumbo box of tissues, watching porn.'

The last microns of colour drained from Simpson's face. 'John, for God's sake.'

'The point is,' said Carlyle, beginning to get exasperated, 'that the wiring in his brain might be off a bit, but only by so much.' He held up a hand, positioning his thumb and forefinger about half an inch apart. 'I'm sure that the boys at MI5 can have lots of fun with his computer, but they're not going to find evidence of a terrorist, just a fairly basic teenage fuck-up.' He stopped, surprised by his strength of feeling on the matter. In total, he had probably only spent about an hour in the presence of Taimur Rage but the inspector knew instinctively what he was dealing with.

'Quite a fuck-up,' Simpson mused.

'No question of that.' Carlyle was pleased that his superior was at least prepared to consider his point of view. 'He'll definitely be spending some time at Her Majesty's Pleasure. But he's just a bit thick. As far as I can see, he wasn't motivated by money and he's definitely not part of some sleeper cell. Go and talk to him for five minutes and you'll see what I mean.'

'Is he still here?'

Carlyle shook his head. 'Nah. They took him to Belmarsh this morning – which is overkill in itself. Putting him in a high security prison is just for show. This is all about internal politics and external PR.'

'You might be right.'

As always.

'But that doesn't matter.'

'Sorry?'

'I got hauled down to the Yard today because of this.'

Ah, thought Carlyle, *that explains the mood.*

'Didn't have a bloody clue what Whitehead was banging on about.'

The inspector frowned. *Who's Whitehead?*

'And I had to swear that you would do a proper job.'

'I *am* doing a proper job.'

The Commander gave no indication that she supported that assertion. 'The Commissioner wants action.'

'Good for him,' Carlyle snorted.

'Don't come the petulant schoolboy with me, Inspector.' Swaying slightly, Simpson almost slipped off the edge of the desk. *She definitely looks like she's going to throw up*, Carlyle thought. 'You know how difficult the current financial and political context is in which we have to operate. We need more than just a confession.'

The financial and political context? 'What the hell does that mean?'

'It means that you have to get your arse back out there and find out exactly who put this boy . . .'

'Taimur Rage.'

'Who put him up to it. Go and speak to his family, friends, associates. We need a more rounded picture of this young man, his thought processes, his networks. His connections.'

Christ, thought Carlyle sullenly, *talk about creating work.* 'But—'

'We need more action,' said Simpson, cutting him off. 'We need more arrests. The public want to know that we can protect them.'

We can't always protect them, that's the point.

'It has to be zero tolerance.'

For the truth.

'Otherwise the security boys take over. You lose your

conviction and the MPS is seen as being sidelined when it comes to keeping London safe.'

So that's what it's about. Carlyle had no time for turf wars. 'Let them have it.'

'No, I will not let them have it,' Simpson insisted. 'The Commissioner will not let them have it. This is our responsibility. To hand a case like this over to someone else would be seen as an admission that the Metropolitan Police can't do its job; that we can't protect our own city. I will not allow it.' She pointed towards the window. 'So get out there right now and damn well find me something.'

Carlyle was taken aback. It had been a long time since he had heard the Commander sound so strident. Looking round the room, he realized that a group of colleagues had stopped to listen in on their conversation. Irritated, Simpson waved them all back to work. As he watched them slope off, the inspector considered arguing back. He had done his job – and done it in double-quick time too. The idea that he was somehow failing to protect his fellow Londoners was ludicrous. He was about to open his mouth but, catching Simpson's glare, he thought better of it. 'Okay,' he sighed, 'okay. You're the boss. I'm on it.'

'Inspector.'

Bollocks. He was just about to make a dash for the exit when he was cut off by a slack-looking woman pushing a baby buggy. Narrowly avoiding falling on top of the child, the inspector admitted defeat. Trying to escape was futile. He turned to face his pursuer.

Dressed in a garish Prince of Wales check suit, Chris Brennan had gone to seed since their last meeting. His cheeks were puffy and his hairline not so much receding as running away. The deep lines around his eyes suggested that decades of partying were finally catching up with him.

'I wondered if I could have a word.'

You've got a bloody nerve, turning up here. Sticking his hands

89

firmly in his pockets, Carlyle glared at the lawyer, 'Mr Brennan. What can I do for you?'

Brennan waved for him to come closer. Reluctantly, the inspector complied. 'It's about my colleague,' he said quietly.

'Yes.'

'Brian Winters.'

'Uh-huh?'

'His briefcase.'

Get to the point. Hopping from foot to foot, the inspector was keen to get going. He didn't want Simpson to find him still here when she made her own exit. 'What about it?'

'You have it.' Brennan smiled, like a fox might smile at a chicken. 'I need it.'

Carlyle frowned. 'I do?'

'Poor Brian had a fatal cardiac arrest while crossing Waterloo Bridge,' Brennan explained. 'I understand that you were the officer on the scene. He had certain important client documents in his briefcase. I need to get hold of them.'

The briefcase in the evidence room. He'd forgotten all about it. Out of the corner of his eye, he saw Simpson heading down the corridor in his direction.

'Well?'

'Sorry, you've got that wrong.' Carlyle began edging towards the door. 'I was dealing with something else.' Ignoring the dark look on Brennan's face, he ploughed on. 'Your colleague was handled by a couple of officers from the Waterloo station. You'd better go and talk to the desk sergeant over there.'

Brennan knew that he was being fobbed off and he didn't like it one little bit. 'But—'

The Commander was getting closer. Catching Carlyle's eye, she scowled.

'Sorry, but I've really got to run.' Turning on his heel, Carlyle broke into a trot, heading for the relative sanctuary of the street.

NINETEEN

The Persian Palace was a nondescript kebab shop in the middle of a row of single-storey properties on the north side of Shepherd's Bush Green. Catering for punters eschewing the more refined delights of the nearby Westfield shopping centre, it served fare of largely indeterminate content from 11 a.m. until 2 a.m., seven days a week. Like all coppers, Carlyle knew that peak hours for this kind of takeaway establishment were 11 p.m.–1 a.m.; the two-hour window after most of the pubs closed accounted for something like 80 per cent of kebab sales and probably in excess of 90 per cent of sales of whatever illegal shit was being peddled under the counter at any given time. In the middle of a weekday afternoon, however, the place was devoid of customers, save for a girl sitting in a back booth, underneath a tattered poster of Kylie Minogue that had to be at least fifteen years old. Bursting out of a pair of tiny gold lamé shorts, the young singer was in the kind of nubile nymphet pose that the inspector had frequently admired across the decades. *That would have been back in the days before Michael Hutchence got his paws on her*, he thought jealously.

Putting such generic disappointment behind him, Carlyle looked around the shop. The floor was filthy and the windows had clearly not been cleaned in an age. The inspector didn't want to think what the kitchen was like; presumably the health inspectors hadn't been round in quite a while. There was no one behind the counter but he could make out movement in the back. *Barge*

91

straight in, or wait? There was no need to be pushy – this was supposed to be a pastoral visit, after all – so he decided to hang on.

Shuffling from foot to foot, Carlyle waited for a member of staff to put in an appearance. Gazing out of the window, the girl in the back did not acknowledge his presence. In a leather jacket, wearing too much eye-liner, she looked barely fourteen. On the table in front of her was a plate containing the remains of a burger and a few chips, next to a can of Coke with a straw poking out of the top. From a small speaker stuck to the wall next to the counter, the radio started playing 'Call Me Maybe'. The inspector recognized the song; it was one of Alice's current favourites and he liked it too. Even in his advancing years, Carlyle wanted to think that he recognized good pop music when he heard it – timeless, meaningless, cheery. When the song was playing at home, he would join in on the jaunty chorus, happily oblivious to any of the other words. There was no chance of that happening here, however. The Persian Palace was not the type of place for a cheery sing-along. Instead, he pulled out his BlackBerry and began checking his emails.

Of the sixteen unread messages in his inbox, fifteen were junk. The other was a reminder from Helen to pick up some groceries on the way home. *The joys of modern technology. Always on call.*

As he slipped the handset back into his pocket, the song finished and was quickly replaced by an annoying advert for car insurance. There was still no sign of anyone coming to see what he wanted. With a sigh, Carlyle watched the girl pick up a chip. Tipping back her head, she opened her mouth and tried to drop the chip inside, somehow managing to miss from less than two inches; she was left with tomato sauce on her chin and the chip on the floor. Laughing, she wiped her mouth with the back of her hand while mashing the chip into the floor.

Carlyle shook his head sadly. On a waste bin standing on the pavement outside the shop, he could make out an advert for the council's truancy hotline. For a moment, he thought about making a call and shopping the girl. However, the idea faded from his brain almost as soon as it had emerged. Even by the subterranean standards of local government, social services were uniquely useless. If he dialled the number, chances were no one would answer the call. If he did manage to talk to someone, would the girl get picked up? At best, there would be lots of hanging around and lots of form filling for little if any end result. Upon reflection, the inspector quickly decided that he didn't have the time to chase up a lone schoolgirl playing hooky.

A banging door alerted him to the fact that someone had finally arrived behind the counter.

'You wan' somethin'?' The boy was wearing some sad approximation of a fast food operative's uniform, a blue and yellow striped polo shirt, complete with a fine selection of stains, complemented by a matching baseball cap. From under the brim, a pair of brown eyes viewed Carlyle suspiciously. If anything, the boy looked even younger than the girl in the back. The down on his upper lip suggested that his efforts to grow a moustache were destined to be a struggle.

'No, thanks.'

The kid frowned. 'Drink?'

'No. I'm looking for Calvin Safi.'

The frown dissolved into the kind of blank look that the inspector had seen a million times before.

'Calvin Safi,' Carlyle repeated, 'the owner of this place. Where is he?'

The shop door opened and there was the sound of laughter – hostile, male laughter. Carlyle stiffened slightly, but kept his gaze on the lad behind the counter. At his shoulder, two hoodies appeared. One was white, the other Asian. Both of them were taller than the policeman and, he estimated, the best part of forty years younger.

'Hey, man,' the Asian guy shouted at the boy behind the counter in a West London accent that covered all the neighbourhoods this side of Heathrow. Unzipping his jacket, he flicked off the hood to reveal an impressive mane of jet-black hair which reached down to his shoulders. 'Get us two doners and two large Cokes.' Producing a rubber band from his pocket, he pulled his hair back into a ponytail, checking his reflection in a glass cabinet, before heading into the back of the shop with his mate in tow. 'And make it quick,' he shouted over his shoulder, 'we're hungry.' Dancing round the remains of the chip on the floor, he slid into the booth next to the girl.

Nodding, the boy pulled out a tray and set about filling their order. Grimacing, Carlyle stepped closer to the counter. The food smells were beginning to give him a headache. 'Calvin Safi.' The boy didn't look up. His lips were moving but no sounds were coming out. *You're really beginning to piss me off*, the inspector thought. He waved a hand in front of the kid's face to remind him that he was still here. 'Hey.'

'Hey yourself, man.' The Asian guy slipped back out of the booth and wandered back over until he was about five feet from where Carlyle was standing. 'What do you want with Calvin?'

Standing his ground, the inspector took a moment to read the legend – *'WHAT U SAYIN'?* – on the left breast of the guy's black hoodie. 'Who are you?'

'Never you mind,' the guy scowled, edging forward, 'Who the fuck are *you?* Comin' here and askin' questions.'

'Aqib, siddown.' A burly guy appeared from round the end of the counter, wiping his hands on a souvenir London 2012 tea towel that was draped over his right shoulder. Waiting for the youth to slink back to the booth, he eyed the policeman suspiciously.

'Calvin Safi?' Carlyle asked.

'Yeah.' The kebab shop owner couldn't have looked any less pleased if Carlyle had dropped his trousers and shat on the floor of his kebab shop. He was in his mid-to-late thirties, roughly the same height as the policeman but about twice as wide. Giving up on the tea towel, he wiped his hands on his grubby blue and white T-shirt bearing the hopelessly out of date legend: *Chelsea – Champions of Europe.*

'I'm—'

Safi cut the inspector short with a wave of the hand. 'Not here.' Turning on his heel, he headed back towards the food preparation area. 'Come with me.'

TWENTY

The kitchen led to a small paved courtyard at the back of the building about ten feet by twelve, with a gate in the far wall for deliveries. Each side of the gate were stacked piles of cardboard boxes full of takeaway containers. Scattered across the concrete was an impressive collection of cigarette butts, along with the odd chocolate-bar wrapper. Standing in the middle of the yard, Calvin Safi eyed the inspector, hands on hips, waiting for him to explain himself.

Carlyle pulled out his ID and held it up for Safi to inspect. 'I'm from Charing Cross police station.'

Safi waved the warrant card away as if he couldn't care less if it was real or fake. 'Another policeman,' he grunted. 'What a surprise.' Under the manufactured annoyance, however, Carlyle could detect more than a little tension in the man's demeanour. 'Are you here for a freebie, or to ask some more questions?'

'Huh?'

Safi's eyes narrowed. 'What do you want?'

'I'm in charge of the Joseph Belsky investigation.'

Pouting, Safi stuffed his hands into the pockets of his jeans. 'Who?'

Are you for real? Carlyle wondered. 'Joseph Belsky is the guy who Taimur attacked.'

'Yeah, yeah.' Letting his hands fall to his sides, Safi seemed to relax a little.

A thought popped into the inspector's head. 'By the way, Taimur's surname . . .'

Safi glanced up at the heavens. 'He changed it by deed poll. I was amazed he managed to get the forms filled in properly, but there you go. He said he didn't want to have the same name as me or his mum. Rage – hah. He thought he was making some kind of statement.'

'About his view of society?'

'What are you, some kind of social worker?' Safi shook his head in disgust. 'Taimur couldn't even spell "society", never mind tell you what it means. He was pissed off at me and his mum for being such crap parents.'

'But he lived with you?'

'More or less,' Safi sighed. 'More than he did with his mother, anyway. Taimur's not quite right in the head, or haven't you worked that out yet?'

'That's not my call,' Carlyle said primly.

'Suit yourself.'

'While he's in Belmarsh, he'll have a number of evaluations.'

'Ah,' Safi grinned, 'he's gone there, has he? Maybe that'll finally knock some sense into the silly bugger.'

'You didn't know?'

Safi shrugged.

'No one told you?' Carlyle frowned. 'Have you not spoken to his lawyer?'

'Mich-el-ang-elo?' Safi hopped from foot to foot as he sang the name. 'Do you think I can afford a guy like that? He works for Taimur's mother, not me.'

'Can I go and see Taimur's room?'

'Sure,' Safi said wearily. 'There's not a lot to see, though. You're a bit late. Everything that wasn't nailed down, including his computer, was carted off yesterday.'

'By whom?'

Safi gave him a quizzical look. 'Shouldn't you know that?'

Yes, thought Carlyle, *I suppose I should.* He turned to head back inside just as the Asian guy who had tried to face him down appeared in the open doorway.

'Calvin. Steve's here.'

A look of boundless exasperation crossed the kebab shop owner's face. 'Tell him to come back later.'

'But he's brought a mate.'

'Tell them to come back *later*.'

The youngster scowled at Carlyle. 'Okay, okay, you're the boss.' Disappearing inside, he bounced the door closed.

'Bloody kids.' Safi shepherded the policeman towards the door. 'Anyway, if you want to go and have a look at Taimur's room, help yourself. The stairs are inside, to the left. It's right at the top.'

Taimur Rage had lived in what might charitably be called a garret at the top of the building. In reality it was a half-completed loft conversion with a lovely view of the discount shopping centre on the south side of the Green. The place looked like it had never been decorated, with a dirty rug covering bare floorboards. Aside from a child's single bed, there was a small wardrobe, a desk and a chair. *Good preparation for living in a cell*, Carlyle thought.

Looking around listlessly, he wondered whether it had been worth making the trip across London at all. Safi was right – the place had been stripped of anything of interest. Apart from a well-thumbed copy of *Men Only* under the bed and two unopened cans of Red Stripe on the desk, all that had been left by the previous visitors – presumably the boys at MI5 – was a poster of a sports car taped to the wall. Never having owned a car in his life, Carlyle had no idea what kind it was. At the same time, he knew an expensive motor when he saw one; it was not the kind of vehicle that a lad like Taimur could ever hope to own, or even take for a test drive.

'All in all,' he mumbled to himself, 'not very al-Qaeda, is it?' To be fair, the inspector was only too aware that he had no idea what an actual terrorist hideout might look like. At the same time however, he didn't imagine that it would be like this.

After a desultory glance through the empty wardrobe, he sat on the bed and again checked his BlackBerry. He had a grand total of three new emails, all of which were junk. Deleting each of them in turn, he watched a spider scurry across the floor before flopping back on to the bed and staring at the ceiling, pondering his next move. Should he pick up some groceries in Shepherd's Bush before he jumped on the tube, or wait till he got back to Covent Garden?

Decisions, decisions.

Making his way gingerly back down the stairs, Carlyle stopped on the second-floor landing. In front of him were two doors, one painted an off-white colour, the other not painted at all. On his toes, he stepped quietly up to the first door and listened, trying to separate out the background noise from the traffic outside from anything that was going on behind the doors. After several seconds he was sure that he could make out no voices, no TV or other signs of life. Carefully, he turned the handle and pushed. The door was locked. He tried the second one and found the same thing. 'That would explain why Safi was so relaxed about letting me have the run of the place,' he told himself, 'if everywhere is locked.'

Back on the ground floor, he found Safi sitting at a table by the door with a cup of tea and a copy of the local freesheet. The kid behind the counter had once again abandoned his position. Aqib, his mate and the girl in the leather jacket had gone; the back booth was now occupied by a couple chatting happily over a pizza.

'Find anything?' Safi asked, not looking up.

'Nah. Like you said, it's all been cleaned out.' Carlyle pulled up a chair and sat down. 'What can you tell me about his friends?'

'He didn't have any,' Safi said firmly.

'C'mon,' Carlyle said, failing to keep the irritation from his voice. 'He must have had some.'

'Look,' said Safi patiently, 'like I told the other guys, he knew

99

a few of the kids that came into the shop, but he never really hung out with any of them.' Glancing at the couple in the back booth, he lowered his voice. 'He certainly didn't belong to any bloody terrorist cell or any nonsense like that.' The kid behind the counter announced his reappearance by turning up the radio. 'Mushudur,' Safi snapped, 'leave that alone.' Without acknowledging his boss, Mushudur reduced the volume to a more acceptable level. The owner returned his attention to the policeman. 'Your mates spend too much time watching Hollywood movies.'

They're not my mates, Carlyle thought. 'Anyway,' he said, moving the conversation along, 'you don't seem too stressed by everything that's happened.'

Returning his attention to the newspaper, Safi carefully turned the page. 'Look, I told you, the kid's not been right in the head for a long time. I'm just glad that he didn't manage to kill anyone.'

'That remains to be seen.'

'The guy had a heart attack, right?' Safi looked back up from his paper. 'But that was *after* Taimur had been arrested.'

'Who knows what the experts might decide in terms of cause and effect. The CPS will offer him some kind of deal, but it may still be in relation to a murder charge.'

'He wouldn't have done it.' Letting his mask slip for the first time, Safi's face showed the all too familiar strain of an anguished parent. 'If he'd caught the guy, Taimur wouldn't have buried that axe in his head. He didn't have it in him.'

'We'll never know one way or the other.' It irritated Carlyle, the manner in which people would always try and mutate hope into fact. In his own pendantic way, he knew that, obviously, Taimur Rage *could* have planted his axe in Joseph Belsky's skull. Would he have done it if the cartoonist hadn't escaped into his panic room? That could only ever be a matter of speculation. In Carlyle's book, speculation wasn't worth anything much.

Safi let out a deep breath. 'Anyway, whatever happens he can claim diminished responsibility.'

'Maybe.' Despite everything, the inspector felt a pang of

sympathy for Taimur. Everyone was so keen to write him off as a sad nutter, the lad really didn't have a hope. 'It will be a struggle for him in prison,' he said. 'You really should go and see him.'

Safi made a face but the inspector sensed that the earlier hostility had dissipated. For whatever reason, the kebab shop owner no longer seemed so annoyed by the policeman's presence. 'No.' He shook his head. 'That's his mother's job.'

'Couldn't the pair of you manage to put on a united front?' Carlyle asked. 'Under the circumstances?'

'Ha.' Safi tossed the paper on to the table. 'Have you met Elma?'

'Not yet,' Carlyle admitted.

'What you've got to realize is that she is even crazier than he is.'

You married her, Carlyle thought.

'It wasn't like that to start with,' said Safi, as if reading his mind. 'But after Taimur was born she had a complete personality change. Totally lost the plot.'

'Ah.'

'She got religion, big time.' Safi grimaced at the memory. 'It was like her brain went completely haywire. In the end, when she did a runner, it was a bit of a relief, to be honest.'

'So Taimur got into religion from his mother?' the inspector asked.

Safi looked at him blankly.

'She exposed him to Islamic fundamentalism?' The words made him sound like one of those MI5 berks, but he ploughed on. 'Got him into the life that led him to go after Joseph Belsky with an axe?'

'Islamic fundamentalism?' Pushing his chair back against the window, Safi began to laugh. 'No, no, no. You've got it all wrong.'

Wouldn't be the first time, Carlyle thought.

'Elma is a kind of . . .' Safi waved his hand in the air as he tried to find the right words, 'a born again Christian. An evangelist.

Started preaching sermons, stuff like that. She has her own church down in South London now, trying to convince people that she can work miracles.' Seeing the look of confusion on the inspector's face, he shrugged. 'I know, I know. There are people who not only believe that rubbish, they'll pay good money for it.'

'I thought that kind of thing only happened in America,' Carlyle said. 'Still, there are fools everywhere.'

'That's true enough. Anyway, the one thing that little Miss Born Again could most definitely *not* have was a Muslim husband.' Safi prodded himself in the chest with his index finger. 'That is to say, me. Not that I was practising or anything, but it sure as shit wouldn't have looked good on the promotional literature. Anyway, she divorced me for God and I've hardly seen her since.'

'Bummer,' said Carlyle, getting to his feet.

'To be honest, I stopped caring long ago. Like I said, when she finally left, it was more of a relief than anything else. I'm sure it didn't do Taimur any good. But I didn't expect he'd do anything like this, though.'

The inspector extended a hand and they shook. 'You should go and see him.'

Safi sighed. 'I'm sorry, Inspector, but I think I'll leave that to his mother. She's probably trying to arrange Bible classes as we speak.'

'Up to you,' Carlyle said. 'If I need anything else . . .'

Safi spread his arms wide. 'I'm always here. Open or closed.'

'Thank you. We'll be in touch.' Carlyle reached for the door.

Safi scowled at Mushudur, who was sprawled across the counter, picking his nose. 'You wanna kebab to go?'

'I'm good.' Pulling open the door, the inspector made a break for the relatively fresh air of the street. 'Thanks.'

TWENTY-ONE

Grimacing, Carlyle dropped the two plastic bags full of groceries onto the kitchen floor and set about massaging the circulation back into his fingers. Plastic bag technology; one thing that hadn't apparently evolved all that much over the years. When he had finally recovered feeling in both hands, he stepped over to the fridge and pulled out a well-deserved bottle of Tiger beer. Taking a bottle opener from the drawer next to the sink, he flipped off the cap and drank deeply. 'Aah.'

'So you're back then?'

Smiling, Carlyle offered his wife the bottle.

Keeping her expression neutral, Helen shook her head. 'No, thanks.'

'Tough day?'

'Just the usual,' she sighed. 'Arguing over how to spend the money we don't have. Deciding who lives, who dies. That sort of thing.'

Not for the first time, Carlyle wondered if it was perhaps time for Helen to think about a change of job. Twenty years of working for a medical charity where – literally – you had to take life and death decisions almost every day was enough to take its toll on anyone. Placing the beer bottle by the sink, he stepped over to give her a kiss. As he did so, she bent down to pick up the shopping, leaving him to brush past the top of her head.

'What did you get?' she asked.

He watched nervously as she hoisted the bags onto the

worktop next to the cooker and began decanting his purchases. This domestic ritual was like having your homework marked – except that you always knew in advance that you had failed. 'Er,' he stammered, 'I got most of what you wanted.' *I hope.*

Helen pulled out a jumbo box of Jaffa Cakes and waved them at him accusingly. 'What about these?'

'You can't beat a nice Jaffa Cake,' Carlyle observed, well aware that they had not been on her list.

'Hm.' Next out of the bag came the jumbo tin of fruit cocktail, one of his favourites, followed by a large can of baked beans. 'And these?' He shrugged helplessly as she began rummaging through the bags with increasing exasperation. 'Bloody hell, John, where's the spinach I asked you to get? And the onions?'

Christ. He knew he'd forgotten something. 'They didn't have any,' he lied.

She looked at him suspiciously. 'Why is it that a man of your age can't even go to the supermarket and get some simple—' Grabbing his choice of toilet roll, she looked like she was going to cry. 'And what is this?'

The apparent simplicity of the question made him nervous. 'It's . . . er, loo paper.'

'Yes, but it's the wrong colour.'

The wrong colour? Walking down the aisle of the supermarket, the inspector had just picked up the first thing that had come to hand. 'It is?'

'Of course it is,' she wailed. 'It's blue.'

For the first time in his life, the inspector pondered the issue of the right colour for toilet paper. 'What would be the right colour, then?'

Resisting the urge to throw it at him, she dumped the pack back down on the counter. 'I wanted white.'

'Ah.' Attempting to defuse the situation, he tried to pull her towards him for a cuddle. But Helen was having none of it and she pushed him brusquely away. 'For God's sake, you are so useless! Why is it I have to do everything around here?'

Jesus, he thought, *here we go again*. It was a familiar refrain and he was wearied by it. Overall, he reckoned that he did his share of the family chores – but what he saw as a daily point-scoring exercise was increasingly driving him mad. *We're both getting older*, he thought, *and more crotchety*. 'I'm sorry,' he whined, 'but they just didn't have any.'

'Hm.' Helen started putting the food away. 'Did you get some butter?'

'Yes.' *Thank God for that.*

'Salted?'

'Er.' He held his breath as Helen pulled a small block wrapped in golden foil from one of the bags and carefully inspected the labelling.

'Salted.' Shooting him a rueful smile, she pulled open the fridge and placed it on one of the shelves on the inside of the door. 'Very good.'

Phew. Carlyle reached for his bottle.

'By the way, I spoke to Christina today. She'd love us to do some babysitting.'

I'm sure she would, thought Carlyle unhappily, sucking down the last of the beer before dropping the empty bottle in the waste bin under the sink.

'So I said we'd take Ella tomorrow night.'

Shit.

'Christina wants Umar to take her to a Chinese restaurant in Soho that they liked to go to before Ella was born.'

'Okay.' He tried not to grimace.

'What's happening tomorrow night?' Alice appeared in the doorway. She was wearing jeans and a Stiff Little Fingers 'Nobody's Hero' T-shirt. Carlyle smiled. His daughter's interest in punk rock had lasted far longer than he would ever have expected. Having expropriated Carlyle's collection of Clash, Jam and Elvis Costello CDs, she had moved on to the likes of SLF and the Buzzcocks, happily mixing Ian Dury and Graham Parker with whatever pop fluff was currently flavour of the moment among teenage girls. God knows what her friends at school made of it, but her father was chuffed to bits.

Alice caught him staring at the T-shirt. 'Cool, eh?'

'Great.'

She started into a tuneless rendition of 'Alternative Ulster', bobbing and weaving like a miniature facsimile punk. Carlyle wondered if she had the first clue what the song was actually about.

'Where did you get it?'

She stopped pogo-ing. 'I found it in the vintage shop on Drury Lane last week.'

'Result.' He didn't dare ask how much it had cost.

'They've got a concert coming up soon, in Kilburn. I thought maybe we could go?'

Carlyle glanced at Helen. It was a long time since he had been to a rock concert.

'Don't look at me,' his wife smirked. 'All this stuff was after my time.'

'As if . . .' Carlyle snorted.

'The tickets are only twenty-five quid,' Alice persisted. 'And Spear of Destiny are the support act.'

Spear of Destiny? *Bloody hell*, he thought, *are they still going as well? Don't any of these bands ever die?* 'Well, maybe. We'll see.'

Alice seemed happy enough with that response. 'Okay,' she said cheerily. 'And in the meantime, what's happening tomorrow night?'

'We're babysitting Ella for Christina and Umar,' Helen explained, carefully putting the last of the groceries in a cupboard and stuffing the empty plastic bags under the sink. 'So they can have a night out.'

'Maybe you could give us a hand,' said Carlyle hopefully.

'Ha.' Alice laughed. 'No way.'

'I'll pay you.'

'Sorry, I'm going round to Martha's house tomorrow night. We're revising for a history exam.'

'Oh.' Martha Railton was one of Alice's schoolfriends. Her father was an entrepreneur of some description and the family lived in a massive pile in Bloomsbury. She was also Alice's *get out of jail free card* – a 24/7 excuse for getting out of unwanted Carlyle family activities.

'That's great,' said Helen, filling the kettle and fishing a box of white tea from a cupboard behind Carlyle's head. 'Anyway, I'm sure that your father and I will be able to manage.' She gave Carlyle a gentle poke in the ribs. 'Just make sure that you're home at a reasonable time.'

TWENTY-TWO

Taking a deep breath, Melville Farasin took a step forward and hesitantly offered the envelope to his boss.

'What's this?' Elma Reyes asked, making no effort to take it from him.

Melville could feel his pulse throbbing in his neck and his heart was racing faster than he had ever felt it before. His mum would be mad as hell when she heard what he'd gone and done, but he was sure that she would be all right when he explained it to her and told her of the job waiting for him at Tesco. She wouldn't be too impressed about him stacking supermarket shelves, but at least it was a start. If he stuck with it, there would be other opportunities down the line.

Elma, however, was another matter altogether. Only God Himself could explain things to *her*. Melville looked down at the letter in his shaking hand. It was too late to back down now. *Take it*, he silently urged his boss. *Just take it.* Bracing himself for the inevitable volley of abuse, he did a little jig from foot to foot. All he could hope for was to get through this conversation without wetting himself.

In no mood for any nonsense, Elma glanced at Michelangelo Federici. Not knowing what Meville wanted, the lawyer just shrugged, so turning back to her assistant, she said curtly, 'Spit it out, boy.'

'It's my letter of . . . resignation.' As the words settled, Melville was relieved not to feel a damp warmth spreading across his crotch. 'I'm sorry, but I don't want to work for the Christian Salvation Centre no more.'

'What?' Grabbing the letter from the boy's hand, Elma tore it into little pieces, tossing them up in the air. Once they had fluttered to the floor, she pointed to the door. 'Get outta here, you ungrateful little creature. Your resignation is refused.'

'But—'

'But nothin',' Elma snorted.

'Elma . . .' Federici said, trying not to laugh.

Keeping her gaze firmly on her underling, Elma waved away the interruption. 'Wait till I speak to your mother about this.' When Melville hesitated, she grabbed his shoulder and pushed him towards the door. 'Get back to work. Go.'

Reluctantly, the boy did as he was told.

'My, my,' Federici chuckled as Melville disappeared and the door clicked shut behind him. 'You really do have a way with the staff.'

Elma shot him a dirty look. 'Great help you are.'

'Elma,' the lawyer pouted, 'I didn't come here to do your HR.' Dressed in Boss Jeans and a lime-green Fred Perry polo shirt under a Paul Smith pinstripe jacket, Federici settled back into Elma's chair. From behind her desk, at the Salvation Centre's Global HQ, he had a fine view of the number 96 bus stop across the road. Two teenage schoolgirls were sitting in their uniforms, backpacks at their feet, scoffing packets of crisps while they waited for their bus. Federici glanced at his watch. *You two should be in class*, he thought, *rather than bunking off.*

'That boy simply doesn't know what he's sayin',' Elma scoffed. 'He's a bit simple in the head.'

Seems okay to me, Federici thought. *Just a bit quiet. And not that daft. I wouldn't want to be your gofer either.*

'His mother'll have to sort him out – again.' Elma stepped around the desk and shooed the lawyer out of her chair. 'The things I have to put up with! It's not like Melville could get a job with anyone else.'

'No.' Federici retreated to a ratty sofa – a gift from a recently deceased parishioner – that took up most of the far wall.

Elma slipped on a pair of wire-rimmed glasses and leaned across the desk. 'So, Mr Lawyer, to what do I owe this three hundred and fifty pounds an hour pleasure? Why are you here?'

Positioning himself directly beneath a poster of a white cloud in a blue sky bearing the legend *He is watching over you*, Federici smiled. 'We need to talk about Taimur . . . and also about Jerome Mears.'

'Jerome?' Elma frowned. 'What about him? Isn't he safely back in the Bible Belt by now – with all the true believers? Home territory, where all the easy money is.'

'He's back in Texas. But he's not happy.'

'Awww.' Sitting back in her chair, Elma wiped a fake tear from her eye. 'And why would that be? Were the hookers in King's Cross not to his liking?'

'His complaint is rather more specific than that. I got an email from him last night. He's threatening to sue you.'

'Sue me?' Elma spluttered, bouncing up and down on her chair. 'Sue me for what?'

Sitting forward on the sofa, Federici placed his hands on his knees. 'He is claiming breach of contract.'

Taking off her glasses, Elma chucked them onto the desk. 'For Christ's sake, Mikey,' she complained, pinching the bridge of her nose, 'I paid the smug bastard, didn't I?'

Federici held up his hands in supplication. 'Yes, yes, you did. But he is claiming that you failed to deliver the agreed audience for his sermon to the Miracle and Healing Conference.'

Don't I know it, Elma thought.

Federici pulled a piece of paper from his jacket pocket, unfolded it and squinted at his scribbled notes. 'Mears says that both in terms of numbers and quality, the turnout was, quote-unquote, "substantially below the level which had been agreed, in order to allow for the Mears Ministry to participate".'

'What the hell does that mean?'

Federici looked up from his notes. 'It means that performing to a handful of folk in a hotel in North London could be deemed to be damaging to the Ministry brand.'

'I thought that we had hundreds there,' Elma objected, somewhat optimistically.

'The Reverend Mears claims that he counted no more than eighty-seven what he calls "bona fide participants". He also claims that the lack of a decent crowd seriously undermined sales of the pay-per-view event on his website.'

Elma felt that her head was about to explode. 'What pay-per-view event?'

Federici shrugged. 'Apparently, he decided to charge people in the States to watch his sermon from King's Cross, both live and on a catch-up basis.'

'Hell!' Elma thundered. 'But it was *my* conference.'

'There was nothing to stop him doing that,' Federici told her. 'It simply wasn't covered in the contract.'

Elma's eyes narrowed. 'Wasn't the contract *your* responsibility?'

Federici smiled. Elma was right, this had been an oversight on his part but, having anticipated the question, he smoothly delivered his pat answer. 'Yes, of course. But it was a standard agreement that allowed both sides to exploit new media rights as they saw fit.'

So that crook Jerome was going to diddle me out of my share of the revenues, Elma thought sourly. *And now that his plan has backfired, he wants to sue me.* She shot the lawyer one of her famous fire and brimstone looks. 'Tell him to go fuck himself.'

Federici raised an eyebrow. 'I could do that.'

'But?' Elma slumped back into her chair.

'But,' Federici repeated, 'if I do that, the danger is that he'll go to a friendly judge in some hick town in Texas and get some kind of preliminary judgement to start a legal process that could tie you up for years. Worse than that, depending on what the judge decides, you could face arrest and possible incarceration the next time you go to the United States.'

Arrest and possible incarceration. Elma thought about that for a moment. There were three trips to the US booked into her diary before the end of the year, starting with a guest slot at the San Diego Hispanic Rebirth Festival in a little over a week's time. If she had to cancel any or all of the trips it would be a disaster for her attempts to crack the American market. And without America, she might as well close down the Salvation Centre right now. London just wasn't big enough on its own. There was no way she was going to keep slogging round the budget hotels of the capital for the rest of her career. No way. It was America or bust for her.

'How much does he want?' she asked resignedly.

'Another ten thousand, sterling.'

'Wha-at?' Elma squawked. 'Is he on crack?'

Probably, Federici thought. 'Reading between the lines,' he explained, 'the balance of the original fee was stolen from Jerome's London hotel room before he went back home. It looks like his insurance company doesn't want to pay up and he's trying to recoup his losses by gouging you.'

Elma eyed her lawyer carefully. 'And how do you know all this?'

The man gave a modest shrug. 'I have my sources.'

'Can we afford it?'

'The ten k? Just about. It doesn't leave you with much left over, though.'

'Cashflow's a bitch.'

'Haven't you got that new CD coming out?'

'Not for a couple of months,' Elma sighed, 'and these things don't sell much these days.' Closing her eyes, she began humming a tune he didn't recognize.

'I suppose not.' Federici let his client ponder her options a little longer. 'Do you want me to pay him off?'

'Lemme think on it.'

'Okay. I'll play for time.'

'Good,' Elma mumbled. Torn between pragmatism and poverty, her indecision was final. After a couple of moments, she opened her eyes. 'Are we done?'

'We still have to talk about Taimur.'

'Not any more.' Elma gave Federici a dismissive wave of her hand. 'That boy's a totally lost cause. There's nothing more I can do for him right now. He'll have to find his own salvation. We have to focus on the important stuff – like how to generate some more cash.'

The smiling blonde pulled her hair away from her face to give a better view of her ample chest. 'I like Army guys,' she purred, 'but firemen too.'

'What the hell are you doing?'

'Nothing.' Pushing the chair away from his desk, Umar looked up at his boss like a naughty schoolboy. 'Just a bit of surfing.'

From a nearby desk, WPC Sonia Mason observed them both coolly. 'He's not on sexyuniforms.com again, is he?'

'Just having a look,' Umar admitted sheepishly.

Carlyle squinted at the girl in the small video in the top corner of the screen. 'But she's not wearing a uniform.'

'No,' Umar explained. 'She's a normal member of the public.'

Carlyle grinned. 'Normal member of the public' wasn't the kind of phrase he came across too often at the station.

'She wants to go out with someone in a uniform,' the sergeant said.

'Ah,' said Carlyle, none the wiser.

'Most of them want soldiers,' Mason chipped in, 'not coppers. But Umar lives in hope.'

'So, it's a dating site?'

Umar hit a button on his keyboard and the video containing the blonde disappeared. 'Isn't that what I said? It's a dating site for punters who want to go out with people who wear uniforms. Some people like that kind of thing.'

Gang of Four's 'I Love a Man in a Uniform' started playing in

Carlyle's head. He hadn't heard the song in years, perhaps decades. *Whatever happened to the Gang of Four?* He pointed at the computer screen. 'Why are you looking at this?'

'No reason.'

'He's still trying to pull,' Mason laughed. 'Playing away.'

'Bollocks,' Umar protested. 'I was only having a look.'

'It's quite common among men whose wives have just had kids,' Mason observed. 'Not getting the attention at home and feeling a bit sorry for themselves.'

Carlyle gave Umar a sympathetic pat on the shoulder. 'God help you if Christina finds out.'

'I'm only looking,' the sergeant repeated, sounding rather more irritated.

Carlyle looked sceptical. 'Good luck with that line of defence.' A thought popped into his head. 'Anyway, shouldn't the IT department block this kind of stuff?'

'Oh no,' said Mason cheerily. 'We need access to the whole worldwide web to do our job properly. It's essential that we know what all the nasty people are up to, as well as the needy.'

'Lucky us.' Carlyle pulled up a chair next to his sergeant and lowered his voice. 'Anyway, about tonight . . .'

'Yeah. Thanks for agreeing to do the babysitting.'

'Happy to do it,' Carlyle lied.

'Thanks.'

'It's no problem. Helen's really up for it. But . . . er, how long do you think you'll be?'

'Not long,' Umar shrugged. 'A couple of hours, max. It's the first time we've gone out on our own since Ella was born. Christina's looking forward to it but she'll get too stressed if we leave the baby for too long.'

'Okay. Good.' Getting to his feet, the inspector began heading towards the stairs. 'I'll see you later.'

'You still remember how to change a nappy?' Umar called after him.

'Naturally,' Carlyle muttered, hurrying away.

TWENTY-THREE

At the front desk, there was a message for him. Chris Brennan, the oleaginous lawyer, had called again and was insisting that they spoke again as soon as possible. *Why don't you just sod off?* the inspector thought sourly. He was sick of people telling him what to do. Carlyle knew well enough that dealing with authority – real or imagined – had never been one of his strong points. Indeed, he had long clung to the belief that the man who had many the masters had none. The problem was that the masters, like buses, tended to all turn up at once – usually after long absences – to put that theory to the test. Well, Brennan was not one of his bosses. He simply had no authority to swan into the station and demand that the police hand over Brian Winters' bag.

That was not to say that Brennan's lumbering attempt to recover his ex-colleague's effects had not piqued Carlyle's interest. After giving the strictest instructions that the lawyer was not to be allowed anywhere near his presence, the inspector headed downstairs in search of the mysterious briefcase.

Located between the canteen and the media room, the evidence room at Charing Cross was, in fact, no more than an outsized broom cupboard. After punching in the security code on the entry pad, Carlyle pulled open the door and stepped inside. Switching on the overhead strip light, he stood in the middle of two lines of shelving, four rows high and about two feet deep, lined up against each wall. There was just enough room to walk between the shelves, as long as there was only one person in the room at a time. The place had the air of a lost luggage deposit. The shelves contained items that had been lost, or pinched from tourists, in and around Covent Garden – cameras, watches, mobile phones and the like. Few, if any, were ever returned to their original owners; after a few months, anything with a residual value would be scooped up and sent to Mile End, to be auctioned off for the benefit of the Police Benevolent Society.

The briefcase was where he had left it, in the middle row on the left, sitting between a battered laptop and a pair of Nike trainers, which were still in their box. Grabbing the handles, Carlyle signed the case out in the evidence log and made his way back upstairs. After a quick detour into the canteen to pick up a sandwich and a Coke, he grabbed an empty interview room on the first floor. Placing the bag on the table, he sat down and ate mechanically before turning his attention to the bag, pressing the catch on the lock and giving it a gentle push. Happily, it sprang open without any protest. 'Not locked – very good.' Carlyle peered inside. The case was divided into three compartments. The ones at the front and the back were stuffed with papers. The inspector carefully removed them, setting them on the table in two separate stacks. The middle compartment was zipped shut. Opening it up, he stuck in a hand, pulling out a passport, a wallet and a pile of credit-card receipts.

'Very good,' he repeated.

Predictably enough, the passport was made out to Brian Winters. Carlyle looked at the picture of a silver-haired guy. According to the details in the book, he had been born in 1953. The document itself had been issued in London less than a year ago but already the pages contained visas for Nigeria, Israel, Russia and Brazil, as well as the United States. Clearly, its owner spent a lot of time on the road. And equally clearly, he had not been expecting to keel over so suddenly on Waterloo Bridge. Pulling out his phone, the inspector scrolled through his contact list until he found WPC Mason's number upstairs.

She picked up on the second ring. 'Mason here.' Her chirpiness made him smile.

'It's Carlyle. Is Umar still gawping at that website?'

'Nah,' she laughed, 'he's gone out. On bike ride-duty.'

'He's on a bike?' Carlyle frowned. He had never known Umar to do anything remotely athletic – apart from flirting – in all the time they had worked together.

'No, no,' Mason giggled, 'he's not riding a bike. He's signed up to cover the naked bike-ride protest. Him and half the station.'

'Figures,' Carlyle grunted.

'They should be coming down the Strand right about now. He can't be that far away. D'ya want me to find him for you?'

'It's okay. But there is something else.'

'Yes?'

'Can you speak to the Waterloo station and get their report on the guy who dropped down dead on Waterloo Bridge the other night? His name was Brian Winters.'

'Sure.'

'Also, check whether he's ever been in any trouble with us before. And, if you've got time, do a quick online search and see what you can find out about him, generally speaking.'

'No problem. What am I looking for?'

'Nothing in particular,' Carlyle mumbled. 'Just see if anything interesting pops up.'

'Okay, I'm on it.'

Ending the call, he rang Susan Phillips. After three rings, her voicemail kicked in and he left a short message, asking her to call him back. Then, after finishing the last of his snack, he wiped his fingers on a paper napkin and began sifting through Winters' papers.

After several minutes of aimless searching, he was interrupted by the sound of his phone buzzing across the desk. It was Susan Phillips.

'Hi. Thanks for calling me back. I just wanted to check about the guy on Waterloo Bridge.'

'Just done him,' Phillips replied cheerily. 'Interesting character.'

'How so?'

'Well, you don't normally find sixty-something men with traces of cocaine in their system, at least not in London.'

Carlyle sat back in his chair. 'I thought he died of a heart attack?'

'He did. Not a bad way to go, if you ask me. *Bam*. He didn't know anything about it.'

'Brought on by the coke?'

'That wasn't clear but I rather doubt it. Just general wear and tear. Could have been brought on by the stress of the rush hour.'

'Yeah?'

'It's not that uncommon. What we found was evidence of long-term drug use, rather than of any massive recent binge. He certainly didn't OD. The guy was a lawyer as I understand it.'

'Apparently so.'

'So, presumably, it was just a recreational habit he'd developed over the years. Nothing that exciting.'

'Hm. Have your findings gone over to Waterloo?'

'Not yet. But they've had the basics, like you. I'll probably get a written report to them sometime tomorrow.'

'Will they do anything with it?'

'Nah, you know the score. Natural causes. It's gonna be *case closed* as soon as my findings reach their inbox.'

'Fair enough,' Carlyle mused, knowing that, in their position, he would do exactly the same. 'Thanks again for calling me back.'

'No problem. Any time.' The pathologist ended the call. Tossing the phone onto the desk, Carlyle contemplated the papers spread out in front of him. Phillips was right – it all seemed very straightforward. Winters' property should quickly be returned to his next of kin, who could then hand the relevant bits back to his employers. One thought, however, kept nagging at him: if Winters' death was so routine, why was that little shit Chris Brennan getting so agitated about the contents of his briefcase?

TWENTY-FOUR

Wearing nothing but a cycling crash helmet and a pair of aviator shades, Melissa Graham pedalled slowly down the Strand, heading towards Trafalgar Square. Trying to keep her gaze firmly on the patch of tarmac two feet beyond her front wheel, she hoped that none of the gawkers standing on the pavement could see how deeply she was blushing.

All around her, people were laughing and joking. Every so often, someone would break into an impromptu, invariably tuneless, song. After more than an hour on the road, however, the collective determination to have fun felt increasingly oppressive. Her shoulders were starting to burn under the London sun and, all in all, Melissa felt thoroughly miserable. Not for the first time that afternoon, she cursed her boyfriend for talking her into getting naked and riding through the middle of bloody London at about three miles an hour for the amusement of all and sundry. Her friend Laura, who was supposed to be riding alongside her, had pulled out at the last minute, claiming bad PMT. *Laura*, Melissa thought ruefully, *was no mug. She instinctively knew when something was just too uncool for words.*

The rider in front of her got out of the saddle, giving Melissa a perfect view of his hairy arsehole. Grimacing, she looked away. What the hell had she been thinking? All the talk of making a protest – about *what*, by the way? – was a load of old nonsense. The whole thing, she realized sadly, was just a chance for a group of pervy men to talk a bunch of stupid girls into taking their kit off.

Stupid girls, just like her.

Somewhere in the distance a siren wailed. 'Nice tits!' came a cry from the crowd, followed by peals of plebeian laughter. Melissa looked up to see who had been shouting, only to be greeted by a random mixture of bemused and lecherous faces – a united nations of wankers. Even the small knot of policemen – and one WPC – standing in front of a taxi that had stopped to take in the show seemed to think that the whole thing was hilarious. A few yards further on, a reporter was doing a piece to camera while a couple of other TV crews were filming the cyclists, many of whom were waving or mooning as they went by, flourishing their little anti-nuclear and anti-capitalist flags and banners as they did so.

Shit, shit, shit. She felt like crying. *What happens if they see me at work? What if my parents are watching this, live, on News 24?*

Melissa badly wanted to stop, get off her bike, pull out some shorts and a T-shirt from her pannier and get dressed. But that would only serve to draw attention to her and her embarrassment. All she could do now was try and get to the end as quickly as possible and slink off, putting it down as a never-to-be-repeated learning experience.

One thing was for sure, clothed or unclothed, she would never be getting on a bloody bike again.

A man on the bike next to her began scratching his balls vigorously. Catching her watching, he gave her a cheeky grin. Melissa quickly returned her gaze to the road. She was careful to remain tucked into the middle of the group, well away from any would-be gropers lurking between parked cars. But the turnout for the ride had been poor – at most, only about a third of the number that had been confidently predicted by the organizers had turned up – and there was really nowhere to hide. The whole thing made her skin crawl. By her tally, there were at least four times as many men on the ride as women. There were a broad range of specimens – a wide variety of ages and physical conditions – but all of them seemed ecstatic at the opportunity to let their willies dangle from the side of the frame of their bike while they ogled some naked female flesh.

As the cyclists picked up pace slightly, she glanced over at Will. About two bike rides in front, off to the right, her boyfriend was holding the position that he'd taken from the very start of the ride – up close beside Kara Johnson, whose massive breasts had been painted bright red for the occasion. Will was transfixed; Melissa was convinced that he'd had a semi-chub on for the last mile and a half, at least. He looked like he wanted to jump Kara on the spot. And she didn't look too dismayed at the idea, either.

What annoyed Melissa more than anything was the knowledge that if she and Will had sex tonight, he would be thinking about Kara and her gigantic – no doubt fake – tits.

Tosser.

The pace of the riders had slowed once again, this time to little more than a crawl. Taking a drink of lukewarm water from her bidon, Melissa spat the water out onto the tarmac. 'Urgh.' She was thirsty but she also really needed to pee. She recalled the case of the London marathon runner who'd squatted down in the gutter, mid-race, to go. Somehow she didn't think she'd be able to get away with that not so close to Nelson's Column at least.

As the front of the ride reached the south-east corner of the square, everything came to a complete standstill. Amid the general grumbling, Melissa gleaned that the police were holding them up to let regular traffic through first. This was not what the organizers had promised would happen and she could sense the group's humour levels begin to ebb still further. Doubtless she wasn't the only participant who was tired and fed up. She tried to catch Will's eye but he remained focused on the Amazonian Kara, his head so close to her arse that he looked like he was poised to lick the sweat from her glistening buttocks. Catching sight of ripples of cellulite on the backs of her thighs, Melissa felt a grim glimmer of satisfaction. 'You should cover that up,' she hissed to herself, 'you fat bitch.'

The need to pee was now becoming more urgent. Hopping from foot to foot, she tried to make out what was happening up ahead. Still there was no sign of the riders moving off. Melissa realized that if she didn't find a loo soon, she would just have to go in the street after all. To her left, she caught sight of a teenage boy in a replica Manchester United shirt standing on the pavement with his left arm aloft, filming her on his mobile phone. His right hand was shuffling in the pocket of his jeans. Their eyes met and the boy's grin grew wider.

Fuck this, Melissa thought. *I've simply got to get out of here.* Turning around, she had just reached for her pannier when an ear-splitting scream suddenly cascaded down the road towards her. Looking up, she could see people ahead jumping off their bikes and letting them drop to the ground as they ran to converge on an hysterical woman in a red bikini. Through gaps in the crowd, Melissa could see that the woman was standing over a bearded man who had apparently fallen from his bike and was lying on his back in the road. A couple of the police officers who had been watching the ride go past were trying to make their way through the crowd towards the prostrate man. A third was calling for an ambulance.

'Excuse me.' Melissa felt a hand on her shoulder and looked round to see a tall Asian guy gently manoeuvring her out of the way so that he could get past.

'I think the police are dealing with it,' she mumbled, grateful that the guy was at least making an effort to look at her face, rather than her chest. He was wearing jeans and a navy T-shirt bearing the legend EVERTON'S.

Handsome, Melissa thought, *but knackered-looking.*

'I *am* the police,' he replied with a slight Northern accent, producing an ID badge on a chain and pulling it over his head.

'What's going on?'

'I don't know,' the officer replied. 'But don't worry. Just stay here for the moment and we'll find out.' Stepping backwards, he took a moment – a long moment – to check her out from tip to toe. 'Maybe put some clothes on,' he said, giving every indication of liking what he saw. 'This may take a while.'

Not for the first time in his police career, Umar was almost completely distracted by the naked woman in front of him. The girl was very pretty – petite, slim, with pert breasts that ended in enormous nipples – and it took him a moment to tune back in to the screaming just down the road. There were various uniforms milling about but no one appeared to be taking control of the situation.

'Police!' he shouted, waving the ID in front of his face. 'Let me through.' Slowly a narrow pathway opened up in front of him. Moving away from the girl, he slalomed past a series of cyclists until he came to the guy on the ground. A WPC was kneeling over him, searching for a pulse. She looked up at Umar and shook her head. Behind her, he could see a dark mess sticking to the tarmac – blood. Lying in the blood, glinting in the sunlight, was what looked like a kitchen knife.

Not natural causes then, Umar mused.

'Looks like he's been stabbed,' said the uniform. The woman who had been screaming was now sobbing quietly into the chest of a fellow rider whose yellow Speedos left nothing to the imagination. All around him, Umar could make out a low murmour among the onlookers, the sound of curiosity rather than fear.

Christ, he thought, *how are we going to secure this scene?* From the direction of Charing Cross Road came the sound of an ambulance siren rushing towards them. Speaking into her walkie-talkie, the WPC was asking the station for more officers to help secure the scene and corral witnesses. Already, however, people were beginning to slip away. There was no way that the police officers would be able to stop them. Another group of cyclists had peeled off to buy ice creams from a van parked by one of the exits to Charing Cross tube station. Already, the dead man was no more than a mildly diverting topic of conversation.

Hands on hips, Umar watched a buxom wench, her breasts painted red for the occasion, chatting happily to some chinless wonder. As the ambulance pulled up in the eastbound lane, the paramedics jumped out and began retrieving their kit. They went about their task with practised efficiency, but lacking the high tempo that marked a life and death situation. Ten yards further down the road, a couple of uniforms were cordoning off the street, much to the annoyance of a bus driver who'd just had his route abruptly curtailed. More uniforms started trickling out of the nearby station. Umar watched to see if any more senior officers followed them. What he needed was someone to take charge as quickly as possible, so that he could slink off. Otherwise, his evening would go up in smoke. He would have to cancel dinner. Doubtless, Carlyle would be delighted at having avoided babysitting duties, but Christina would kill him. And the sergeant knew full well which of the two scared him most.

'My God. What's happened?'

It took Umar a couple of seconds to recognize the girl he'd spoken to just minutes before. Having slipped into a pair of white shorts and a Nike T-shirt, she looked completely different – if anything, even prettier. 'The bloke over there,' Umar pointed at the prostrate cyclists, 'it looks like he's been stabbed.'

Pulling off her sunglasses, Melissa Graham squinted at the victim. 'Is he dead?'

Umar shrugged. The hovering paramedics told their own story. 'Yeah.'

'Holy shit.' She giggled nervously.

'Do you know who he is, or, rather, who he *was*?'

'No idea.'

Umar pointed at the woman in the red bikini. 'Or her?'

'No, sorry.'

'Do you know who's in charge here? Who are the organizers?'

'I'm not really the person to ask, Officer.' Melissa perched the sunglasses back on her nose. 'I just came along for the ride, so to speak.' Half-turning, she pointed to the chinless bloke talking to the girl with the red chest. 'Will should know, though. He was the one who got me involved in this.'

Umar thought he detected a hint of bitterness in her voice. 'Okay, thanks.' Digging out a business card from the pocket of his jeans, he handed it over. 'This is me. What's your name?'

'Melissa . . . Melissa Graham.'

'Okay, Melissa. You have to stay here now until someone takes a statement.'

'But I didn't see anything,' Melissa complained, 'and I need to pee.'

'It shouldn't take long,' Umar lied.

'But I need to pee right now,' she protested. 'Otherwise I'm going to look like the woman in that Harvey Nichols advert.'

The policeman looked at her blankly.

'The advert of the woman pissing herself with excitement at the Harvey Nicks sale?'

Umar shrugged. The upmarket department store was way out of his league. 'Must've missed that one.' From the corner of his eye, he saw Detective Inspector Julie Postic marching down the empty eastbound lanes of the Strand, her faithful lackey, Sergeant Lawrence Shames, in tow, along with a couple of uniforms who were having to jog to keep up. Postic was already waving her arms in the air and generally asserting her authority.

'Thank God for that,' Umar mumbled to himself, carefully plotting an exit route that would keep him away from the beady eyes of the DI. 'The cavalry have finally arrived.'

'What?'

'Never mind.' Once again, he placed a hand on Melissa's shoulder. 'Tell you what, come with me.' He pointed in the direction of Agar Street. 'My station is just up there. You can come and use the facilities and then we'll take a quick statement. Then you can be on your way.'

125

'That would be great, thanks.' With a final glance towards the chinless wonder, Melissa began pushing her bike back through the crowd, towards the pavement. With a broad grin, the sergeant followed on, right behind her.

'Police. Coming through.'

TWENTY-FIVE

After an hour or so of semi-careful reading, the inspector had sorted the papers from the dead lawyer's briefcase into three piles. The first was personal: a series of letters and statements relating to a two-million-euro mortgage on a property Winters had bought in France. Two million euros was what? Carlyle's best guess was something like one point seven million quid or thereabouts. *One point seven mil.* That was a lot for a mere copper, but not necessarily such a big deal for a City lawyer.

The second pile of papers were also personal: a series of letters from a legal firm in North London asking for details of Winter's assets – bank accounts, pensions, property and so on. Apparently, Mrs Giselle Winters – née Aceveda – was seeking a divorce on the grounds of 'unreasonable behaviour'.

'Unreasonable behaviour,' Carlyle mumbled to himself. 'That doesn't exactly narrow it down.' He felt a sudden stab of male solidarity. 'No wonder the guy was so stressed.' On the other hand, the disaffected widow must now be sitting pretty.

The final set of papers was presumably what Chris Brennan was after: three copies of unsigned contracts concerning the merger of WBK – Winters Brennan & King – with an American legal firm called Austerlitz & Co. Nothing particularly interesting as far as Carlyle could see.

'Here you are.' He looked up to see Sonia Mason's head popped round the door. 'I've been looking for you all over the station.'

'Sorry,' Carlyle shrugged. 'I just wanted somewhere quiet to sit and do some reading.'

Mason slipped through the door, waving a set of papers of her own. 'I've been doing some reading too.'

'Oh?'

'Yes, your man Winters – very interesting.' Pulling out a chair, she dropped the documents on the table and sat down opposite him.

Behind her head, Carlyle caught sight of the clock on the wall. *Christ*, he thought, *is that the time?* If he wasn't home in the next forty-five minutes or so, Helen would kill him.

'Gimme the quick version.'

'Brian Winters seems to have had a fairly spectacular mid-life crisis, or rather, *late* mid-life crisis.'

Carlyle watched his mobile vibrating across the desk. He didn't need to check the screen to know that it was his wife. As the phone's voicemail kicked in, he eyed Mason. *Get on with it*, he thought.

'According to the gossip column in *the innkeeper* . . .'

'The what?'

'It's a website for lawyers. The name references Lincoln's Inn, where the legal bods hang out.'

'Yeah, yeah.'

'He had set up home on the Cote d'Azur with an escort, was getting a divorce and threatening to scupper his firm's merger with some American outfit.'

'Why the latter?'

'Because, *allegedly*, he didn't think he would get enough of a pay-out.'

Money and sex, Carlyle mused. *It always came back down to money and sex.* In a way that was reassuring. It certainly made life a lot simpler. However, it still didn't mean that the guy had died of anything other than a bog standard heart attack. His mobile phone started ringing again. Once again, without looking at the screen, he knew that it would be his wife.

You can run, but you can't hide.

He picked up the handset and hit receive.

'I'm coming right now.'

'Good,' said Helen firmly, 'and make sure you bring Umar with you.'

He found his sergeant sitting at his desk, chatting away happily to a young blonde girl. It was impossible not to notice that she was wearing nothing more than a flimsy T-shirt and the skimpiest pair of shorts that the inspector had seen in a long time.

'Managed to tear yourself away from sexyuniforms.com then?' Carlyle asked as he hovered behind Umar's chair.

The sergeant chose to ignore the bait. 'Inspector, this is Melissa Graham.' The girl smiled at him politely. 'She was on the bike ride today.'

'Glad to see you've managed to get some clothes on before you came in here,' Carlyle quipped, gesturing round the office, 'or the forces of law and order would have ground to a complete halt.'

Melissa's smile wavered but she said nothing.

'And the bike ride,' he asked, 'how did it go?'

'Not too good,' Umar said. 'A bloke got stabbed.'

'Not seriously, I hope.'

'Dead.'

Carlyle looked at the girl and frowned. 'By her?'

'No, no,' said Melissa, blushing violently. 'I was just—'

'She was just a witness,' Umar explained. 'I was taking a statement.'

Yeah, right, Carlyle thought. *Along with an email address and a phone number, you dirty little sod.* 'I see.' Slowly, he looked around the room. 'So where are all the other *witnesses*?'

'Lawrence Shames and DI Postic are rounding them up now; it looks like it's gonna be their case.'

Thank God for that. The last thing he wanted at the moment was more on his plate. 'I'm sure they'll get to the bottom of it . . . no pun intended.'

Umar raised his eyes to the heavens.

'It's really Sergeant Shames you should be talking to.' Carlyle smiled at the girl. 'He's a very nice man.'

'I needed to pee,' Melissa said, 'so Umar brought me back here.'

Umar, is it?

The sergeant shrugged. 'All part of the service.'

'Very good.' The inspector stepped forward, half-turning so that he could better look his colleague in the face. 'Anyway, *Umar*, we'd better get going.' He smiled maliciously. 'You don't want to be late for your date with your *wife*.'

Steve Metcalf dropped the last of the lamb kebab into his gaping maw and wiped his hands on the front of his faded T-shirt. Washing it down with the last dregs from a half-litre bottle of Kingfisher lager, he looked expectantly across the table at Calvin Safi.

'You shouldn't be drinking that in here,' Safi pointed out. 'You know I don't have a licence.'

'Calvin, old son, relax. Why do you let yourself get so wound up about shit?'

'I could get shut down,' Safi grumbled.

'Ha.' Metcalf let out a ferocious belch. 'Who's gonna complain?' With the empty bottle, he gestured round the almost empty kebab shop. Aside from Aqib and his mate Rasheed, sitting near the counter, their faces a study in concentration as they wolfed down a couple of hamburgers, there were no other customers.

God knows how anyone is supposed to make money selling fast food, Calvin thought unhappily. If he'd taken £200 so far today, it would be a miracle. There was no way he could cover his costs simply by selling kebabs. He watched Metcalf wipe some brown sauce from his chin and wished that he'd never come across the sick bastard. As usual, the whole thing was Aqib's fault; the idiot wanting to look good in front of one of his Chelsea mates. Calvin knew that they should never have let white guys in on their little scheme. White guys always fucked things up.

Why had he gone along with it? Basically, Aqib had whined like a child – well, he was a child, more or less – but still, he had moaned endlessly and Calvin had given in. It had been a big mistake, even before all this stuff with Taimur had brought the police round. Now he felt very nervous about the whole thing. But stopping it seemed impossible, particularly now that this stupid sod had discovered how to get laid by someone other than his wife.

'So,' Metcalf sat back in his chair, scratching his balls through the dirty denim of his trousers, 'what have you got for me tonight?'

Calvin felt sick. 'I thought Aqib told you,' he replied, trying to sound as forceful as possible, 'we need to quieten things down for a while.'

Metcalf glanced over at the other two, still chomping away on their burgers. 'Aqib din' tell me nuffink,' he asserted, turning on the hard mockney accent to remind the foreigner who was the bloody boss here. 'And I want a shag.'

Gritting his teeth, Calvin tried to stand his ground. 'After the last time . . .'

'After the last time, nuthin'.' Flinging the bottle past Calvin's head, Metcalf watched with grim satisfaction as it smashed against the wall, sending pieces of brown glass scattering across the dirty floor. Calvin flinched. Stuffing the last of the bun into his mouth, Aqib looked up at Calvin and laughed, giving him a look that said *don't pretend you can fuck with Steve – you're not in charge any more*.

'It was a one off and we dealt with it,' Metcalf said cockily. 'It's history.'

Calvin nodded, not believing a word of it.

'There's nuthin' that can come back to any of us.'

'Let's hope not.'

'Why do you say that?' Metcalf's eyes widened. 'Has anyone come sniffin' round?'

'No. But—'

'But nothin'.' Debate over, the fat man folded his arms. 'So it's business as usual, my friend.'

'Sure, Steve.'

'And who's this new girl Aqib's told me about?' Metcalf enquired eagerly. 'I hear she's a right slag.'

TWENTY-SIX

After maybe three hours adrift in the orange gloom, Taimur Rage realized that the shouts and the screams from the other cells were not going to stop. They would go on all night. He was in a loony bin.

At least the guy he'd been put in with wasn't a nutter. Lying back in his bed, Taimur listened to the snoring coming from the bunk above him – his cellmate was some foreign bloke who'd been fighting deportation for more than a year – and felt the pills in the palm of his hand. He had been expecting to get a visit from his mum, or at least his lawyer. Instead, it was Aqib who turned up at visiting time. He had a girl in tow that Taimur had never seen before. She was wearing a flimsy T-shirt and no bra. The warders certainly couldn't get enough of her; when Aqib had passed him the pills no one was paying a blind bit of attention.

'Your dad would've come,' Aqib sniffed as he watched Taimur slip the small clingfilm packet into his boxers, 'but he's got the shop and that.'

'Yeah.'

Aqib tugged at his hoodie. 'That's a 24-7 operation right there. You know the chavs working the till will rob him blind if he leaves them alone for a minute.'

Taimur shrugged. He glanced at the girl across the table. She was grinning aimlessly at a monster bloke with a tattoo – some kind of snake that went all the way up his left arm – who was sitting at the next table. Tattoo Man was so taken by Taimur's visitor that he barely acknowledged the woman who was sitting opposite him. She was a hard-looking bottle blonde with a baby on her lap and an unlit cigarette between her fingers. Yammering away at great speed, the blonde was laying in to Tattoo Man, complaining about money or something. She didn't seem to notice that her man wasn't listening.

'Anyway,' Aqib continued, lowering his voice theatrically as he gestured across the table, 'those are good stuff.' He whispered a designer-sounding name that Taimur didn't recognize. 'Got 'em wholesale from my man Steve.'

The pills were probably aspirin or some shit like that, Taimur thought. *Aqib was such a dick.*

'They'll help take the edge off in here,' Aqib explained, mistaking the amusement in Taimur's face for enthusiasm. 'Keep you mellow.' He allowed himself a sneaky peek down the top of the girl's T-shirt, licking his lips as he did so. 'Or you can trade 'em with your mates, or whatever.'

What mates? Taimur wondered.

Without warning, the girl pitched forward in her chair. Showing decent reflexes, Aqib grabbed her arm, pulling her towards him before she could hit her head on the table. The blonde woman at the next table turned to see what was going on and gave the three of them a nasty grin.

'Fuck, Nat!' Aqib shrieked. 'What you doing?'

The girl started to giggle as a pair of guards watched them suspiciously.

'C'mon. We need to walk.' Getting up, Aqib dragged her to her feet. 'Sorry, man, we better get outta here before someone decides she needs a drugs test. Be strong, hear?' He waved his free hand in the air. 'You a big man now, in here. Maximum security. Enjoy it.'

His mind blank, Taimur watched the pair of them stumble towards the exit. The blonde woman at the next table went back to her complaint, and Tattoo Man tried to find something else to stare at. When the guard came to take Taimur back to his cell, he was already on his feet, good to go.

The sound of footsteps on the landing outside died away as the warder continued his rounds. Above his head, his cellmate mumbled something in a language that he didn't recognize and then promptly went back to sleep. As the man's snoring resumed, Taimur reached down for the bottle of water he had placed on the floor. Propping himself up on his elbows, he pulled Aqib's gift from inside his boxer shorts and carefully unwrapped the cling-fim. Inside it were six unmarked white tablets. Knowing Aqib, they were probably useless, but it was worth a go. Dropping them into his mouth, Taimur unscrewed the top of the bottle and took a long swig.

TWENTY-SEVEN

Where exactly was he? Page 378? 379? It had to be around there.
Harry was just about to shoot someone and save the day.

Good man, Harry. Good name, too.

Harry Hole.

Great name for a cop.

Shame about his drinking problem.

And his relationship problems.

And all his other problems.

Feeling rather smug, sitting pretty in his domestic cocoon,
Carlyle looked over at Helen, perched on the edge of the sofa,
her mobile jammed under her ear.

'Well,' she said, speaking into the phone, 'if you can't come up
next week, maybe we could come down to the coast for a few days.'

Uh, oh, Carlyle thought, *she's cooking something up with her
mother*. He shifted uneasily in his seat. It wasn't that he had any
particular cause to dislike his mother-in-law; it was just that
he preferred it when he was in London and she stayed down in
Brighton.

'No, no, I think we would all come.' Helen glanced up at her
husband but he pretended not to notice. 'John would like to come
too. He could do with a bit of time by the sea. The fresh air would
do him good.'

Finding his page, the inspector shrank as far behind his book
as possible and began reading. The bad guy was just about to
be stopped in his tracks, as promised. *This is what policing is*

supposed to be about, he thought happily. *Shoot first and ask questions later.*

If only.

Sadly, it was about as far removed from reality as he could possibly imagine. You didn't get many serial killers howling at the moon in Covent Garden.

Waaa.

The cry from down the hall was faint but clear. Carlyle steadfastly refused to look up from his book. *Ignore it*, he told himself. *It might go away.*

Waa. Waa.

Just ignore it.

'Hold on a second, Ma.' Stretching across the sofa, his wife prodded him with a stockinged toe. Reluctantly, he looked up. From down the hall, the crying had mutated into a continuous complaint that was becoming steadily louder. 'Go and see that Ella's all right. Her nappy might need changing.'

When he didn't move, Helen waved the handset in front of his face. 'I'm on the phone.'

WAAA.

Why don't you get off the bloody phone, then? he thought grumpily. But Helen had already returned her attention to the conversation with her mother.

'Yeah, just making John get off his backside to go and see to the baby . . . yes, she's lovely . . . I know . . . no, it would be far too late for us to have another one now.'

Too damn right, Carlyle thought. With a weary sigh, he tossed his book onto the table, struggled to his feet and padded towards the hall.

Ella was lying in a travelling cot on their bed. By the time he reached her, the noise level had gone up another notch. As he bent down to pick her up, the inspector realized that Helen had been right. He wrinkled his nose. 'Shit.'

Taking a moment out from her wailing, the child looked up at him suspiciously. Even Carlyle had to admit she was a very

137

pretty kid, her dark features showing traces of both of her parents. He tried a smile.

Waa.

'Okay, okay.' He held up his hands in supplication. 'Let's get this done.' Gently removing the child from her cot, he carefully carried her next door, breathing through his mouth as best he could.

In anticipation of just such an occurrence, Helen had laid out a changing mat on the bathroom floor, along with all the required paraphernalia. Thankfully, Ella lapsed into a bemused silence as she watched the inspector free her legs and lower body from her romper suit and begin the delicate operation of removing the soiled nappy. 'God,' Carlyle grimaced, reaching for a nappy sack. 'What the hell have you been eating, eh?' Looking up, Ella gave him something that could have been interpreted as a smile. 'That was a monster.' Dropping the nappy into the sack, he tied the drawstrings and lobbed the offending article into the bath. *How long is it since I did this for Alice?* he wondered, knowing that his daughter wouldn't want to be reminded of those not so long ago but long gone days. He looked at Ella and smiled. 'You'll be grown up too, before you know it.' All he got by way of reply was a broad yawn. 'Understood.' Reaching for the wipes, Carlyle began carefully cleaning the child's arse. 'Give me a minute and we'll get you back in bed.'

When he made it back to the living room, Helen was still on the phone to her mum. She looked up and he gave her a nod to signify that everything was all right. Ella had fallen asleep almost before he had left the room. Domestic peace had been restored. Reaching over, he kissed his wife gently on the top of her head. For a moment, it was almost as if they had gone back in time. Returning to the sofa, he picked up his book and returned to his page. Finally, it was time to learn a thing or two about proper policing.

TWENTY-EIGHT

Three missed calls from Bernie Gilmore were by no means the ideal start to the day. The journalist would either want to berate the inspector for not dropping a tip in his lap or, alternatively, try and winkle something out of him. There was nothing that Bernie liked more than some nice piece of juicy information that Carlyle should sensibly keep to himself. 'God, Bernie,' he grumbled to himself, 'what makes you think *I* know anything?' He didn't have any such titbits to share, whether he wanted to or not. Hell, that was the whole point of being a copper – you spent your entire life coming to terms with your basic *lack* of information.

Happily, by the time the inspector reached the front steps of the station, Bernie Gilmore had been completely forgotten.

Slipping unobtrusively through the reception, keeping an eye out for any familiar faces on the benches, he was intercepted by Michelangelo Federici, creeping up on his blindside.

'Inspector.'

Oh shit. 'To what do I owe this pleasure?' Carlyle asked grumpily.

Federici looked around nervously. Clearly, the lawyer was not keen to be discussing his business in such a public space. 'Can we talk upstairs?'

Carlyle sighed. He had a lot to get through this morning and already he was running late. But Federici seemed a decent enough sort – for a lawyer. The inspector pointed past the front desk, towards the doors leading into the station proper. 'Sure. Let's go and find a room. It'll need to be quick, though.'

'Thank you.' Smiling, Federici immediately signalled to a small black woman in an expensive-looking business suit sitting on a nearby bench. The woman jumped up as if she had been given an electric shock and scuttled over. 'Inspector, this is Taimur Rage's mother.'

Hovering beside her lawyer, Elma Reyes shot Carlyle a hard look but said nothing.

Nice to meet you too, Carlyle thought, scowling at the lawyer who had so shamelessly tricked him. 'Uhuh.'

'We need to discuss developments,' Federici continued.

So now, all of a sudden, she wants to get involved? Well, it's a bit bloody late. The only development we're going to get now is her lad going to jail for a long time. Turning on his heel, the inspector headed towards the doors. 'Follow me.'

Finding an empty interview room on the first floor, Carlyle pushed open the door and ushered his guests inside. 'Please, take a seat.'

'Thank you.' Michelangelo Federici pulled out a chair and invited his client to sit down. Silently, Elma Reyes obliged. Federici took the seat next to her.

The inspector stepped over to the window. There was a pause while his guests waited for him to speak. When he failed to oblige, Federici took the initiative. 'What happened last night was truly devastating.'

'Hm.' What the hell was he talking about? Gazing through the glass, Carlyle kept his back to the table.

'For Taimur to be able to take his own life while under the care and protection of the state is a dreadful indictment of the prison service.'

Shocked, Carlyle maintained his silence.

'The fact that this vulnerable young man was able to obtain and use as yet unidentified drugs while supposedly under round-the-clock supervision will,' the lawyer continued, 'surely be a matter of some detailed investigation.'

Why had no one told him about this?

'In the meantime, it almost beggars belief that these services were outsourced to a private contractor.'

In the courtyard below, he caught sight of the top of WPC Mason's head as she climbed into a squad car. *Maybe that's what Bernie was ringing about*, he thought. It wouldn't be the first time that the shaggy journalist had known more about one of his investigations than Carlyle himself.

'Legal action will almost certainly follow.'

Get to the point, Carlyle thought, *you've used up all of my goodwill already.*

'However, our main interest is in truth and justice for the family.'

Yeah, right, you ambulance-chasing bastard.

'Ms Reyes has lost her son. And nothing anyone can say or do can bring him back.'

'Yes.' Finally, the inspector turned away from the window and took a seat on the opposite side of the table, holding the mother's stony gaze as he did so. 'Please accept my deepest condolences.'

Elma Reyes gave the merest of nods. A grim mask had settled on her face. If she had shed any tears for her son, they were long gone.

'This must be a very difficult time for you.' The inspector paused, counting to three in his head. 'What is it that I can do to be of assistance?'

Federici started to say something but Elma Reyes held up a hand to silence him. 'Arrest the people that killed him,' she said, jabbing an accusing finger at the inspector. 'Do your job for once.'

Gritting his teeth, Carlyle looked at the lawyer. Regardless of the circumstances, he didn't like being criticized, and certainly not by a civilian.

'Ms Reyes believes that her ex-husband, Calvin Safi, and his associates are ultimately responsible for this tragedy,' said Federici.

'By *ultimately responsible*, you mean . . .'

'They gave him the drugs,' Elma said flatly.

The inspector thought about that for a moment. 'When he was

141

arrested, Taimur was tested for drugs – I don't think they found anything. Are you saying that he had a history of—'

'No.' Elma glared at him as if he was a stupid child, trying her patience. 'Taimur never did anything like that. That's why it was so easy to lead him astray.'

'And why would they want to do that?'

'Good God.' Elma turned her wrath on her lawyer. 'I thought you said this one wasn't totally stupid.'

Federici shrugged apologetically. Whether the gesture was for the benefit of his client or the policeman, it was not clear.

Looking at the lawyer, Carlyle tried to change tack. 'I thought that Mr Safi was your client also?'

'I pay the bills.' Elma Reyes angrily slapped her hand down on the table. 'Those heathens corrupted my boy, they're the ones to blame. My son would never have ended up dead on drugs if he'd been under *my* roof.'

But he wasn't, Carlyle thought, *was he?* All these people who came crying to him after the event; why didn't they manage to pull their finger out before the shit hit the fan? It was so much easier just to whine about it afterwards. Taking the deepest of breaths, he tried to locate an atom of sympathy from somewhere in his being. 'Mrs . . .'

'Ms,' Federici reminded him. 'Ms Reyes.'

'Ms Reyes,' the inspector repeated, 'do you have any evidence to support what you are saying here?'

A look of such pure fury passed across Elma Reyes' face that for a moment he thought she was about to reach across the table and try to rip his face off with her bare hands. However, as it passed, she slumped back into her chair and folded her arms. 'Isn't that your job – to find the proof?'

Carlyle looked over at the lawyer, who was staring at his hands. 'Yes, but—'

'As God is my witness, I told you what happened,' she said defiantly, her eyes shining with an emotion that Carlyle couldn't quite place. 'Now surely it's up to *you* to go and get the damn evidence.'

TWENTY-NINE

Deeply irritated by Elma Reyes' crude attempt to bully him into hassling her husband, Carlyle was in a foul mood as he climbed the stairs to the third floor. Ignoring the two guys hovering near his desk, he scanned the room looking for his sergeant. Where the hell was Umar?

With a weary sigh, the inspector sat down and began banging on his keyboard. He still hadn't submitted his final report on Taimur Rage to Simpson. It was a bit academic now, but the Commander liked her paperwork. If he didn't get it over to her soon-ish, she would be on his case.

'Inspector John Carlyle?'

'Yeah,' Carlyle mumbled, not looking up as he continued typing, 'that's me.'

Why couldn't people just bloody leave him alone? Holding up his left hand, he continued typing with his right. 'Look, I'm kind of busy right now, so if it can wait . . .'

'It can't.' The stony reply was followed by a warrant card being waved in front of his face.

'Fuck.' Pushing back his chair, the inspector looked up to see a small round guy with a completely bald head and a rather spectacular handlebar moustache staring back at him. He was wearing a brown corduroy jacket and a navy polo-neck jumper of the kind that had rarely been seen in London since the late 1970s. Behind him stood a younger, taller guy sporting a T-shirt showing a line of guitars over the legend *Choose Your Weapons.*

With hair down to his shoulders and a dopey expression on his face, he looked like something out of a Bill & Ted movie.

Not the fashion police, then, Carlyle thought unkindly.

'I'm DI Ron Flux and this is Sergeant Adrian Napper. We're from the Hammersmith station.'

'Nice to meet you guys,' Carlyle lied unconvincingly. 'How can I be of assistance?'

Scratching his 'tache, Flux made a show of giving Carlyle the once-over. 'We want to talk to you about Sandra Middlemass.'

Trooping his colleagues back down the stairs, Carlyle took them to the interview room that had just been vacated by Elma Reyes and her lawyer. Flopping into the seat last used by Michelangelo Federici he gave a thin smile. 'Okay, so who is . . .'

'Sandra Middlemass,' said Napper, taking the seat opposite.

'Sandra Middlemass,' Flux repeated, leaning back against the wall, 'was a fifteen year old from White City who disappeared three months ago.'

'Okay.'

'Before she vanished, one of the last places she was seen was the Persian Palace.'

It took the inspector a moment to place the name. 'Calvin Safi's kebab shop?'

'Exactly.' Pulling out a chair, Flux finally sat down. 'Sandra used to hang out there a lot.' Taking a photo out of the inside pocket of his jacket, he flicked it across the table. Carlyle stopped it before it fell off the edge, picked it up and made a show of studying the girl's nondescript face.

'In fact,' Flux continued, 'she spent more time there than she did at school. One of the worst attendance records at Phoenix High School. By all accounts, a complete waste of space. But just a kid, nonetheless.'

Handing back the picture, Carlyle recalled his visit to the shop and the girl in the rear booth. *Leather jacket and eye-liner. Looked like she was off her face on something.*

Flux stuffed the picture back in his pocket.

Napper idly scratched one of the guitars on his T-shirt. 'What were you doing at the Persian Palace?'

'After we arrested Taimur Rage,' Carlyle explained, 'I went to see the father.'

The two officers looked at each other. 'What did Taimur do?' Napper asked.

'Are you serious?' Carlyle laughed. All he got in return was a couple of blank looks. 'Where have you been the last few days? Have you not seen the papers?'

Flux shifted uncomfortably in his chair. 'I'm just back from holiday. Two weeks' fishing in Ireland. I was in the middle of nowhere.' Looking down at the table, his sergeant said nothing.

'Okay, well . . .' Carlyle gave them the two-minute version of events.

'So Taimur finally lost the plot,' Flux observed. 'Doesn't really surprise me. The boy never struck me as being all there.'

'The whole family's fairly fucked up,' Napper mused.

Flux smiled at Carlyle. 'Nice for you, though.'

'What?'

'The kid confesses and then tops himself. If only it were always that simple.'

'Yeah,' Carlyle agreed, 'but back to the matter in hand, what do you want from me?'

'When you went round there,' Napper asked, 'did you find out anything interesting?'

'Not really.' Carlyle pretended to think about it for a moment. 'The boy's room had been cleaned out by MI5.'

'Those muppets,' Flux groaned. 'What do they want?'

'They see this as an organized terrorist attack,' Carlyle said.

'An attack on the very fabric of civilized society,' Flux quipped, parroting the standard line in official bullshit for such occasions.

'Exactly. As such, they want to track down other members of Taimur's cell, so that we can all sleep more easily in our beds.'

'Ha. What cell? That boy couldn't organize shit,' Flux scoffed. 'It's a miracle that he was able to get out of bed in the morning.'

'I know,' Carlyle agreed, 'but they have to tick all the boxes. Imagine if someone else popped up and they hadn't been seen to take it seriously?'

'I suppose so,' said Flux, clearly as unconvinced as the inspector.

'Anyway,' Carlyle continued, 'I had a look around and a chat with Calvin. He just seemed a bit worn down by the whole thing.'

'I wouldn't be taken in by that struggling small businessman act,' Flux snorted. 'He's a right bastard.'

'Two drugs convictions,' Napper chimed in, 'for possession with intent to supply.'

Maybe Elma Reyes had a point, Carlyle thought glumly.

'Plus one for assault. And another for false imprisonment.'

Carlyle raised an eyebrow.

'A twenty-year-old girl claimed he locked her in a room on the first floor for a couple of hours.' Clasping his hands together as if in prayer, Flux leaned across the table. 'And four months before she went missing, Sandra Middlemass turned up at Shepherd's Bush police station to make a complaint.'

'About Safi?'

Flux grimaced. 'We don't know. It wasn't properly investigated.'

You mean it wasn't checked at all, Carlyle thought. 'So how did you guys get involved?'

'I know Sandra's family.'

Carlyle waited for further explanation. When it wasn't forthcoming, he pushed his chair back from the table and stood up. 'Fine. Okay, well, sorry I can't be of more help. From my end, the Taimur Rage investigation is more or less done. But if anything that might be of interest comes up, I'll shout.'

'Thanks.' Pulling a business card from his pocket, Flux handed it over.

'No problem.' Taking the card, Carlyle shuffled from the room, leaving his visitors to find their own way out.

THIRTY

'Even by your standards, this is a bit of a mess.' The outsized reporter took his empty crisp packet in both hands and began carefully folding it into quarters.

Carlyle wasn't going to disagree. 'Kind of you to point that out,' he said morosely from behind his demitasse.

'Just an observation.'

Bernie Gilmore had chosen the small café in a side street off Soho Square, just south of the permanent traffic jam that was Oxford Street. The original Uruguayan owner of the Café Montevideo had gone decades ago. But his successors had kept its name and also its reputation for good, cheap food. A great spot for people-watching, it was also far enough from his home turf for the inspector to be able to relax a little over his elevenses.

Ringing up to suggest the meeting, Carlyle had requested that they go somewhere not too close to Charing Cross. In his book, that basically meant west of Charing Cross Road and north of Old Compton Street. It wasn't that he was embarrassed to be seen in Bernie's company, but there was no need to be seen *too* close to the station while in the act of shamelessly breaking bread with such a notorious muck-raker. After all the recent scandals concerning police officers selling information to reporters, the inspector didn't want to get a reputation for being too chummy with journalists. As a rule of thumb, he normally gave most hacks short shrift. But he had an occasionally symbiotic relationship with Gilmore based on the careful exchange of information. No money ever changed hands.

Bored with his origami, Bernie tossed the crisp packet amidst the remnants of food on his plate. Then he toyed with his Coca-Cola can, taking a swig before asking: 'Have you seen Seymour Erikssen recently?'

Wondering how much more baiting he would have to endure before they got down to business, Carlyle shook his head. 'Nope.'

'So the world's crappest burglar is not on the Met's Most Wanted list any more, then?'

Finishing his espresso, the inspector returned the cup to its saucer. 'As you know, I've been rather busy.'

Stroking his chin, Bernie grunted his commiserations. Their last face-to-face meeting had been months earlier, in a pub just down the road. Since then, the journo had shaved off his beard and invested in a new hairstyle, a rather severe all-over number one. The effect was to make his face look fatter than ever, even though the inspector guessed that Bernie might actually have lost a little weight in recent times, given the reduced swell beneath his grubby T-shirt.

'I hear that Seymour's been quite the busy bee, up the West End. Knocked off a couple of high-end hotel rooms. Rich pickings. A few tourists have been taken to the cleaners.'

Good for him, Carlyle thought irritably. He vaguely remembered having heard something about it, but hadn't connected it to Seymour. Maybe he should go and pay him a visit – see if he could manage to nick the old bugger properly this time. Even better, he could get Umar to do it. The thought of delegating such a chore made him perk up.

Bernie waved the Coke can in front of his face. 'Shame you couldn't manage to keep hold of him.'

'Don't worry, you know he'll be back behind bars soon enough.'

'That's a nice picture story,' Bernie grunted. 'I'm more interested in words. Do you know anything about the bloke who was stabbed on the bike?'

'The guy on the naked bike ride?' Carlyle shook his head. 'Nah. That isn't me. Postic and Shames are dealing with it.'

'Okay, I'll give them a call.'

Is there anyone on the force you don't know? Carlyle wondered.

'Strange way to go, totally naked in a London Street.'

'Yeah.'

'Probably some kind of domestic.'

'You reckon?'

'Oh yeah.' Bernie made a face. 'Guy was probably wiggling his willy at the wrong bird – or the wrong bloke – on the wrong bike.'

'Maybe.' Carlyle couldn't care less.

'Postic's on it, you say?'

'Yeah.'

'Excellent,' Bernie beamed. 'Julie Postic's a good sort.'

I hope you're not saying that about me to anyone.

Leaning forward, Bernie gave the inspector a gentle pat on the arm with his free hand. 'Almost as good as you.'

Fuck. 'Can we get down to the matter in hand?' Carlyle asked, his patience exhausted.

Downing the last of his drink, Bernie daintily placed the empty can back on the table. '*You* called this meeting, Inspector. What exactly is the matter in hand?'

'Taimur Rage.'

'Ah, yes. I wrote about him this morning.'

'I read it,' Carlyle lied. 'Nice piece.'

'I did what I could. But really, it's watery gruel.'

'Not according to the spooks.'

'Ha. All this terrorist stuff is just so much nonsense.'

'Tell me about it.'

'What I don't understand is why you didn't go and speak to his psychiatrist.'

Psychiatrist? What bloody psychiatrist? 'Well,' Carlyle blustered, 'to be fair, once he topped himself, it was case over.'

'Surely you have to tie up the loose ends?'

The inspector chuckled. 'That would be a waste of precious time and resources.'

'Well, anyway, I thought that she was a very eloquent and engaging woman.'

'Name?'

'Janice Anderson. She works at a place called the Doppio Clinic.'

Carlyle pulled his BlackBerry out of his pocket and began typing. 'How do you spell that?'

Bernie obliged. Then: 'It's just off Southampton Row, up towards Euston.'

'Okay. Thanks.'

'Like I said, Janice is very impressive. I think she tried very hard to bring the young man out of his dreamlike state. In the end, some people are just beyond help.'

'Hm.' Carlyle didn't set much store by this. He knew that journalists were very much like policemen – very good at making snap judgements based only on their superficial first impressions. Even so, it would be worth chasing down the shrink to see what she had to say about her patient.

'Surely it's clear to anyone who bothers to look that poor Taimur Rage was just another social inadequate living in a fantasy world,' Bernie said. 'There are so many of them these days.'

'Yes.'

'Maybe you should mention it to your colleagues in MI5 – save them wasting their precious time and resources in the fight for freedom.'

'They're not my colleagues,' Carlyle said stiffly. 'Hopefully, they'll have read your wonderful article and gone off to chase someone else.'

'The price of freedom,' Bernie sighed, 'is eternal vigilance.'

'Handy, that.'

The fat man laughed. 'You are such a complete cynic, Inspector. That's why I like you.'

Carlyle gave a small bow. 'Don't you get fed up,' he asked, 'writing about this bollocks all the time?'

Sitting back on his chair and gazing out at the endless stream of people floating past, Bernie adopted a sage tone: 'It is, simply, the stuff of life.'

'And death.'

'Of course. Poor Taimur. But he is yesterday's story. Gone and forgotten. It's as if he never existed. Happens to everyone.'

'What about his father?'

Bernie raised a quizzical eyebrow. 'What about him?'

'I hear that he's quite a character.' Carlyle recounted what the Hammersmith officers, Flux and Napper, had told him about Calvin Safi and the missing girl, Sandra Middlemass.

'So, the Hammersmith plods, they think . . . what?' Bernie asked when he had finished. 'That the guy was using his kebab shop as a brothel?'

'Dunno,' Carlyle shrugged. 'Maybe.'

'And he killed the girl because she wanted to get off the game?'

'No idea.'

Bernie let out a deep breath. 'It's all a bit speculative – even for me – but it might make a story. I'll take a look.' He scratched his nose, distracted by the engine of a canary-yellow Porsche as it roared sixty yards down the road at what seemed like eighty miles an hour. He waited until the car disappeared round the next corner. 'The boy Taimur lived with his father?'

'Yes.'

'So where's the mother?'

'They divorced years ago.' Looking across the room, the inspector signalled to the girl behind the counter that he wanted the bill. 'She seems quite a piece of work, as well.'

'You've met her?'

'Yeah.' Carlyle struggled to remember the woman's name. 'Very in your face.'

'Aren't they all?' Bernie sighed.

'Ella . . .' no, he was getting his names muddled up, 'or rather, Elma. Elma Reyes.' The waitress appeared and placed the bill on the table. Carlyle hesitated for a second, just in case Bernie felt like offering to pay. He should have known better; when the two of them dined out, the convention was always that the inspector picked up the tab.

'Elma Reyes?' Bernie watched as Carlyle found his wallet, reluctantly pulled out a twenty-pound note and put it with the bill. 'A small black woman who likes speaking in tongues?'

'Small black woman, yes. But when I met her, she was speaking normally.'

'You're kidding.'

'No, no. She was speaking the Queen's English. More or less.'

'No, I meant: Elma is Taimur Rage's mother? Are you sure? *The* Elma Reyes?'

'I suppose so.' The inspector had no idea what Bernie was banging on about. 'How many of them are there?'

The waitress appeared to scoop up the cash and Bernie cheerily waved her away. 'Keep the change.' The girl smiled and scuttled back behind the counter.

That's very generous of you, Carlyle thought resentfully. 'What's the big deal about Elma Reyes?'

'She runs her own church in South London,' Bernie explained. 'The Salvation Church of Something or other. I did an exposé on her a couple of years ago. It was a nice little scam she had going, fleecing the lame-brained of Crystal Palace. And she was shagging her masseur, or someone, if I remember rightly.'

'Yeah, yeah.' Carlyle recalled what Calvin Safi had told him. 'She runs her own church. So what?'

'So what?' Bernie cackled. 'So what? You really don't know what makes news, do you?'

'No, that's why I'm a policeman.'

Bernie quoted: '*Suicide bomber's mum born-again preacher* – good story.'

'Taimur had an axe, not a bomb.'

'Whatever.'

'And he wasn't trying to kill himself.'

'You can be so bloody literal. It's a broad term – the readers

152

will know what I'm banging on about. Anyway, he died in the end, didn't he?'

Carlyle groaned. The meeting had gone tits up and lunch had cost him twenty quid. Why did he bother? 'Bernie . . .'

An alarming gleam had appeared in the hack's eye. He smiled at a little old woman shuffling along on the street outside. Studiously ignoring him, the woman went on her way. 'I can get the front page for this. With a bit of luck. On a slow day'

'She's got a lawyer – a guy called Federici.'

'Doesn't matter. Even if Elma won't talk to me, it's gonna be page two or three. I have good contacts in her organization.' The journalist jumped to his feet. 'Looks like you might have redeemed yourself after the Seymour Erikssen fiasco.'

The inspector's mood lightened somewhat at the thought of redemption. 'Jolly good.'

'This is one of those stories that writes itself.' He patted Carlyle on the shoulder. 'They're the best kind.'

'I'm sure.'

'And, as my special bonus gift for you, I'll see what I can find out about the father.'

'Thanks.'

'My pleasure. I'll be in touch.'

THIRTY-ONE

Feeling rather sorry for himself, Umar Sligo walked down the Strand, his hands shoved deep into his jacket pockets as an unseasonably chilly wind whistled past his head. His dinner with Christina had been flat; a combination of poor food, poor service and continual fretting about Ella meant that their date had been only marginally more fun than the night spent trying to rescue Joseph Belsky from his toilet. Christina had insisted on calling Helen as soon as they had arrived at the table. When the number had been engaged, it had taken him almost five minutes to talk her out of immediately fleeing the restaurant and rushing straight back to the Carlyles' flat. Even then, she had managed another three calls and two texts in the course of a meal lasting barely an hour and a quarter.

Ella, of course, had been fine. When they had gone to pick her up, the child had been fast asleep. But that didn't stop her from kicking off on the cab journey home. The usual fractured night followed; his dreams of Melissa Graham regularly interrupted by extended periods of pacing the living-room carpet trying to ease the baby back to sleep.

It was after 4.30 a.m. when he'd finally got to sleep himself. Then, of course, he'd slept through the alarm and only woken up an hour after his shift had been due to start. As he rounded the corner into Agar Street, he braced himself for the inevitable dressing down that Carlyle would only too happily deliver.

As if on cue, the mobile in his pocket started rumbling.

'Boss . . .'

The inspector didn't stand on any ceremony. 'Where are you at the moment?'

'Just heading into the station.'

'Busy morning?'

'Er, yeah.'

'Okay, well, look, there's something I need you to do.' As Carlyle explained what he wanted, Umar's mood began to brighten. It looked like the aforementioned bollocking was not going to materialize after all.

Problems on the Bakerloo Line meant that it took Umar about forty-five minutes to make the journey from Charing Cross to St John's Wood. Although still in the centre of London, Boyle Avenue was a different world, a suburban tree-lined road where mock-Tudor mansions hid behind tall hedges, thick security gates and state-of-the-art CCTV systems. If you wanted to buy into this neighbourhood, a property would cost well north of ten million.

Placards on the lampposts informed any unwelcome visitors that the residents were being protected 24/7 by a private security firm. That was the thing about having too much money, Umar supposed: it made you paranoid.

Crossing the street, something didn't feel right. It took him a few moments to realize what it was: the place was empty. No cars on the road. No pedestrians on the pavements. No security guards anywhere. Since arriving in London, this was the first time Umar could ever recall being alone on a street.

Number 72 stood behind a ten-foot brick wall. In the middle was a large grey metal gate which slid open to allow vehicle access to the property. Beside it was a smaller gate which allowed pedestrian access under the gaze of a fish-eye lens. Stepping in front of the lens, Umar pressed the intercom and waited. A few moments later, a maid answered and, after checking his ID, buzzed him inside.

As he walked up the short gravel driveway, the front door opened. The woman standing beside it, however, was clearly not the help. Wearing tight white jeans and a paisley silk blouse, she swayed slightly in the doorway as he approached. On first glance, Umar put her at maybe early forties. Tanned, with blonde hair that reached her shoulders, she had a well-preserved look that suggested both plenty of money and the time to spend it.

Approaching the door, he held up his ID for a second time. 'Mrs Winters?'

'Yes.' Ignoring the warrant card, Giselle Winters looked at the young sergeant and licked her lips. 'Another policeman?' Her accent was noticeable, but he couldn't place it.

Umar held up the bag he was carrying. 'I have your husband's briefcase.'

'You'd better come in then.' Turning, she disappeared back down the hall. 'Close the door behind you.'

The hallway ran the length of the house to a kitchen at the rear. Through patio doors was a large garden, which backed on to the house on the next street. At the far end, a couple of women were on their knees planting a flowerbed.

'It's such hard work.'

'Sorry?'

Mrs Winters gazed at the expanse of green that was the lawn. 'The garden. It costs an absolute fortune to keep it looking good.'

'Hm.' *I bet it's not the only thing.*

'Take a seat.' The woman pointed to a series of stools lined up against an island that looked bigger than the entire kitchen in Umar's flat. 'Drink?'

'That would be great, thanks.' Trying not to gawp too openly, the sergeant took in his surroundings.

'What would you like?'

'Tea would be good.' Umar hoisted himself on to one of the bar stools. 'Maybe peppermint?' He ran a hand along the cool black granite work surface. The place was straight out of one of those magazines that Christina liked to read, *Homes & Gardens*.

Everything looked shiny, expensive and unused. Surrounded by such wealth, he suddenly felt energized for the first time in months.

'I was thinking of something maybe a little stronger.' From the other side of the island, Winters lifted her glass without taking a sip. Standing next to a vase filled with white roses, Umar noticed the half-empty bottle of vodka.

At this time of the day? The signals from his brain, however, weren't reaching his mouth. 'Sure,' he grinned, 'why not?'

'Good for you.' As she reached for the bottle, Umar's eyes were inevitably drawn to the front of her blouse.

Catching his gaze, Giselle Winters leaned a little further forward to give the young policeman a better view. 'Ice?'

'No, thank you. Straight is fine.' Trying to re-focus on the matter in hand, Umar hoisted her late husband's briefcase onto the worktop. 'I have to apologize that it has taken so long to return this to you.'

'Don't worry about that.' Winters poured a large measure into a tumbler and handed him his drink.

'Thanks.'

Slinking round the island, she raised her glass. 'Cheers.'

'Cheers.' Umar took the tiniest sip of his drink.

Gulping her vodka, Giselle Winters nodded towards the bag. 'I can't believe that there is anything of much interest in there, anyway.'

'Perhaps not. But it is my responsibility to make sure that it is returned to you. And there were also a couple of things I was wondering if I could ask you about.'

A sly grin passed across the widow's face. 'First things first,' she purred, slipping her free hand between his thighs. 'We can talk later.'

THIRTY-TWO

Sitting up in bed, Giselle Winters reached over and plucked a packet of Rothman's King Size from the bedside table. 'Want one?'

Scratching his balls, Umar shook his head.

Pulling a cigarette from the packet, she placed it between her lips and reached for a lighter. After lighting up, she inhaled deeply, holding in the smoke for five or six seconds before exhaling towards the ceiling. 'I needed that.'

Me too, thought Umar. If there was to be any guilt attached to what he had just done, it would have to come later. At the moment, he just felt pleased with himself.

'That was really quite something. Not bad for a first run.'

A first run?

'You know, before now, I hadn't had sex for almost a year.'

'Really?'

'Yes.'

The tell-tale scars confirmed what he already knew – but the breast-enhancement surgery had not been too outrageous. Clocking her erect nipples, Umar felt himself begin to stiffen again.

'Ever since my husband started seeing his whore, I made him sleep in his own room.'

'You were getting a divorce?'

'Of course. What else should I have done?' Taking another drag on her cigarette, she patted him on the shoulder. 'Anyway, it seems that I wasn't the only one who needed to get laid.'

Saying nothing, Umar propped himself up on his elbows and

looked around the bedroom for the first time. On the far wall was a large oil painting in a heavy gilt frame. The smiling nude, hands on hips, breasts thrust forward, looked familiar. 'Is that you?'

'Do you like it?'

'Very nice.' He squinted at the picture for a few seconds. *Maybe airbrushed a bit . . .*

Winters mentioned the name of an artist that Umar had never heard of. 'He said I was a great subject.'

'Cool.' He wanted something to eat. 'I'm starving.'

Giselle Winters, however, had other ideas. Stubbing the remains of her cigarette into an ashtray on the bedside table, she caressed him under the duvet. 'More of this,' she murmured, 'then food.'

He was just about to hang up when a bright and breezy voice came on the line.

'This is the Doppio Clinic. How may I help you?'

'I would like to speak to Janice Anderson,' Carlyle replied, trying not to sound too grumpy at being kept on hold for so long, 'please.'

'I'm afraid that Dr Anderson is with a patient at the moment.'

'When will she be free?'

'Hold, please . . .'

Stay calm, he told himself, *it's not a big deal.*

After a short while, the receptionist came back on the line. 'I can book you in for an appointment, next Wednesday at three. Or we have a slot available on Friday at eleven thirty.'

'I don't want an appointment,' he said snappishly, 'I just want to know when Janice . . . Dr Anderson will be free today.'

'Are you a new patient?' the girl asked, sounding more like a machine now than a human being who could hold an actual conversation. *Maybe that's it*, Carlyle thought. *Maybe I'm not talking to a person at all, just some high-end automated booking system.*

'I am not a patient,' he said firmly.

'We have Wednesday at three . . .'

He glanced at his watch. His sugar-levels were plummeting. Lunch was overdue. 'What time does the doctor's last appointment finish today?'

There was a pause. 'We cannot give out that information. Do you want to leave a message for the doctor?'

'Don't worry. I'll sort it out.' Ending the call, the inspector slipped the phone back into his pocket. The shrink could wait; it was time to eat.

The gardeners had left. Dropping his head, Umar gave himself a discreet sniff. Even after a shower, he could still smell the not-so grieving widow on his skin. For sure, he couldn't risk presenting himself in front of Christina like this. But that was okay, since he had a plan: after work he would go for a swim at the Oasis, before heading for home.

What he was going to do about the scratches was another matter. He was certainly going to need a decent story to cover his afternoon activities. The Swiss railway clock on the wall told him that he should have been back at the station a couple of hours ago. And a glance at his mobile told him he had four messages. He was in no hurry to check them.

Catching the worried look on the sergeant's face, Giselle Winters gave him a consolatory smile. Placing a bowl of cherry tomatoes on to the table, she stared at the wedding ring on Umar's hand. 'Feeling a bit guilty?'

'No, no,' Umar lied. 'Everything's good.' *Anyway, even if it isn't, it's too late to do anything about it now.* He watched as his hostess placed some ciabatta, cheese, olives, water and a bottle of white wine on the work surface in front of him. His appetite, however, had gone. Helping himself to a small bottle of Evian, he made no effort to reach for the food.

'Not hungry?' Winters asked. 'I'm ravenous.' She began piling food on her plate. 'You must have burnt off some calories up there. Don't you see anything you fancy? Eat.'

'Looks good, thanks.' Reaching forward, Umar grabbed a tomato and dropped it into his mouth.

Nibbling on a piece of cheese, Winters poured herself a large glass of wine and immediately downed half of it. The marathon sex session had sobered her up and it was time to get pissed again. 'So, down to business. What did you want to know?'

'Well . . .' For a moment, Umar struggled to remember anything about the dead lawyer or, indeed, why he was here.

'Yes?' Winters refilled her glass almost to the brim.

'Was there anything about your husband's death that was suspicious?'

'Not really,' she shrugged. 'He had a heart attack, didn't he?'

'Yes. But he was under a bit of stress, wasn't he?'

'Ha. I'd say.' Putting down her glass, Winters placed her hands palms down on the counter. Looking up, her face was all business. 'He had over-extended himself with the house in France, and my lawyer was going to take him to the cleaners on the divorce. Worst of all – from his point of view – his legal business was being sold on the cheap to the Americans by that bastard Chris Brennan, so he wasn't going to be able to use his equity to raise enough cash to bail himself out.' A gleam appeared in her eye. 'Best-case scenario? He was going to have to work until he was eighty, in order to pay back his debts.'

'So he'd had a falling-out with Brennan?'

'Sure.' Winters slipped onto a bar stool and recovered her drink. The maid appeared in the hallway and was waved brusquely away. 'They spent 90 per cent of their time arguing over the deal with Austerlitz & Co. and the rest of their time doing lines of coke together.' She shook her head. 'Men.'

Umar tried to look suitably apologetic for his sex.

'Anyway,' she continued, 'Brennan was happy to take the Americans' paper but Brian wanted cash – quite rightly, in my opinion. You know what they say: *money talks, bullshit walks.*'

'So there was a deadlock?'

'Not really,' Winters sighed. 'The company is called WBK

– Winters Brennan & King – but Chris effectively owns it. Sid King sold up when he retired and Brian had to keep selling off parcels of shares to fund his . . . lifestyle. Brennan now has something like 80 per cent of the shares. Effectively, he could do what he liked. Brian wasn't happy, but he was powerless to stop him.'

Umar pointed at the briefcase which was still standing on the island. 'After your husband died, Brennan tried to get us to hand over Brian's case. We couldn't do that, obviously, but any idea why?'

Taking a sip of her wine, Winters looked at him suspiciously. 'Why do you want to know?'

'Just curious. After all, Chris Brennan is quite a well-known character down at our shop.'

'I bet he is.' The woman laughed. 'So you hate him too, huh?'

'Well, I think my boss has had a few run-ins with him over the years.'

'He is such a total bastard,' she spat, the wine glass hovering in front of her pale lips. 'I can think of a couple of reasons why he wanted the case. One, if there were any drugs in it . . .'

Umar shook his head. 'No drugs; just different sets of papers.'

'Okay. Well, in that case, it must be something to do with Kenneth Ashton.' She gave the young sergeant an amused look. 'I presume you know who *he* is?'

THIRTY-THREE

With the receiver wedged between shoulder and ear, Carlyle tuned out of the conversation as he flicked through the BBC Online news pages: 'record' drug seizure in Portugal; 25 per cent rise in homelessness in Britain; and, in Russia, a girl pop group called Pussy Riot were in court on charges of hooliganism.

'God bless the Russians,' he mumbled.

'What?' squawked an irate DI Julie Postic.

'Nothing, nothing.' Re-focusing on the matter in hand, the inspector sat up in his chair.

Postic returned to her rant. 'It is completely unacceptable that you go briefing journalists behind my back on a case that is nothing to do with you.'

'Julie, Julie,' he said soothingly, 'I haven't briefed anyone about anything. I don't speak to journalists, full stop. Everyone knows that.' Out of the corner of his eye, he caught a glimpse of Umar approaching across the floor.

'But Bernie Gilmore said—'

Carlyle quickly cut her off. 'Bernie Gilmore will say anything to get you to talk to him. Personally, I never take his calls.' As Umar reached the desk, he held up a finger, to indicate that the conversation was almost over. 'Anyway, Julie, I've got to go. Good luck with the investigation and don't let Bernie wind you up.' Without waiting for a reply, he quickly dropped the receiver on to the cradle.

'What was all that about?' Umar asked, pulling up a chair.

'Nothing, nothing.' Carlyle dismissed all thoughts of the Detective Inspector with a wave of his hand. 'And where the hell have *you* been?' He looked his sergeant up and down. The boy looked crumpled, as if he'd just had a nap in one of the interview rooms downstairs, which for all Carlyle knew he might well have done.

'I did what you told me,' Umar replied defensively.

'What did you get from the widow?'

'She was quite helpful; went on a bit, though. It took me ages to get out of there.'

Carlyle grunted. 'Good-looking then, was she?' He knew Umar well; his sergeant wouldn't have hung around for long if the lady of the house wasn't seriously fit. Married or not, he was still a ladies' man.

Umar made a show of thinking about the question. 'Not bad, I suppose, for her age. Anyway, why do you have it in for Brennan?'

'He's a lawyer,' Carlyle grumbled.

'Yes, but there are lots of lawyers. Did you have a run-in with him?'

The inspector sighed, said, 'Some other time. It was a long while ago.'

'Fair enough.'

'What did you find out?'

'Right, okay. Brennan and Winters were at loggerheads over the sale of the business, but there was nothing that Brian Winters could do about it because, essentially, it belongs to Brennan.'

'So where does that get us?' Carlyle wondered.

'Giselle ... Mrs Winters thinks that the real issue was Kenneth Ashton.'

'Bloody hell.' The inspector was surprised. 'What's that crooked bastard got to do with any of this?'

'Apparently he was one of Brian Winters' major clients. Brennan was pushing for Winters to drop him. The new

American owners of the business were not best pleased about having one of London's most senior criminals on their books.'

'Senior is the word,' Carlyle said. 'He's got to be eighty, at least. He was a name even before I started on the Force. He was mainly into dodgy property deals and tax scams, but he wasn't beyond getting his boys to break your legs – or worse – if you got in his way. I could see how he could be an embarrassment to Chris Brennan.'

'Enough to have Brian Winters killed?'

Carlyle thought about it for a moment. 'No idea. Maybe it's just a coincidence. It certainly looked like a heart attack. But I could ask Susan Phillips to take another look.'

'Too late. They cremated him the day before yesterday.'

'So much for that idea.'

'The widow reckons that there must be something in her husband's papers relating to Brennan that he needs to get his hands on.'

'Good job I made some copies, then.' Pulling open the top drawer, Carlyle took out a sheaf of photocopies and placed them on the desk.

Umar frowned. 'Are we allowed to do that?'

'No idea.' Carlyle jumped to his feet. 'Take a look at these with a fresh eye. See if you can find anything relating to Ashton.'

Umar glanced at his watch. 'I was going to go for a swim.'

'It won't take long,' said Carlyle firmly. 'Give me a call when you're done.'

'Where are you going?'

'To talk to a man . . .'

THIRTY-FOUR

The latest anti-smoking laws had clearly not reached the executive suite above the Clivenden Club, a Members Only establishment located behind a discreet green door in an alley off Wardour Street. Angus Muirhead contemplated the inspector through a haze of cigarette smoke while the incessant beat of some techno music rose up from the bar next door. Muirhead wore a navy blazer and a white shirt, with a red cravat at the neck. It was, more or less, the same uniform he'd worn for the last forty-five years. Stubbing out his Macanudo cigar in an already overflowing ashtray, he immediately reached for a replacement from the box on his desk.

'How long do the doctors say?' Carlyle asked, hoping his voice sounded suitably sympathetic.

Muirhead grunted. Underneath his shock of white hair, his face was gaunt. Maybe it was his imagination, but it seemed to the inspector that the figure in front of him had shrunk since their last conversation. For sure, some of the sparkle had gone out of the old fellow's eyes. 'They say I could keel over at any time,' he cackled. 'Nice of them to spare my feelings, isn't it?'

'That's doctors for you,' Carlyle observed, 'social skills of plankton.'

'Quite. Anyway, however you dress it up it seems that even on a best-case scenario it's going to be a matter of months rather than years.'

'Sorry to hear that.'

'What can you do?' Angus waved the unlit cigar in the air. 'You just have to keep going. Then again, the doctors have been saying the same thing for the best part of a decade now.'

'Bummer.'

'No, not really.' Muirhead reached for his Zippo lighter. 'Apart from anything else, there are plenty of people who are really pissed off that I've lasted this long. That is some consolation in itself.'

'I suppose you've got to take all the positives you can,' said Carlyle doubtfully.

'Look, the thing that I've discovered is that it's really not worth worrying about. Once I could see the end of the tunnel, I felt a strange calm descend on me. Anyway, we've all got to go sometime.' Lighting up, Angus took a couple of quick puffs and settled back into his chair. 'And at least I'll go happy.'

'Fair enough.' Carlyle glanced at the window, wondering if it would be rude to ask if he could open it.

'Go ahead,' Muirhead chuckled. 'I wouldn't want to take you with me.'

'Thanks.' Getting to his feet, Carlyle unlocked the window and pushed up the frame.

'Not too far though, the noise is terrible.'

'Okay.'

Muirhead waited for the inspector to sit down again. 'So, why are you interested in Ken Ashton all of a sudden? He's a bit old hat these days.'

'Is he?'

'As far as I know,' Muirhead took another drag on his Macanudo, 'he is more or less legit, which is as much as you can say for anyone, just about.'

'Yes.'

'At least, I don't think he douses people in petrol and threatens to torch them any longer,' Muirhead joked. Thirty years on, he could laugh about it. At the time, shivering in the dark, in a damp Soho basement, it wasn't so funny. He shook his head.

'You know, that building on Harley Street is worth more than fifteen million now.'

Carlyle let out a low whistle.

'Fifteen mil that should be in my pocket.'

'That's the law of the jungle,' Carlyle sympathized.

'Naturally.' Muirhead gave a rueful smile. 'It took me a long while to get over that; if I ever did. It was only around the time that we first met that I was getting back on my feet.'

Carlyle looked around the room. 'You've done okay in Soho.'

'I could have done a bit better but, equally, it could have been a *lot* worse.' Leaning across the table, he stabbed the cigar in Carlyle's direction. 'Now, if you hadn't sorted out those bloody drug dealers next door . . .'

It was a conversation that they'd had many times before and Carlyle knew his lines well. 'I was only doing my job,' he said defensively.

'*Only* doing your job?' Muirhead snorted. 'That's what you've never understood, Inspector. Maybe 1 per cent of people do their job properly; the other 99 per cent don't get anywhere near. If everyone *only* did their job, the world would be a much better place.'

'Mm.' They both knew that there was no way that the Met could have ignored a bunch of bikers trying to sell heroin and ecstasy out of a Georgian townhouse slap bang in the centre of tourist London. The fact that they were also destroying the takings at Muirhead's club was hardly a significant consideration, from the police's point of view.

'If you hadn't stepped in, I would have been driven out of this place.'

The inspector shrugged. It hadn't even been his operation. But he had been the liaison officer for Angus Muirhead and the old guy had been hugely grateful. Since then, they had stayed in regular contact. Carlyle had always been more inter- ested in Muirhead's stories about the old days, rather than his tips about current bad boys. Stories like the time Kenneth Ashton had threatened to turn Angus into a Roman Candle if he didn't sign over the lease to his most lucrative Central London property.

Matter in hand, he told himself. *Matter in hand*. 'Ashton's name has come up in something I was looking at. His lawyer dropped down dead on Waterloo Bridge a few nights back.'

Muirhead carefully balanced the smouldering cigar atop the remains of its predecessors in the ashtray. 'What was his name – this lawyer?'

'Brian Winters.'

'Never heard of him.'

'He was a partner of Chris Brennan.'

'Ah.' The old fella rubbed his hands together with glee. 'Now we're getting somewhere. If your man was hanging out with that little runt, he must have been as bent as a nine-bob note.'

'That was my general thinking.'

'Was the death suspicious?'

'No, I don't think so – looks like it was a heart attack.'

'So this is not a murder investigation?'

'No, I'm just curious. The suggestion is that Ashton was Winters' biggest client, but Brennan wasn't happy about it. Brennan wanted Ashton off the books before he sold the business.'

'In which case, the heart attack was perfectly timed.'

'Most definitely.'

Sitting back in his chair, the old man contemplated the ceiling. Outside, the techno music abruptly ended, to be replaced by some indistinct sound that blended into the background traffic noise. 'Like I said, Ken is more or less straight these days. But the key phrase is *more or less*. I can only think of one thing that he's up to at the moment that would be so dodgy that even someone like Brennan, who has the morals of a syphilitic rent boy, would want to steer clear of.'

'Oh, yes?' Ignoring the dangers of passive smoking, Carlyle leaned forward in his chair. 'And what would that be, then?'

Muirhead retrieved his cigar. 'That would be the sale of my old property.'

Fumbling with his BlackBerry, Carlyle wished he'd brought something to write on. 'Let me understand I've got this right. Ken Ashton wants to sell the freehold to 749 Harley Street, but you've still got the papers?'

'I've still got *some* papers.' Angus Muirhead stubbed out his cigar in the ashtray. 'I've still got the original deeds. What Ken has is a "contract" ' – he waved his hands in the air, to signify the quotation marks – 'where I signed the property over to him.' He let out a guffaw. 'It probably still stinks of petrol.'

'Could you get it back?'

'Perhaps.' Muirhead made a face. 'The lawyers can argue the toss forever. As far as I'm concerned, it's a bit too late.'

'But Ken doesn't know that?'

'No.' The old man smiled menacingly. 'As far as Ken's concerned, we're going to fight him all the way. You know what they say about the best revenge being a dish served cold? Well, this is about as cold as it gets.'

'Aren't you worried he might come back with his petrol can?'

'Why bother? The tobacco industry has beaten him to it.' He coughed, as if to prove the point. 'My life is done. Anyway, he's an old man, too. You lose your edge.'

Tell me about it, Carlyle thought.

'I would have thought,' Muirhead continued, 'that the guy who had the heart attack was probably getting a lot of grief from Ken. He can see legal proceedings dragging on for years and wants it wrapped up quickly. Apart from anything else, the fees will be mounting up.' He grunted. 'God knows, mine are.'

'Expensive game,' Carlyle mused.

'Yes, it is. Meanwhile, Ken's lawyer . . .'

'Brian Winters.'

'Winters will be reluctant to push things along. As far as he's concerned, the taxi meter is ticking over nicely. Aside from that, he doesn't want to go in front of a judge to discuss the detail of how his client came to acquire such a prime piece of property in the first place.'

'Interesting.' Carlyle wasn't sure whether this information added up to much, but his instinct told him that it was worth knowing. 'Presumably, it's not the kind of thing that Brennan would want to have to explain to his new American partners, either.'

'In my experience,' Muirhead agreed, 'the Americans are rather funny about that kind of thing. They tend to see the world in very black and white terms.'

'With them being the good guys at all times.'

'Quite. I remember once . . .' In the distance, a siren wailed. Catching the rather glazed look on the inspector's face, Muirhead turned back to the subject under discussion. 'Anyway,' he asked, 'how do you know our Mr Brennan?'

'That,' Carlyle said, 'is a long story.'

Muirhead settled back into his chair. The look on his face said: Entertain me. 'I'm an old man, Inspector. I've nothing better to do.'

THIRTY-FIVE

Yawning, Umar neatly stacked the pile of papers on his desk, weighing them down with a roll of Sellotape that he'd nicked from the stationery cupboard. He had gone through the photocopies twice and nothing had jumped out at him. The overall impression was of a man in the throes of a post-mid-life crisis. Brian Winters' life – and his finances – appeared to be in complete disarray. It looked extremely doubtful whether Giselle would be able to keep the house in St John's Wood once everything was sorted out.

That would be a shame.

His thoughts of the widow lying naked on the bed were interrupted by the sound of Flo Rida's 'Whistle'. Lifting his mobile from the desk, he looked at the screen – Christina.

'Hi.'

'When are you coming home?' She sounded tense and irritable. At least, for once, there wasn't any crying in the background.

'I won't be long.' He tried to sound soothing. 'I've got to check a couple of things for the inspector and then I'll be on my way.'

'But it's almost six.'

Umar looked up at the clock on the wall. 'Bloody hell.' *Where had the day gone?* He knew only too well the answer to that question. 'Okay, sorry. I didn't realize that it was so late.'

A suspicious grunt came from the other end of the line.

'I won't be long,' he persisted. 'How's Ella doing?'

'Just hurry up,' she hissed, ending the call. With a sigh, Umar tossed the phone on to the desk and sat back in his chair. Closing his eyes, he counted slowly to fifty, breathing deeply as he did so. When he had finished, he jumped to his feet, switched off his PC and headed for the stairs.

Standing at the edge of the outside pool, he caught the eye of a skinny Asian guy with a great six-pack, wearing bright red Speedos. The guy smiled and Umar quickly looked away. The last thing he needed was for someone to try and pick him up at the Oasis. Scanning the swimmers in the water, he decided that the outside lane looked the best bet. Pulling on his goggles, he took a couple of steps to his left. *Fifty lengths*, he told himself as he dived in, *and then it's home*.

Annoyingly, all of the lanes were too crowded for him to be able to establish any kind of rhythm. Every time he managed to get up a bit of speed, Umar would find himself stuck behind some pensioner doing the doggy paddle. Frustrated, he jumped out after only twenty lengths and headed for the showers.

Ten minutes later, he was ready to finally head for home. Pushing through the turnstiles, Umar smiled at Moira, the pretty brunette from Stirling, who worked late shifts on the front desk while studying at UCL. Outside, stepping into the stream of pedestrians making for Shaftesbury Avenue, he was just about to turn right to the tube station when it hit him.

'Shit.' Why hadn't he seen it before? For a moment he hesitated. Then, dodging a couple of Australian tourists with their heads stuck in a map, he did a 180-degree turn and began jogging back to the station.

THIRTY-SIX

'Ha.' Angus Muirhead stood up creakily from behind his desk. 'That really is quite a story. Most amusing.'

Carlyle gave a small bow.

The old man ushered him towards the door. 'I can understand why you don't have any time for Mr Brennan, but I'm not sure you'll be able to get to him through this. You might be able to arrest him for . . . *something* . . . but pressing charges will be another matter altogether.'

There speaks the voice of experience, Carlyle acknowledged. Muirhead knew his way around the law far better than your average copper.

'Maybe not,' the inspector shrugged, 'but I just hope that I'm around to watch the spectacle when he crashes and burns.'

'That seems perfectly reasonable to me.'

Pulling open the door, the inspector hovered on the threshold. 'Good to see you, Angus.'

'I'm always here.' The old man offered his hand. But when they shook, his grip was weaker than a child's.

Bloody hell, Carlyle thought. *He really is on the way out.*

'Let me know how you get on with Ken Ashton.'

'I will.'

'Thanks. I wouldn't want to miss being around to see *him* come unstuck.' Muirhead followed the inspector on to the dingy landing. 'And just before you go, there's one other thing . . .'

'Yes?' Carlyle started down the stairs.

'Seymour Erikssen.'

His heart sinking, Carlyle stopped in his tracks and turned to look back up at Muirhead.

'I thought I'd read in the paper that you'd nicked him?'

'That's another long story.'

'Anyway, he's been seen here in the club a few times recently. And a couple of people have had their pockets picked. Coincidence?' The old man shook his head. 'I don't think so.'

'No.'

'It's a hassle I can do without.'

'Of course.'

'The thing about Seymour is that he's not as hopeless as you like to think. Sometimes he can be a bit *too* successful for his own good. Maybe you could have a word. Sort him out.' Muirhead spread his arms wide. 'Otherwise . . .'

He didn't have to spell it out. 'No problem,' Carlyle said. 'Will do. Seymour was on my To Do list anyway. I'll let you know when I've spoken to him.'

'Good.' Muirhead slowly retreated into the gloom. 'We'll speak soon.'

Carlyle listened to the office door closing. 'Bloody Seymour,' he grumbled to himself, 'why can't he just fuck off to someone else's patch?' For a few moments he stood on the stairs, wondering how best to track down the burglar. When nothing immediately sprang to mind, he continued on his way.

By the time he had finished with Muirhead, it was too late to drop in on Janice Anderson, Taimur Rage's shrink, at the Doppio Clinic. Reaching Charing Cross Road, he hovered on the kerbside, opposite what used to be Blackwell's bookstore, toying with the idea of heading home until his conscience got the better of him. Turning left, he went south, towards the station.

Back on the third floor, he was surprised to see Umar still at his desk.

'What are you doing here? Hiding from Christina again?'

'I've found something.'

'Oh yes?' Carlyle asked, always willing to be pleasantly surprised.

'Look at this.' Umar handed him a sheet of paper from the top of the pile on his desk.

Carlyle scanned the rows of figures that filled the page. 'What am I looking at?'

'Here.' Getting to his feet, Umar pointed to a small box at the top, underneath the WBK logo. 'This is a print-out of a timesheet at Winters Brennan & King. The client is Hanway 58 Associates.'

'Ok-ay.'

'Hanway 58,' Umar explained, 'is Ken Ashton's company. I should have realized earlier – I remember reading about it somewhere.'

'Funny name.'

'He set up shop in Hanway Street in 1958. Anyway, the point is, this shows the number of hours that Brian Winters was billing Ashton.' Umar pointed to the sterling figure at the bottom of the page. 'That is just for a single month. Before VAT.'

'Jesus. This has got to be almost all of his working hours.' Carlyle looked again at the numbers. It didn't seem likely that Winters could be spending so much time on the sale of a property on Harley Street, however controversial that might be. 'What the hell was he doing for the guy?'

Umar shrugged. 'I guess that's what we've got to find out.'

THIRTY-SEVEN

Sitting in a humid, windowless room off Tottenham Court Road, Chris Brennan pondered the wisdom of his earlier wardrobe choices. If he had known that he was going to end the day with a beating, he would have left the Brioni pinstripe in the wardrobe. Looking around the dirty room, his thoughts turned to the late Brian Winters, and he was filled with a mixture of rage and self-pity.

'Brian, you tosser,' he muttered to himself, 'this should be you.'

As he was fuming at the injustice of it all, he heard the door click open. Looking up, Brennan watched the two goons who had earlier 'escorted' him from his office step inside. They were followed by an old man, small and sprightly, wearing a double-breasted suit that was almost as wide as he was tall. In his left hand was a wooden Derby cane.

The old man pointed at Brennan with his walking stick. 'Do you know who I am?'

The lawyer signalled that he did.

'Good. Do you know why you are here?'

'My colleague—'

'Your *ex*-colleague,' Kenneth Ashton corrected him with a flourish of his cane.

'Yes.'

'Who billed me an enormous sum on behalf of *your* company,' Ashton pointed out.

'Imagine my dismay,' Ashton continued, 'when I find out that my long-time adviser, Mr Winters, and his junior colleagues had been ripping me off, over-billing month after month, while failing to properly progress the sale of my Harley Street property – a transaction which is very important to me at the present time.' Lowering the cane, he demanded somewhere to sit. One of the goons darted outside and quickly reappeared with a chair, which he placed behind his boss. Slowly, Ashton lowered himself onto it, his face a study in concentration.

What Harley Street property? Brennan wondered. He had a raging thirst and a powerful need to pee at the same time. In his head, he went through a list of nearby pubs, settling on one just off Charlotte Street. If he ever managed to get out of here, it would be straight down to the Bearded Lady for a slash and a very large G&T.

'To put not too fine a point on it, Mr Brennan, I want to get my hands on the cash from the sale of the building before I die.' Placing his hands on his knees, Ashton leaned forward. 'Look at me.'

Reluctantly, Brennan did as he was told.

'These guys' – he invited the goons to take their bow – 'are really rather unfortunate. Forty or fifty years ago, their job would have been a lot more fun. Some of the things that they would have got to do . . .' Ashton smiled at the happy memories. 'But now? Now, the world is different. Standards are different. They have to release their tensions in the gym. It is no world for a proper man.'

Brennan tried to speak but all that came out was a squeak.

'Which happens to be good news for a weakling like you. The people who stole directly from me will pay . . . one way or another. You, on the other hand, get the chance to put things right.' Pulling a small square of paper from his jacket pocket, he offered it to Brennan. 'Take it.'

Extending an arm, Brennan let Ashton drop the square into his open palm.

'Open it.'

Unfolding the paper, Brennan looked at the large number scribbled in blue biro.

'All that you have to do is deliver that amount – in sterling – into my Jersey account by the end of the week.'

Knowing that it would be almost impossible to come up with the required sum, Brennan grimaced. 'But—'

Ashton lifted the cane so that its tip hovered just in front of the lawyer's nose. 'By the end of the week. That's more than reasonable, don't you think?'

Brennan gave a non-committal whimper.

'Once that is sorted,' Ashton continued, 'I need you to come to my office and tell me how quickly you can resolve the Harley Street issue.'

'I'm sure we can do that, no problem.' Brennan still had no idea what the precise issue was, but it couldn't be that complicated. Winters was probably asleep at the wheel and it just needed someone to look at it properly.

'A sensible, professional approach – that is exactly what we need.' Ashton smiled at his two goons. 'Otherwise, Bruno and Jason here might get some additional fun after all.'

'That won't be necessary,' Brennan stammered.

'In that case, we'll let you get on your way.'

'Ah, yes, good.' Jumping to his feet, Brennan's smile was a mixture of relief and discomfort. If he didn't get out of here right now, he would piss himself. In his Brioni suit. Without a backward glance, he rushed for the door.

THIRTY-EIGHT

Even before he had the key in the lock, Umar could hear Ella's wailing. Resisting the urge to flee, he opened the door and stepped inside. Immediately, he was accosted by Christina, who was pacing the hall, arms folded.

'Where the hell have you been?'

Reaching forward, he tried to kiss her, but she reared away. Gritting his teeth, he fought to keep his annoyance in check. 'Why not let me see to Ella,' he said, 'while you go and put your feet up.' Not waiting for a reply, he slipped down the hall and into the darkness of his daughter's bedroom.

At least Ella seemed happy to see him. As he picked her up out of the cot, her crying subsided. He kissed the jet-black hair on the top of her head – her mother's hair – cooed gently in her ear. Happy with the attention, she seemed content to burrow into his chest. Umar sniffed the chlorine on his skin. 'Sorry I'm a bit smelly,' he whispered, 'but it's good to see you.'

By way of reply, she gave him a wide yawn. Bending his knees, Umar carefully sat down, before stretching out on the floor, Ella cradled on his ribcage. After a few minutes, he had tuned out the background hum of the city as he synchronized his breathing with that of the baby. As he felt her rise and fall on his chest, the sense of peace and wellbeing was overwhelming. Closing his eyes, he smiled.

THIRTY-NINE

Lying back in the bath, Kara Johnson glanced down at her breasts. You could still just about make out the lines where she had painted them red for the naked bike ride. Trailing through London wearing nothing but a splash of body paint wasn't as much fun as she had expected, but you never know about these things until you try them.

It was the same with men, really.

Yawning, she looked over at the naked figure of Will Carter as he pissed into the toilet bowl. The boy was a bit pale but he certainly had a nice bum – it was just a shame that his dick was so small. Almost as bad, the little twerp simply didn't know how to use it properly. If Kara had any regrets about seducing Melissa Graham's boyfriend it was only because the last hour would have been considerably more satisfying if she had spent it in the company of her Rampant Rabbit.

Poor old Melissa No Tits. Then again, maybe she relies on a vibrator of her own. Kara watched Will shake himself off and flush the toilet. She gestured at the stall in the far corner of the room. 'Why don't you take a shower? I just want to lie here for a while.'

'Okay.' Turning to face her, or rather her breasts, Will continued manipulating himself. Reminded of a wildlife documentary about masturbating monkeys, Kara had to resist the urge to laugh. Closing her eyes, she slipped below the surface of the water and began counting.

1 . . . 2 . . . 3 . . .

Maybe if she held her breath long enough, he would be gone when she resurfaced.

17 . . . 18 . . . 19 . . . Kara pushed herself back up. But as she did so, she felt a hand around her neck, another pressing down on the top of her head. 'Hey.' Panicking, she swallowed a mouthful of bathwater and felt herself gag.

23 . . . 24 . . . The harder she pushed, the further down she went, until she was pinned against the bottom of the bath. Frantically, she tried to claw at the hand around her neck, to no avail.

28 . . .

Am I suffocating or drowning?

31

FORTY

He recognized the song, but couldn't put a name to it. Music was coming from somewhere nearby. It took him a moment or two to realize that it was coming from the back pocket of his jeans. While keeping hold of the baby with one hand, he pulled out the mobile and hit a button at random to stop the noise.

Happily, Ella was still asleep. Carefully getting to his feet, Umar put her in the cot and covered her up before retrieving his phone from the floor. Looking at the screen, it took him a moment to realize that the line was still open. Feeling light-headed from his unscheduled nap, he lifted the handset to his ear.

'Hello?'

'Umar? Are you there?' It was a female voice that the sergeant didn't immediately recognize.

'Yes,' he whispered. 'Hold on a sec.'

Quietly closing the bedroom door behind him, Umar switched off the harsh hall light, preferring to use the more gentle illumination from the streetlamps outside.

'Umar?'

'Yes. Sorry, who is this?'

'It's Melissa Graham. I was on the bike ride when the guy got stabbed. We talked at the station.'

'Ah, yes. The bike ride.' Presumably, she was ringing for a date. He began flicking through his mental calendar, thinking about times and possible venues.

'Sorry for calling you so late.'

From down the line, someone started banging around in the background, followed by some shouting. *Maybe she's at a party, or something*, Umar thought. 'Not at all,' he replied cheerfully. 'What can I do for you?'

There was a pause before she blurted it out: 'I've been arrested. For murder.'

As he processed that little nugget of information, Umar listened to Christina stomping about in the kitchen, almost immediately followed by the resumption of Ella's cries.

'Are you there?'

The baby's crying was getting louder. Umar rolled his shoulders, trying to ease his tension. 'Where are you?' She gave him an address in Islington, off Upper Street. 'Okay, I know it. Just sit tight. I'll be right there.'

Leaning against the bonnet of a Chelsea tractor parked in the corner of Bonetti Square, Sergeant Lawrence Shames took a long drag on his JPS Black as he eyed Umar walking towards him. Exhaling, he pushed himself off the Porsche, careful not to set its alarm off in the process. 'What are you doing here?'

'I was just going to ask you the same thing,' Umar responded. Although their respective bosses had a frosty relationship, the two sergeants got on well enough.

Shames tossed the remains of his cigarette into the gutter. 'You first.'

'I got a call from Melissa Graham.' Umar explained how he'd met the girl, and her panicked message to his mobile.

'Waste of a phone call,' Shames grunted, quickly adding, 'No offence.' Umar made a gesture signifying that none had been taken. 'She'd have been better off calling a lawyer. Melissa Graham is in deep shit.' Shames pointed at the blue door of number 39. 'Top-floor flat, you've got her boyfriend bludgeoned to death and the bird he was shagging's been drowned in the bath. Graham's got his blood all over her, and her fingerprints are on the suspected murder weapon – a cycling trophy in the shape of a pedal; quite a handy weapon as it turns out.' There was a pause as both men watched a trio of white-suited forensics technicians appear from round the corner and go inside the building.

Umar scanned the neighbouring properties. All of them had lights burning on the upper floors, despite the late hour. 'At least the locals are being kept entertained.'

'We aim to serve,' Shames snorted. 'A woman next door heard screaming and called 999. When the first uniforms arrived, they found Graham sitting on the floor, staring into space. Her first words to the officers were, quote-unquote, "that bitch was screwing my boyfriend." ' He shot Umar a look that said *Open and shut case.*

'She denies killing them, though, doesn't she?'

'Her story is that she found them in the bathroom and tried to revive the boyfriend. But you know what it's like – she'll get a lawyer, decide that she can't remember anything and then go for some kind of temporary insanity defence. Get enough women on a jury who think playing away should be a capital offence and you're off at the races.'

Or perhaps she's telling the truth, Umar thought. 'Maybe I should go and see her.'

Shames shook his head. 'You're too late. They took her to the station about twenty minutes ago.'

'Islington?'

'Don't think so. They're full, apparently. There was some gang fight up near Highbury tube earlier in the evening. I think she's at Holborn.'

'Okay, thanks.' Looking up, he saw Shames' boss watching them from a second-floor window. 'How's Postic doing?'

Shames followed Umar's gaze, holding up a hand of acknowledgement as the Detective Inspector signalled for him to come inside. 'Same old, same old. She's pissed off with your guy, though. Thinks Carlyle dropped her in it with Bernie Gilmore with regard to Bradley Saffron.'

'Who?'

'The guy who was knifed on the naked bike ride. Bernie's story only ended up as a couple of paragraphs on page 30, but Postic doesn't like to have anything to do with the press.'

'Neither does Carlyle.'

'Hm.' Shames edged back towards the house. 'Anyway, that's why we're here. Three people who were on that bike ride are now dead. Something's going on. Even if Melissa Graham did kill the two upstairs, she didn't stab Saffron.'

'No.' Umar knew that himself. He had been there at the time.

'And if she *didn't* kill the two upstairs, well, we have to make sure we've covered all the possibilities.' Shames gestured up at the flat. 'I gotta get back inside. It's a mess up there and it doesn't look good for your girl. But go and talk to her, see what she says. We can catch up later.'

'Fine.' Umar turned and headed back in the direction from which he had arrived. As he reached Upper Street, his mobile started ringing. 'Christina,' he mumbled morosely as he plucked it from his pocket, 'or Carlyle?' Without looking at the screen, he placed the handset to his ear.

'Yes?'

'Sergeant Sligo?'

'Yes, Commander.' Recognizing the voice, Umar stiffened slightly. What the hell was Carole Simpson ringing him for?

'Is Inspector Carlyle with you?'

'No.' The sergeant relaxed again. She wasn't after him at all. 'I'm up in—'

'Do you know where he is?'

'In bed, I would have thought, at this time of night.' Umar stepped round a couple of young white guys coming the other way on the pavement. One of them took a drag on a large spliff while the other chatted away in an animated fashion. As he continued on, Umar breathed in deeply from the trail of Lebanese Black left in their wake.

'Hm.' The Commander had learned the hard way that her

troublesome underling could get up to mischief at any hour. 'When you next see the inspector, tell him to call me. I need to see him.'

'Of course.'

'Good night,' Simpson clicked off. The sergeant continued on his way, wishing that he had a joint of his own.

Tossing the empty can of Stella into the gutter, Jade Jones let her foot dangle over the edge of the kerb. Through her alcoholic haze, she wondered what time it was. One thing was clear, the last train out of Paddington had left and services would not resume until sometime after five. She was in for a long wait.

Was Paul out looking for her right now? Her boyfriend was okay, but sometimes he could be a right pain. She hoped that he was worried; it served him right for picking a fight and calling her a 'stupid slag'. Concentrating hard, she tried to remember what it was they had been arguing about, but her mind was totally blank. *Whatever.* When she arrived back home in the morning, he had better have learned his lesson.

Jade looked along Praed Street. Back home, the streets would have been long since deserted, but here there was still plenty of activity. A bus rumbled past, full of tired passengers heading home. Across the road, a 24/7 mini-market was still doing a brisk trade. Sticking a hand in her pocket, she found a handful of coins, more than enough for another couple of cans of lager. Just as she was about to step off the pavement, a car pulled up. The driver, an Asian guy, wound down the window and gave her a friendly smile.

'Missed your train home?'

'Uh-huh.' Jade placed a hand on the car roof to steady herself.

'Need a place to stay?'

'Nah.' Jade shook her head. 'I'm okay. Just gonna get another drink and wait in the station.'

'We've got a nice place just round the corner. Lots of booze. And you can have a kip until it's time to get your train.'

Jade looked up and down the road. Suddenly, the place seemed deserted. She gripped the vehicle more tightly for support. 'Nah. It's fine.'

'Come on, it will be fun. We can have a party.'

There was a loud click. The back door of the car opened and a big white bloke struggled out.

Why didn't I notice you before? Jade thought. She suddenly realized how tired she felt. Her head was swimming and she wondered if she was going to be sick.

'You don't want to be stuck out here in the middle of the night,' the white guy said, taking her by the arm. Jade noticed he had a CFC tattoo on his forearm and her face broke into a crooked grin.

'Chelsea,' she slurred. 'JT and the Special One. My boyfriend's a Chelsea fan.'

'Top man,' the guy smiled, carefully ushering her into the back of the car.

FORTY-ONE

Pushing open the door of his battered Vauxhall Corsa, Sergeant Adrian Napper stepped out into the deserted alleyway, yawning as he stretched. Three hours sitting in the car watching sweet fuck all happening was exhausting. Surveillance work was invariably a pain in the arse, and this was a complete waste of time. He was ready to call it a night. First, however, he needed a piss.

Slipping round the back of the vehicle, Napper lined himself up facing a garage door and unzipped his fly. 'Aaaah,' he breathed contentedly as a stream of piss slammed against the metal, 'that feels good.'

He was still in full flow when he heard the sound of an engine coming towards him. Keeping his head down, he continued about his business as the car rumbled slowly past, coming to a stop thirty feet down the road. There was the click of a door opening and then the sound of footsteps on the cobbles behind him. Zipping himself up, Napper turned to face a large bloke standing in front of him with a crooked smile on his face. Under the sodium lighting, he could see that the guy had a tattoo on his arm and a hammer in his hand.

Shit. Tensing, Napper realized that he had left both his radio and his pepper spray in the Corsa. He glanced down the alley, trying to distinguish the remaining figures in the other car.

Catching the direction of Napper's gaze, the guy let the hammer swing limply at his side. 'What are you doing?'

Napper held up his hand in a conciliatory manner. 'Just taking a piss, mate.'

Grimacing, the guy took a step forward. 'Fucking filth. What are you doing here?'

The guy knows who I am. How does he know that? Has he seen me before?

The questions could be saved for later. Keeping his eyes on the hammer, the sergeant moved on to the balls of his feet as he quickly contemplated his options for escape. There was no way he could get back inside his car without taking some heavy blows. But if he could somehow get himself back to the main road, he was fairly sure that he would be safe. If he had to make a run for it, he decided he would go left. It was maybe two hundred yards to the end of the alley and he had a start on his would-be attacker. He could feel the adrenaline pumping through his system and knew that he would be able to out-run the fat bastard. The people in the car shouldn't be a problem, either. By the time the driver realized what was going on and started reversing down the road, the sergeant would be free and clear.

That was the theory, anyway.

Fear mingled with excitement as Napper's heart felt like it was about to jump out of his chest. *Stop thinking about it*, he admonished himself. *Just run*. Taking a couple of deep breaths, the sergeant watched the guy edge closer. *Go, go, go.* With a grunt, he pushed off, slipping between the Vauxhall and the garage, heading for the traffic on the Uxbridge Road.

'Hey. Fucker!'

Head down, arms pumping, the sergeant saw something fly past his left shoulder, clattering across the cobbles before bouncing into the gutter. Rather than try and chase after him, the bloke had thrown the hammer. And missed. *Heh, heh*, Napper chuckled, *fuck you, you fat bastard, I'm outta here*. Lifting his right arm in the air, he gave his attacker the one-fingered salute while careful not to slacken his pace. Focused on the end of the alley, he lengthened his stride, planting his left foot straight into a pothole about a foot deep. 'Aargh.' Sticking out his arms, he cushioned his fall as best he could as he went arse over tit. Sprawling across the cobbles, he slammed head first into a row of wheelie bins with a sickening thud.

For a moment, there was silence as he felt the cool of the stone against his cheek. *Up, up, up.* Shaking himself out of his daze, Napper struggled to his feet. Foot to the floor, he tried to resume his flight but was halted by the intense pain shooting up his left leg. Supporting himself on one of the bins, he looked despairingly towards the safety of the main road. Standing unsteadily on his one good leg, he turned to look back down the alley at the hulking figure of his assailant. Pausing only to bend down and recover his weapon, the man moved steadily towards his prey.

The clock high on the wall said that it was well after three in the morning. After a couple of hours' dozing on a chair in the corridor, Umar Sligo felt as if he'd been trampled by a herd of bulls. What he needed was a minimum of twelve hours' uninterrupted sleep in a nice, warm bed. But, like someone once said, you can't always get what you need.

Yawning, he pushed open the door to Interview Room 4 and stepped inside. Nodding at the WPC sitting in the corner, he placed two small paper cups on the desk and pulled out a chair.

'Here you go.'

'Thanks.' Melissa Graham picked up the nearest cup and took a tentative sip of the steaming coffee. 'Urgh.'

'I know,' Umar replied, sitting down, 'it's terrible.'

'At least it's hot.'

Melissa seemed to be holding up reasonably well, under the circumstances. He knew that she had already made an initial statement. DI Postic had called it a night and gone to get a few hours' kip. Unless anything interesting came up while the DI was in the Land of Nod, she would probably charge Melissa later in the morning. Every police officer was the same: you go for the obvious answer until proven otherwise. It seemed an open-and-shut case.

Melissa's clothing had been taken away for forensic examination. Sitting opposite Umar, she was wearing a cheap pair of jeans and a shapeless red sweatshirt. It wasn't a good look.

Leaning forward, the sergeant placed his forearms on the desk and clasped his hands together. 'Sorry it's taken me so long to come and see you. I am not part of this investigation, so I had to get the permission of the officer in charge. And I also had to wait until you'd seen a lawyer.'

'I've spoken to a lot of people already,' she said quietly. 'I can't remember all of their names.'

'That's understandable.' Umar sat back in his chair. 'It's quite a situation you find yourself in.'

'But why would anyone want to kill . . .' her voice trailed off. Sniffing, she wiped her nose on the back of her sleeve. He could see that she was working hard to try to hold back the tears.

Umar gave her a supportive smile. 'That's what I was hoping you might be able to tell me.'

She looked at him quizzically. 'I thought that this wasn't your investigation?'

'It isn't. But I *am* a policeman. And the only reason I'm allowed in here at all is because you want to talk to me.'

Placing the cup on the desk, she shot him a hurt look. 'You want me to confess?'

'I want you to tell me precisely what happened,' Umar said gently. He pulled out a small black notebook and a biro from the back pocket of his jeans and tossed them on the table. 'If your story is going to check out, we need to find some evidence to support it . . . quickly.'

Walking out of the police station, Umar saw Sergeant Lawrence Shames coming the other way. As he bounded up the stairs, there was a spring in his step suggestive of a man contemplating a quick win in a big case.

'Did you see her?' Shames asked, stopping on the top step.

'Just spoken to her.'

'And?'

Umar tapped his notebook against the back of his free hand. 'And nothing, really. She says she walked in and found them there. Tried to revive the boyfriend, which is how she got covered in his blood. Doesn't have any idea who might have done it.'

'There you go,' said Shames cheerily, patting him on the shoulder. 'We are *sorted* on this one.'

'What about the forensics?'

'Ach, we'll have to wait and see, but you know . . .'

'Yeah.' Umar *did* know. The wheels of justice were moving fast and it would take something spectacular to slow them down.

'What are you going to do?'

Umar made a face. 'Not much. I'll speak to a few people. But it's not really my investigation.'

'That's right,' Shames headed inside the station, 'and don't you forget it.'

FORTY-TWO

No trains were listed on the electronic indicator. However, the board above the platform helpfully reminded her that the time was now four fifty-eight and thirteen seconds. The first service of the morning should arrive in around twenty minutes. Shivering in the pre-dawn gloom, Chantelle Malloy gazed vacantly at the lights burning in the office block across the road. From this distance, the large, squat building which housed a large part of the BBC's London operations looked like it was made of tinfoil. At this time in the morning, the place would be largely empty, but still, most of the windows were shining brightly. *Stupid bastards*, she thought, *what a waste of electricity. Haven't they heard of global warming?*

A mail van barrelled down Wood Lane, accelerating through a red light and disappearing in the direction of Shepherd's Bush. Yawning widely, Chantelle kicked the bucket of dirty water along the empty platform of the westbound platform of White City tube, cursing her supervisor for putting her on cleaning duty again. She had been forced to wash down the station platform for three of the last four mornings. It simply wasn't fair: the other members of her crew, Marlon, Pavel and Anton, all got to sit inside, reading the paper and having a kip while she slogged her way from one end of the station to the other, picking up litter and cleaning up after the dirty bastard passengers. Nothing surprised Chantelle any more – in less than a month on the job, she'd had to retrieve everything from false teeth to used condoms. People were so disgusting. Not for the first time, the girl wished that she had stuck with her hairdressing course at Goldhawk Road Technical College.

Wearied by the injustice of it all, Chantelle pushed her mop across the sticky concrete. This was exploitation, pure and simple, but there was bugger all that she could do about it. The supervisor, Crina, was a skanky bitch from Romania or some other Eastern European hell-hole. She had all of them reporting for duty at four o'clock in the morning so that her employment agency could claim workfare credits from the Department of Work & Pensions. Meanwhile, Chantelle had to work for six and a half hours a day for no money or risk losing all of her state benefits.

'What do they want you to do?' her father had asked when the letter from the DWP had arrived, instructing Chantelle to report for their latest welfare-to-work programme. 'Go on the game?'

'Probably,' Chantelle grumbled. The idea had crossed her mind. Her useless bastard father wouldn't give a toss if she did but, instinctively, the girl knew that she didn't have the stomach for it.

'I would tell them to get stuffed,' her dad huffed, retreating behind his copy of the *Daily Express*.

Easy for you to say, Chantelle thought. Her dad hadn't done a day's work for more than thirty years. Good luck to anyone trying to get *him* back into a job.

In the end, however, there was no alternative. Two weeks later, Chantelle had reported for duty with her career reorientation provider, a company called New Life Horizons, which operated out of a two-room office in the basement of a crumbling office block just south of Brook Green. The place smelled of cigarettes and piss. All the people looked like they were on medication. After filling in a handful of forms, Chantelle was informed that she had been assigned to an environmental services crew who would be providing outsourced services to London Underground.

'What are outsourced services?' she'd asked the young guy behind the desk.

'You'll be doing the cleaning,' he told her, not looking up. 'Make sure you pick up your uniform before you go.'

'Hey. Do it all.' The Romanian slag, all peroxide hair and fake fingernails, appeared from behind a pillar and took a deep drag on her Lambert & Butler cigarette. Exhaling into the dark morning sky, she pointed towards the far end of the platform, past an advert for the latest James Bond movie.

'Fuck off,' Chantelle whispered to herself.

'What you say?' Crina jabbed an angry finger in Chantelle's direction. 'I'm watching you.'

'Yeah, yeah.'

Standing about five feet four inches tall, the Romanian woman was dressed in jeans and a red puffa jacket. Not for her the green jumpsuit with the letters NLH in black on the back that Chantelle and the other 'employees' were forced to wear. Behind her slapdash make-up, the woman could have been anywhere between thirty and fifty. Taking another drag on her cigarette, she glanced at her watch. 'The station opens in less than half an hour – you have to finish soon.'

Looking up, Chantelle caught sight of Anton through the staffroom window. He was pointing at her and laughing. 'Sod you,' Chantelle mouthed, flipping him the finger.

'Leave him alone,' the woman snapped.

'Get *them* to do some work,' Chantelle demanded, stomping along the platform like an angry eight year old.

'They work,' Crina said flatly.

'Yeah, right.' *You don't tell them others what to do*, Chantelle thought bitterly, *'cos they'd kick your bony arse all the way back to the shitty little country you came from. Get you deported, so you can spend the rest of your life standing by the side of the road, sucking off Russian truck drivers for a living.*

'Hurry up!' the woman squawked.

With her foot, Chantelle pointed at the cardboard box containing a selection of industrial-strength cleaning materials. 'I need more disinfectant.'

Shaking her head, Crina took a final drag on her smoke and flicked the stub towards the empty train tracks. 'There's more stuff over there.' She pointed at a small concrete shack, a glorified cupboard about six feet high by three feet wide, set to the side of the station building. To the right of its metal door was a keypad. 'The code is 1026. Don't take forever.' Lecture over, she headed back inside.

'*Dunt tek fowevvva,*' Chantelle parroted in a cod Eastern European accent. Letting the mop fall from her hand, she watched the woman disappear into the ticket hall. '*Fuuukkk uuu.*' Slouching across the platform, she stepped up to the shed door.

'Urgh.' White City really was an outdoor khazi. Something didn't smell good and the cleaner looked around to see if she could locate the offending excretions. Wrinkling her nose, she punched in the key code, waiting for the lock to click open before reaching for the door handle. As she did so, the door swung open and the stink intensified.

'Bollocks.' The cleaner jumped backwards as a large black bin bag fell out on to the platform. As the sack hit the concrete, it split open to reveal its contents. As Chantelle realized what was inside, her eyes grew wide and she felt her legs wobble.

'Crina.'

Slowly she backed away.

'CRINA!'

What time was it? Where was she? Jade Jones tried to sit up in bed but the searing pain bouncing around her skull caused her to abandon that idea pretty damn quickly. She didn't remember drinking that much, but this sure was a monster hangover. Her mouth was dry and her head felt like it had been split open with an axe. She could feel some noxious brew bubbling away in her stomach, all too eager to force its way back up her throat.

Concentrating on not throwing up, Jade waited for the nausea to subside, before trying to piece together the events of the night before. Slowly, it started coming back to her – the row with her boyfriend, the spur-of-the-moment trip to London, the guys in the car, the bottle of Smirnoff Black, the party . . . The bit she didn't want to remember. Gently easing herself off the bed she sifted through the crumpled pile of clothing lying on the floor. Where were her knickers? Deciding that it didn't matter, Jade picked up her jeans and checked the pockets. To her relief, she still had her return train ticket, ATM card and some spare cash. Her mobile phone was still in her jacket. It was time to get the hell out of this shit-hole, get back home and have a nice bath, forget all about last night. Hopefully Paul had learned his lesson. She had certainly learned hers.

Flopping back onto the bed, Jade struggled into the jeans before slipping on her trainers. Pulling on her jacket, she stepped gingerly towards the door. When she turned the handle, however, it didn't budge. It took her a couple of moments to realize that the door was locked. She gave it a smack with her fist, followed by a series of rapid kicks.

'Hey! Open the bloody door!'

When no one responded, she sat back on the bed and took out her mobile. Paul's number was at the top of the dialled list. She hit call and listened to it ring. As it went to voicemail, she didn't know what to say. The whole thing just seemed too stupid, too *embarrassing*. Ending the call, she wondered who to try next. No one came to mind.

At least the headache was gone. 'Who you gonna call?' she asked herself. In the absence of Ghostbusters, she dialled 999.

FORTY-THREE

The morning sun sneaking through the West London cloud glinted off the bald dome of Ron Flux, causing Carlyle to shield his eyes with the back of his hand. This morning, the Detective Inspector from Hammersmith was wearing a gruesome green blazer with a red check, and a pair of chinos that seemed too small at the waist and too long in the leg. Nothing, however, could distract from the look of agitation on the man's face.

Carlyle looked down at the body laid out on the platform under a blue plastic sheet as a trio of technicians buzzed around the shed where it had been dumped. A familiar sense of despair and anger washed over him. He tried to remember the girl's name, but his mind was blank. 'Is that her?'

'Sandra Middlemass? Yeah, that's her.' Hands on hips, Flux stared at the board indicating that all west-bound Central Line services had been suspended. He signalled towards a couple of women standing further down the platform, just inside the police tape. The pair of them looked like they would do a runner at any moment if it wasn't for the attentions of a couple of uniforms hovering nearby. 'The cleaner found her about six this morning and got her supervisor to call it in. How long she'd been there, we don't know yet.'

Couldn't have been that long, Carlyle thought, *otherwise someone would have smelled something.* 'So, what's next?'

'Get her out of here,' Flux replied, 'find out how and when she died. See if we can link it back to the Persian Palace.' He took out his mobile and made a call.

'Fair enough.' The inspector still wasn't sure why Flux had called him out here. 'How can I help?'

Flux made a face, indicating that the call was being diverted to voicemail. He hung up without leaving a message. 'I just want to make sure you don't get in the way.'

'Don't worry about that. We won't do anything that obstructs you and your sergeant.'

Flux toyed with the phone in his hand. 'Bloody Napper,' he said. 'Where the hell is he?'

Bloody Umar, for that matter – where is he? 'And, of course, if there is anything we can do . . .'

Still playing with his phone, Flux gave him a perfunctory nod. A couple of paramedics appeared on the platform, sliding their gurney under the police tape. Carlyle thought back to his meeting with Calvin Safi and the vacant girl in the leather jacket sitting in the back booth. He turned his attention back to Flux. 'Are there any other girls who have been reported missing?'

'There are plenty of girls that are reported missing,' the DI sighed, 'but none that we have been able to connect to the kebab shop.'

'Okay.' Carlyle stepped aside to let the paramedics past. 'I'm going to head off, but let's keep in touch.'

'Yeah, sure,' Flux replied, his thoughts elsewhere.

On his way out of the tube station, Carlyle tried calling Umar. When the sergeant's voicemail kicked in, he hung up and stomped unhappily across a zebra crossing, forcing an onrushing Vauxhall Corsa to slam on the brakes. The driver, a skinhead with a tattoo on his forearm, looked as if he wanted to give the pedestrian a piece of his mind, but thought better of it when the inspector gave him a defiant glare. As he reached the kerbside, it occurred to Carlyle that the man looked vaguely familiar, but he dismissed the notion without even looking round. 'All these wankers look the same,' he mumbled to himself as he scanned the horizon in search of sustenance.

In the end, he chose a café with strawberry tablecloths run by a couple from Thailand. In the background, a commercial radio station was playing at a mercifully low volume. Aside from an old guy sitting under a poster advertising holidays in Phuket, the place was empty. Stepping up to the counter, the inspector considered the modest fare on offer.

After ordering toast and a mug of green tea, he grabbed a copy of *Metro* from one of the tables and took a seat by the window. Looking across the Green, he had a reasonable view of the Persian Palace – good enough at least to see that the place was closed. Carlyle carefully scrutinized the windows on the upper floors for signs of life. There were none. With a sigh, he turned his attention to the newspaper.

He was halfway through a story about an MPS staff survey when his breakfast arrived. Thanking the waitress, he picked up a slice of toast and took a large bite as he continued reading. The survey, which had been released after a request under the Freedom of Information Act, looked at officers' attitudes towards the job and towards the public. 'Nobody bloody asked me,' Carlyle muttered, washing down the toast with some tea as he scanned the findings. One stat caught his eye: *32.7% of officers agreed with the statement: 'It's a waste of time trying to help some people'.*

'That must make the other 67.3 per cent liars,' he mused, reaching for another piece of toast. An Assistant Commissioner was quoted as saying: *'We strive to be an organization which is as open and transparent as possible and within which all our staff support each other in providing the best service possible to the public.'*

'You make it sound like the Waltons,' Carlyle snorted, turning to the sports pages. Folding the paper in half, he began to read a story about Fulham's latest transfer target when he was distracted by a pair of pretty black girls walking past the window. As they disappeared from his field of vision, the inspector noticed activity at the kebab shop. He watched as a fat white bloke put a key in the front door, went inside and locked the door behind him. Dropping the newspaper onto the table, Carlyle slurped down the rest of his tea before reaching into his pocket. Pulling out a tenner, he headed over to the counter to pay his bill.

Crossing the Green, he looked up at the clouds. The early morning sunshine had given way to more familiar grey skies. The forecast was for rain. For once it looked like the Meteorological Office had got it right. It was only a matter of time. Outside the Persian Palace, he gave a short sharp blast on the buzzer and waited.

No response.

He pressed again.

Still nothing.

I know you're in there. He left his finger on the buzzer and started counting in his head as he listened to its insistent whine inside the shop. Breathing in the smells of old kebabs and car exhausts was making him feel dizzy, and Carlyle tried to shake the fuzziness from his head. Despite his breakfast, he was still feeling hungry and his mood darkened with every passing second.

He had reached seventy-six when the white guy he had seen going inside a few minutes earlier appeared from the back of the shop. 'What're you doing?' he snarled through the glass as he scratched at a tattoo on his forearm. He was wearing a red Fred Perry polo shirt under a black Harrington jacket. Dirty jeans and a pair of white Nikes made up a fairly standard blue-collar ensemble.

Was this the guy who'd nearly run him over at the zebra crossing? He might have been, but the inspector was by no means sure. 'Open the door.'

'We're closed. Fuck off.'

Carlyle pulled up his ID and held it up against the glass. 'I want to talk to Calvin.'

The man scratched his head. 'Guess what? He's not here. So fuck off.' Stepping to his left, he hit a switch and a security

202

shutter started descending on the inside of the shop. Not waiting for it to fully close, the man turned and headed further inside.

Standing on the pavement, Carlyle considered his options. A sign next to the door said that the shop wasn't due to open for another three hours. He could come back later. Or what? Unsure of his next move, he began walking aimlessly along the pavement in the direction of Shepherd's Bush tube. Twenty yards before the station, a bus pulled up at the stop and a dozen or so passengers swarmed onto the pavement. Brought to a halt, Carlyle noticed a narrow passageway leading behind the row of shops that included the Persian Palace. For want of anything better to do, he decided to take a look.

The passageway led to a cobbled alley that was barely wide enough to accommodate two cars. One end was blocked off by the tube, while the other led back to the main road. Looking towards the road, Carlyle surveyed the scene. To his right was a row of single-storey garages, backing on to the shops in front. Between each garage was a small yard, each with a metal gate set into a brick wall. Each section of wall was topped by its own style of razor wire fencing. The wire must have been deemed sufficient to keep out any unwanted visitors for there was no sign of the otherwise ubiquitous CCTV cameras that covered the city.

On a metal gate he noticed a black and white sticker: *BEWARE OF DOG: KEEP OUT*. Right on cue came the sound of vigorous barking. Carlyle stopped; he didn't like animals at the best of times. After a few moments, however, it became apparent that no one was paying any attention and the animal quickly stopped.

Moving along the alley, the inspector glanced at the graffiti sprayed on the brick wall to his left. In black paint, someone had written: *some people do this for fun – I'm just a cunt*. Laughing, he kicked an empty Sprite can across the cobbles into a nearby pothole.

Running the full length of the alley, the wall gave on to the railway line. This was the point where trains heading west on the Central Line came up to the surface. Sticking his hands in his pockets, Carlyle listened to a train rumble past, making for White City and the distant suburbs beyond.

Looks like the service is back up and running, he thought. *They must have removed Sandra Middlemass's body from the platform.* Whether the forensics guys would have been given enough time to properly do their job was another matter. The inspector knew from his own experience that the Mayor's office would always prioritize the needs of the transport network over an inconvenient murder. Poor old Flux would have been under immense pressure to get the station open and have trains running through it again as quickly as possible. Preserving the crime scene was always a major struggle.

Moving past a parked Mercedes, Carlyle came to a stop where he estimated the back of the kebab shop should be. He wrinkled his nose as the familiar smell of ammonia caressed his nostrils. Looking down, he could see where someone had relieved himself on a rusted garage door. 'Dirty bastard.' Carlyle tutted. There were times when London just seemed like one big outside toilet.

At least it seemed that the guy hadn't pissed on the door handle. After glancing up and down the alley, Carlyle gave it a cautious tug. Locked. Stepping to his right, he tried the next gate along – a solid metal construction, painted military green: same story.

Okay . . .

At least the small handwritten sign stuck to the gate – *Persian Palace ring bell for deliveries* – told him that he was in the right place. Taking a step backwards, the inspector looked up aimlessly at the back of the building, as if that might reveal his next move. Just then, there was the sound of a door opening and footsteps in the yard on the other side of the wall. Carlyle froze, his eyes on the gate. It didn't open. Instead, there was a sound of coughing, followed by a stream of smoke appearing behind the barbed wire. Someone was having a smoke. More footsteps. Voices. Edging back towards the gate, the inspector strained to hear above the traffic noise in the distance. It sounded like Safi and the guy with the tattoo, but he couldn't be sure.

'*Bloody policeman.*'

'*You need to calm down.*'

A cigarette butt flew over the wire and landed on the cobbles near his feet. Standing to the left of the gate, Carlyle pressed himself against the wall, trying to catch more of the conversation.

'*What about the girl?*'

'*That's your problem, you didn't have to—*'

At that moment, the dog in the nearby yard started up again. Looking round, willing the barking to stop, Carlyle saw a guy – presumably the dog's owner – appear in the alley, glancing in both directions. The inspector hesitated: should he stay? Or had he pushed his luck far enough already? The sight of a large Alsatian at the guy's side made his decision a lot easier. Turning on his heel, he headed for the far end of the alley at a brisk clip.

Back where he started, the inspector made his way along the north side of Shepherd's Bush Green, his intended destination the Central Line. He was literally walking round in circles; doing nothing but wasting time. As he walked past the Persian Palace, he saw that the shutters remained down. Further along, he glanced back down the passageway – it was empty and there was no sign of the Alsatian or its owner. Grumbling to himself, he reached the tube station and fished out his Oyster card. As he went through the barriers, he felt his mobile start to vibrate in his pocket. Ignoring it, he let the escalator take him down towards the east-bound platform.

Twenty-five minutes later, he was back at his desk. He had barely sat down when WPC Mason came in and perched on the edge of his desk. She looked tired, as if she was just coming off a night shift.

'What can I do for you?' he asked.

She stifled a yawn. 'I've been looking for Sergeant Sligo.'

Good point. Where the bloody hell is *Umar?*

'Giselle Winters has been trying to get hold of him,' the WPC went on.

'The lawyer's wife?'

'She says he's not responding to his mobile.'

'I wouldn't worry about it,' Carlyle said. 'He's probably just catching up on some sleep.'

'Probably.' This time Mason did yawn. 'He's not the only one who needs to do that.'

'Anyway, I'll tell him when I see him. I'm sure he'll be only too happy to go back and speak to the lady again.'

Ignoring the innuendo, Mason slipped off the desk and set off towards the stairs. 'Okay. Thank you, Inspector.'

'Hope you manage to get a decent kip.' He knew from experience how difficult it could be to sleep during the day. Whenever possible, he avoided working nights. It buggered up your body clock and was bad for your health.

'I'll be fine.'

'Good. See you later.' As he watched her disappear, his mobile started up again. Pulling it out of his pocket, he answered. 'Yes?'

'Carlyle? It's Flux. I've been trying to get hold of you for ages.' The irritation in the DI's voice was clear. 'Don't you ever answer your bloody phone?'

Not one of my strong points, Carlyle had to admit. His ability to miss calls and lose voicemails was something that many people had commented on over the years. 'I'm back at Charing Cross.'

'Well, *I'm* back at the Persian Palace,' Flux said sharply. 'Look, you need to get over here pronto.'

'But I've just come from there,' Carlyle complained.

'Well, you might want to come back. Another girl's gone missing.'

FORTY-FOUR

Why the hell am I chasing backwards and forwards across London for the sake of someone else's case? With the argument still raging in his brain, Carlyle found Flux waiting for him outside the kebab shop. The shutters had been raised and the place was open, but there was no sign of any activity inside. The Detective Inspector, meanwhile, looked like he'd aged five years in the last couple of hours. The guy looked so weary, Carlyle felt energized by comparison.

'What have you got?' he asked brusquely, by way of introduction.

'Jade Jones,' Flux told him, 'nineteen years old. She went missing from Maidenhead last night after a row with her boyfriend. This morning, she makes a 999 call saying she's being held captive by some guys who picked her up outside Paddington station.' He pointed towards a dry cleaner's three doors down from the Persian Palace. 'They traced the call to a mast on the top of that building. When I heard it come over the radio I came right down here.'

'And?'

Flux shrugged. 'And nothing. Safi was still in bed. No sign of the girl. No one else on the premises.'

'Hm.' Carlyle thought about the white guy and the inaudible conversation in the back yard. 'Have you tried ringing her mobile?'

'Of course,' Flux snapped. 'It's switched off. We've lost track of her. Safi, naturally, claims he knows nothing about her.'

'Can I go and talk to him?'

Flux's expression said *Be my guest*. 'I've got to get back to the station. Let me know if you manage to get any more out of him.'

'Sure.' Carlyle watched the DI weave between the almost stationary traffic and disappear across the Green. On the side of a bus, an advert for the nearby shopping centre caught his eye; the latest American teenybopper was due to make an appearance at the weekend, sing a few songs, sign a few autographs. *Do they still call them teenyboppers?* he wondered as he headed inside the kebab shop.

Ignoring the fetid atmosphere, he turned the lock and flipped the *Closed* sign before walking through to the back. Calvin Safi was in the yard smoking a cigarette. He was wearing a pair of light grey sweatpants, along with a ratty-looking navy V-neck jumper over a white T-shirt. Unshaven and bleary-eyed, he looked like he'd had a heavy night.

'Good party?' Carlyle asked.

Safi eyed the inspector sullenly. 'What do you want?'

Stepping forward, Carlyle replied with a fist to the gut.

'*Pfff* . . .' Surprised as much as winded, Safi made a noise like a deflating balloon. Doubling over, the cigarette fell from his lips on to a cracked paving stone. Grabbing the back of his jumper, Carlyle smacked his face into the wall. 'Argh.' There was a thud, and the shop owner slid to the ground, blood pouring from his nose. Scrambling into a sitting position, he watched warily, ready to defend himself from further blows. 'What are you doing?' he managed, wiping his nose on his sleeve.

Stomping on the smouldering cigarette butt, Carlyle moved forward, readying himself to give Safi a good kick.

'Hey!' Safi shrieked, adopting the foetal position. 'This is assault. It's GBH, man. Wait till my lawyer hears about this.'

'Federici? He's your wife's lawyer. Somehow I don't think she's going to lend him out for you on this.' The inspector hovered over the prostrate man, making it clear that a good shoeing was still very much at the top of his agenda.

'I'll get my own bloody lawyer,' Safi mumbled from behind his hands.

'Like fuck.' Carlyle gave the man a prod with the toe of his boot to keep him focused on the matter in hand. 'And anyway, it'll be too late by then.'

Safi let out a satisfying whimper.

It's fun being a bastard, Carlyle thought as he felt the frustration of a morning spent running around in circles draining away.

'Where's the girl?'

'What girl?'

Once again, the inspector grabbed the guy's jumper, this time dragging him up. 'Jade Jones, the girl you picked up from Paddington last night.'

'I don't know what—'

'Fuck you,' Carlyle hissed. Releasing his hold, he let the man fall back to the concrete and administered two swift kicks to his ribs. Not hard enough to break anything, but hard enough to hurt. Tears appeared in Safi's eyes. 'I've seen the CCTV pictures. I know you were there.' It was a decent enough lie; most Londoners assumed that security cameras covered their every waking move. And, most of the time, they were right.

Safi hesitated before trying one last time. 'I wasn't—'

'Don't fuck with me.' Almost revelling in his loss of control, Carlyle stepped forward until he was almost standing on the prostrate man. 'Tell me the truth, or I am going to do you some serious damage. Good luck being able to speak after I've done with you – even if you can find a bloody lawyer.' He gave another quick kick for emphasis, a little harder this time. 'Now, where is the girl?'

'He took her back to Paddington,' Safi cried, 'The little slag's gone home.'

'Who took her back to Paddington? When?'

'Steve . . . Steve Metcalf.'

'The white guy with the tattoo?'

'He was the one who fucked her, not me. I didn't touch her.'

209

'We'll see about that. When did they go?'

'An hour ago.'

About the time I was snooping around out the back, Carlyle thought. *I must have just missed them. Or maybe I passed them on the pavement without realizing.* Annoyed with himself, he gave Safi another kick, although with less venom this time. 'Do you have a mobile?'

Reaching into the pocket of his pants, Safi pulled out a battered Nokia and offered it to the inspector. Grabbing the handset, Carlyle pulled off the battery and took out the SIM card. Dropping the SIM in his pocket, he tossed the rest of the phone over the wall into the alley. Safi started to protest but quickly thought better of it.

'Stay here,' Carlyle commanded. 'If you move one inch before I get back, I will give you a proper kicking.' Not waiting for a reply, he went back inside.

Standing in the kitchen, he wondered exactly what he might be looking for. Above the hum of traffic came the sound of someone thumping on the locked door at the front of the café. Peeking towards the street, he caught a glimpse of the kid who worked behind the counter. 'Looks like you might be getting the day off,' Carlyle murmured, as he headed for the stairs.

He started at the top of the building, working his way down through a series of dirty, messy rooms that had been converted into bedsits. When he found a door that was locked, he unceremoniously booted it open. It was the first time he'd done this kind of donkey work for a long while.

Bloody Umar, Carlyle thought grimly. *Where is he when you need him?* He checked the last room; like the others, it was empty, apart from an unmade bed and a nasty smell.

Downstairs, the kid had given up banging on the door and had gone away to enjoy his unexpected day off. A steady stream of pedestrians passed by the window, none of them apparently put out that the kebab shop wasn't open for business. *Hardly surprising,* Carlyle reflected. *There must be at least half a dozen*

210

fast-food places within a minute's walk from here. Feeling peckish, he walked into the kitchen. A loaf of white sliced bread sat next to a filthy grill. Out of the corner of his eye, the inspector caught some movement. A cockroach – or something bigger? It crossed his mind that maybe he should put a call in to the local health inspectors. First, however, he needed to put something in a sandwich. Filling the far corner of the room was an upright, stainless-steel double door refrigerator.

Gotta be something in there.

Stepping across the room, Carlyle yanked at the right-hand door.

'Holy fuck!' Jumping sideways, he just managed to avoid being hit by the body that tumbled out, hitting the floor with a gentle thwack.

FORTY-FIVE

Surveying the scene, the inspector let out a nervous chortle. 'As far as I can recall, that's the first time a dead man has ever tried to headbutt me.' At least his reflexes were still good enough that he was able to escape the corpse's attention. Hands on hips, he took a couple of deep breaths, watching a small cockroach scuttle under the sink as he waited for his heart-rate to return to something approaching normal. He should definitely contact the health inspectors.

As he regained his composure, Carlyle realized that he was still hungry. Stepping over the body, he recovered an almost-full packet of processed cheese slices and carefully closed the fridge door. Could he be about to eat some important evidence? Highly unlikely, he decided. Flipping over the packet, he contemplated the best-before date. 'Only a couple of days overdue,' he said aloud. 'They'll do.'

Looking down at the deceased's frosty face, he recognized the guy immediately. Even though he had clearly been given a battering, the victim still wore the same dopey expression that Carlyle remembered from their first meeting. The *Choose Your Weapons* T-shirt had been replaced by one displaying a Star Wars DJ Yoda design but the overall look was still that of an outsized twelve year old.

Shit. Carlyle belatedly remembered what he had been up to before being so rudely interrupted. As a matter of routine, he stuck his head out of the back door and checked the yard. Safi was gone. *No surprises there*, the inspector thought grumpily. Even the damn kebab shop owner wasn't dumb enough to hang around with a corpse stuck in his fridge.

Closing the kitchen door, he turned and looked down at the lifeless body. 'What the bloody hell did you think you were doing?'

Gazing helplessly up at him, Adrian Napper did not reply.

Shaking his head sadly, Carlyle tossed the packet of cheese on to the counter next to the bread and reluctantly pulled out his mobile phone.

By the time someone at Hammersmith police station managed to track down Ron Flux, the inspector was munching on his second sandwich. The combination of white bread and plastic cheese was totally tasteless but it filled a hole. Washing it down with a can of Diet Coke he'd nicked from the cabinet out front, he gave a satisfied burp just as someone came on the other end of the line.

'What?'

The inspector placed the can onto the counter by the sink. 'Flux? It's Carlyle.'

The DI sounded tired and harassed. 'What is it?'

Carlyle popped the last of his sandwich into his mouth and swallowed quickly. Now was not the time to be talking with your mouth full. 'Bad news,' he said, adopting a suitably sombre tone. 'I've found your sergeant.'

DI Flux was pacing up and down on the cobbles, his head bobbing around as if he was being attacked by an angry wasp. 'Bloody Napper,' he fumed. 'What the fuck was he doing?' It was the same lament that he had repeated maybe a dozen times in the last five minutes.

Not for the first time, Carlyle shrugged helplessly. *How would I know?*

The two policemen had retreated into the alley as a small army of uniforms and forensic technicians descended on the kebab shop in order to process the crime scene. Watching them going about their business, Carlyle felt a familiar sense of weariness descend on his shoulders. They were the cavalry who always arrived too late.

Staring blindly into the middle distance, Flux looked like he wanted to cry. 'The stupid sod should never have tried something like this.'

'No.' The inspector stared down at his shoes. There was still the distinct whiff of ammonia in the air and he wished he was standing somewhere else. Above all, however, he regretted not giving Calvin Safi more of a kicking when he'd had the chance. No matter, he told himself, he would catch the guy soon enough.

The Alsatian down the alley started barking. Carlyle thought about going to speak to its owner but decided against it. One of the uniforms could go and tick that box. He had other priorities.

'Stupid bugger,' Flux groaned.

'Did he have any kids?'

'No,' Flux shook his head. 'Not married.'

Carlyle thought back to the Yoda T-shirt. Not a garment for a grown man. Probably didn't have a girlfriend. 'That's something, at least.'

Flux took a reluctant step down the alley. 'I need to go and speak to his girlfriend. She's going to be devastated.'

Rather you than me, Carlyle thought. Breaking that kind of bad news never got any easier. 'Yes.'

'And his mum, as well.'

'Okay.' Carlyle hopped from foot to foot. He really had to get out of here. 'I'll set about tracking down Safi and this guy Steve . . .'

'Metcalf?' Flux pawed the ground with his shoe. 'That piece of shit will be up to his neck in this, for sure.'

Carlyle gave him a consoling pat on the shoulder. 'Don't worry, we'll get them.'

'Oh, I know that,' Flux said, as if it didn't count.

214

'And the girl made it home.'

Flux looked at him blankly.

'Jade Jones,' Carlyle explained. 'She made it back to Basingstoke. I checked. Her phone had died. That's why we couldn't get hold of her before.'

'Silly cow.'

'It's something, at least.'

'Maybe.' Shoving his hands in his pockets, Flux turned away. 'But really, who gives a fuck?'

Carlyle watched the Detective Inspector as he slouched down the alley, heading towards the hustle and bustle of Shepherd's Bush Green. A succession of car horns blared in the distance, a reminder that, whatever cruelties were dispensed in its dimly lit back alleys, London never stopped moving forward. He thought about Adrian Napper slowly defrosting on the kitchen floor of a dirty kebab shop and felt a pang of jealousy. *Would anyone on the job care that much if it was me that had been stuffed in a fridge?* he wondered. *Somehow, I doubt it.*

FORTY-SIX

'I don't suppose that you know anything about this, do you, Mr policeman?' Elma Reyes hurled the newspaper across her desk. Keeping his expression neutral, the inspector watched the tabloid land at his feet, making no effort to pick it up. He glanced towards Michelangelo Federici, who was sitting in a chair to his right, grinning like a naughty schoolboy. Behind him, one of Elma's minions was standing, head bowed, with his back to the wall. The boy had an envelope in his hand, like he was waiting to deliver a letter to his boss.

'Terror suspect's mum runs church scam,' the lawyer chuckled.

'Huh?'

Federici pointed towards the paper with the toe of his badly scuffed shoe. 'That's the headline. It's a complete hatchet-job on the Christian Salvation Centre and its work in the miracle and healing market. The usual garbage – riddled with factual inaccuracies and contentious opinions – wrapped up in a pseudo public-interest defence because of Elma's relationship with the poor unfortunate Taimur.'

You mean the fact that she was his mother. Carlyle adopted an exasperated look. 'Journalists . . .'

'It was written by a man called—'

'Bernard Gilmore.' Elma spat out the name as if it was the Devil's own smouldering sperm.

'Thank you,' Federici smiled at his client. 'It was just on the tip of my tongue. Bernard Gilmore.' He turned to the policeman. 'Do you know him, Inspector?'

Bloody Bernie. Carlyle mimed pondering the question for a moment, carefully scanning his memory banks before slowly shaking his head. 'No. Not as far as I can recall. I don't think so.'

'That damn journalist has been harassing me for years,' Elma complained. 'He pays people to spread lies and tittle-tattle. If I ever find his source within my organization, I'll kill 'em.' She shot the boy hovering by the wall a suspicious glance. 'I swear to God I will.'

'You could sue,' Carlyle ventured. 'There are limits. Even for the press.' *And Bernie knows better than anyone how to stay just the right side of them.*

'Of course we're gonna bloody sue,' Elma thundered. 'We're going to sue his bloody arse off.'

Trying to keep a straight face, her lawyer said nothing.

'Anyway,' the inspector continued, moving swiftly along, 'that's not really why I'm here.'

Elma gave a grunt that suggested she couldn't care less about his agenda.

'The thing is,' getting down to business, Carlyle fixed the preacher woman with his most serious stare, 'I need to find Calvin as a matter of some considerable urgency.'

Some considerable urgency. When needs be, he could invoke his inner plod and talk the talk like the best of them.

Blank faces all round.

'I need to find the guy,' Carlyle repeated. 'So where should I look?'

Elma frowned. 'What's he done now?'

'I just need to speak to him. Quickly.'

'Is he in trouble?'

Even more than you, love. But Carlyle was able to evade those kind of questions with ease. 'He's not at the kebab shop, so where else might he be?'

'He *is* in trouble, then. Why am I not surprised?' The woman's eyes glistened malevolently as for a nano-second she contemplated problems other than her own.

'Where might I find him?' Carlyle persisted.

'How the hell should I know?' Elma threw up her hands. 'I've hardly spoken to him over the past few years. The last thing I want to know about is what the grubby little so-and-so gets up to when he's not selling outsized portions of food poisoning in a Styrofoam box.'

Looking for some assistance Carlyle glanced at the lawyer.

'Sorry, Inspector,' Federici said smoothly. 'I'm afraid that I can't help you on that one either.'

'Very well, if you think of anything, let me know.' Carlyle got to his feet. 'In the meantime, good luck with your legal action. I'm sure that Bernie will be delighted to be on the receiving end of another lawsuit.'

Raising an eyebrow, Federici gave him a bemused look. '*Bernie*? I thought you didn't know him?'

Me and my big mouth. 'Only by reputation,' Carlyle stammered. 'I think he tried to sue one of my colleagues once. A rather messy business, if I remember correctly.'

Federici's eyebrow stayed raised, making him look like a poor man's Roger Moore.

Avoiding eye-contact, Carlyle headed for the door. 'It came to me while we were talking.'

Elma looked at him with contempt. 'Melville,' she said threateningly, 'will you please show the *po-lice-man* out?'

Escaping the tangle of his own lies, the inspector hurried from the building. Stepping out on to the pavement, he looked around in vain for his car.

'Fuck.'

With a groan, he realized that his driver had scarpered. Hadn't he told the guy to wait? He couldn't remember.

'Fuck, fuck, fuck.'

Stranded in the middle of a seemingly endless suburban street somewhere in deepest, darkest South London, the inspector had no idea how to get back to civilization. Central London, WC2, seemed a *long* way away. Thanks to the vagaries of the public transport system, it probably was.

Overwhelmed by weariness, he felt rooted to the spot. According to Lao-Tzu, a journey of a thousand miles begins with a single step. Then again, the Chinese philosopher had never found himself stranded in a dump like this

Slowly, Carlyle scanned to his left, and then to his right. As far as the eye could see, there was nothing but row upon row of tiny terraced houses. At this time of day, the streets were deserted; there was not a soul to be seen. Even the ubiquitous background hum of the city seemed to have melted away. For a moment, he felt like the only human survivor in a post-apocalypse zombie movie.

Almost.

He turned to the boy who was hovering on the step behind him. 'How do I get back into Town?'

With a helpful smile, Melville Farasin pointed down the road with the envelope that remained glued to his hand. 'Go to the end then take a right. Cross the road and there's a bus stop on the far side. Four or five diff'rent buses stop there. Most of 'em go to Crystal Palace. You can get trains to Victoria from there.'

Great, Carlyle thought. Even after he made it to Victoria, it would be a half-hour schlep back to the police station. *Life in the fast lane. What a totally wasted day.* He looked up and down the street again and then back at the boy. 'You don't know where Calvin Safi might be, do you?'

Melville shook his head. 'Nah.'

'Fair enough.'

Moving down onto the pavement, the boy glanced over his shoulder. 'I spoke to Bernie, though,' he said quietly. 'He says that you're a good guy.'

'Did you now?' Carlyle laughed. 'Well, I would keep that to yourself if I were you. I don't think your boss would be too chuffed if she found out.'

'She'd go mental.' Melville waved the envelope at Carlyle. 'Elma's a bit of a nutter.'

219

'You can say that again.'

'That's why I'm handing in my resignation.'

'Don't blame you, son.' Digging a business card out of his jacket pocket, Carlyle offered it to the boy. 'In the meantime, if you hear anything . . .'

'Let you know, yeah, yeah.' Melville took the card, staring at the numbers as if trying to memorize them by heart. 'That's just what Bernie told me.'

'Yeah, well . . .' He was used to being beaten to the punch by the journalist but it was still more than a little tedious.

Satisfied that he had properly processed the information, the boy slipped the card into his trouser pocket and looked up. 'I'm gonna get a job at Tesco. Start in a store then see if I can get on some kind of management trainee programme.'

'That seems like a much better bet than—' Carlyle pointed towards the dilapidated prefabricated building that looked more like a warehouse than a church – 'this place.'

'Yeah,' said Melville with feeling. 'I've come to the conclusion that the Christian Salvation Centre is a bit of a con, really.'

'You don't say.'

'My mum likes it an' all, but why so many people hand over their cash to Elma is beyond me.'

'In my experience,' the inspector sighed, 'people do strange things.' He started walking slowly down the road. 'Anyway, good luck.' Upping the pace, he scanned the horizon, keeping a careful watch for any loitering zombies.

Thanks to a defective train which had broken down near Clapham Junction, reducing train speeds to a crawl, it took the inspector more than two hours to make it back to the safety and security of Charing Cross. He was in a foul mood by the time he hurried up the steps and entered the police station, a mood that wasn't improved by the uncommonly jovial atmosphere that he found waiting for him inside.

'What the fuck?'

Standing on the front desk, swigging from a can of Sprite, was a man barely four feet high, dressed in white Nikes and washed-out jeans. His green T-shirt had a picture of a crown, under which was the legend *KEEP CALM AND SMOKE SOME BLOW* in white lettering. Hopping from foot to foot, the midget was dancing to a silent beat that only he could hear, clearly enjoying his newly found role as impromptu entertainment for the grubby and dispirited members of the public waiting in the reception area.

'What's going on, Jazz?' Carlyle asked, stepping in front of the desk.

Maradona Wilson – aka Jazz, on account of his *smooth* moves – stopped dancing and took another mouthful of lemonade. 'The usual, Inspector,' he said, looking down on Carlyle from behind the can. 'The usual.'

Sat at her computer terminal, the desk sergeant, a sour woman from Bow called Celina Roper, muttered: 'Ebert nicked him outside Ladbrokes.'

Who was Ebert? Some uniform playing at being undercover, the inspector supposed. He looked at the pint-sized pusher and tutted. 'How many bloody times is that now?'

'The man wanted some white,' Wilson observed. 'What can I say?'

'Bloody hell, Jazz,' the inspector grumbled, 'we don't need this nonsense. You should fuck off back to Tottenham, there's a much better market for crack up there. Down here, it's only tourists. They don't want that shit.'

'But people pay more down here,' the dwarf shrugged. 'It's your basic market forces at play, innit?'

Carlyle let out a long breath. What was the world coming to when even midget pushers thought they could lecture you about the economics of the bloody drugs trade? He got enough of that business school gobbledygook from his mate, Dominic Silver, a former copper turned dealer. But Dom was a one-off, a serious businessman, unlike Jazz here. 'So what are you telling me?' he asked. 'You can't buck the market?'

'That's very true.'

'The customer is always right?'

'The customer is always right,' Jazz parroted.

'Even when it's illegal?'

Jazz held up a hand. 'Don't get me started on the failure of political leadership that gives us the so-called war on drugs.'

'Okay,' Carlyle said quickly, 'I won't.'

'I'm not trying to cause you any problems here.'

'That's good to know,' the inspector said drily.

'What you've got to remember,' Jazz explained, 'is that I'm not into volume. That's where too many people go wrong. I'm focused on the bottom line, man, not the top line.'

Carlyle had no real idea what the annoying little sod was talking about. 'Good for you.'

'Profit's what counts, not turnover. Got to get the margins right.'

'Hm.'

Their effortlessly erudite banter about the profitability of the crack trade was unceremoniously interrupted by Celina Roper, who appeared from behind Jazz, waving a blue biro at Carlyle. 'The Commander's here. She wants to see you.' The sergeant pointed her pen towards the heavens. 'Third floor.'

Great, Carlyle thought, beginning to move towards the stairs before he could manage to think up a reason to head the other way. 'I'd better go and see her then. Catch you later, Jazz.'

'Sure thing, Inspector.' Wilson gave him a small bow and resumed his slow-motion dance moves.

'And remember to fuck off back to N17 as quick as you like.'

'Don't worry,' Jazz laughed, 'I'm going. The coppers are much nicer up there for a start.'

'Ha.' Reaching the top of the stairs, the inspector hesitated, before sneaking back down, heading for the basement canteen.

'I thought the desk told you I was upstairs?'

Carlyle grunted something that could not be definitively nailed as a lie.

Not waiting for an invitation, Carole Simpson pulled out the chair opposite and sat down at the canteen table. 'Bloody hell, John. Do you know how long I've been waiting? Why is it you think you can waste my time willy-nilly?'

Willy-nilly? The inspector cleared his throat in order to stifle a laugh. 'Sorry,' he told her, 'I was starving.'

The Commander did not look sympathetic.

'It's already been a hell of a day.' He shovelled another forkful of chips and beans into his mouth. 'I had to venture south of the river.'

'Poor you,' Simpson snapped, unsympathic. Staring into the middle distance, she waited for a woman to appear at her shoulder.

'Here you go, Carole.' The woman handed over a paper cup containing a peppermint tea bag and some hot water.

'Thanks.'

Still smiling, the woman placed a second cup on the table and sat down.

'Emma,' said Simpson as she blew on her tea, 'this is Inspector Carlyle. John, this is Emma Denton.'

Somewhat disconcerted by the new arrival, Carlyle set down his knife and fork. He didn't like an audience while he was eating. Grabbing a paper napkin from the table, he wiped his mouth and gave her a friendly nod.

'Emma is a Crown Prosecutor.'

I know who she is, Carlyle thought, *which is hardly surprising, given Emma Denton's fondness for sticking her face in front of TV cameras.* He must have seen her on the news at least half a dozen times in the last year or so.

'*Chief* Crown Prosecutor,' Simpson corrected herself.

Dropping her gaze, Princess Di style, Denton gave a practised, ever so slightly embarrassed smile.

Do you ever stop smiling? Carlyle wondered. He made a show of looking her up and down in best police officer fashion. A good-looking woman, but getting a bit worn around the edges.

Too many late nights, stuck in stale rooms eating takeaway pizza while ploughing through witness statements were clearly taking their toll.

'What can I do for you?'

Looking up, the Chief Crown Prosecutor flicked a stray lock of expensively dyed blonde hair away from her face. 'I want you to get me Calvin Safi.'

FORTY-SEVEN

Overcoming his modesty, Carlyle speared the last of the chips, waving the fork above his plate. 'It's a bit bloody late.'

The Chief Crown Prosecutor waited patiently for him to place the food in his mouth, chew – mouth carefully closed – and then swallow.

'Why is that?'

'When we catch up with him, which hopefully will be sooner rather than later, there will be a lot of people who want to talk to him.' Picking up his mug, the inspector shot Simpson a look of grim amusement. 'Assuming he makes it back to the Hammersmith station in one piece.'

'For Christ's sake, John,' the Commander complained, 'now is not the time for your bloody—'

'For my what?' Carlyle snapped. Holding the mug in front of his face, he gripped the handle tightly. He was tired and he was pissed off, and in no mood to kiss some prosecutor's arse just to appease his boss. 'For my bad attitude?'

A couple of uniforms passing the table, their trays laden with food, exchanged a knowing look. The station's resident chippy bastard was going off on one again; in front of the brass, to boot. It was no wonder that the stupid sod had never managed to make it beyond inspector.

'I was going to say,' Simpson said sharply, 'that now is not the time for your vigilante tendencies.'

Keeping her eyes on the inspector, Denton said nothing.

Glowering, Carlyle waited until the two uniforms had moved on, plumping for a table beyond eavesdropping distance. Placing his mug back down, he leaned forward, lowering his voice, just to be on the safe side. 'A cop died last night. I found him. Whatever happens to Calvi before he makes it into custody, he deserves it.'

Denton gave him a patronizing look. *You are being grossly unprofessional* was the message. 'So, what you are saying is—'

'I am not saying anything,' Carlyle hissed, cutting her short with an angry wave of his hand. 'This is a murder investigation. A lot of people want to get their hands on the guy. There are protocols and procedures to be followed. If it is down to me, I can assure you that this will be handled properly, but you'll have to wait your turn.'

Glancing at Simpson, Denton fiddled with a button on her expensive-looking leather jacket. 'I appreciate that, Inspector,' she said calmly, 'but I want you to be aware of the big picture here.' Carlyle began to protest but now it was her turn to cut him off. 'The Commander tells me that, despite some presentational issues . . .'

Presentational issues? Carlyle looked at his boss. Sipping her tea demurely, Simpson did not meet his eye.

'. . . you are a very motivated and principled colleague.'

'Depends on what your principles are,' Carlyle muttered.

'And,' Denton continued, 'that this is particularly the case in situations involving children and young adults.'

Don't try and butter me up. 'So?'

'I need to speak to Mr Calvi about matters that go far beyond the murder of Sergeant Adrian Napper. It is extremely important for us that he *is* taken safely into custody and processed properly so that I can do this. However, I assure you that it will not – in any way – negatively impact the Napper investigation.'

'What could be more of a priority than Napper?' Carlyle asked, genuinely wanting to know.

'Calvin Safi is part of a network of men around the country

who we know are involved in the grooming and sexual exploitation of young girls,' Denton explained, keeping her voice even. 'These are primarily cases of white girls being exploited by Asian men.'

'So you can see,' Simpson interjected, 'why the whole thing is so delicate.'

'Last month,' Denton went on, 'three men were convicted of raping or assaulting four drunken young women in Blackburn. Another three are awaiting trial in Middlesbrough on similar offences. Last year, there was the case of seventeen-year-old Lisa Evans who was stabbed twenty-two times and thrown into a canal near Sheffield. For six years, social services had her on an "at risk" register. The man convicted of her murder admitted paying her for sex with cigarettes when she was just fourteen. And I've got testimony from girls as young as twelve, being sent fifty text messages a day from men pestering them for sex.'

Enough already. Feeling somewhat sick, Carlyle took a deep breath and said, 'So men can be total bastards – tell me something I don't know.'

'Yes, but as Carole says, there is rather more to it than that; in all of these cases, the girls are white. And all the men are Asian.'

The inspector thought back to the kebab shop and the man with the tattoo. 'There's at least one white guy who hangs around the Persian Palace.'

'All I'm saying,' Denton persisted, 'is that there are definitely cultural issues at play here.'

'Cultural issues?'

'That's the polite way of putting it. We are tiptoeing through a minefield of race relations and political correctness here. Trying to be as anodyne about it as possible, it seems to me incontrovertible that the status of women in some social groups contributes to an environment where some men think that they can do what they like without any regards for either the law or any kind of moral standards.'

'You know just as well as I do,' Simpson chipped in, 'that there is exploitation and abuse in all parts of society. However, if nothing else, there is a growing body of evidence that group grooming is a particular problem with regard to Asian men.'

'Unlike other offenders,' Denton said, 'these guys don't act on their own. And we have a growing amount of evidence that groups around the country are linked up. It's a kind of social network for abusers. Sometimes they exchange videos; sometimes they exchange girls.'

'Okay, okay,' Carlyle sighed. 'I get the message. We have to multi-task on Calvin Safi. What do you want me to do?'

'When you find him, bring him to me first. I will only have a small window of opportunity before it becomes widely known that we have him and everyone else goes to ground. I want to see if I can use that time to bring some of those other bastards down with him.'

'*If* I find him,' Carlyle corrected her. 'It's not like I'm the only one looking for the little shit.'

Denton's smile grew wider. Taking a slip of paper from the pocket of her jacket, she passed it across to him. 'Yes, but as of right now, you are the only one who knows where he is.'

Carlyle looked at the piece of paper.

'There's the address. It's accurate information – somewhere in the Midlands.'

Carlyle grunted. Arguably, having to flee to Birmingham was a rather worse fate than being sent to jail.

'Go and collect him. Then bring him to me.'

'Okay.' Without asking where it had come from, the inspector shoved the address into his pocket.

'Don't worry,' Denton reassured him, 'I won't keep him for long. I'll make sure that Hammersmith gets him in good time, and in good order – after I've had the chance to speak to him.'

As he reached the third floor, Carlyle felt his mobile start to vibrate in his hand. Looking at the screen he saw the number of

DI Ron Flux. 'Not now,' he pleaded, letting the call go to voice-mail. Looking up, he could see Umar sitting at his desk across the room, bashing away at his keyboard while munching on a sandwich. *Good to know you're still alive*, the inspector thought unkindly.

Engrossed in whatever was on the screen, the sergeant didn't look up when Carlyle approached the desk.

'You could have bloody called.'

'Sorry?' Finishing his email, Umar hit send, closed Outlook and looked up.

Scowling, Carlyle folded his arms as he came to a stop next to the monitor. 'Where the hell have you been?' he demanded.

Umar arched an eyebrow. 'Nice to see you too.'

'I was beginning to wonder if someone had stabbed you with a knife and stuffed you in a fridge.'

'Yuk.' Umar placed the remains of his sandwich on a napkin lying on the desk beside the keyboard. 'I heard about that. Poor bastard – Napper seemed like a nice bloke.'

'A poor bastard who paid the price for going off on his own and not telling his boss what he was up to.'

'You knew what I was up to,' Umar protested. 'Anyway, if it was a big deal, you could always have given me a call.'

'I tried.' In Carlyle's pocket, the mobile started vibrating again. It would be his voicemail offering up Flux's message. Ignoring it, he glanced at the sergeant's monitor. On the screen was a page from a gossip site, featuring a story about the divorce of some celebrity he'd never heard of. *Ah well*, the inspector thought, *at least it's not online dating.*

Umar was now bringing up another story, concerning a blind grandfather who had been tasered by a pair of police officers who mistook his white stick for a Samurai sword. He pointed at the screen. 'Did you see this?'

'Yeah,' Carlyle said. 'What a joke.'

'I know those guys,' Umar laughed. 'We did our training together.'

'It's no wonder they're still constables. Just as well they only had tasers. Imagine if they'd shot the bloke.' Carlyle frowned, 'Anyway, I thought only firearms specialists could use them.'

'Nah,' Umar shook his head. 'That was before.'

'Before what?'

'Before they sent everyone on a training course.'

'I didn't get sent on a course,' Carlyle complained.

'Well, not everyone, but a lot of people. I went on one. It was good fun.'

'Did you get tasered yourself?' The inspector smiled maliciously at the thought of it. 'To see what it was like?'

'No chance,' Umar scoffed. 'No one's going to fire fifty thousand volts at me.'

'I always said that you were a smart boy.'

Umar ignored his boss's sarcasm. 'Have they caught the guy who killed Napper yet?' he asked, finally getting back to the matter in hand.

'Funny you should mention that,' said Carlyle. 'That's what we're off to do right now.'

Umar glanced at the remains of his sandwich. 'We?'

'That's right, super-sleuth. Go get a car and meet me outside in ten minutes.'

A wicked grin crossed Umar's face. 'Shall we take a taser with us? We've got a bunch of them downstairs.'

Carlyle thought about it for a moment. 'Up to you,' he decided. 'Can't do any harm, can it? Just make sure that you don't go using it on the wrong bloke.'

FORTY-EIGHT

Stuck in a line of slowly moving traffic, Umar peered out through the grimy windscreen, trying to work out which lane they needed.

'Is that it?' he asked, pointing at a large sign that simply said THE NORTH.

'I suppose so.' A pained expression crossed the inspector's face. The further they edged away from Central London, the more he felt his humour drain away.

Umar squinted as they approached the sign. 'Not very informative, is it?'

Tells me all I need to know, Carlyle thought grimly.

'I guess it must be the right lane.' The sergeant pointed at another sign nearby. 'It's not as if we want to go to Oxford, is it?'

'No.' Carlyle had no idea, either way.

'This traffic is lousy.'

'Just as well we're not in a hurry.'

'Eh?'

Carlyle looked at Umar, his face scrunched up like a little old man as he gazed into the middle distance, and said, 'You need to get your eyes tested.'

'You can drive if you want.'

'No, thanks.' Carlyle tried to remember the last time he'd been behind the wheel of a motor car. Driving simply wasn't his thing. Living and working in Central London, he didn't have much need for a motor. Most of the time, a car was a liability. And he found driving incredibly stressful; most people seemed to use it as an opportunity to unleash their inner idiot. When it came to his police work, it was a chore that he was invariably happy to leave to others. After opening the window to expel the stale air inside the vehicle, he reached for the glove compartment. 'Was this shit-heap all you could get?'

'Yeah,' Umar shrugged. 'Not much of a choice.'

'There never is,' Carlyle groused.

'Three of our cars were involved in accidents last week, so we were lucky to get anything.'

'How is that possible? This is a city where the average traffic speed is less than ten miles an hour. Cars move at the speed of chickens.' Pulling out a battered road map, he slammed the compartment door shut. 'We're supposed to be the police. How the hell do we manage to have so many bloody accidents?'

A gap opened up in front of them and Umar clumsily manoeuvred into the correct lane. 'Chickens?' he sniggered.

'I read somewhere that the average speed of a running chicken – apparently – is about ten miles an hour, the same as a car in London or maybe even a bit faster.'

'And who the hell measures something like that?' Umar asked as they edged forward at a speed considerably below 10mph.

'Dunno.' The inspector watched fumes spewing from the exhaust of a black cab in front of them, cursed and wound his window most of the way back up. 'The Department of Transport, I suppose.'

'No, no, no,' Umar chortled. 'Not the traffic – the chickens. Why would anyone want to measure the speed a chicken runs at? What's the point of that?'

Carlyle thought about it for a moment. 'That is a very good question,' he grinned, 'but one for which there is no immediately obvious answer.'

'Christ Almighty,' Umar said. 'I imagine being some poor scientist who has to measure running chickens. How do you make them run in straight lines, for a start?'

'Do they have to run in straight lines?'

'I dunno. You'd have thought so. Anyway, chicken analyst – that's got to be an even worse job than ours.'

'I wouldn't be so sure of that.' Carlyle shifted in his seat. 'By the way, did you get the taser?'

'It's in the boot.'

'You can give me a lesson later on. I feel I've been missing out when it comes to handling the latest in police technology.'

'It's not a toy,' Umar warned him.

'No, no, of course not.'

'I had to sign it out.'

'Yes.'

'If anything goes wrong, I'm responsible.'

Don't be such a tart. 'Yes.' Gazing out of the window, the inspector was mesmerized by the sight of a woman wobbling along the inside lane on one of the mayor's hire bikes. 'But that doesn't mean you can't show me the basics. It's good to learn new tricks.'

'Mm.' Still hunched over the wheel, Umar seemed less than convinced.

'Don't worry,' his boss said soothingly, 'I'll be careful with it.' All too predictably, a single-decker bus cut in front of the cyclist, almost sending her into the gutter, face first. *It's a miracle that more people don't die on those things*, Carlyle thought. *Or maybe they do, and no one notices.* He vaguely remembered reading a piece a few months earlier in the *Standard* that claimed on Oxford Street alone a dozen or so cyclists died in accidents each year. One person a month – on one street. And no one batted an eyelid. As far as Carlyle could see, more and more people were getting on bikes. Therefore, more people would die. It stood to reason. For sure, you would never see *him* cycling around London. It was way too dangerous. He did not have a death wish – unlike the woman in the inside lane. 'How much does a taser cost, anyway?'

'Dunno.' Umar shrugged. 'Seven, eight hundred quid.'

'Bargain.'

'Although knowing the police force,' Umar added, 'they probably managed to hook up with some supplier who let them have a job lot at a grand and a half each.'

'That wouldn't surprise me in the slightest,' Carlyle reflected. 'We're very good at wasting taxpayers' money.' He watched as another bus went past. Once again, the woman cyclist was almost run over. After a few more seconds of precarious wobbling, she was finally forced to give up the fight. To his considerable relief, Carlyle watched her dismount, haul the bike onto the pavement and start pushing it along the street in search of a docking station.

Wise move. Unfolding the map, the inspector tried to work out the route that they needed to take. After a few moments, he realized that he was wasting his time. A Chinese subway map would have made more sense to him than the mass of lines swimming in front of his face.

'What are you doing?' Reaching forward, Umar tapped a small screen that was stuck to the car's dashboard. 'Type in where we're going and that will show you the way.'

Trying to refold the map, the inspector looked at the Sat Nav suspiciously. 'Isn't that the kind of thing that tells you to drive off a cliff?'

'Don't be such a bloody dinosaur,' Umar laughed.

'Me?' Carlyle protested.

'These things are very handy,' Umar told him. 'And somehow, I think that the computer will prove to be a much more reliable guide than you.'

'Okay, okay,' Carlyle sighed, 'the technology wins.' Unable to get the map back into a reasonable shape, he tossed it over his shoulder towards the back seat, where it joined a selection of old newspapers, plastic bottles and other rubbish that had been kindly left by the car's previous occupants. 'I suppose we might as well give it a go. Just don't blame me if we end up in a river or something.'

* * *

After fighting their way out of London, they headed north on the M40, stopping for a comfort break at the Cherwell Valley services. Car journeys made the inspector nauseous and he was extremely glad for the chance of some fresh air. Standing in the car park with a Coke and a Mars Bar, he let his mind go blank as he contemplated the names on the procession of lorries heading north.

Eddie Stobart.

Willi Betz.

Tillers Turf.

Good God, he thought, shaking himself from his daze, *you're turning into a bloody lorry spotter – assuming such people exist.*

After a while, Umar appeared at his shoulder, his hand deep in a bag of crisps. 'Want one?'

Carlyle thought about it for a moment. 'What flavour?'

'Cheese and onion.'

Urgh. Deal-breaker. The inspector was a strictly salt and vinegar man. 'Nah. Thanks all the same.'

'Suit yourself.' Umar shoved another handful of crisps into his mouth and began munching happily.

Carlyle downed the last of his cola and looked around in vain for a bin. 'What do you make of all this stuff?'

'What?' Umar asked. 'You mean the group grooming business?'

'Yeah.' Carlyle frowned. *Why were there no bins? What was wrong with this country?* Doubtless it was some kind of security measure. *What was he supposed to do with his rubbish? Eat it?*

'It's a grim business,' Umar replied, staring at his crisps.

'Mm.' Resisting the urge to toss his litter onto the tarmac, the inspector stuffed the Mars wrapper into the can, which he then crumpled in his hand. 'But do you think it's a cultural thing? Or is this another monster Met fuck-up in waiting? Will we be hailed as the protectors of young girls, or vilified as racist bastards?' He thought about it further for a moment. 'Or, indeed, both?'

'How should I know?' Umar said, tipping back his head and pouring the last of the crisps down his throat.

'No?'

'No,' Umar repeated. 'You can't have a view on everything, you know. Well, not unless you're a politician, of course.'

Carlyle made a face. 'I would have thought you'd have a bit more of a view on this one – at least, more of a view than me.'

'Why?' Umar frowned. 'Because I'm half-Asian?'

Uh oh. Wishing now that he'd never raised the subject, the inspector said awkwardly, 'Yeah, I suppose.'

'Hardly,' Umar told him. 'I'm from Manchester. Whatever you might think down here, we came into the twenty-first century at exactly the same time that you London buggers did.'

'I know, but—'

'Just because my mother's Asian,' the sergeant continued, 'it doesn't mean that I have any particular *insight* into the thinking of some Asian men who happen to be criminals. I'm British. I don't have any of the kind of so-called "cultural baggage" that we're talking about here. Who knows what those guys are thinking? And really, who cares? As far as I can see, they're not *Asian* dickheads. They're just dickheads.'

It was just a bloody question.

Reading the irritation in his boss's face, Umar softened his tone. 'Look,' he said evenly, 'I understand the theory. But I wouldn't get too hung up on why bad people do bad things. All we need to worry about is how we stop them from getting away with it.'

'Fair point,' Carlyle conceded.

The sergeant did a little jig on the tarmac. 'And we're going to get those fuckers *good*.'

'Well, if we're to do it any time soon, we should get going.'

'Yeah. Fair enough.' Umar held out a hand. 'Gimme your rubbish and I'll go and find a bin.'

Back on the road, Umar took a few minutes to talk his boss through the situation with Melissa Graham, the naked bike rider with the dead boyfriend.

'Sounds like she did it,' was the inspector's only response as he stared out of the window at the bland countryside speeding by at something greater than seventy miles an hour. 'What about the other guy – the one who was stabbed on the Strand?'

Umar drummed his fingers on the steering wheel as he tried to recall the name. 'Bradley something . . .'

'Yeah. Presumably your girl didn't kill *him*.'

'She's not *my* girl,' Umar objected.

'Yeah, right,' Carlyle snorted. 'Your interest is purely professional and nothing to do with the fact that she looks good naked.'

Umar steered the car into the outside lane and accelerated past a dawdling Skoda. 'How do you know she looks good?'

'Ha,' Carlyle cackled. 'So you're saying that she doesn't?'

'She certainly didn't kill Bradley Saffron,' said Umar, finally remembering the victim's surname.

'Well, it's like Meatloaf said,' Carlyle mused, 'two out of three ain't bad.'

'Eh?' Umar glanced into the rearview mirror as the Skoda retreated into the distance behind them.

'Never mind.'

'I never do,' the sergeant observed, slipping back into the middle lane.

'The great pushbike palaver,' Carlyle said, stifling a yawn, 'is most definitely not our problem.'

'No, but—'

'Leave it to Shames and Postic,' the inspector said firmly. Reaching forward, he tapped the Sat Nav screen. 'Is that thing working? It looks to me as if it says we're heading for France.'

'Like I said, you're a bloody dinosaur.' Umar gave a resigned sigh. 'Don't worry, we're right on track.'

FORTY-NINE

'Okay, according to the computer, this is it.' Pulling over to the kerb, Umar brought the car to a halt.

'Thank God for that,' Carlyle groaned. 'I thought we were never going to make it.'

Umar glanced at his watch. 'We didn't do that badly.'

'Bloody machine. We almost ended up in Wolverhampton. That would have been a fate worse than death.' Unlocking his seatbelt, the inspector looked through the windscreen with dismay. In front of them was an empty street straight out of a 1960s kitchen-sink drama, lined on each side by a row of two-storey redbrick terraced houses for which the word 'modest' might have been invented. Out of a nearby side street appeared a stray dog of some description. It looked inquisitively at the two policemen before cocking its leg against a rusting lamppost and going about its business.

'Welcome to the real world,' Umar muttered.

The inspector felt an immense reluctance to get out of the car. 'Where precisely are we?'

Umar pointed at a street sign on the wall of a house on the far side of the road. 'Powke Street. Cradley Heath.'

'That doesn't tell me much,' Carlyle objected. 'Anyway, come on, let's go and find the address that Denton gave us.' He pulled out the slip of paper the Prosecutor had given him and unfolded it. 'Uncle Didier's. 147–149 Puke Street.' Stuffing the paper back in his pocket, he pushed open the car door. 'It's some kind of takeaway joint.'

Struggling out of the car, Carlyle stretched, yawning as he looked up and down the street. To his right, maybe two hundred yards away, was what looked like a small cluster of shops that had been plonked between the houses in an apparently random fashion. He squinted but they were too far away for him to be able to work out what they were. Patting his jacket pockets, he tried to find his glasses. Coming up empty, he tried again, checking more carefully this time. The end result, however, was the same: no spectacles. *Shit.*

'Left your specs at the station again?' The sergeant opened up the boot.

Just you wait till your eyesight starts going. The inspector pointed in the direction he had been looking. 'It'll be down there – let's go take a look.'

Slamming the boot shut, Umar slung a grubby-looking backpack over his shoulder and fell into step with his boss.

'What's that?' Carlyle asked as they headed down the road.

'Got the taser in there,' Umar said.

Carlyle grunted. He had forgotten all about the device.

'So what's the plan?' Umar asked.

'The plan,' Carlyle said decisively, 'is to get something to eat. I'm absolutely starving. We can nick the little scrote after lunch.'

On first glance, Uncle Didier's was a pretty good facsimile of the Persian Palace back in Shepherd's Bush Green. As they got closer, Carlyle could make out a handwritten sign in the window offering Burgers – Kebabs – Chips. Apart from an acne-ridden girl behind the counter, the place was empty.

The look on Umar's face suggested he considered it no more appetizing than his boss. 'What do you fancy?'

Next door to Didier's was a bookmaker's and then a launderette, followed by a grocery store. Next to the grocer was another café. It didn't look up to much but it looked better than Didier's. 'Let's try that place,' the inspector said.

'Fine by me.'

Carlyle walked along the pavement, then stopped at the door of the café to let an old woman with a shopping trolley shuffle out. As he did so, he looked up. Thirty yards further down the road, a familiar figure turned out of a side street and strolled towards them, head down, a carrier bag in each hand. 'Fuck me,' he breathed.

'Language, language,' the woman scolded him, in a broad Black Country accent.

Ignoring the unhappy granny, Carlyle half-turned towards Umar. 'That's our man,' he hissed, gesturing down the road.

'Shit.' Slipping the bag from his shoulder, Umar fumbled inside for a moment, before pulling out the taser.

'Hey,' the woman squawked. 'Is that a gun? What you doin'?' She took a half-step backwards, towards the sanctuary of the café. 'Put that thing away. I'm going to call the police.'

'We *are* the police, madam,' Carlyle said wearily, his gaze still fixed on his approaching prey. 'There's nothing to worry about here. Please be on your way.' At that moment, Calvin Safi looked up. Recognizing the inspector, he stopped in his tracks. For a heartbeat, he pondered his options, before dropping his bags, swivelling round and fleeing in the direction from which he had come.

'He's legging it!' Carlyle shouted, stating the obvious as he rocked back on his heels. 'Get after him.'

Umar set off down the road, arms pumping. *Nice technique*, Carlyle thought, happy that he didn't have to bust a gut himself in pursuit of their prey. Pulling out his warrant card, he flashed it at the woman. 'Sorry about that,' he said, belatedly trying to inject some warmth into his voice. 'That man is a wanted criminal. But don't fret, we'll have him apprehended in a minute.'

The woman scanned his ID. 'So you're a policeman, then?' she said.

'Yes,' Carlyle tried to smile.

The woman pointed in the direction of the fleeing suspect. 'Shouldn't you be getting after him, then?'

* * *

Confident in his colleague's abilities, Carlyle set off at a leisurely pace. By the time he caught up with the pair of them, Umar had Safi face down on the Tarmac with his hands behind his back.

'Nice of you to join us.' The sergeant snapped a pair of Safariland speedcuffs on to the suspect's wrists.

'I knew you had it well under control.' Looking down at the prostrate man, Carlyle noticed a gash on his forehead. 'What happened?'

'He tripped and fell,' Umar explained.

'He shot me,' Safi whined. 'The bastard *shot* me.'

Umar pointed at the taser lying on the road. 'It worked a treat.'

'It's police brutality,' Safi cried, his voice rising an octave, 'pure and simple.'

'You ain't seen nothing yet,' the inspector muttered grimly. Standing over the fellow, he had to resist the temptation to give him a hard kick in the ribs. He could feel his mood darkening faster than a November night in Glasgow. 'Shut the fuck up, you little shit, or I'll show you what police brutality really is.' Out of the corner of his eye, he noticed a couple of young boys on bikes twenty yards down the road who had stopped to see what was going on. Stepping forward, he waved them away angrily, shouting, 'Fuck off.' Reluctantly, they did as requested. Watching them disappear round a corner, he turned to Umar. 'Let's go. Get him up.'

Swallowing a mouthful of pasta, Umar gestured out of the window with his fork. 'Do you think we should leave him there?'

Carlyle looked at Calvin Safi, who was standing on the pavement, handcuffed to a lamppost, looking suitably pissed off. 'We won't be long.'

'But what if someone sees?'

Carlyle considered the empty streets. The old lady was long gone. Even the stray dog had disappeared. Nothing moved. Calvi's shopping bags remained where he had left them, untouched on the pavement. 'Like who?'

'What if some of his mates turn up?' Umar persisted.

'Okay, okay,' Carlyle sighed. 'You go and put him in the car and I'll pay the bill.' Discarding the last of his cheese toastie, he watched the sergeant release Calvin Safi from the lamppost and march him across the road towards the car. Taking his mobile from his pocket, he pulled up Flux's number. After a moment's hesitation, he hit call.

The Detective Inspector answered on the third ring. 'I've been trying to get hold of you,' he said gruffly.

'I've got Safi.'

'Where is he?'

'He was holed up in a place in the Midlands. We're bringing him back to London now.'

'When will you get here?'

The inspector paused.

'Carlyle?'

'Look, I just wanted to give you a heads-up. Don't lose your rag but we're not bringing him back to Hammersmith.'

'You've got to be joking.'

The inspector could hear the desperation and frustration in his colleague's voice. Watching Umar carefully deposit Safi into the back of the Focus, he slowly explained the deal that he had struck with Chief Crown Prosecutor Emma Denton.

'But that bastard – he's mine.' Flux was almost pleading. 'Who is this woman?'

'She's the one who found Safi,' Carlyle said firmly. 'She needs to talk to him. Then he will get handed over to us. I will make sure you get your hands on him as quickly as possible.'

'It's not right.'

Maybe this job is getting too much for you, Carlyle thought. 'Denton found him,' he repeated. 'Otherwise, the little wanker would still be in the wind.'

'How did she know where he was hiding?'

'No idea. Does it matter? We're all on the same side here.'

'*Fu-uck.*'

Carlyle pictured Flux pacing up and down some corridor in Hammersmith station, trying to pull out his non-existent hair.

'I went to see Napper's girlfriend and his mum. That was a real barrel of laughs.'

'I'm sure.' The inspector tried to sound sympathetic but he was already bored with his colleague's whining.

'I promised them that we'd get this guy.'

'And we have got him.'

'But I promised them that *I'd* get him.'

'It's a team game,' Carlyle said flatly. 'Anyway, when it comes to it, we can give them an alternative version of events if it's going to make them feel better.' Looking up, he saw Umar glaring at him through the window. Gesturing that he would be a minute longer, Carlyle got to his feet.

'How long is it going to take you to get back?' Flux asked.

'Depends if we get lost again,' Carlyle laughed.

'Which route will you be taking?'

The inspector thought about it for a moment. 'We came up the M40, with a stop at Cherwell Valley.'

'Hm. That makes sense.'

'I reckon that we should be back at the services in a couple of hours.'

'Okay. Good.'

'Give or take.' Fishing some money out of his pocket, the inspector went over to the counter. After picking out a couple of doughnuts for the journey, he paid the woman at the till, before dropping the change into the otherwise empty tips jar.

'We found blood in various locations inside the Persian Palace,' Flux continued.

Smiling at the woman, the inspector turned and headed for the door. 'Napper's?'

'No. We think it might belong to one of the missing girls. If we're lucky, it's from Sandra Middlemass and we can link the body to the shop. Even if it's just from Jade Jones it still gives us proof that these wankers were locking the girls up.'

'Yes.'

'There was also some blood in the yard.'

'That'll be Safi's,' he said. *The same as on the toe of my boot.*

'How would you know that?'

Ignoring the question, the inspector stopped at the door. 'Any news on the sidekick?' he asked, changing the subject.

'Metcalf? Not yet. But he knows that the net's closing. He didn't turn up for work today.'

'Where does he work?'

'He's a driver for London Underground. Normally works on the Central Line.'

'One of Sam Reilly's finest,' Carlyle quipped, referring to London's last great union boss – a man so talented that he could keep his members in lucrative jobs almost fifty years after technology had – in theory, at least – made them all redundant. Despite introducing 'driverless' trains in 1968, when the Victoria Line was opened, London Underground was still paying out around £150 million a year in drivers' salaries, with the bonus of regular strikes thrown in for free.

'Yes, indeed,' Flux said tiredly. 'Let's hope we don't find ourselves in the middle of an industrial dispute. We don't want the union arguing that we're trying to victimize one of their members.'

'Yeah,' Carlyle grinned as he stepped out on to the street. 'That would be just our luck. But let's cross that bridge when we get to it. We have to find the bugger first.'

'Calvin might know where he is.'

'He hasn't had much to say for himself, so far,' Carlyle replied. Crossing the road, he glanced over at Uncle Didier's. The place still looked dead. If it was another nest of perverts, none of them were intent on riding to Safi's rescue. 'If we get anything out of him on the road, I'll call you straight away.'

'Thanks. Appreciate it. See you soon.'

I'm sure I will, Carlyle thought as he pulled open the car door.

FIFTY

Umar gave the inspector a quizzical look as he slipped into the passenger seat. '*Another* bloody cake?'

Carlyle tossed the paper bag containing the two iced doughnuts on to the dashboard. 'It's a long way back.'

Sticking the car into gear, the sergeant tutted as he pulled away from the kerb. 'It's no wonder you're so unfit.'

'Me?' Carlyle protested. 'Unfit?' Stung by his underling's observation, he tried to recall the last time he had visited the gym. It certainly wasn't any time in the last month. A vague sense of shame washed over him.

Taking one hand off the steering wheel, Umar jerked a thumb at their passenger. 'If it hadn't been for me, he'd be halfway to Dudley by now. You'd never have caught him.'

'Of course I would,' Carlyle lied.

From the back seat, the prisoner piped up: 'He beat me up, you know.'

'Yeah, yeah,' Carlyle snorted. 'You told me.'

'Gave me a shock.'

Umar glanced in the rearview mirror. 'Shouldn't have run away then, should you?'

'My lawyer will get you for this.'

'Look,' Carlyle snapped, 'you have been arrested for abduction, rape and murder. You killed a policeman. I don't really think your human rights are going to be too much of a priority here.'

'It wasn't me who killed that copper,' Safi bleated, leaning forward so that his head appeared between the front seats. 'It was Steve Metcalf.'

Carlyle looked at Umar. 'The guy with the tattoo?'

'Yeah, that's right.'

'So where is he?'

'I dunno.'

The inspector shook his head. 'Not much use then, are you? If you've got nothing to say, why don't you just shut up and enjoy the ride?'

Safi slumped back in his seat. 'I need a piss.'

'You'll have to wait,' Carlyle said heartlessly, as Umar pulled out of Powke Street, heading for the motorway.

'But—'

'Look,' the inspector said firmly, 'if you piss on the seat, you really will be a victim of police brutality.'

An accident near Bishop's Tachbrook had closed one of the southbound lanes on the motorway, slowing their progress to a crawl for more than twenty miles. By the time they reached the service station at Cherwell Valley, Safi was crying from the discomfort caused by his aching bladder. When the inspector finally opened the back door, the prisoner shot out of the car in search of a toilet.

'Just as well he didn't run that fast when you were chasing him,' Carlyle mused.

Umar yawned. 'I'd still have caught him, no problem.'

Rushing towards the entrance, Safi swerved past a granny and almost ran head-first into a bloke carrying a tray of drinks. 'I hope he makes it in time,' Carlyle chuckled.

'Yeah,' Umar agreed. 'It can be tricky when you've got hand-cuffs on.'

'Hm.'

'Anyway, I don't want that stink in the back all the way home.'

'If he pisses himself, he goes in the boot.'

246

'That's the great thing about you, Inspector,' Umar chuckled, 'you're all heart.'

'So they tell me,' Carlyle smirked as he watched their prisoner disappear inside the service station. 'Anyway, I'll go with him, make sure he doesn't try and do a runner. You go and get some drinks. I'll have a green tea.'

Inside, it was clear that the southbound facilities were laid out in the exact same way as those on the other side of the motorway: newsagent and mini-market to your left, café to your right, with the bogs straight ahead. The place was moderately busy, but not heaving. It was an unremarkable weekday afternoon with normal people going about their normal business. As he walked through the foyer, Carlyle did not break stride as he gave Flux the slightest of nods. The Detective Inspector was standing by a kiosk selling breakdown insurance. Next to him stood a tall, well-developed bloke with a vacant expression who may or may not have been a fellow police officer. Either way, Carlyle had never seen the guy before. Flux put down the leaflet he had been holding and said something to his acquaintance, who nodded and set off for the toilets.

Here we go. The gents was empty, apart from a guy washing his hands and a cleaner who was mopping the floor with disinfectant. Carlyle stepped up to a long row of urinals and unzipped himself.

'Aahh . . .'

Aiming at the small yellow chemical cube, the inspector heard the cleaner being ordered out. There was the sound of one, two, three hand-dryers springing into action, over which he could just make out footsteps squeaking on the freshly washed floor, followed by the sound of a cubical door being kicked in. There was a scream . . . then a series of grunts and groans.

Tuning out Safi's protests, Carlyle gave himself a shake and zipped up his jeans. Stepping over to the wash basins, he passed Flux who was standing, arms folded, next to a yellow sign on

247

the floor that read: *Sorry. Closed for cleaning.* A middle-aged man in a polo shirt and checked trousers walked in, read the sign and hesitated. Flux glared at him until he got the message and left.

Washing his hands, Carlyle glanced into the mirror. It was not a pretty sight. He looked old. Much too old to be hanging around in motorway service-station toilets while a suspect was given a good beating. The dryer in front of him died as he stuck his hands in it; irritated, he hit the button and it roared back into life. Once his hands were a reasonable approximation of dry, he finished the job by wiping them on the backside of his jeans and stepped back outside. Scanning the café, he found Umar, stuck in a queue for the till. Two minutes later, Flux appeared at his shoulder.

'We're done. Thanks.'

'No problem,' Carlyle mumbled, then counted to ten before looking up. Flux and his henchman had already disappeared.

'What was that all about?' Umar asked, coming over.

'I'll explain later.' Carlyle glanced at the cardboard tray his sergeant was holding. It contained three cups. 'You didn't get that muppet a drink, did you?'

'Well,' Umar shrugged, 'it seemed a bit unfair not to.'

The inspector whistled out a breath. 'Sometimes, you're just too soft.' He noticed the paper bag in Umar's other hand. 'I suppose you got him something to eat as well?'

Ignoring the question, Umar looked over his shoulder, towards the toilets. 'Where is he, anyway?'

'Enjoying his last moments as a free man,' Carlyle grinned. 'I'll go and get him. See you back at the car.'

FIFTY-ONE

'What the hell happened?'

Emma Denton fiddled nervously with the top button on her Chanel jacket as her gaze moved from Umar, to Carlyle and back to Calvin Safi.

Carlyle looked up at the clock on the interview-room wall. He knew that he would have to take some flak, but time was pressing. Safi looked a mess, but not that much of a mess. The full extent of his beating wouldn't become apparent until he got to see a doctor – which, hopefully, wouldn't be for a while yet.

'Well?' the Chief Crown Prosecutor demanded.

'They hit me,' Safi complained. 'Shot me with a stun gun. Bloody *e-lectro-cuted* me. Chained me to a lamppost while they ate their lunch. And then . . . then they let the other guys hit me, too.'

Denton's frown deepened.

Realizing that his boss was not going to immediately respond to the prisoner's all too justifiable complaints, Umar let out a nervous cough.

Denton looked at him expectantly.

'Mr Safi fell and hit his face while trying to run away,' the sergeant said finally, adopting his most official tone. 'Despite making repeated, violent attempts to resist arrest, he was eventually apprehended and restrained in the appropriate manner, in line with official regulations and protocols. Then he was brought directly here, to Charing Cross, as per your instructions, ma'am.'

Ma'am? I'm not the bloody Queen, you know. Trying to suppress a smile, Denton sucked in her cheeks and raised an eyebrow. The sergeant was a good-looking guy, for a copper. It was just a shame that he was such a poor liar. 'In that case,' she enquired, 'will you be looking to press charges against Mr Safi?'

Safi began to protest but she cut him off with a raised hand.

Umar pretended to think about the question for a moment before responding. 'Under the circumstances,' he said equably, 'given all the other charges that Mr Safi is currently facing, which are far more serious than those that I have just outlined, there isn't really much point, is there?'

'Perhaps not.'

Safi stomped his foot in frustration. 'They beat me up in the toilet,' he rasped. 'It's not right.'

Denton narrowed her eyes and looked over at the inspector, who was trying, and failing, to project the image of a 1950s choirboy. 'What do you have to say about this?'

'This guy,' Carlyle said quietly, 'is an inveterate liar, a child molester and a cop killer. As my sergeant explained, he did not come quietly once we'd tracked him down. As you know, DI Ron Flux in Hammersmith is waiting to speak to Mr Safi about the death of his sergeant, Adrian Napper. The Detective Inspector was not very impressed that you wanted to speak to Mr Safi first and, frankly, I can understand his feelings. However, here is Mr Safi, as promised.' Monologue over, he got to his feet and pointed at the clock. 'Now, if you'll excuse me, I've got another appointment. I promised DI Flux that we would hand Mr Safi over to him at your earliest convenience. Umar will make sure that the prisoner is taken across to Hammersmith when you are finished with him.'

'I want a lawyer,' Safi shouted.

'That is your right,' Denton said flatly.

Carlyle adopted a pained expression. 'We have tried to reach Mr Federici – he isn't answering his phone at the moment.'

'Not him,' Safi squealed. 'He works for my wife. I need some-one else.'

'Do you have your own lawyer?' Denton asked.

'Nah,' Safi shook his head. 'But you need to get me one, don't you?' The thought cheered him and he let out a brittle cackle. 'It's the law, innit?'

Denton gave him a look that Carlyle interpreted as her itch-ing to give the little shit a good slap herself. Allowing himself a smirk, he realized that he was warming to the woman.

'You've gotta get me a lawyer,' Safi persisted, 'and he's gonna sue your arse off.'

'That will take a bit of time,' Denton said, trying to sound as calm as possible, 'but let me set the wheels in motion.'

'Good.' Safi flashed a set of chipped, yellow fangs that Carlyle had not noticed before.

'In the meantime,' Denton added primly, 'anything that you tell us of your own volition will be to your benefit.'

Looking at her suspiciously, Safi immediately shut his mouth.

Good luck with that, Carlyle thought. Reaching for the door handle, he slipped into the corridor.

Leaving the prisoner with Umar, Denton swiftly followed him outside. 'Inspector – can I have a quick word?'

Carlyle half-turned, giving her an apologetic smile. 'I really do have to go.'

'I just wanted to thank you for bringing Safi in as we agreed.'

'Ah.' Wrong-footed, he wasn't quite sure how to respond.

'I'm sure that you must have been under a lot of pressure from Flux.'

'We had a deal.' Looking past Denton's shoulder, he saw Sonia Mason come sashaying down the hallway, carrying a stack of green files. As she passed, the WPC gave him an inquisitive look. He ignored her as best he could, waiting until she had disappeared round the corner before adding, 'I did what I said I would do.'

'True,' the prosecutor continued, 'but still, I know what it's like when you're being pulled in two directions at once.'

'Mm.'

'Even so, you have to be careful. Whatever actually happened, the guy looks like he's been beaten up – quite badly, too. Lucky for you he asked for a lawyer and not a doctor.'

Rocking back on his heels, Carlyle stared at his shoes. As usual, they could do with a polish. 'There is nothing to worry about.'

'I'm not worried. I will conduct my interview with Safi right now and get him out of here as quickly as possible, before he can hook up with the duty solicitor. Flux can sort out any loose ends.'

'He'll be happy to do that.'

'Good.' The prosecutor pushed a rogue strand of hair behind her ear. 'Still, it's not clever, bringing him in like that.'

'No.'

'Commander Simpson said you had anger management issues.'

Did she now? Allowing himself a rueful smile, Carlyle gestured towards the interview room with his chin. 'I didn't lay a finger on him.'

'Carole also said something about poor impulse control.'

'Maybe she was being ironic.'

'Ha.' Denton shook her head. She was trying to look stern but her eyes sparkled with mischief. 'I don't think so. That's not really her style.'

'No, I suppose not,' Carlyle chuckled. 'Anyway, as it happens, I'm off to see a psychiatrist right now.'

'Really?' Denton failed to hold her curiosity in check. 'In a personal capacity?'

As if. 'Isn't that supposed to be confidential?' he teased her.

'Of course, of course,' she agreed. 'But either way, I hope it's useful.'

'*Either way*,' he quipped, 'I'll mention my boss's concerns about my various personality flaws; see if the shrink has got any tips.'

FIFTY-TWO

Sitting in the under-lit reception of the Doppio Clinic, Carlyle browsed a discarded copy of that morning's *Metro*. On page four of the freesheet – opposite a full-page MI6 recruitment advert inviting applicants for Security Officers – was a story about a group of Muslim extremists who had been jailed by a court in Epping Forest for encouraging attacks on British soldiers. Halfway down the story, he noted a paragraph that claimed that the four men had taken part in a protest against a rival newspaper that had published Joseph Belsky's controversial cartoon featuring the Prophet Muhammad. Amongst other things, they called for a repeat of the 7/7 bombing attacks in London and vowed to see British troops in Afghanistan coming home in body bags.

Why do they call them 'extremists'? Carlyle wondered. *'Nutters' would be more appropriate.* He thought back to his experience of growing up in London during the 1970s and 1980s. Back then, it was all about Irish terrorism. 'Northern' and 'Ireland' were, by common consent, the two most boring words in the English language. At that time, the man in the street had never even heard of Islam, and Holy Wars were confined to the history books.

Now the world seemed a much different place. IRA boss Martin McGuinness was shaking hands with the Queen, and Public Enemy No. 1 was now some bloke called Abu something-or-other. *At least the security services still had a new bunch of morons to fight. That was the thing, wasn't it? Always have a new enemy up your sleeve, ready for when the old one packs it in.*

Over the top of his newspaper he saw the door to Dr Janice Anderson's office open slightly. A small, pinched woman slipped through the gap and scuttled towards the exit. From inside the office, the door was pushed shut. The inspector returned to his paper. A few moments later, the door opened again and a woman's head popped out.

'Inspector Carlyle?' She fixed him with a professionally blank expression that suggested neither irritation nor pleasure at his presence. 'Please come in.'

Jumping to his feet, Carlyle tossed the paper onto the chair and headed inside.

With its white walls, varnished wooden floors and empty bookcases, the room was functional and rather depressing. There were three uncomfortable-looking wooden chairs facing a large wooden desk and, rather disappointingly, no couch. The desk itself was empty apart from a stack of papers, a telephone and a half-full glass of water. Behind the desk, with its back to the window, was an outsized executive leather chair.

'Take a seat.' Janice Anderson sat down on the chair behind the desk. Her dark hair, showing streaks of grey, was cut into a short bob, with a pair of tortoiseshell glasses perched on the top of her head. Wearing a black polo-neck sweater, she had a thin gold bracelet on her left wrist, and an expensive watch on her right one. All in all, it was a fairly standard casual-professional look. Reaching over, she grasped the glass of water, taking a sip to buy a little time while she eyed up her new visitor.

Listening to the comforting traffic noise outside, the inspector waited patiently for his host to ready herself. *It's a bit like the Sopranos*, he thought. *Except I'm not Tony Soprano and you're not Dr Melfi.*

'So,' she said finally, having taken his measure, 'what can I do for you? Is this business or personal?'

'Business.' Crossing his legs, Carlyle sat back in his chair. 'I have an interest in one of your patients, Taimur Rage.'

'Ah, yes, of course.'

'I spoke to a journalist called Bernie Gilmore. I believe that he has already contacted you.'

The smile wavered. 'We had a brief conversation. Mr Gilmore is a most engaging character.'

'Bernie certainly talks a good game.'

'How do you know him?' the woman asked.

'Our paths cross from time to time.'

'And what did he say about Taimur?'

He described him as a social inadequate living in a fantasy world. 'He said that Taimur was a very troubled young man and that you tried very hard to help him.'

'Hm.' Anderson glanced at her watch. 'How *precisely* can I be of assistance, Inspector? There is a limit to what I can say about a patient, even a dead patient.'

'I understand. The issue for me is that I need to put the investigation into the death of Joseph Belsky – the guy that Taimur attacked – to bed. Basically, it comes down to a difference of opinion between myself and certain colleagues as to whether Taimur could have been acting alone or whether he was part of an organized group.'

A wry smile crossed the doctor's face. 'You mean whether he was just a crazy guy or a bona fide terrorist?'

Carlyle shifted in his seat. 'Kind of.'

'Does it matter?'

Good question. 'It might.'

The therapist plucked a red and black striped pencil from her desk and started twirling it between the fingers of her right hand. 'I am happy to talk to you.'

'Thank you.'

'But only on the basis that this is all strictly off the record.'

'Of course.'

Sitting back in her chair, the shrink let out a deep breath.

'Well . . . I think it was fairly clear that Taimur lived in his own little world. His social interactions were very limited. I would be extremely surprised if he was able to function as part of any organized or even semi-organized grouping.'

'So, as far as you know, the boy was acting alone when he attacked the cartoonist?'

Nodding, Anderson let the pencil fall on to the desk. 'I would bet my practice on it. The defining event in his young life was the divorce of his parents. He was still, even after several years, hugely resentful about that, while still remaining under their sway to a surprising degree for a young adult of his age.'

Carlyle frowned. 'Under the sway of the father, you mean? Do you think Calvin Safi could have put him up to it?'

'No, no.' Anderson shook her head. 'I think you're barking up the wrong tree there. I hosted a couple of sessions for the family as a group. The father was fairly useless – he didn't even turn up to one of them. The mother, though . . .'

'Elma Reyes? I've met her a couple of times.'

'Then you'll know what I mean. To describe the lady as "forceful" would be something of an understatement.'

'Yes, Elma gets in your face all right.'

'Considering that she had kept the boy at arms' length for so long, it was interesting to see the amount of control she still exerted over him.'

That's interesting, Carlyle wondered if he had given enough thought to the importance of the mother-son relationship in his investigation. *Maybe I should go and have another chat with Elma Reyes.* 'Do you think that *she* could have put Taimur up to the attack on Belsky?' he asked.

An annoyed expression crossed the shrink's face, crumpling her forehead so that she appeared to age about thirty years. 'No. Elma runs her own Christian church. For her, it's all business. I don't really see why she would bother.'

Carlyle shrugged. 'People do strange things.'

'Don't I know it,' Anderson laughed. 'But even so. Elma was

not my patient, you understand – so ultimately, I do not have a view.'

'Of course not.'

'My comments are just observations and thoughts suited to this casual, off-the-record conversation. But my *impression* would be of an ego-driven individual with a great deal of self-control. She believes in careful planning and precise execution, in order to achieve the desired outcome in any given situation.'

'Makes sense.'

'That would make it unlikely for Elma to risk using her rather *unworldly* son to launch a violent attack on the unfortunate Mr Belsky.' A fly landed on the desk. The psychiatrist flicked it away with her hand. 'Anyway, what would be her motive? What could she possibly have against the unfortunate cartoonist?'

'Maybe she wanted Muslims to take the blame for another apparent hate crime,' Carlyle offered, realizing just how weak his words sounded as they came out of his mouth.

'I don't think so,' Anderson disagreed gently. 'As part of my preparation for the family sessions, I took a look at the Christian Salvation Centre's website.'

I should have done that, Carlyle realized.

'It doesn't say anything about Islam. To be honest, it doesn't say much about anything apart from Elma, her wonderful personality and her God-given healing powers. I would say that the woman is too self-obsessed to have any interest in hate crimes.'

'What about her husband?' Carlyle said. 'He's a Muslim. Maybe she was trying to get back at him?'

'Pfff. I would have thought that you would be at least as much of an expert on domestic disharmony as I, Inspector. If the wife wanted to manipulate the son to get revenge on the husband, why not just get Taimur to stick an axe in Calvin's head?'

'So,' Carlyle sighed, 'that brings us back to the basic question: why did Taimur do what he did?'

'Does there have to be a reason that we consider valid?'

'No, but there has to be a reason.'

'Not necessarily.' Anderson crossed her arms. 'Maybe – and let me slip into common parlance here – it's as simple as the wires in his brain got crossed that day and he went a bit off-piste.'

Crossed wires? The inspector suspected that he was being patronized but he didn't know what to do about it. Maybe he would go back and talk to the miracle-working mother anyway. The idea that he was running around chasing his tail because some lame-brained kid happened to get his wires crossed was just too depressing to accept.

'Anyway,' Anderson continued, jumping to her feet, 'common parlance or not, that's all off the record. And I have to be going.' She lifted her gaze to the door. 'So, I'm afraid that your time is up.'

'Yes, of course.' Carlyle immediately got up, happy at least that he wasn't having to pay for the session. 'Thank you very much for your time. What you had to say was very interesting.' *If totally useless. Crossed wires, indeed.*

FIFTY-THREE

Turning off Drury Lane and into Macklin Street, the inspector instantly noted the large guy with the crew cut, wearing jeans and a green Adidas tracksuit top. Standing by the front door of Winter Garden House, the block of flats where the Carlyle family lived, he was playing on his smartphone, with a cigarette dangling from his lips.

The man waited until Carlyle was almost about to pass him.

'You the policeman?' he asked, his voice a low grumble of estuary English.

Carlyle keyed in the entry code and pulled open the door. Looking up, he gave the slightest of nods. The guy must have been at least six two, maybe taller. He didn't look particularly fit, but then again, he didn't have to. All in all, he was not the kind of bloke you wanted standing outside your front door.

The inspector paused in the doorway. 'Who are you?'

The guy dropped the phone in the back pocket of his jeans, took a deep drag on his smoke and gazed down the street. 'Mr Ashton would like to have a word with you.'

At the mention of the old gangster's name, Carlyle stiffened slightly. 'So why can't he just phone me, like anyone else?' He stepped aside, holding open the door to let an elderly woman whom he didn't recognize slip between them and enter the building. 'This is the twenty-first century, after all.'

'Dunno.' Taking a final puff on his cigarette, the man flicked

259

the stub towards the gutter. 'Maybe he hasn't got your number. Anyway, he's not a big fan of mobile phones.'

'Great.' *There are more mobile phones than people in this world but Ken bloody Ashton isn't a fan.*

'He's just down the road. It won't take long.'

Carlyle looked across the road, towards Il Buffone. The old café was shuttered and closed up, like it had been for months, a board above the door still proclaiming the promise of a low rent for a new tenant. In the current economic climate, there was next to no chance of anyone taking it on. If someone was foolish enough to do so, he reckoned they would last six months, at the outside. It was a shame, but then lots of things were a shame.

Pining for a raisin Danish and a double espresso, the inspector wondered what Marcello, the old owner, was up to. Hopefully, he was sat at home in North London, enjoying a well-deserved and prosperous retirement with his wife.

'I was going to have my tea,' he mumbled, talking more to himself than anyone else. 'I need something to eat.'

'Won't take long,' the man repeated, ambling off in the direction of Drury Lane. 'C'mon. Mr Ashton doesn't like being kept waiting.'

'And I don't like missing my tea,' Carlyle muttered under his breath as he reluctantly let go of the door and followed after him.

They found Ken Ashton sitting in the upstairs snug of the Royal Circus pub on Endell Street, his cane resting on the table in front of him, next to a half-empty pint of London Pride. Ashton looked very dapper in a grey suit with a thick pinstripe that, up close, smelled slightly of mildew, with a white shirt and a ruby red tie. Flicking through a copy of the *Evening Standard*, he didn't look up as they approached.

The messenger boy in the green tracksuit top took a seat near the stairs as Carlyle stood in front of the old man's table.

'Bloody hell,' Ashton snorted, 'listen to this – *French police left a four-year-old girl stuck in a bullet-riddled car with her dead family for eight hours because they didn't realize she had survived a suspected carjacking gone wrong.*' He looked over the top of his newspaper. 'Those Frogs,' he cackled, 'they're almost as useless as you.'

Carlyle gave a pained smile and took a seat.

Closing his newspaper, Ashton folded it carefully and placed it on the table. 'How are you, Inspector? Long time no see.'

'I'm fine, Ken, how are you?'

'Mustn't grumble.'

'Good.'

The old fellow smiled malevolently. 'I see that Seymour Erikssen has been running rings round you again.'

Why is it that everyone likes talking about Seymour? Carlyle wondered.

'Must be very embarrassing for you.'

Carlyle took a deep breath. 'Hardly.'

'Anyway,' Ashton continued, 'this is not primarily a social chat. I hear that you've been wanting to see me.'

'I was wanting to have my tea,' said Carlyle, glancing at the thug who'd brought him to the pub.

'But you came anyway.'

'I'm interested in Brian Winters.'

'Oh?'

'I was on Waterloo Bridge when he keeled over.'

Ashton made a face. 'Good for you.'

'He was your lawyer.'

'I have lots of lawyers,' said the gangster, not sounding that happy about it. 'You collect quite a few of them when you are in my line of work.'

I'm sure you do, Carlyle thought.

'And, for his part, Mr Winters had lots of clients,' Ashton went on.

'Did you do a lot of work with him?'

'A bit. Brian worked for me for, oh, I suppose more than fifteen years. When he died, he was handling the sale of my property in Harley Street, as I believe you know. All very straightforward stuff – at least, it should have been.' He shot the inspector a quizzical look. 'Anyway, he had a heart attack.'

'That he did.'

'So why are you so interested, copper? Given that you should be out dealing with anti-social little scumbags like Seymour.'

'I hear that Winters had a falling-out with Chris Brennan,' Carlyle said evenly. 'I was just wondering . . .'

'Ha!' Ashton chortled, cutting him off. 'Now we're getting to it. You're still trying to get even with Brennan, are you?'

Christ, how do you know about that? The inspector tried to look both surprised and offended at the same time.

'Talk about grasping at straws.'

'I'm just being thorough,' Carlyle said primly.

Waving a dismissive hand at the policeman, the old man leaned across the table, careful not to knock over his drink in the process. 'Come on, son,' he grunted, 'don't kid a kidder. Everyone knows that you're not the kind of bloke to let something like that slide.'

Sitting back in his chair, Carlyle folded his arms. 'That's bollocks.'

Ashton took a sip of beer. 'Suit yourself. To be honest, I'm really very surprised that you allowed someone like Brennan to get the better of you in the first place.'

'Bollocks,' Carlyle repeated.

Ashton placed his glass back on the table. 'If it's bollocks, I suppose that means you're not interested in my proposal then?'

Carlyle eyed the old man suspiciously. *Fuck it*, he thought. *I'm here. I might as well take the bait.* 'What proposal?'

'Simple.' Ashton's eyes narrowed. 'You get that muppet friend of yours, Angus Muirhead, to stop messing me about on the Harley Street deal and I'll give you more than enough on Mr Christopher Brennan to put him away for a long time.'

FIFTY-FOUR

'He's not here, boss.'

'Fuck.' Ron Flux kicked out at the open can of Tennent's Lager standing on the bare floorboards. The can went flying across the room, sending an arc of ill-defined yellow liquid through the air. His new sergeant jumped backwards, to avoid getting any of the mess on his boxfresh trainers.

'Sorry,' Flux said.

Grunting, the sergeant – an unprepossessing bloke called Jordan Henderson – lifted his left foot an inch off the floor and gestured towards the tattered navy blue sleeping bag lying in the corner of the room. Next to it was a copy of the programme from Chelsea's last home game, along with a tattered edition of *Readers Wives* and an empty Styrofoam takeaway container. 'At least it looks like he was here last night.'

'Lot of good that does us,' Flux sniped as he scanned the rest of the room.

Wrinkling his nose, Henderson hovered in the doorway. 'What is that smell?'

'Dunno.' Ignoring what looked suspiciously like a pile of shit next to the boarded-up fireplace, Flux stepped over to the first-floor window and pushed it open, breathing in as a blast of cold air hit him in the face.

'What do you wanna do?'

Flux silently contemplated the cars neatly parked in the street below.

'Boss?'

'Dunno.' He could barely force the word out.

'Is it gonna rain?'

Why does that matter? 'Probably.' It was a typically grey, charmless West London day, in line with his mood, and for a moment, Flux wondered what it would be like to jump. *Don't be so self-indulgent*, he told himself. *You still have work to do here. Get on with it.*

At least Carlyle had been true to his word. The inspector from Charing Cross was a bit of a cold fish but at least he seemed reliable. After looking the other way at Cherwell Valley services, he had ensured that Calvin Safi had been delivered to Flux, as promised, immediately after the Crown Prosecutor had finished interviewing him.

By the time he'd arrived in Hammersmith, however, Safi was fully lawyered up and keeping schtum. As expected, the lawyer had insisted on an immediate medical inspection of his client. After a delay of more than four hours, a Greek locum had declared that Safi's injuries were sufficiently serious that he should be taken immediately to A&E. After a frank exchange of views, Flux had managed to prevent the prisoner being whisked off to Hammersmith Hospital. The quid pro quo was that Safi was to be allowed a night's rest in the cells before any further questioning took place. As a result, the detective inspector hadn't been able to conduct a proper interrogation before a tip-off had come in about Steve Metcalf being holed up in an abandoned Bloemfontein Road squat.

There was a shuffling of feet behind him. 'Should we wait here?' Henderson asked.

No idea, Flux thought, not turning round. 'Maybe.'

'Do you think Metcalf'll come back?' the sergeant persisted.

'Good question.' Flux watched a couple of uniformed school-boys, maybe twelve or thirteen, strolling down the road. He glanced at his watch. Not only were they an hour late for school, they were heading in the wrong direction. For the first time in

264

what seemed like years, Flux allowed himself a small smile, recalling the days when he used to skive off from school himself, stuff his blazer into a battered Gola holdall and head off to explore the fleshpots of Soho. *You enjoy it, boys*, he thought. *Bunking off now and again is good for the soul.* Certainly, the odd day off had never done him any harm.

None at all.

'Shit.'

Looking past the boys, the DI broke out of his reverie as he recognized the figure ten yards behind the boys, lumbering along the road towards the house. 'It's him!' he shouted with more than a hint of glee in his voice. 'Metcalf's back already.'

Sergeant Henderson appeared at his shoulder and peered down the street. 'Are you sure that's him?'

'Oh yes.' Flux thought for a moment. Metcalf was only about four doors away now – he would be with them in less than a minute. There wasn't really much they could do, other than wait to welcome him back. The DI fingered the knuckleduster in his jacket pocket. 'Come on, you bastard,' he hissed under his breath. 'Come right in and say hello.'

As Metcalf approached the front gate, he paused and looked up. Flux jumped back from the window, but it was too late – he had been spotted.

'Shit.' Pushing the sergeant out of the way, the DI raced to the door and down the stairs, three at a time. Tearing open the front door, he hurdled the low brick wall at the front of the house, slamming into a taxi parked by the kerb. Regaining his balance, Flux set off after his quarry. Showing an impressive turn of speed for such a big man, Metcalf was already fifty yards down the road. Flux guessed that he was making for the Cleverly Estate, a sprawling 1920s development located a couple of blocks to the west.

'Bastard,' Flux wheezed. If Metcalf made it into the estate, he knew that he would lose him amidst the warren of buildings and walkways it contained. The DI tried to kick on, but it felt like there was a fire in his chest and he was struggling to breathe, while his legs were turning to jelly. The rueful thought crossed his mind that this was one of those times when being one of the 75 per cent of Met officers who were overweight wasn't that clever. Trying not to throw up, he felt desperation wash over him as he watched Metcalf disappear round the corner and into Sawley Road.

'Hey! Watch where you're going!'

'Huh?' Pulling up with a start, Flux glared at the cyclist who had blindsided him.

'Idiot,' the middle-aged man hissed from behind a pair of designer sunglasses.

'What are you doing on the pavement?' Flux wailed, casting a forlorn glance down the road.

'You need to watch where you're going, dickhead,' the lycra-clad hooligan repeated as he jumped off his expensive-looking mountain bike and tried to walk it around the quivering policeman.

Out of the DI's frustration, an epiphany bloomed. 'Give me the bike!' he shouted, making a grab for the handlebars.

'What?' The cyclist tried to jerk the bike away but he was too slow. 'What the hell are you doing?'

'Police,' Flux croaked. 'I need to commandeer your bike.'

'Fuck off, you nutter.' With a grunt, the cyclist pulled the bike free, staggering backwards into the waiting arms of Sergeant Henderson, who had belatedly emerged from the squat.

'Arrest that bastard,' Flux commanded, grabbing back the bike and pushing it into the road.

'What for?' the sergeant asked.

'Anything you like,' Flux giggled, jumping on to the saddle.

The pain in his chest had subsided slightly although his legs still felt funny. As he wobbled into Sawley Road, it occurred to Flux that it must have been more than thirty years since he had been on a bike. 'Just keep peddling, you stupid bastard,' he laughed nervously, wondering what had happened to the burnt orange Chopper of his youth, while scanning the middle distance for a sign of the fleeing Steve Metcalf. After swerving to avoid a couple crossing the street, he saw a man dart between two parked cars and cross the street about 150 yards in front of him. *'Gotcha.'*

Metcalf seemed to be keeping to a reasonable pace. Even so, upping his speed, Flux felt the wind in his face as he closed the gap steadily – and silently – on his target. Still making for the sanctuary of the Cleverly Estate, not looking backwards, Metcalf was unaware that he was being gradually reeled in. Gritting his teeth, the detective inspector ignored his accelerated heart-rate and gave it one final effort. 'C'mon,' he grunted, 'like Lance Armstrong on crack. Just do it, baby.'

With the gap down to less than twenty yards, the game was up. Flux raised a fist in triumph. As he did so, he caught a sudden flash of red out of the corner of his eye. There was the screech of brakes, followed by an almighty bang, and he was suddenly flying through the air, landing in a heap on the road. As he lay on his back, staring up at the grim clouds, wondering why he wasn't feeling any pain, he heard a vehicle door open, followed by the sound of footsteps on the Tarmac. The sky was suddenly obliterated by the face of an angry-looking man in an Army jacket.

For the sake of appearances, Flux let out a groan.

'You stupid cunt!' screamed the man. 'What the fuck do you think you were doing?'

FIFTY-FIVE

'Didn't you bring me any grapes?'

Carlyle looked at Umar, who shrugged. 'Er, no . . . I didn't think that you would be a grape kind of guy.'

'It's supposed to be the thought that counts,' Flux groused. 'Didn't your mother ever tell you that?'

Looking at the irate detective inspector propped up in his hospital bed, Carlyle laughed. 'No.'

'Thanks a lot.'

'My mum wasn't that kind of woman,' Carlyle added ruefully. 'But we didn't come empty-handed, though.'

'No?' A flicker of cautious optimism spread across Flux's face.

'Of course not. That would be rude.' The inspector pulled the copy of *Cycling Weekly* from the pocket of his raincoat and tossed it on the bed.

'Pah.' Disgustedly, Flux kicked it off.

'I'm afraid we're gonna have to drug test you,' Umar snickered. 'That van driver said you were going like a bat out of hell. You gave him a terrible fright, by the way.'

'*I* gave *him* a fright?' Flux squawked. 'What happened to the idiot, by the way? Did he get nicked?'

Carlyle yawned. 'Not as far as I know.'

'However,' Umar said cheerily, 'we do have some good news.'

'Oh?' Watching on a pretty Asian nurse floating past the end of the bed, Flux didn't seem immediately interested in what the sergeant had to offer.

'We got Metcalf,' Carlyle explained. In the breast pocket of his jacket his phone started vibrating. Ignoring the call, he let it go to voicemail.

Flux quickly brought his gaze back to his colleagues.

'He's in hospital too. In a secure unit up the road at Wormwood Scrubbs.'

'Ha! Did that bastard in the van run him over as well?'

Umar shook his head. 'The silly sod fell into a six-foot hole on the Cleverly Estate and broke his ankle. British Gas was doing some emergency work and he didn't look where he was going. A couple of officers from the Wormholt & White City Safer Neighbourhoods Team who were on the estate looking for some teenage crack dealers found him trying to crawl out. Metcalf freaked when he saw the uniforms and tried to leg it. They radioed back to the station, realized who he was, and nicked him.'

'Result,' said Flux, perking up before their eyes. 'Now I just need to get out of here and interview him.'

Carlyle held up a hand. 'It can wait twenty-four hours or so, there's no rush. Best if you rest up a bit. It's not like Metcalf's going anywhere. We've got both of the bastards now. It's game over.'

'Yes, but—'

A loud electronic chirping began issuing from the mobile in Umar's hand. Glancing at the *No mobile phones* sign above the bed, Carlyle gave him a pained look. 'Swedish House Mafia,' the sergeant explained nonchalantly, hitting the receive button.

'Okay.' The inspector didn't recognize the name.

'Not your thing,' Umar continued, stepping away from the bed to take the call.

Flux lifted a small bottle of apple Lucozade from his bedside table, unscrewed the cap and took a long swig.

Folding his arms, Carlyle stood at the end of the bed, hopping from foot to foot in slow motion. He was still trying to think of something to say when Umar sidled back up to him, holding out the handset.

'It's for you.'

Carlyle frowned.

'Simpson,' Umar whispered.

Reluctantly, Carlyle took the phone, striding towards the exit. 'Boss—'

'Why are you ignoring me?' the Commander demanded.

Taken aback by the icy tone, Carlyle took a deep breath. *Be cool*, he told himself. *Don't let her wind you up.* 'What can I do for you?' he asked, pushing through the swing doors and stepping into the corridor.

'What the hell do you think you were playing at?'

Not sure which particular transgression he was about to get hauled over the coals for, he waited for her to explain. A sign above his head pointed towards a café. He decided to follow it.

'I have just been reading the medical report on Calvin Safi. You won't be surprised to know that the doctor's verdict is that our Mr Safi is in a right old mess.'

'I never laid a finger on him, Boss.'

'No,' said Simpson, her voice simmering with rage, 'you just bloody tasered him, didn't you?'

'How did you know that?' he blurted out, unable to contain his surprise.

'Because, you stupid sod, I'm sitting here watching it on bloody YouTube. One minute and four seconds of media gold just waiting to be mined. The damn thing has only been up three hours and it has already had more than sixteen thousand views. It's only a matter of time before some sodding journalist sees it.'

'How did that happen?'

'You tell me.'

Turning a corner, Carlyle reached the cafeteria. Standing by the door, he closed his eyes. He thought back to Safi lying in the road with Umar standing over him. 'Those bloody kids . . .'

'What?'

Carlyle opened his eyes. 'There were a couple of lads on bikes

270

who watched us make the arrest. One of them must have filmed it on his mobile phone.'

'You berk,' said Simpson, with feeling.

The inspector didn't argue the point. 'Can't we get it taken down?'

'The lawyers are trying to do that right now, but you know what these internet people are like, freedom of speech and all that. Even if they manage to get it removed, it'll probably be too late. You really have fucked up this time.'

From the café came the sound of Squeeze's 'Cool for Cats'. After more than thirty years, Carlyle could still remember every word. Smiling, he started singing along in his head. Immediately, his spirits began reviving, along with his appetite.

'John?'

'Look,' said Carlyle, pushing through the doors and scanning the menu written on a blackboard above the counter, 'just let the lawyers get on with doing their thing. I've got some other stuff to sort out. We can catch up later.' Not waiting for the reply, he ended the call, beaming at the middle-aged woman behind the counter. 'Could I have the pie and chips, please?'

FIFTY-SIX

Feeling a spasm in his guts, Carlyle winced. 'I shouldn't have had that pie,' he told his sergeant. Umar mumbled something that could plausibly pass for sympathy, before adding: 'You should have been more careful.'

Taking a gulp of his Jameson's, the inspector scanned the room as Umar supped his pint of Guinness. The Monkey's Uncle pub was only a couple of minutes' walk from the police station, but it hardly counted as a regular haunt. Indeed, this was the first time he'd been in here for a drink in what – more than six months? It was probably longer than that. Easily. By and large, Helen wasn't keen on the idea of him neglecting his family duties and going off drinking after work. For his part, the inspector was content to head straight home at the end of the day. The long and short of it was, he wasn't that much of a pub man.

Tonight, however, he fancied a drink. With a lot on his mind, Carlyle felt the need to let his brain decompress slowly before he reached the flat. The day had filled his head full of irritating stuff that he saw no point in offloading on to his wife. So when his sergeant had suggested a drink, he was quick to agree.

For his part, Umar was in no hurry to go home either. Sure enough, during the working day he missed his wife and baby daughter. He knew, however, that the moment he walked through the door, Christina would hand him Ella and launch into a well-rehearsed monologue about how all he did was go to work to skive off. Once she got started, it was all he could do to keep his head down and his mouth shut.

The two men were lucky to have grabbed a table by the door for the place was heaving with a mixture of tourists, theatregoers and off-duty office workers. Not to mention the odd policeman. Since they had arrived, the inspector had already spotted three or four familiar faces manoeuvring their way to and from the bar. Still a steady stream of people arrived, barely making it through the door before having to dive into a crowd six or seven deep in an attempt to make it to the bar. *So many people.* Carlyle shook his head. The recession might have been going on for longer than anyone cared to remember but, by and large, the pubs and bars of Covent Garden seemed immune to the vagaries of the economic cycle.

Umar sat back in his chair and placed his pint glass down on the table. 'What was it?'

Carlyle frowned. 'What was what?'

'The pie. What kind was it?'

'Dunno.' The inspector finished his drink and got to his feet. It was his round. 'It just said meat pie.'

'You know what they say about hospital food.'

'Yeah, but this was some kind of outside chain, a franchised thing.' He mentioned the name of one of the outlets that had popped up everywhere over the last decade. 'I thought it would be okay. Obviously I was wrong.' He wiggled his empty glass across the table. 'Another one?'

Umar considered for a moment. 'Just a half.'

'Fair enough.' Carlyle contemplated the crush of bodies between the table and the bar. 'Make sure no one nicks my seat. I may be some time.'

Pulling out his mobile, Umar started tapping at the screen. 'Will do.'

When he finally made it to the bar, Carlyle found himself next to a youngish American couple in matching green North Face ski jackets who seemed incapable of deciding what they wanted to drink. The man wanted to know the barman's opinion of each of the half-a-dozen single malts on the shelf above the cash register, while the woman was caught in an existential crisis – should she choose the Australian Chardonnay or go with the Chilean Sauvignon Blanc?

They'll both be shit, love, Carlyle thought, *so it doesn't really make any difference.*

'What do you recommend?' the woman asked.

'The Chardonnay's nice,' said the barman with all the enthusiasm of a man picking fag ends out of a pint pot.

The woman sucked air through her teeth. Clearly it was not the answer she had been looking for. She glanced at her partner. 'I don't know, Henry. I don't normally go for South American wines.'

How hard can it be to choose a bloody drink? Carlyle tried to catch the eye of the girl next to the barman. As she handed another customer his change, he held up his hand. 'Can I—'

Avoiding eye-contact, the barmaid turned on her heel and went in search of a customer on the other side of the bar.

Henry pointed towards the bottles of Scotch. 'What about the Glenlivet?' he asked in a whiny, East Coast accent.

'They're all good, mate,' said the barman, staring vacantly into the middle distance.

'Gee.'

Gee? At that moment, Carlyle experienced that rarest of feelings, a desire to be somewhere other than in the middle of London. 'Bloody tourists.'

The woman gave a nervous twitch but tried to ignore him. For some reason, this annoyed the inspector even more.

Carlyle was just about to throw in some gratuitously offensive observations on the shortcomings of the United States and its citizens when the barmaid reappeared and signalled that it was finally his turn. 'A Jameson's, please.'

Just as he was finally giving his order, someone elbowed him hard in the back, pushing him into the American woman.

'Hey!' she squeaked, jumping backwards.

'Sorry.' Carlyle turned to face the idiot who had shoved him, ready to give him some grief. As he saw who it was, however, the inspector's face broke into a broad smile. 'Well, well.'

A look of profound dismay passed across Seymour Erikssen's face. 'Oh shit.'

'How very nice to see you. We need to have a little chat.'

'I don't think so.' Already backing away, Seymour turned and pushed his way roughly past a Goth girl, heading for the door.

'Seymour!'

'Hey,' Goth Girl squealed, 'your mate spilled my gin and tonic.'

'He's not my mate,' Carlyle said, sharpening his elbows as he dropped his head and set a course for the door.

By the time the inspector had made it on to the pavement, Erikssen was halfway down Bow Lane. Carlyle shook his head. 'What's got into you?' he wondered.

Glancing over his shoulder, Seymour upped his pace, darting in front of a well-heeled couple and diving through a set of revolving doors that led into the Royal Opera House.

Stepping off the kerb, the inspector ignored the blast of the horn from an approaching taxi driver and ran to the other side of the road. Jogging to the side-entrance, he hopped from foot to foot as he waited behind a small queue of operagoers to get inside. Once through, he was standing in a long corridor, with the box office counter to his right. As a few stragglers collected their tickets, there was the sharp ring of a bell, warning patrons that they had three minutes to take their seats. At the entrance to the auditorium, the ushers began directing patrons inside with increasing vigour. Hanging from the ceiling in front of him was a giant screen advertising upcoming performances of Benjamin Britten's *Gloriana*. He had no idea what it was about but remembered Helen commenting on its good reviews. She had mentioned a desire to take Alice to see it. *Good luck with that*, the inspector thought. Their punk-rock-loving daughter was about as likely to be up for it as he would be himself. *A bit too highbrow for my tastes.*

Parking his plebeian shortcomings for a moment, the inspector looked towards the man wrestling his way through the far exit, which led on to James Street and Covent Garden's Piazza. 'Got you.' Upping the pace, the policeman happily left the world of culture behind.

'Just my luck,' Seymour muttered to himself as he swerved round a woman gawping at a poster of some beefcake dancer. 'Of all the sodding people to bump into.' The last thing he needed right at the moment was a nice little chat with Inspector bloody Carlyle. Not when he'd just lifted the fat wallet of that American geezer in the Monkey's Uncle. It was rotten timing, making his best score of the night and then coming right up against the most annoying copper in the whole of London. What were the odds? Seymour frowned at the injustice of it all. At least he'd managed to get out of the pub sharpish. The plod was giving chase but the thief knew that he should be able to lose him quite easily amidst the early-evening crowds in the Piazza.

Exiting the Opera House, he trundled along the colonnade and found a path through the knot of tourists watching a tuneless busker go through his set of ropey U2 cover versions. Head down, the pickpocket ignored the potential booty on offer as he concentrated on not running in to anyone and so delaying his escape. Only when he had passed the Apple Store and stepped on to King Street, did he allow himself a glance over his shoulder. Following behind at a steady pace, Sherlock Holmes still had him in his sights. Cursing, Seymour contemplated the possibility that he might not be able to make a clean getaway. Just in case the policeman did manage to catch him, he needed to dump the wallet. And sharpish.

Instinctively, Seymour veered to his left, slipping behind a performance artist juggling a couple of roaring chainsaws in front of the Tuscan portico of St Paul's Church, and disappearing into the churchyard. With five different entrances – and exits – the Actors' Church had long been one of Seymour's favourite properties for facilitating his departure from the scene of a crime. Trotting down the steps, he jogged across the greasy flagstones, taking care not to slip on his arse, and reaching the side door of the church, he headed inside.

Carefully closing the door behind him, the thief took a moment to catch his breath and let his eyes adjust to the gloomy interior. The quiet was disconcerting; the roar of the flying chainsaws in the Piazza reduced to a low growl as the city outside was kept at bay by the seventeenth-century walls. Inside, it appeared that the place was empty, apart from an elderly woman to his left. Reading from a guidebook as she stood by the font, she gave no indication of noticing his arrival. Head down, Seymour quietly made his way towards the West entrance. From past experience, he knew that there was a large wooden box for visitor donations, set to the side of the main door. At best, the box was emptied once a week, allowing Seymour to use it as an occasional over-night safety deposit box. Keeping to the shadows, he removed the American's wallet from the pocket of his jacket and pulled out the pleasingly thick wad of Euro and sterling notes that it contained. Checking that the woman by the font was still engrossed in her book, he stepped over to the box and quickly stuffed them inside. As he did so, he checked the padlock which secured the box and grunted his approval. Rudimentary was not the word. It would only take him a few seconds to have that off on his return visit.

Stepping out into the chill of the church garden, he considered his next move. The bloke's credit cards, an Amex and a MasterCard, were worth a few bob, but only if he could hand them on immediately. Tomorrow would be too late. The guy would have discovered the theft and alerted his card provider. The window of opportunity would be a few hours at most.

A familiar mixture of fear and greed coursed through Seymour's veins. It was a case of selling the cards now or just tossing them away. Looking round, there was still no sign of the damn copper. Fuck it, he would take a punt. Stuffing the cards into the back pocket of his jeans, he tossed the wallet into a nearby bin, before scooting out of the Henrietta Street exit.

Less than a minute later, he glided into Agar Street, saluting as he wandered past the CCTV cameras mounted outside the Charing Cross police station. 'See you later, Inspector,' Seymour chortled, as he upped the pace, heading in the direction of Soho.

FIFTY-SEVEN

There was a gasp of delight from the crowd as the blade of the chainsaw sparked against the cobbles and bounced away from the juggler. *Is that part of the act?* Carlyle wondered. *Or was it a mistake? Either way, it seems a bit risky to me.* Presumably the act had been licensed by the council, but all it would take was one maimed tourist and all hell would break loose.

Breaking off from gawping at the juggler, the inspector looked around, resigning himself to the fact that he had lost Seymour Erikksen in the throng. As he scanned the tramps loitering in the portico over a few cans of Carling Zest, his eye was caught by a poster advertising St Paul's Jubilee Garden Appeal. Next to it, the churchyard gate was being locked up for the night by one of the staff as he shooed away a couple of visitors who had missed their chance for the day.

The inspector felt his phone start ringing. Moving away from the chainsaws, he pulled it from his pocket and answered without checking the screen to see who was calling him.

'Yeah?'

'What happened to you?' It sounded like Umar had left the pub and was walking down the street. Carlyle explained about Seymour. 'The lengths some people will go to, to avoid getting their round in,' the sergeant observed wryly.

'Sorry,' Carlyle replied. 'I can be back there in a couple of minutes.'

'Another time. Christina's on my case – I'd better get home.'

'Fair enough.'

'See you in the morning.'

'Okay.' Ending the call, Carlyle watched the juggler's mate go round the crowd with a hat, touting for donations. A few children stepped up to toss in some coins, but the inspector could see from the expression on the bloke's face that pickings were slim. 'Times are tough,' he mumbled to himself, walking smartly away before the hat could get thrust under his nose.

From the church, it was a three-minute walk home, heading past the tube station, cutting across Long Acre and up Endell Street. By now, the girls would have eaten, so he decided to pop into the Ecco Café on Drury Lane for a takeaway pizza. He was halfway along Shelton Street when his phone went again. Assuming that it was Helen, he lifted the handset to his ear.

'Hi.'

'John?'

Shit. Reluctantly, he came to a halt outside the Good Vibes Fitness Studio. 'Boss . . .'

'Where are you?' the Commander demanded.

'In Covent Garden. I was just on my way home.' As Carlyle stared into the gutter, a groan came from the Sun pub across the road, followed by a collection of choice expletives. There must be a game on. Most of the locals were Gooners; presumably Arsenal were making a mess of things again.

'Fine.' Simpson thought about it for a moment, before mentioning the name of a nearby bar. 'I need to give you an update on developments. Why don't you meet me there in half an hour?'

'Sure.' Ending the call, the inspector looked up at his flat in Winter Garden House, just across the road. The lights were on, but he wasn't going home. Presumably Helen and Alice were snuggled up on the sofa watching some rubbish on TV. Feeling sorry for himself, he suddenly realized that he did at least have time to grab his pizza. Turning into Drury Lane, he walked slowly up the road while texting his wife to let her know that he would be out for a while yet.

On the thirty-first floor of Centre Point, a notorious 1960s tower block located at the bottom end of Tottenham Court Road, the inspector waited patiently for the girl behind the desk to finish her phone call.

It took a minute or so for her to complete the booking. 'Good evening, sir,' she said brightly once it was done, 'and thank you for waiting. Welcome to the Seifert Club.' Looking him up and down, her smile stiffened somewhat. 'Are you a member?'

Carlyle frowned. 'Er, no.'

'Might you be interested in our membership options?'

'Not really.' Looking over the girl's shoulder, he scanned the room, looking for his boss. But most of the tables were empty and the Commander was nowhere to be seen. 'Actually, I'm here to meet Carole Simpson.'

'Ah, yes.' The girl looked down at the reservations book and made a mark by Simpson's name. 'A table for two.'

Somehow, that just didn't sound quite right. 'Ye-es,' Carlyle acknowledged, 'I suppose so.'

'In the corner, by the window. Let me take you there now.'

Carlyle held up a hand. 'That's fine. I think I can just about manage to find my way over there on my own. Thank you.'

By the time the Commander finally appeared, the inspector was on his second glass of Jameson's and was beginning to feel quite mellow.

'Sorry to keep you waiting.' Simpson gave him a brittle smile as she took the seat opposite him.

'No problem.' Carlyle gestured with his tumbler in the direction of the spectacular glass and steel roof of the British Museum's Great Court. 'I was just enjoying the view.'

'Not bad, is it? Then again, we're so high up here.'

'Yes.' Never having been a great one for heights, Carlyle didn't really want to dwell on that point too much. 'Presumably you're a member here?' he asked, moving the conversation briskly along.

Simpson's face clouded as she gazed into the night sky. 'Joshua was a founder member.'

'Ah.' Carlyle looked at his drink. His boss rarely mentioned her late husband, which was not surprising. Before being diagnosed with cancer, Joshua Hunt had been convicted of a large-scale fraud. Traumatic and embarrassing, the episode had threatened the Commander's very future in the Metropolitan Police Service. In the end, she had survived. However, any hope of progressing beyond her current rank was gone. Like Carlyle, Simpson had to accept that her career had peaked. Like Carlyle, she knew that she could live with that and still come in to work every morning, keen to get on with the job.

'He bought a fifteen-year membership for some ludicrous amount of money,' Simpson explained. 'Presumably it was deemed a justifiable business expense, tax deductible and so on. Anyway, I only found out about it after his death. One day, I came for a look round and found that I quite liked the place.' She let out a feeble laugh. 'After all, it's paid for. And it's one of the few things he left me with. So why let it go to waste? Being stuck out in Paddington most of the time, I find it quite useful for meetings in this part of Town.' A waiter appeared at their table and she asked him for a large glass of Chardonnay and a copy of the food menu before turning her attention back to her colleague. 'Have you had dinner yet?'

'Yes, thanks.' Carlyle found himself regretting his trip to Ecco.

'Good. Let's get our business over with and then you can go and see the family.'

Carlyle sat up in his chair. 'Thanks.'

'They're all well, I take it?'

'Fine.'

'Good.' Pleasantries out of the way, she went straight on to the business end of things. 'There's good news and there's bad news.'

'Okay.' Carlyle allowed himself to be distracted by the lights of a jet following the river as it headed towards Heathrow.

282

'Which do you want first?'

'You can decide.'

The Commander watched the waiter approach with her wine. She let him place it carefully on the table and hand her a menu before heading off to serve a couple of girls who had just arrived at a nearby table. 'We'll start with the good news,' she said, lowering her voice.

'Okay.'

'You are in the clear over the assault on Calvin Safi.'

Carlyle made a show of frowning but kept his voice even. 'What assault?'

Simpson took a sip of her wine. 'Don't piss about, John. We are talking on our usual, completely private basis. You know I'm not going to grass you up.'

'Fair enough.' He felt flushed. Maybe it was the alcohol. 'Sorry.'

'You are the most suspicious-minded little sod that I have ever come across.'

'But in a good way.'

'And also one of the luckiest. The video footage of Calvi Safi being tasered prior to his arrest is no longer online. Apparently it was shot using a stolen iPhone. The young man responsible for recording it agreed to take it down as part of a deal that will see him return the mobile on a "no questions" basis and thereby avoid prosecution.'

The inspector took another mouthful of whiskey. 'Excellent.'

'The local plod did a very good job for me there.' Simpson mentioned a couple of names. 'You need to get in touch to say thanks.'

'I will.'

'However,' she continued, 'that is not the end of it.'

'Oh?'

'No. In order to pre-empt the inevitable squealing from Safi's lawyer, the footage is now being reviewed by the Independent Police Complaints Commission, as is the CCTV footage from Cherwell Valley Services.'

'These things happen,' Carlyle said, adopting the air of a man for whom a brush with the IPCC was all in a day's work – which it was, more or less.

'How very philosophical of you,' Simpson said sarkily.

'It's not such a big deal.'

'Not so much for you, although you'll probably get some kind of reprimand. Sergeant Sligo and DI Flux, however, are on trickier ground.'

A pained expression crossed Carlyle's face. 'I can't believe you have anything on Ron,' he said. 'All the cameras were outside the toilets and there were no witnesses to whatever may have happened while they were in there.'

'No?' Simpson raised an eyebrow.

'No,' said Carlyle firmly.

An amused smile played on the Commander's lips. 'But why was Flux there in the first place?'

'No idea,' Carlyle shrugged. 'Just a coincidence.'

'I don't believe in coincidence.'

'I do.' *When it suits me.*

'Anyway,' Simpson continued, 'what happened there may well turn out to be academic. I think the detective inspector could be on the road to early retirement, what with the stress of losing his colleague and so forth.'

'I wouldn't be surprised.'

'Which brings us to the conduct of your sergeant,' said Simpson, staring into her glass, 'which could be the *really* bad news.'

FIFTY-EIGHT

Swaying slightly, Umar caught sight of himself in the mirror in the hallway just as he was about to lick his lips. He was pissed. And he was horny. In recent months it was not an unfamiliar combination.

For about the tenth time in the last five minutes, he felt his mobile vibrating insistently in his pocket, next to the packet of Durex Love Ultra-Thin Condoms he'd picked up from the mini-mart round the corner. With a sigh, he pulled out the phone and switched it off.

'Here you go.' Dressed in a man's white shirt, tennis shorts and a pair of expensive-looking driving shoes, Melissa Graham appeared from the kitchen and handed him a small can of Heineken.

'Thanks.' This time, he did let his tongue run along his bottom lip as he took the lager from her.

She pointed at the phone in his hand. 'Was that work trying to get hold of you?'

Grunting something non-committal, he let the phone fall back into his pocket. 'Thanks.' Pulling the ring, he took a long slug.

'Thank you for coming.' Melissa played with the thin gold chain hanging from her neck.

'It's good that you're finally back home.' Umar had been more than a little surprised when Melissa had phoned and told him that she had been released from police custody. The enquiries were continuing into the violent deaths of Will Carter, Melissa's

285

erstwhile boyfriend, and the young woman he had been seeing on the side, but as far as Umar knew, the girl standing in front of him looking as if butter wouldn't melt in her mouth was still the only suspect. The thought aroused him even more.

Leaning against the frame of the door, Melissa folded her arms across her chest as she watched the wheels turning slowly inside his drink-fuddled brain. A couple of days on remand in Holloway seemed to have done her no harm at all; she was looking bright-eyed and rested. 'Didn't you think they'd let me out?' she pouted.

From behind his beer, Umar made a face, playing for time while he thought how best to respond. He didn't want to accidentally say anything that would ruin his chances of getting laid. 'Well, you know, the charges are very serious. And these things are always a bit of a lottery.'

'Well, they finally arrested the guy who stabbed Bradley Saffron on the naked bike ride,' Melissa told him.

Shames and Postic will be relieved about that, Umar thought. *I wonder if they mentioned it to Carlyle?* Hopefully not; it would be good to have a nice bit of information to share with his boss in the morning.

'Some random nutter, apparently.'

Kettle, Umar thought, *pot*, *black*. But he kept his own counsel.

'So I'm off the hook for that – assuming that I *was* ever on the hook in the first place.' She gave him a searching look.

Umar held up a hand. 'Not my investigation.'

'No, I suppose not.'

'But I'll see what I can find out.'

'As for Will and that bitch Kara Johnson . . .'

'Yes?'

'Your colleague said that the investigation into their deaths will take a while longer to complete. My lawyer got me bail after my father put up a large bond and I surrendered my passport. I still have to report to the police station every day, though, which is a complete and utter pain in the bum.'

'I can imagine.'

'I suppose I can at least have a drink and—' letting the chain fall between her breasts, she shot him an arch look '—sleep in my own bed.'

Umar lifted the can to his mouth and tipped back his head.

'Speaking of which, I need a glass of wine. A large one.' Turning in the doorway, Melissa headed for the fridge. 'Want another beer?'

Following her into the kitchen, Umar crushed the empty can and placed it on the draining board, next to the sink, beside a large bottle of pills with the name Clozaril on the label.

Taking a bottle of Cava from the fridge, she pointed in the direction of his knees. 'The bin is in that cupboard behind you.'

'Come here . . .' Umar pulled Melissa towards him, planting a kiss on her lips, trying to force his tongue into her mouth as he ran his hand across the front of her shirt.

'Hey.' She tried to wriggle free but Umar held her tightly. He had made his move and wasn't going to back down at the first sign of some resistance. 'Get off.'

Had he read this one wrong? Bemused by the girl's apparent change of heart, Umar relaxed his grip slightly – enough for Melissa to take a half-step backwards and attempt to club him with the bottle.

'Ow.' He laughed, more embarrassed than hurt as it bounced off his shoulder.

'You dirty bastard!' she screamed, a wild look in her eyes.

'But—' Umar protested.

'You were going to rape me.' Taking another step backwards, Melissa smashed the bottle against the edge of the worktop, sending a mess of fizz and glass all over the floor. All that was left in her hand was the broken neck, which she waved in front of his face.

'Whoa.' Backed up against the cooker, with nowhere to go, Umar held his hands up in front of his face as Melissa jumped forward, broken glass crunching under her feet.

'I'll kill you.'

'Argh!' He screamed as he felt the jagged glass slash across his left forearm. Instinctively, he threw a punch with his right, connecting with the side of the woman's head and sending her sprawling across the kitchen floor. Not waiting for her to get back to her feet, he rushed from the kitchen and made good his escape.

'How are you getting on with your sergeant at the moment?'

'Umar?' Polishing off his third glass of Jameson's, Carlyle vowed not to have another. He had suddenly noticed how hot it was in the club and wanted both some fresh air and a return to ground level. Feeling woozy, he struggled to marshal his thoughts. 'We're getting on fine,' he replied finally. 'He's become a father, so there are some inevitable issues at home but, on the whole, he's doing okay.'

Wondering exactly why it was taking so long for the chicken salad she'd ordered to arrive, Simpson looked at him carefully. 'Are you sure?'

'Yeah. There was the case last month, the muggers on bikes who were targeting tourists around the area . . .'

'I remember that, the papers were all over it.'

'Well, they're not any more. Umar, with some help from WPC Mason – she's a solid officer, by the way – traced it back to a gang of teenagers on the local Peabody Estate, and sorted it out with a minimum of fuss. They closed more than a dozen, if I remember rightly.'

'I hear he's a bit of a serial shagger.'

'He was a bit of a ladies' man before he was married,' Carlyle conceded, looking wistfully at his empty glass.

Simpson followed his gaze. 'One for the road?'

'No, I should get going.' The inspector pushed himself out of his chair. 'Umar's a good colleague. Professional. I would genuinely be very disappointed if he came a cropper over this Safi business. Apart from anything else, I've struggled to keep a sergeant in recent years; it would be a shame to lose another one.'

'Yes,' Simpson murmured. 'Ever since the unfortunate Joseph Szyszkowski – may he rest in peace – there has been a bit of a turnover, hasn't there?'

Staring out of the window, Carlyle stuffed his hands into his trouser pockets and took a deep breath. Gazing into the illuminated darkness, he thought back to the day when his long-term colleague was gunned down barely twenty minutes' walk from where they were sitting.

'Do you ever see the family?' Simpson asked.

Not once. Anita never forgave me for what happened to her husband. And who can blame her? As for the kids . . . I probably wouldn't recognize William and Sarah these days. 'Not really.'

'It must still be difficult.'

'Yes.'

Simpson smiled at the waiter as he finally returned to place her salad on the table. 'I'm going to have another glass of wine. Sure you don't want another drink?'

Thinking of Joe, he was hit by a sudden desire to sit down with the bottle and get thoroughly hammered. Gritting his teeth, he waited for it to pass. 'I'm good. Enjoy your dinner. Let me know how things develop with the IPCC.'

Taking a mouthful of rocket, Simpson dismissed him with a wave of her fork.

Conversation over, Carlyle headed for the lifts.

FIFTY-NINE

It was a cold, grey morning in Soho. The lounge lizards and the perverts were still tucked up in bed and, apart from the street cleaners and the traffic wardens, the inspector had the place to himself, which was just how he liked it. Sitting in Bar Italia, he lingered over breakfast, watching highlights of the previous night's Juve–Milan game, reluctant to begin the working day.

'*Cazzo*,' complained the guy behind the counter as he watched Milan's centre-forward put away the only goal of the game in slow motion. 'That was never a penalty.' He glared at Carlyle as if the shortcomings of the officials were the policeman's fault. Slipping off his stool, the inspector took that as his cue to leave.

Making his way along Old Compton Street, he arrived at the Clivenden Club in a matter of minutes. Passing a couple of cleaners at the front door, he bounded up the stairs and presented himself to a sleepy-looking receptionist on the first floor.

'I'm here to see Angus.' The statement seemed to cause the girl some confusion. Carlyle, however, was happy enough taking a moment to admire the framed *Emmanuelle* movie poster on the wall behind the desk while waiting for a response.

'He's not here,' she said finally.

'When will he be in?' Carlyle asked, keeping his gaze on the poster.

'I don't know,' came the flat reply.

Carlyle began to feel the good humour engendered by

daydreaming about Sylvia Kristel starting to fray around the edges. 'I need to speak to him.' He reached into his pocket for some ID then changed his mind. Better not to make too much of his police credentials when he was essentially freelancing; engaged on a mission from Ken Ashton.

'I'm sorry, Inspector, but Mr Muirhead may not be back.'

So much for staying undercover. Carlyle didn't remember seeing this particular girl before, but she obviously knew who he was. 'He may not be back today?' he huffed. 'Or for the rest of recorded time?'

'The latter,' the girl said promptly, taking a sip from the bottle of Evian that stood on her desk, next to an unopened box of Angus's Macanudo cigars.

'Huh?'

'He had a stroke.'

'Fuck.'

'Yesterday afternoon.'

'That's serious.'

'Yes,' she agreed, perking up considerably at the thought of her boss's travails. 'But you've gotta face facts. Angus had been living on borrowed time for a while.'

Angus? It was Mr Muirhead a moment ago.

'He's on the way out.'

Glad to see that you're holding up so well. Parking his bemusement at the girl's attitude, Carlyle wondered where this left his mission. Coming to no obvious conclusion, he asked: 'Where is he now?'

'They took him to A&E at UCH in an ambulance,' the girl said. 'I assume he's still there. I rang the hospital this morning but couldn't get through to anyone who could tell me anything.' Replacing the cap on her bottle, she screwed it on tight. 'Do you want to leave a message, just in case he comes back?'

'It doesn't matter,' said Carlyle, already backtracking towards the stairs. 'I can always call back later.'

* * *

For once, he was happy to wait. Standing in a lobby on the first floor of University College Hospital, looking out across the Euston Road, Carlyle watched the snarled-up traffic and was overcome by an unusual but not unpleasant sensation. His mind was blank, his body idle. In the middle of the city, he had achieved something approximating a state of Zen-like calm.

More or less.

'Inspector . . .'

'Hi.' Turning away from the window, he bent forward and planted a kiss on the cheek of the woman in the white coat who had appeared at his shoulder. 'Thanks for seeing me at such short notice.'

'Sorry to keep you waiting.' Taking a step back, Dr Elizabeth Crane gave him a tired smile. There was considerably more grey in her hair than he remembered and there were dark rings under her eyes, but she still looked good.

'Not at all,' he said. 'Sorry for popping up out of the blue and buttonholing you at work.'

'Isn't that your job – buttonholing people?'

'I suppose. Some of the time at least.' As he spoke, she stifled a yawn. 'Tough day?' he asked.

'I had to help out in A&E,' Crane told him. 'On a normal day they get a couple of hundred people. Today, there was a big smash on the Camden Road, a load of injuries, as well as a fatality, I'm afraid – a bloke on a bike who got completely mangled.' As if on cue, an ambulance appeared outside, its siren growing more insistent as it got caught up in the traffic. 'That's not why you're here, is it?'

'No, no,' he assured her. 'How're Ben and the family?' The Cranes lived in a townhouse just off Seven Dials, a few minutes' walk from Carlyle's flat. Ben and Elizabeth were stalwarts of the Covent Garden Residents Association; a few years earlier, they had helped run a successful campaign to block a kebab shop setting up on Macklin Street, much to the inspector's relief.

'All fine, thanks. Everyone's fit and well.' She gave him a wry smile. 'But I'm assuming that this isn't a social call either, is it.'

'No.' Carlyle explained about Angus Muirhead. 'He was brought in sometime yesterday afternoon. I'm trying to track him down.'

'Is this an official enquiry?'

Carlyle took a deep breath and exhaled. 'Yes and no. He's helping me with something.'

'Okay.' Crane thought about it for a moment. 'Let me find out if he's still here and we can take it from there.'

'Thanks. I really need to see him if at all possible.'

'If the guy has had a stroke, I would be very surprised if he's going to be able to talk to anyone.' Crane's tone was gentle but firm. 'It would be difficult to even try to speak with a patient in Intensive Care without going through the official channels.'

'Yes.' Carlyle realized that he should be careful not to push his luck too far.

'Why don't you grab something from the café? Give me fifteen minutes or so to see what I can find out.'

Finishing his cheese and tomato roll, Carlyle wiped the crumbs from his jumper and went back to checking the messages on his BlackBerry. It was the first time he'd looked at the device for more than a week. After opening a dozen or so of his 176 unread emails, he realized that they were all junk of one sort or another. Even the Police Federation seemed determined to send him nothing more interesting than some 'exclusive' insurance offers. With a sigh, he clicked on the blue band at the top of the screen and selected the *Delete Prior* option. Confirming his decision, he felt a fleeting moment of pleasure as all the messages disappeared into the ether. 'Job done,' he mumbled to himself, turning his attention to the ebb and flow of people across the hospital lobby. A digital clock next to the lifts told him that he had been waiting for more than twenty minutes. He was wondering about having another espresso when a shambolic figure shuffled into view.

Catching Carlyle's eye, there was a moment's hesitation before he reluctantly headed over.

'What are you doing here?' Carlyle asked, nodding at the large bandage wrapped tightly around his sergeant's forearm.

Even by his usual standards, Umar looked washed out. 'I had to go to A&E,' he replied, trying not to look too shamefaced. 'The bastards kept me waiting forever.'

'What happened?'

'Nothing. Just an accident.' Moving from foot to foot, the sergeant made no move to sit down. 'It hurts a bit but it's really no big deal.'

Uh-huh. Keen to interrogate his underling further, Carlyle was distracted by the sight of Elizabeth Crane walking towards him. As she got closer, he could see a mask of professional detachment descend across her face. Instinctively, he knew what was coming.

Emboldened by his boss's loss of focus, Umar suddenly launched a belated counter-attack. 'Why are *you* here?'

'Work,' Carlyle grunted, gesturing past Umar's shoulder. 'I need to have a word with the doctor.'

'Sure.' Grasping this opportunity, Umar turned on his heel, keen to make a hasty retreat. 'See you back at the station.' Not waiting for a reply, he set off, the soles of his red Converse All Stars squeaking noisily as he jogged towards the exit.

If Crane was curious about the sergeant, she didn't let it show. 'Well,' she said, pulling up a chair, 'that took a little bit longer than I expected.'

Getting to his feet, Carlyle watched Umar disappear into the street. 'Let me get you a drink,' he said, giving her a sympathetic pat on the shoulder. 'And then you can tell me about Angus.'

'Here you go.' Placing a latte on the table in front of Elizabeth Crane, Carlyle eased back down into his chair, taking a sip of his own espresso as he did so.

'Thanks.' The doctor cradled the paper cup in her hands

without showing any desire to lift it to her lips. 'Was he a friend?' she asked, not looking up.

'Angus?' Carlyle made a face. 'I've known him a long time but he was an acquaintance rather than a friend – a professional contact. Someone I dealt with now and then for work.'

'I see.' Glancing round the café, she leaned forward. 'Well,' she said, keeping her voice low, 'anyway, sorry to have to be the bearer of bad news, but Mr Muirhead passed away at just after four this morning. The death certificate was signed at 4.37.' She mentioned a couple of medical terms that he didn't understand. 'Basically, he died as a result of complications following the stroke. It seems that he had been in poor health for a while. What happened yesterday just pushed him over the line.'

Where did this leave his deal with Ken Ashton? Carlyle finished his espresso and let his gaze drift to the comings and goings at the entrance. A child in a bright red coat entered the lobby, grimly holding the hand of an attractive blonde woman.

'Did you know that he had been quite unwell for some time?'

'Yes.' Carlyle dragged his attention back to the doctor. 'He told me that he was on borrowed time.'

'Not any more.'

'No.' *So what happens next?* 'What is the situation with next of kin?'

Crane finally took a sip of her latte. 'How do you mean?'

'Does he have any?'

'Ah, yes. Just the one close relative. A daughter. Name of Louise Schapps.'

'A daughter.' Carlyle pondered that piece of information for a second. 'You wouldn't know if she's still here in the hospital, would you?'

'No.' Crane placed her cup back on the table and pushed it away. The beverage was obviously not up to scratch. 'She's gone to speak to the funeral director at Levertons. It's on Eversholt Street, up past Euston station on the way to Camden Town.'

'Brilliant. How did you know I would need that?'

'You're a policeman. I knew that you would want to know as much information as possible. I spoke to the staff dealing with Mr Muirhead who were still on duty.' Crane gestured over her shoulder towards the lift. 'I didn't want you sending me back upstairs with a set of supplementary questions. Apart from anything else, people would get suspicious. You're hardly going through the normal channels, are you?'

'I know. And I'm very grateful.' Carlyle stood up, leaned over and gave her another quick peck on the cheek. 'I've gotta run, but you've been a big help.'

'It was no trouble,' Crane lied, making him all the more grateful for the effort she had put in. 'Say "hi" to Helen for me. Hopefully we'll see you guys soon.'

'That would be great. Maybe go to Wagamama's or something.'

'There's a Residents Association meeting next week. Maybe you could come along,' Crane suggested rather optimistically. 'There's some important stuff on the agenda; the council wants to allow another nightclub on Drury Lane. We could do with as many people attending as possible.'

Carlyle's heart sank. 'Sounds good.' With a cheery wave, he scuttled towards the exit. 'I'll get Helen to give you a call about it.'

The phone refused to stop ringing. Knowing that he would have to take the call sooner or later, he prodded the receive button and lifted the handset to his ear.

'Christina, look—'

'Umar?' The brittle voice on the end of the line cut him off. 'It's Giselle.'

It took a moment for the sergeant to flick through his mental Rolodex and come up with the entry for Brian Winters' wife. An image of the widow sprawled across the marital bed wearing nothing but a smile washed through his brain, leaving him squirming with embarrassment. The dalliance was just another error of judgement to add to his growing list of misdemeanours.

'Umar?'

'Yes, hi.' He looked ruefully at his gashed arm. Giselle might have been a mistake but at least she hadn't tried to glass him, unlike the crazy cyclist, Melissa Graham. A number 48 barrelled down the bus lane, heading towards him. For a brief moment, the sergeant fantasized about stepping in front of it.

'You have to come up to the house.'

Closing his eyes, he felt the wind on his face as the bus rushed past. 'Actually—'

'No,' she insisted, 'you have to come. Right now.' For the first time, he noticed the tension in her voice.

'Is there something wrong?'

'Yes,' she sniffled. 'There is something wrong.'

'What—'

She cut him off with a sob. 'I need your help. Don't be long.' There were some muffled sounds in the background and the line went dead. Umar stared at the phone, wondering what to do.

SIXTY

The legend on the window of Leverton & Sons said *Funeral Directors since 1789*. As Carlyle approached, an elegant woman in cowboy boots, jeans and a short fur jacket came out of the front door and started towards him. Assuming that this was his quarry, the inspector held up a hand. 'Ms Schapps?' Slowing down, the woman stared at him from behind a pair of chic sunglasses. 'Apologies for buttonholing you on the street,' Carlyle persisted, 'but are you Angus Muirhead's daughter?'

'Who are you?' Lifting the sunglasses onto the top of her head, the woman peered at him suspiciously. Her face was pale and free of make-up. It showed no sign of sorrow, only a mixture of anger and grim determination. Trying to affect an air of professional detachment, the inspector took in the mouth, the cheekbones and the large ebony eyes, looking for signs of a family resemblance, but none was immediately apparent.

'Inspector John Carlyle, from the Metropolitan Police.' Finding his warrant card, he held it up for her to inspect.

'I would have hoped the bloody police could leave me alone, today of all days,' Louise Schapps whined, buttoning up her coat. *Is that real fur?* the inspector wondered. *Or is it fake?* He had no idea. He tried to make eye-contact but she was having none of it, ostentatiously scanning the middle-distance in search of a cab. 'My father's dead – surely you lot can leave him alone now?'

'This is not about any ongoing investigation,' he pointed out.

'All the crap that my family's had to put up with over the

298

years . . .' Schapps ranted, giving no indication that she was listening to what he had to say.

'I knew Angus for a long time. I'm very sorry for—'

'What do you want?' she snapped, holding out an arm and clicking her fingers. Almost instantly, Carlyle heard a taxi pull up behind him. He realized that it had been a mistake to come here. Any attempt to force the Harley Street issue was doomed to failure. *Inspector Carlyle?* he thought morosely. *Bloody Inspector Clouseau, more like.*

'It can wait,' he said, giving a thin smile as she stepped over to the cab and leaned into the open window to give the driver an address in Hampstead.

Opening the cab door, she reluctantly returned her attention to the policeman. 'If you knew my father,' she said tersely, 'I'm sure that you must know his lawyer. Speak to him, not me.' Slipping inside, she slammed the door shut, not giving him a second glance as the cabbie did a U-turn and barrelled off, heading north. A poster in Leverton's caught his eye: *Planning your funeral the Independent Way.* 'Maybe I should give it a thought,' he chuntered to himself, heading off down the street.

Standing once again on the doorstep of 72 Boyle Avenue, Umar glanced around nervously. An endless stream of questions bounced around a brain that was devoid of any answers.

Why did I come back here?

Should I do a runner?

What should I say to Christina?

Caught in a mire of indecision, he heard the door open and Giselle Winters ushered him inside. This time, she had not bothered to dress up for his arrival. Grey sweatpants and a baggy sky-blue jumper did a pretty good job of hiding her figure. Her hair was pulled back into a ponytail and her face kept hidden behind an outsized pair of sunglasses.

'Thank you for coming,' she whispered, not quite managing to muster a smile. Keeping his gaze fixed on the expensive-looking print hanging on the wall, Umar grunted a nothing response. Despite the early hour, he could smell the booze on her breath.

'Drink?' she asked, following him into the kitchen.

'I'm fine.' Looking out into the garden, he could see that the flowerbed was still a work in progress. There was no sign of any gardeners at work this morning. Leaning against the wall, he watched her reach for a less than full bottle of vodka on the island and then appear to think better of it. 'So what's the problem?' he asked, his tone sharper than he had intended.

Stifling a sob, she removed the sunglasses and let them drop next to the bottle. 'Chris Brennan paid me a visit . . .'

Gritting his teeth, Umar contemplated the mess of her face. It wasn't pretty but he'd regularly seen worse. Nodding, he tried to retrieve signs of the woman who had seduced him on his last visit. It wasn't easy – she looked as if she'd aged twenty years or more since then.

'My husband's partner.'

'Yes, I remember.' Umar's brain was telling him to say something consoling, but somehow, his mouth couldn't quite manage it.

Pulling up a stool, she sat down. 'I didn't know who else to call.'

'Yes.' The sergeant knew that Brennan's appearance on the scene meant that he should really call Carlyle. For the moment, however, he didn't dare. Maybe he would have something to drink, after all. Stepping over to the fridge, he helped himself to a Diet Coke. 'Why did he hit you?' he asked, cracking open the can and drinking deeply.

'He says Brian owes him five hundred thousand pounds.' Giselle wiped her nose on the sleeve of her jumper and for the first time he felt a stab of sympathy. 'And that means *I* owe him five hundred thousand pounds.'

Waiting for her to explain, Umar tipped back the can and emptied the remaining contents down his throat.

'Chris says that Brian was stealing from a client. The client has found out and now Chris has to pay it back. If he doesn't get the money by the end of the week, he's in deep shit.'

Placing the empty can on the island, Umar raised an eyebrow. *Carlyle will like that.* 'How deep?'

Giselle made a face. 'I don't really know. I think the client was threatening him. And he's worried about this derailing his merger with the Americans – the Austerlitz guys. Anyway, whatever mess he lands in, he says that he's going to drag me down into it too.' Now the sobs came and didn't stop.

With a heavy sigh, Umar stepped over and placed an arm lightly around the woman's shoulder. 'Let me guess,' he said gently, 'this client . . .'

'Yes,' she gulped through the tears, 'it's Ken Ashton.'

The voice on the line made no effort at any pleasantries. 'What have you got for me, Inspector?'

Standing by the kerb on Tower Street, by the stage door of the Ambassadors Theatre, Carlyle gazed at a poster advertising *Little Charley Bear and His Christmas Adventure – Live on Stage.* 'I thought that you didn't like using mobile phones,' he said sullenly.

Ken Ashton chuckled down the line. 'Sometimes I do, sometimes I don't.'

'You heard about Muirhead?' Carlyle asked, scratching his head as he watched a gleaming Porsche lumber past. A familiar stab of envy pricked at his guts. The car easily cost more than he earned in a year.

'A stroke.'

'Yeah.' Behind the wheel of the Cayenne, some identikit Sloane bird was yakking away on her mobile. Overwhelmed by a sense of irritation, he dragged himself back to the matter in hand. 'He died up at UCH early this morning.'

'Better late than never,' Ashton grunted. 'I won't be sending flowers.'

'Very generous of you,' Carlyle quipped.

'I think of it as being honest, Inspector. Why should I buy in to this *everybody loves you when you're dead* crap?'

'Fair enough.'

'I hated the man when he was alive and I still hate him now.'

'I get the message.' For want of anything better to do, Carlyle dangled a foot over the kerb as he waited for a reply.

'So, now that he's dead, where does that leave us?'

Pretty much up shit creek without a paddle, Carlyle reflected. He hoped that this phone conversation wasn't being recorded. Then again, he knew that he could probably rest easy on that score; phone hacking had rather fallen out of fashion recently.

'Did you make any progress on the Harley Street issue?' Ashton asked.

'Not really.' There was no point in bullshitting the crime boss. 'I tried to speak to Angus's daughter this morning,' the inspector explained, 'but she wasn't interested. Everything's getting kicked back to his lawyers.'

There was a pause then Ashton let out a low curse. 'That's just brilliant,' he snarled.

'Sorry, Ken, but that's just the way it is.'

Another pause. 'I should have known,' Ashton said finally. 'Not much use, are you, copper?'

'What do you want me to say?' Carlyle snapped.

'I guess I won't be handing you Brennan, after all.' Conversation over, Ashton ended the call.

Slipping the phone back into his pocket, Carlyle watched as another 4x4 bounced down the road towards him, hitting a puddle and sending a spray over his shoes and up his leg. Rooted to the spot, he looked down disbelievingly as the dirty water seeped through the fabric of his trousers. Then, raising his gaze to the heavens, he caught sight of Little Charley Bear looking down on him with a mocking smile on his face. 'Fuck you, you little furry bastard,' Carlyle muttered as he stomped off in the direction of the police station.

302

SIXTY-ONE

Recognizing the couple in the green North Face ski jackets, Carlyle upped the pace as he passed the front desk of Charing Cross police station, trying not to smirk as he eavesdropped on the conversation.

'What do you mean,' the man complained, waving an arm in the air, 'all you can do is give me a crime reference number? What good is that?'

'You'll be able to use it with your insurance company,' the desk sergeant explained patiently, 'to claim for the loss of your wallet. Have you spoken to your credit card company, to cancel the cards?' He had dispensed the same advice so many times before, it sounded like he was reading from a script.

'Of course,' the man huffed.

'Well then, I think we are good to go,' the sergeant continued.

'But aren't you going to investigate the theft?' the woman demanded. 'We've been waiting here for almost two hours . . .'

Bloody Seymour, Carlyle thought. He didn't know for sure that Erikssen had stolen the guy's wallet, but the thief had been standing less than three feet from the hapless pair at around the time that the theft took place. Put two and two together and you usually got four. In his book, that was one of the first rules of policing.

Not waiting to hear any more, the inspector headed for the third floor. There he found Umar at his desk, hiding behind a copy of that morning's *Metro*. Looking over his shoulder,

303

Carlyle could see that his sergeant was reading a story about a Jimi Hendrix guitar that had been sold at auction for a quarter of a million pounds. Presumably Jimi didn't really care that much.

Flopping into his chair, Carlyle switched on his computer. 'How's the arm?'

Not looking up from his paper, Umar grunted. In a pair of tattered jeans and a grubby T-shirt bearing the legend TIME LORD next to a picture of Dr Who's Tardis spinning through space, he looked less like a copper and more like a student who had just managed to roll out of bed.

'Have you spoken to your rep yet?'

'Yeah.' From behind the newspaper Umar tried to sound laid-back. 'She seems quite good.'

'Cute?'

The sergeant glared at him. 'I said "good". As in "someone who's going to do a *good* job to get me off the hook with regard to this bullshit complaint by Calvin Safi, which *you* got me caught up in".'

'Me?'

'Yes,' Umar said with feeling, '*you*. The bloke who wanted to play with the bloody tasers.'

Carlyle shifted somewhat uncomfortably in his seat. 'Hardly.'

'Anyway,' Umar continued, 'I gave Miranda my statement yesterday afternoon. She reckons I'll be fine.'

'When's the hearing?'

'Didn't you see the email?' Frowning, Umar dropped the paper on his desk and reached for his mouse. With a couple of clicks he pulled up his Outlook and opened a message. 'It's . . . next Thursday at three.'

'Here?'

'Nah. Liverpool Street. You'll have to go too.' He gave his boss a sour look. 'Even though it's not your neck on the block.'

'Don't worry,' Carlyle said limply. 'We'll both get a rap on the knuckles and that'll be the end of it.'

Umar looked at him doubtfully. 'Did Simpson tell you that?'

'Yeah,' Carlyle lied cheerily. 'Simpson's okay. She won't let the IPCC make a meal of it. The whole thing is a storm in a teacup.'

'Tell me about it.'

'The video didn't get into the media, thank God,' Carlyle went on, warming to his theme, 'and the Federation won't stand for any nonsense. Safi's lawyer can jump up and down all he likes, but no one really gives a toss.'

Umar thought about it for a few moments. 'I'm not that worried, anyway.'

There was some problem with Carlyle's computer which meant that it was taking forever for his log-in to appear. He stared vacantly at the screen before asking: 'Miranda's not so cute then, huh?'

'Miranda is in her fifties,' Umar said flatly, annoyed by his boss's persistent cheekiness. 'Lives in Leyton. Has a pet pug. Likes Spandau Ballet. Is looking forward to retiring in eighteen months and moving to Hastings.'

'Great.'

'All in all,' the sergeant said tightly, 'she's not really up my street.'

'Oh?' Carlyle just couldn't resist winding his sergeant up. 'I thought you were fairly eclectic in your tastes.'

'Not any more,' As WPC Mason walked past, giving him a cheery smile, Umar leaned forward and lowered his voice: 'I think I'm going to knock all that on the head for a while.'

'That'll be the day,' Carlyle scoffed.

'No, seriously. Things have got a little bit out of hand recently.'

'I'll say.' Folding his arms, the inspector sat back in his chair and lifted his feet onto his desk. 'Speaking of which, what happened to . . .' he tried to remember the name but it escaped him '. . . the naked bike-ride girl?'

A pained look spread across Umar's face as he scratched the bandage on his arm. 'Melissa? I spoke to Shames about it earlier on. They took her back in, a couple of hours ago. She's finally been charged with the murders of her boyfriend and his bit on the side.'

'So she did it then?' Carlyle asked.

'Looks like it,' Umar reluctantly admitted. 'She was taking Clozaril – or rather, she was supposed to be taking it.'

'Which is?' Carlyle waved a hand in the air, inviting his sergeant to explain.

'Which is a drug that is prescribed for patients with a psychotic disorder.'

'Ah.'

'Apparently Melissa has a form of schizophrenia – something that she omitted to mention to her lawyer. It was only when they found the pills in her flat and checked with her GP that it finally became clear what was going on.'

'So who tipped Shames off about the drugs?'

The sergeant stared at his desk. 'Dunno.'

'Pff. You really know how to pick 'em, don't you?'

Umar gave a rueful smile. 'For some reason she stopped taking her medicine and her brain got a bit scrambled.'

'So she went berserk and slaughtered the love birds?'

'That's the theory. Shames says they've been haggling with the lawyer about it. Both sides have piled in with their own medical experts.'

'I'll bet.'

'They're looking to do some kind of deal that saves her from having to go to court. The expectation is that Melissa's lawyer will get her to claim diminished responsibility, or temporary lack of mental capacity. Whatever, she'll end up in a secure medical facility.'

'Christ, what a mess.'

'Postic isn't very happy about it, by all accounts.'

'I bet she isn't.'

'She wants Melissa locked up in Holloway.'

'I dare say she does. *Crazed nutter gets off by claiming insanity in what should be an open and shut case* never looks good on your CV. Poor old Julie.'

'No.'

'There but for the grace of God and all that.'

'Hm.'

'Looks like you had a lucky escape there, sunshine. All you've got to do now is bin the widow and you'll be back on the straight and narrow.'

'Well,' Umar said hesitantly, 'funny you should mention that . . .'

Why hadn't she checked the weather forecast before bringing her lunch outside? Sonia Mason squinted at the grey clouds hovering over St Paul's Church in the Piazza. Deciding that it was unlikely to rain for at least the next twenty minutes, she reached into her M&S plastic bag and pulled out a Tupperware box, along with a small bottle of sparkling water. Ignoring the attempts of the guy sitting on the bench opposite to make eye-contact, she opened the box and pulled out one of her mum's ham sandwiches. Taking a bite, the WPC chewed happily as she tapped on her Kindle screen to bring up her latest read.

'Hell.' No sooner had she made it to the bottom of the page than a big, fat raindrop splashed onto the screen, quickly followed by another. Getting to her feet, Sonia gathered up her belongings and put them back into the bag. Then she zipped up her parka and put up the hood.

Should she head back to the police station or nip inside, take a seat on one of the pews at the back and finally enjoy a few minutes with her book? As the rain began in earnest, she decided on the latter, lowering her head and jogging through the garden towards the West entrance of the church. Hurrying up the steps, she bumped into an old guy who'd clearly had the same idea.

'Sorry.' Mason held out a hand to stop the old bloke taking a tumble.

'Watch where you're going,' he scowled, pushing her hand firmly away.

'Sorry,' Mason repeated, flustered by his hostile response. Looking up, she studied the irritated expression on the guy's

307

face. Realizing who it was she had run into, she let out a loud cackle. 'Seymour.'

'Eh?' A startled look spread across the old burglar's face. Taking a backward step, he slipped on the greasy stone steps. 'Ow.'

'Mr Erikssen, I presume,' Mason quipped, stepping forward and pulling him up by the collar. 'How nice to see you again.'

'Gerroff,' Seymour hissed, looking round for someone to intervene and save him. But the rain had emptied the gardens and there was no one to come to his aid.

'Let's go,' Mason insisted, tightening her grip. 'I think you need to come and have a little chat with us down at the station.'

Carlyle paced the office, making eye-contact with Simpson, Mason and Sligo in turn before looking at the clock on the far wall. 'So,' he said at length, 'if there are three funerals, where's the bloody wedding?' The Commander groaned. The WPC, still flushed with her success in nicking Britain's crappest thief, smirked. The sergeant let the 'joke' pass right over his head. 'Who the hell,' the inspector continued, 'managed to organize three funerals for exactly the same time at the opposite ends of London?'

Looking every inch the cheeky fifth-former, Mason lifted a hand in the air. 'Please, sir, can you have three *opposite* ends of London?'

'Whatever,' Carlyle fulminated, 'whose clever idea was it to lay Joseph Belsky, Taimur Rage *and* Adrian Napper to rest all at the same time?'

'Their families, presumably,' said Simpson, getting to her feet. 'I'm sure that they will be distraught to know that they have caused you a diary problem, but we'll just have to divide and conquer. I will represent us all at Napper's—'

'Fine, fine,' Carlyle snapped, irritated by his boss's unnatural reasonableness. 'Give DI Flux my regards.'

'If he's there.'

'Why wouldn't he be there?' Umar asked.

'After he signed himself out of hospital,' Simpson told them, 'he handed in his resignation and headed off into the sunset. Apparently he's got a place in Spain. His colleagues think he's probably gone there.'

Lucky sod, Carlyle thought. 'Makes sense.'

'Yes, I think so.' Simpson looked at her watch. 'I'd better get going. Let's speak later in the day.'

'Okay.' Once Simpson had left, Carlyle turned his attention to his sergeant. 'You do Belsky, I'll do Taimur.'

'Fine,' Umar agreed.

'Good. It will give me the chance to have another word with his mother.'

'Er,' Mason chipped in, 'it doesn't look like Elma will be putting in an appearance today either.'

The inspector threw up his hands in frustration. 'Wha-at?'

'Sorry, Boss.'

'Is anyone going to these bloody funerals,' Carlyle demanded, 'apart from us?'

'I checked with her office at the Christian Salvation Centre,' Mason informed him. 'Elma has gone to the United States to speak at something called the Hispanic Rebirth Festival, whatever that is. According to her assistant, it is quote-unquote "*a key milestone in her move into expanding New World demographics*".'

'And what the hell does that mean?'

'She's trying to make it big in America,' the WPC translated. 'That's where the money is for this kind of thing.'

'God give me strength. She's the boy's mother. What about Calvin Safi? Are we letting *him* go to pay his last respects to his son?'

'No.' Mason shook her head. 'His lawyer asked for him to be allowed to attend, but permission was denied.'

'Poor kid,' Carlyle sighed. 'What does that tell you, if neither parent manages to make it to his bloody funeral?' He gestured at Mason. 'You go to that one then. Give me a call if Elma does actually turn up.'

'Will do.' Mason picked up her coat and hurried through the door.

'Looks like you're off funeral duty, then,' Umar noted.

'Perks of authority,' Carlyle chuckled.

'Fine.' Umar pushed himself out of his seat. 'I'll see you later.'

'Good,' the inspector replied. 'Are we still set for tonight?'

'Yep. Eight thirty.'

'Looking forward to it.'

SIXTY-TWO

'Excuse me, mate, where's the milk?'

'In the aisle nearest the front door, past the line of chiller cabi-
nets, towards the back,' Melville Farasin pointed past a display
of baked beans. Belatedly recognizing the inspector, he glanced
around nervously. 'What are you doing here?' he asked, lowering
his voice as an old woman pushed by them to pluck a packet of
Ritz Crackers from the shelf. 'It's only my second week on the
job and—'

Holding up a hand, Carlyle cut him off. 'Relax,' he said gently,
waiting for the woman to shuffle off before adding: 'I heard that
you'd managed to make the break from Elma. Well done.'

'In the end, she wasn't that bothered about it,' Melville said. 'It
was my mum who had a total fit.' He gestured around the store.
'She just can't see that this has better prospects.'

'Parents can be funny sometimes,' Carlyle commiserated.

'Tell me about it.'

'I'm sure she'll get over it.'

'Yeah.' But Melville seemed doubtful. 'Hopefully the shock of
Elma getting arrested will make her see sense.'

Carlyle did a double-take. 'When was that?'

'They stopped her at the airport in America,' Melville told
him. 'She's being sued by a guy called Jerome Mears . . .'

Carlyle shook his head. 'Never heard of him.'

'He's an American preacher,' Melville explained, 'runs a thing
called the Mears Ministry.'

Now there's a surprise.

'Elma brought him to London to preach at the Miracle & Healing Conference.'

'Must've missed that one,' Carlyle quipped.

'Anyway,' Melville continued, 'Jerome claims Elma didn't pay him all she owed and he is suing her in the United States. That's why she got arrested, apparently. Her lawyer, Federici is running around like crazy, trying to get her out.'

'I bet he is.' *Maybe there is a God after all*, Carlyle thought cheerily.

'Funny the way these things happen.'

'Yes.' The inspector suddenly decided that he would have some crackers himself. 'I think you're far better off in the supermarket business,' he said, reaching for a packet.

'I think so too,' Melville agreed.

'So, are you enjoying it here?'

'It's okay – early days.'

'If ever I can help with anything, you know where to find me.'

'Thanks.'

'Good to see you, Melville.' Carlyle extended a hand and waited for the boy to get over his initial surprise before they shook. 'Good luck.'

'I'll be fine.'

'I'm sure you will.' Carlyle gestured down the aisle. 'I'll go and find my milk. Let you get on.'

Resplendent in his AC/DC *The Switch Is On Europe '84* T-shirt, Bernie Gilmore raised an eyebrow as the inspector carefully placed a box of crackers and a pint of semi-skimmed milk on the table. 'Bringing your own food, I see?'

Carlyle gave him a thin smile. 'When you're on the Highway to Hell, it's always best to have a few supplies to hand.'

'Ha, ha. Very good.'

Carlyle signalled to the Café Montevideo's waitress that he would have a latte. 'Want anything yourself?'

The journalist pawed at his can of Coke. 'I'm fine. Long time, no see.'

'Been a busy boy.'

'So I believe.' Bernie watched a couple of pretty girls pass by the window, each laden down with a selection of designer shopping bags. 'I hear that Seymour Erikssen's back behind bars.'

'We always get our man.'

'I thought it might be worth a little follow-up story.'

'I'd wait until he actually gets sentenced,' Carlyle advised. 'We just nick the guy – if he gets out again, that's not our fault. We just get the shit when you write about it.' The waitress appeared with his coffee as Bernie mumbled some kind of non-committal reply.

'You want anything else?' the waitress asked. The inspector allowed himself a glance at the various cakes and pastries lined up on the counter. Seeing nothing that immediately caught his eye, he shook his head.

'Anyway,' Carlyle continued, once the waitress had left them to it, 'there's plenty of other things you can write about. Did you hear about Elma Reyes?'

Bernie shot him a pained look. 'I wrote about that, the day before yesterday. Don't you read the papers?'

'Not if I can help it.' Carlyle took a sip of his drink and winced. It was far too weak; no bite. 'I find as I get older that newspapers are becoming more and more tiresome.' Pleased with his choice of word he sat back and watched Bernie pour the last of the Coke down his neck.

'So, what else is happening?' the journalist asked once he'd finished his drink.

'Well . . .' Carlyle flicked through the list in his head. 'Melissa Graham looks nailed on for the naked bike-ride murders.'

'Done that, too,' Gilmore grunted.

Making a mental note to remove the Café Montevideo from his list of approved establishments, Carlyle finished his coffee. 'That's your problem, Bernie – you're just too far ahead of the game.'

'Didn't really do it justice,' the journalist mused. 'We didn't have a good enough picture.'

'What about Calvin Safi?' Carlyle explained about Emma Denton and the group-grooming investigation.

'I hear that's not going too well.'

'I dunno about that. At least we've got Safi.'

'Yeah,' Bernie scowled, 'after how many murders – and rapes.'

'You really love giving me a hard time, don't you?'

'That's because you make it so easy for me,' Gilmore laughed harshly. 'Have you got a number for her?'

'Denton?' Carlyle pulled up the Chief Crown Prosecutor's number on his phone. 'Here you go,' he said, handing it over. 'You didn't get it from me.'

'No, no,' the journalist replied, carefully copying the number into his own phone, 'of course not.' Saving the details, he handed the mobile back to Carlyle. 'Thanks.'

'One final thing,' said the inspector. Already half out of his seat, Bernie fell back into his chair.

'Go on.'

'Hanway 58.'

The hack narrowed his eyes. 'Not ringing any bells.'

'It's one of Ken Ashton's companies.'

'Oh yes?' The eyes narrowed even further.

'A little bird tells me that they're being investigated by the taxman.'

Bernie rubbed the stubble on his chin. 'Is that so? And you would know this because?'

Because I spoke to a mate in the Special Investigations Unit at the HMRC, Carlyle thought smugly, *and got him to put it under review.* 'I hear things.'

'Very occasionally.'

'Might make a good story,' Carlyle said hopefully.

'You reckon?' Getting back on his feet, Bernie gave the inspector a friendly pat on the shoulder. 'I might be the world's greatest living investigative reporter,' he whispered, 'but even I draw the line at trying to have a pop at Ken Ashton.'

'Bernie.'

The hack shook his head. 'Not going near it, sunshine. I value my kneecaps.' He spread his arms wide. 'Do I look stupid?'

'Well . . .'

Bernie waggled an admonishing finger. 'Whatever game you are trying to play, my friend – and you are as transparent as a broken window – I would give it a rest. And that's quality advice I'm offering you for free.' Pulling open the door, he lumbered across the road, heading towards Soho Square.

Carlyle watched the reporter disappear round the corner. As usual, Bernie's advice was very sensible. However, it was too late to change things now. He had spoken to the HMRC, and the Ashton investigation was now underway. With the recession showing no sign of ending, the Inland Revenue was under more pressure than ever to check under every rock for unpaid tax. Any tip-off was seized on with alacrity. Even if they found nothing untoward in the books of Hanway 58 – and Carlyle very much doubted that would be the case – Ashton would find the investigation long, expensive and profoundly annoying.

The waitress appeared with the bill, clearing the table before returning behind the counter. Reaching into his pocket, Carlyle dropped a handful of coins on the table, making sure that there was enough to cover the tab as well as a small tip. As he did so, he caught sight of a familiar face. On the wall, next to the till, Little Charley Bear was still smiling, touting for punters for his Christmas Adventure. *That little bugger's everywhere*, the inspector mused sourly. His mobile started vibrating across the table. Picking it up, he lifted it to his ear.

'Carlyle.'

'You bastard. You've shopped me to the Revenue, haven't you?' The hostility swept down the line in waves.

Stifling a laugh, the inspector played dumb. 'Hello? Who is this?'

'Don't play silly buggers!' Ken Ashton shouted. 'I've just had them descend on my office like a plague of bloody locusts. That's down to you, isn't it?'

Carlyle took a deep breath and tried to sound confused. 'What are you talking about?'

'All my books are in order,' Ashton growled

'I'm sure they are, Ken,' Carlyle said equably. 'Do you want me to speak to HMRC for you, see what I can find out?'

'I want you to leave bloody well alone,' the old crook thundered.

'Careful,' Carlyle quipped, unable to contain his glee any longer, 'you don't want to have a stroke. Look at what happened to poor old Angus Muirhead.'

'Bastard.'

'Anyway, if you end up getting a large demand for back tax, I'm sure you can use the refund you get from Chris Brennan.' Waving a fist in triumph, the inspector ended the call, giving Little Charley Bear the thumbs-up as he got to his feet and headed out into the street.

SIXTY-THREE

About time. Swallowing a mouthful of Peroni, Carlyle listened to the footsteps in the hallway coming steadily towards them. The lawyer was the best part of an hour late. Annoyed, the inspector added poor timekeeping to the list of Chris Brennan's many character defects.

As the new arrival appeared in the kitchen, the inspector allowed himself a small smile. Brennan had ditched the Prince of Wales check suit for a pair of faded jeans, some red Puma trainers and a grey overcoat. The bags under his eyes seemed to have grown since their last meeting and he needed a shave. The overall effect was less legal eagle and more legal aid client.

Clocking the two policemen, Brennan hesitated in the doorway.

'Come in,' Carlyle commanded, as Giselle appeared from behind him and darted towards Umar, who had positioned himself on the far side of the kitchen. The lawyer glared at his hostess but said nothing as he entered and planted himself in front of the fridge. Legs apart, arms folded, the look on his face was more resigned than angry.

'We won't offer you a beer,' Carlyle went on.

Brennan cleared his throat. 'Just get on with it,' he grumbled.

Giselle kept her eyes firmly on a spot on the tiled floor. Her face was heavily made-up but the signs of her recent beating at the hands of her late husband's business partner were still clear to see.

'The good news is that Mrs Winters will not be pressing charges against you.' Carlyle paused, allowing the woman's bowed head to give a small nod of agreement. 'That would certainly not be my recommendation,' he let a pained expression flit across his face, 'but I will, after some consideration, respect her views.'

Brennan stared out into the garden, trying to affect an air of boredom. 'And what else?' he asked, not looking at his nemesis.

'You don't get the money.' Giselle Winters finally found her voice.

Brennan turned to face the widow. 'But—'

'You have to walk away from here – now,' Carlyle said. 'And don't come back. If you try to contact Mrs Winters, or threaten her in any way, you will be arrested immediately and charged with grievous bodily harm and attempted extortion.'

'A spell at Her Majesty's Pleasure might well be a better bet than having to face up to Ken Ashton's people,' Brennan reflected.

Carlyle smiled maliciously. 'I should imagine you'll have to do that whether you're inside or outside.'

Brennan rocked back on his heels. 'You could be right.'

'Regardless of that, don't come back,' Umar repeated.

'You know what? She thought you were a useless shag.' Before Umar could reply, Brennan wheeled round to the inspector. 'As for you . . .' He shook his head. 'Always trying to claim the moral high fucking ground. This is all about Yvonne Meyer, isn't it?'

'Just go, Chris,' Giselle hissed. With a snort of disgust, the lawyer headed for the door. Grim-faced, Carlyle kept his own counsel as he watched Brennan disappear back into the hallway. He listened to the retreating footsteps and the front door slamming shut and realized that he'd been holding his breath. Exhaling, he lifted the bottle of beer to his lips and drank deeply.

Umar fidgeted with his beer bottle and looked up at his boss. 'So who's Yvonne Meyer, then?'

Sitting in Giselle Winters' kitchen, the inspector stared at his empty bottle and registered the light buzz that a third beer had bestowed on his brain. That was enough Peroni for him for one night; it was time to move on. He looked around, wondering whether there was any Scotch in the house. Brian Winters, he imagined, would be the kind of guy to have a bottle of something rather nice close at hand. 'Do you know where they keep their spirits?' he asked his sergeant.

Still lingering over his first drink, Umar said. 'Nah.' He pointed towards the stairs. 'I can go and ask Giselle, though – if you like.'

'It's okay. Don't worry.' The moment Chris Brennan had slunk off into the night, the widow had announced that she was decamping to Antibes that very evening, to stay with friends. She had then disappeared upstairs to pack. The inspector thought it a good idea, just in case the lawyer did try to come back. 'Probably best that you stay away from her bedroom, seeing as you've turned over a new leaf and all that.'

Did Umar blush from behind his beer bottle? Maybe the inspector had imagined it. 'What do you think he meant,' the sergeant mumbled, 'about Giselle saying that I was a rubbish shag?'

I would have thought it was fairly self-explanatory. 'No idea,' Carlyle lied. 'People talk shit, just to wind you up.'

'I suppose.' But the young man sounded doubtful.

'I'm sure Giselle wouldn't say anything like that,' the inspector said soothingly.

'No.' The sergeant's face brightened somewhat. 'Anyway, Yvonne Meyer . . .'

'Christ,' Carlyle groaned. 'Maybe I will have another beer.' Going over to the fridge, he liberated another Peroni.

Umar waited patiently for him to remove the cap and take a swig.

'Yvonne Meyer . . . South African, twenty-three years old, working in a bar on Goodge Street and training to become a graphic designer. Pretty girl . . .'

Umar bit his lip, knowing more-or-less what was coming next.

'Brennan raped Meyer at a party – beat her up too. Then he threatened to kill her if she reported it. I persuaded her to make a complaint and – ten months later – we went to trial.' If only he could wish the memories away.

'And?'

'And the bastard got off. When the case was dismissed, Yvonne walked out of court, went down into the underground and jumped in front of a Victoria Line train heading for Seven Sisters.'

'Ah.' Umar didn't know what to say.

The inspector chugged down half of the remaining beer and let out a small belch. 'That was just over a decade ago now – but some cases you don't forget.'

'No.'

'Her parents came all the way from Durban to collect the body. She was their only child. They had no idea what had happened, didn't even know that the court case was taking place. Yvonne had tried to spare them that.'

'*Fu-uck . . .*'

'It can be a shit old world. But I have followed Brennan's career carefully ever since, waiting for him to make a slip. And now he finally has, it's time for some payback.'

'Are you sure that he was guilty?'

'He was as guilty as sin. Basically, he got off because the forensic evidence hadn't been collected properly. And he had a history of violence that wasn't disclosed to the jury. You saw what he did to Giselle.'

'Yeah. So what will happen to him now?'

Carlyle finished his beer. 'That's for Ken Ashton to decide. Brian Winters has really dropped him in it. Brennan is on the hook for a lot of cash.' Placing the empty bottle on the worktop, he headed for the door. 'We'll just have to wait and see.'

Checking to ensure that he wasn't imprisoning any stray Chinese tourists, the Reverend Lincoln McNelis locked the West entrance and carefully set the alarm. It had been a long day and he was looking forward to sitting down with a cup of tea and a couple of shortbread biscuits. His sense of weariness increased as he approached the donations box. It cost more than a hundred thousand pounds a year to run St Paul's Church, and that sum was growing all the time. On top of that, there was the appeal to save and restore the courtyard, a job that would require another six-figure sum. As their need grew, however, the charity of visitors was coming under ever greater strain, their pockets emptied in double-quick time by the more expensive delights of the surrounding city. The weekly take was getting smaller and smaller, and each year it was becoming harder and harder to balance the books.

As he turned the key in the lock, the rector wondered what 'gifts' he might find in the box this time. It never ceased to amaze him what people managed to force through the slot: bits of food; plastic cutlery; condoms. In short, anything but cash.

With a sigh, he opened the lid and peered into the box.

'Oh, my.'

Reaching inside, he pulled out a fistful of notes in various currencies.

A gift from God. Shuffling the collection of pounds, euros and dollars, Lincoln McNelis did a quick calculation in his head. Guessing that he was holding the equivalent of something like three months' takings, he lifted his eyes to the heavens, apologizing for his cynicism and giving heartfelt thanks for the generosity of strangers.

SIXTY-FOUR

Tired but somewhat elated, Carlyle pushed through the slowly thinning crowd of late-middle-aged men in leather jackets and *Suspect Device* T-shirts. With the final, triumphant encore still ringing in his ears, he tried to remember the last time he'd been to a gig. Any gig. It had to be twenty years at least. The last time he'd seen Stiff Little Fingers themselves was in Brixton, way back in 1988. One thing he did remember: Helen had refused to come with him. She had never really been into Punk. Never really been into music, full stop. Certainly not in the trainspotterish way that he had been, back then.

1988.

By that time, the band had already been around for ten years or more. It was a miracle they were still going, really.

It was a miracle *he* was still going.

After a few moments, he caught up with his daughter, who was waving a rolled-up poster above her head.

'I got it signed!'

'Great,' he smiled, energized by her clear delight.

'That was so cool,' Alice burbled, still riding the adrenaline rush of the show. 'Can we do it again?'

'If you'd like.' Putting a protective arm around his daughter's shoulders, Carlyle steered her towards the exit. 'I don't see why not.'

Umar gave WPC Mason a gentle nudge. 'Do you think we should wake him?' he stage-whispered.

'I'm not asleep,' Carlyle said, if a little groggily. Opening his eyes, he lifted his feet off his desk, allowing himself a stretch while stifling a yawn.

'Of course not, Boss,' Mason agreed.

'Just doing a good impression of a man having a kip,' Umar chuckled. 'Late night, was it?'

'Alice took me to a Stiff Little Fingers concert last night,' Carlyle explained.

'Who are they?' Umar asked. 'Some boy band?'

'Not quite.' The inspector reluctantly got to his feet. He needed an espresso – a double. 'Anyway,' he yawned properly, 'haven't you got more pressing things to worry about? Is there any news from the IPCC?' It was more than a week now since the pair of them had appeared in front of the panel investigating the circumstances of Calvin Safi's arrest and, so far, the silence had been deafening.

'Nothing yet,' Umar said cheerily. If he was feeling stressed out by the whole episode, he wasn't letting it show.

'They're taking their bloody time about it,' Carlyle groused.

'My rep says I shouldn't read anything into that,' Umar countered. 'They just have to make a show of going through the motions. She's fairly relaxed about the whole thing.'

'Let's hope she's right.'

'It'll be fine – no more than a reprimand.' The sergeant sounded like he believed it.

'Good. So, where are we in terms of Mr Safi himself?'

'We've got him in relation to Napper's murder and Sandra Middlemass, the missing girl, but that's about it.'

'That's plenty,' Carlyle grunted.

'I'm not sure that the Chief Crown Prosecutor sees it like that. I don't think Safi talked about the grooming network. Denton didn't get much out of him.'

'Ah, well, it was worth a try.' The inspector turned to Mason. 'And how is our good friend Seymour Erikssen?'

'We got lucky. CCTV from the Monkey's Uncle shows him

robbing that American tourist. We never found the wallet, but we've got him in the frame for another half a dozen thefts in the last few weeks. Fingers crossed, he won't be getting out so quickly this time.'

'Good,' Carlyle said, 'Bernie Gilmore will be pleased, if nothing else.'

Sitting in the canteen, the inspector considered the merits of a cheese and tomato panini as he scanned the news pages of that morning's *Metro*. Beneath a picture of a monkey in a sheepskin coat that had been found wandering around an Ikea store, his eye caught a story in the *news in brief* section:

> *A man found beaten to death near Waterloo Bridge last night has been named as Christopher Brennan, founder of the legal firm of WBK. Police are calling for witnesses after Mr Brennan collapsed after being attacked by two men in an underpass leading to Charlie Chaplin Walk.*

That was quick, Carlyle thought, as he watched Umar approach the table. Closing the newspaper, he tossed it onto the next table as the sergeant placed a fresh espresso in front of him and pulled up a chair.

'Thanks.'

'No problem.' Sitting down, Umar tore open the wrapper on his Mars Bar and took a large bite.

You could have got me one, Carlyle thought resentfully.

'Did you hear?' Umar laughed through a mouthful of chocolate. 'Jazz got off.'

'Huh?' Carlyle's frown grew deeper. The fate of Maradona Wilson was not something that had been keeping him awake at night. 'How did he manage that? The little bugger was caught trying to sell crack to a copper.'

'Apparently,' Umar offered, taking another bite, 'he would have lost his specially modified home if he had been jailed.'

Stop talking with your mouth full. Carlyle crushed the cup in his hand. 'My heart bleeds.'

'As well as suffering from achondroplasia.'

'Suffering from what?'

'Dwarfism,' Umar explained.

'As well as being a short arse, Jazz has been diagnosed with paranoid schizophrenia and depression.'

'I bet he has.'

'The judge gave him an eighteen-month supervision order with six months of drug rehabilitation.'

Carlyle tutted. 'What a joke.'

'These things happen,' said Umar philosophically. 'At least it wasn't our arrest.' Popping the last of the Mars Bar into his mouth, he scrunched up the empty wrapper and dropped it on to the table.

'Did you come down here for something in particular?' Carlyle's eyes narrowed. 'Or did you just want to remind me of the vagaries of the legal system?'

Umar leaned across the table. 'Christina's been offered a job,' he said.

'That's nice.'

'As a trainee radio reporter.'

'But she's a stripper,' Carlyle blurted out. Seeing the look on Umar's face, he tried a cheeky smile. 'I mean, isn't becoming a journalist a bit of a step down?'

'Christina's done lots of things,' Umar replied, somewhat defensively to Carlyle's mind. 'And she did a media course at City University before Ella was born.'

'Good for her,' Carlyle said charmlessly.

'This could be a career for her.'

'Hm.'

Umar let his gaze flicker away. 'And she wants me to become a house husband.'

'Excuse me?'

'She wants me to pack it in here and look after Ella, full-time.'

What? After I've just fought tooth and nail to keep you in a bloody job? 'How would that work?'

'I dunno,' Umar shrugged. 'The way these things normally work, I suppose. It would be cheaper than childcare and better for Ella.'

'Take it from me, sunshine, you're not exactly house-husband material.'

A hurt look crossed Umar's face. 'And you would know this how?'

'Wouldn't you go bonkers?' the inspector asked, changing tack.

'Dunno.'

'Jesus,' Carlyle sighed, getting to his feet, 'you don't know much, do you?' He shook his head in a mixture of disappointment and disbelief. How the hell should he handle this? He would need to ask Helen. In the meantime, he should just focus on not saying anything stupid. 'I need to get something to eat.' He pointed at the crumpled paper wrapper lying on the table. 'Fancy another Mars Bar?'

With her finger poised over the mouse, Emma Denton took one last look at her 'final' report into group grooming on the screen of her computer before sending it to her boss at the CPS. Grimacing, she had to admit that the time, effort and money spent on the investigation had not yielded anything like the results she had been hoping for. Calvin Safi had surprised her with his refusal to co-operate, despite the fact that he was facing an extremely lengthy jail sentence. The white guy, Metcalf, had been only too happy to talk; sadly, he knew nothing about any wider grooming network. Denton considered her options. Maybe she should interrogate Safi again? Or maybe she should just cut her losses and move on? After all, it wasn't as if there weren't plenty of other cases on her desk right now.

Gripped by an unfamiliar indecision, the prosecutor stared at the glass sitting next to the keyboard, in front of a half-empty bottle. Reaching out with her free hand, she lifted the glass to her lips, breathing in the fruity aroma of the eighteen-year-old single malt. The Japanese whisky cost £110 a bottle; expensive, but worth it. Taking a slow sip, a new thought popped into her head. Carole Simpson's policeman – maybe she could use him to investigate further. Put the inspector on the case and see if they could break this thing open. Moving the mouse, she placed the cursor over the 'delete' button, right-clicked and watched the report disappear into cyberspace. Pulling up her contacts list, she found the entry for 'Carlyle' and reached for the phone.

What was she going to do now? Allie Simmons sullenly watched the dwindling stream of people heading along Praed Street. In her pockets, she had the princely sum of three pounds and seventeen pence. Allie might have gotten an 'F' in her maths GCSE last summer, but even she knew that her wasn't going to get her very far on that.

As she hovered on the kerbside, a car pulled up. The driver, a young white guy with a cigarette dangling from his lips, wound down the window and blew a stream of smoke towards her.

'Looking for directions?'

A gust of icy wind tore down the street. Shivering, Allie said nothing.

'Need a place to stay?' the man persisted. The back door of the vehicle clicked open. 'C'mon,' he smiled, 'get in.'

Acknowledgements

I would like to thank Michael Doggart for all his help in producing this book. Also, thanks are due to all at C&R, including Krysyna Green, Clive Hebard and Joan Deitch.